GUNDOWN

Readers react to *Gundown*

"This is a fast-paced yet thought-provoking book, muscular in style and ingenious in worldview. Gundown is an unusual novel, both an action-packed thriller and a rational dissection of our legal system. Well worth reading."

"*Gundown* is one of those books you'll find yourself staying up way too late to read just the next chapter... and still be thinking about for a good time to come."

"Read it for the distraction of a well-told action yarn—once. But you will find yourself thinking about one point or another and checking back to seek the clarity of the message—more than once."

"Ideas make this book stand out. Not just another action story, it has compelling notions that stick in the mind. These ideas seem so reasonable (and yet not impossibly Utopian) that they keep coming back, teasing you to make you wonder why they couldn't be tried."

GUNDOWN

RAY RHAMEY

Unbeaten paths to worthy reads.
Ashland, Oregon

The platypus breaks all the rules—it's the only mammal that lays eggs, is venomous, has a duck bill, a beaver tail, and otter feet—and it does just fine, thank you very much.

It can be the same for novels that don't slip tidily into genre pigeonholes. Platypus takes readers on unique paths to entertainment, truth, and enjoyable reads.

This book is a work of fiction. All characters, organizations, and locales, and all incidents and dialogue, are drawn from the author's imagination and not to be construed as real.

Other works by Ray Rhamey

Fiction

Support Your Local Vampire Kitty-Cat
our heroes fight for their lives—er, undeadness?—against
the mob and a vigilante vampire-killer gang.

The Hollywood Unmurders
crimes and dangerous times in La La Land for Patch,
the vampire kitty-cat

The Summer Boy
a murder mystery wrapped around a coming-of-age story
set in Texas in 1958

Final Fire
a speculative thriller: a madman creates a
plague to wipe out humanity

Nonfiction

Mastering the Craft of Compelling Storytelling
coaching on fiction craft and narrative technique
for writers of all levels

This book was written for my children and their children, and for yours, in hopes that the America they inherit is an improvement on the one that gives rise to this story.

And it's for people who work hard to live good lives, to leave this place better than they found it. It's for you.

Finally, I dedicate this work to my wife Sarah, who would prefer that it was a mystery but has always helped me all along the way.

In the time it takes an average person

to read this novel,

six Americans will die

from a handgun bullet.

IN A POSSIBLE NEAR FUTURE

 **MEAN STREET**

The sunny blue sky over Chicago brought a smile to Hank as he sliced through the noontime trudge of pedestrians on Michigan Avenue. His PTSD tried to needle him with a spike of fear that he'd fail today, but he smacked it down. So far, lifted by a rare feeling of well-being, he felt sharp, at his best. He checked his watch—plenty of time to get to his meeting with the NRA guy.

The job the man wanted to talk about sounded like it could be a path back to having a real life again. Yeah, not as a cop anymore, but it might return him to the duty he still felt to serve and protect.

A tiresome clump of a half dozen gang jerks swaggered toward him with cocky menace, three of them with pistols in their hands. Sure, they had the right to carry them, but these guys were pushing it. The gangbangers blocked most of the sidewalk, forcing people to step off the curb or sidle along a building front.

Hank didn't step aside for fools. He slid his hand inside his windbreaker to the familiar feel of the butt of his Colt .45 in its shoulder holster. He locked his gaze onto the eyes of the center guy, who carried a Glock, and walked straight at him.

The kid kept his cool as they came together, but one stride from colliding, he dropped his gaze and sidestepped. Never slowing, Hank walked on.

This was going to be a good day.

Jewel Washington pushed through the lunchtime flow of people that filled the plaza beside the Chicago River, searching for Murphy. The lard-ass cop said he'd be here, and her brother will be hurtin' bad if she doesn't get the pink Timmy needs.

A clot of gangstas swaggered through the crowd, dangling pistols in their hands, radiating dares no one answered. Creeps oughta get a life. Jewel cut wide, careful to avert her gaze even though she'd rather glare at them. But that could set them off.

Instead, she lifted her face to the spring sun. Its warmth promised good things. Maybe it would add to the spray of freckles like chocolate dots against the brown of her cheeks.

She spotted Murphy, a fat blue boulder parting a stream of girly secretaries hurrying to cram in their noontime shopping, a boulder that leered at their bobbing chests.

His piggy eyes stumbled across her when she closed in on him. He sent his gaze on its usual tour of her body—yeah, she was wearing a scoop-neck top and a miniskirt, but what the hell, couldn't a girl enjoy a spring day without some slob feeling her up with his eyeballs?

She held out forty bucks for a packet of pink, the only thing that could stop Timmy's withdrawal agony—for a while.

Murphy ogled her. "I decided to take it in services insteada cash." He aimed a fat thumb at Pioneer Court behind him, and then cupped his crotch. "Got a spot for a quick hummer behind them bushes over there."

In the shadow from the Equitable Building, raised beds of marble broke up the dreary pavement with boxes of green shrubs, trees, flowers, and a fountain.

She didn't have another way to get the drug, but this was bullshit. She lifted her chin and looked him in the eyes. "You don't want my cash, there's dealers in the 'hood."

"Bitch." He snatched her money and handed her a packet of pink just as a bony white teen shuffled up to them, his nose leaking, body shivering, winces flickering across his face. Jewel had seen the same thing in Timmy—it had been too long since the kid's last hit of pink.

He held out a handful of grubby bills. "N-n-need one."

Murphy took his time counting the money while the kid jittered. It hurt to look at him, he was so much like her brother—she turned away. She wasn't gonna go there. Too nice a day and nothin' she could do about it anyway.

The clock on the Wrigley Building said she had time to do a little window-shopping before she had to be back at work, so she headed north toward Water Tower Place, not that she could afford anything in the boutiques there. A breeze reeking of car exhaust swirled between the skyscrapers, but she liked its touch.

She stopped at a restaurant window to eye a cupcake display. Her ice-blue eyes, donated by some honky ancestor, reflected back at her. So did her scar, a three-inch trail curving down from high on her cheekbone.

Jewel gave her body the once-over like Murphy had. Still lookin' good . . . Wait a minute, was that a little bit of extra tummy? She turned sideways. Damn, gettin' poochy. Should she diet? Exercise? Both? She sucked her gut in and walked on.

Two white dudes slouched against a gun store smacked kisses at her. A green stripe ran down the center of the blond's buzz-cut hair, and a red do-rag decorated the smaller guy's shaved head—he cupped his balls and licked his lips. Ugh. What was it with men and their junk? She lengthened her stride, her miniskirt riding high.

They pushed off from the store and swung into step on each side of her. Green-Stripe crowded against her. His sour stink assaulted her, and the skin on her arms goose-bumped. He said, "Hey, brown sugar."

She wanted to say, "I'm not your sugar," but no, she just kept going. Staring straight ahead, she said, "There's a cop back there."

He laughed. "Yeah. Murphy."

Wishing she wasn't wearing heels, she broke into a run and darted between a couple holding hands.

Do-Rag flashed past Jewel and then stopped a few feet ahead, arms spread wide. A hand grabbed at her elbow from behind. She jerked free, cut around a woman pushing a stroller, and then ran back toward Murphy.

Green-Stripe caught her arm and yanked her to a stop. He swung her to face him and leaned close. "You need somethin' to relax you, chocklit, and I'm it."

She yanked free and spun.

His partner stood waiting for her.

They grabbed her arms and forced her toward Pioneer Court. They hauled her behind a clump of bushes—they could be seen from the plaza, but only above the waist. She pulled with all her strength but couldn't tear free.

Thirty feet away, Murphy stared at her.

She cried, "Murphy?"

He didn't move.

But there were a ton of people walking by just a few yards away. "Help! Hellllp!"

Glances flicked in her direction from the throng on the sidewalk and then skittered away. See no evil, don't get involved, stay safe; she'd done the same a thousand times.

Okay, what she had to do now was live through this.

A shout from behind Hank cut into his thoughts. He turned to see two scruffy punks pull a young woman behind a cluster of bushes in a courtyard. A reflexive impulse to go to the rescue fired up . . . but a policeman was close by. She'd be all right.

The woman's cry came again. "Murphy!" The officer, a wide man with multiple chins, faced the action.

Hank stayed where he was. What the hell, he could spare a minute to lend a hand if needed. He still had his old badge and the call to duty that went with it.

The shorter punk held the woman's arms from behind while the blond with a stupid green stripe in his hair ripped her shirt open. She wasn't wearing a bra.

She yelled to the cop, "Murphy! Murphy, it's me!"

Quick, smooth, Clothes-Ripper slipped his hand inside his Bulls jacket and pulled out a pistol. He jammed the muzzle under her chin and forced her head back. Then he gave the officer a screw-you smile.

Hank knew what he'd do, and he was a good-enough shot to do it, but how would the uniform handle it?

The cop moved on, hands clasped behind his back as if just out for a stroll in a peaceful park.

The son of a bitch turned his back on his sworn duty!? Hank clenched his fists, tempted to go after the coward.

The kid stuffed his pistol back under his jacket and unzipped his pants. A yell from the woman shriveled into a wail. "Murphyyyy."

The cop didn't look back. People flowed past, unseeing, as if they wore blinders.

The woman staggered her attacker with a kick to his leg. He slapped her, and then had to dodge a knee aimed at his crotch.

Girl had guts.

Hank moved closer and stepped behind a tall shrub that concealed him from the passing crowd. He drew his Colt, pulled the silencer from his pocket, twisted it on, and settled into a marksman's stance: legs spread, both arms up, his gun steady.

The punk holding the woman's arms saw Hank, and his grin O'd toward a shout. Hank couldn't allow a warning—the one with the gun was fast. Hank's bullet stopped the kid's yell in his mouth and slammed him back.

His hands didn't know he was dead, and he pulled the woman on top of him when he fell away from the little garden. They sprawled on the pavement, and the woman gaped at Hank as he swung his gun to the other guy.

Hank shouted, "Freeze!"

Green-Stripe spun toward him and jerked his gun out of his jacket as he yelled, "You're dea—"

Hank shot him in the heart. The kid staggered back and looked down at his chest and then up at Hank, his eyes wide like those of a scared little boy. His knees buckled and he collapsed, his gun clattering on the pavement.

Hank checked the area—if there was any law nearby he was willing to be late for his meeting to show his badge and square things away, but the chicken-livered cop was gone and there were no other uniforms in sight. Passersby glanced at the bodies beside the garden and then focused on where they were going. He took a deep breath to ease the rush of adrenaline and concentrated on the mechanical rhythm of removing the silencer and stuffing his pistol into his holster. He'd call 911 and report the shooting.

The NRA had the right idea when they said, "The surest way to stop a bad guy with a gun is a good guy with a gun."

The woman scrambled to her feet. Clutching at her torn top, she stared at the mess that had been her attackers, then at Hank.

She looked like she was okay, and he had a meeting. He turned his back on her and stepped into the mindless herd, looking for the cop. He wanted to bury a fist in his fat gut, but there was no sign of the creep. Hank picked up his pace. He needed action to keep his head straight, and maybe this NRA thing could generate something. Too much downtime was . . . well, too much. Stuff kept bubbling up that his meds and pot had trouble handling . . .

Jewel trembled, the scar on her cheek throbbing as though it remembered old trouble. She breathed deep and settled herself down. Her mama had always said, "In this world, you got to be hard. Ain't nobody there for you but you." Hallelujah, Mama.

She'd been lucky this day—somebody *had* been there for her. She had to thank that man, even if he was white—Mama'd taught her manners, too. Jewel hurried after him, trying to arrange her torn top into decent coverage, but one boob or the other kept falling out. Great, now she had to walk down Michigan Avenue with her tits on display. And wouldn't they love it back at the office, especially Ronald Reese the Third, certified asshole.

She spotted her rescuer knifing through the crowd. She really should get back to her job, but, hell, he'd pretty much saved her brown ass. "Hey!" she shouted. No response.

He crossed the street. She hurried after him; damn, the man could move. The crossing signal switched to "Don't" as he entered the Chelsea Hotel.

Jewel ran for the other side of the street.

2 PATRIOTS GATHER

In his hotel room, Mitch Parsons knotted his tie and then added his NRA tie tack, its pewter eagle clutching crossed rifles in its talons. His mission in Chicago wasn't sanctioned by the NRA—hell, his fellow board members were dead set against it, chickens that they were—but he'd be damned if he'd set aside his allegiance because of that.

Anyway, they were dead wrong. The move in Oregon to take away guns would spread if the NRA let things go—if they let *Noah Stone* go—and soon they'd all be disarmed, the whole damn country, man and boy.

He cocked his thumb and aimed an index-finger gun at the *Time* magazine on the dresser where Noah Stone's smile looked up from the cover. The headline read, "The Alliance's Pied Piper."

Mitch squeezed the trigger and wished . . . well, he wasn't sure what to wish for other than Stone gone. Like Daddy used to say, if wishes were horses, beggars would ride. Wishing would do no good. So here he was in Chicago to take action.

He rubbed his belly and then pulled a mini Tootsie Roll from the stash in his pocket. The rush of chocolate soothed him even though it meant trouble later with his ulcer. For the millionth time, he wished smoking wasn't bad for people. Not that Tootsie Rolls were much better.

But he really had no reason to be worried. He was doing the right thing. Noah Stone was weakening American freedom in this troubled world, and that amounted to treason.

Mitch flicked a glance at the *Time* cover. It was a matter of duty. And Hank Soldado sure sounded like the man to get it done. He was a cop and a soldier who had sworn to protect the constitution, one of the heroes who will not obey any order to disarm the American people. Hell, even his name meant "soldier." By God, together they'd stop Stone.

In the Chelsea Hotel's lobby, habits from years of police work set Hank to scanning the room, alert for body language that signaled trouble.

With all the glamour and finery of models posing at a fashion shoot, the usual high-priced hookers littered red velvet furniture. The usual bellboys idled, and the usual on-the-road businessmen eyed the usual high-priced hookers. Except for a long table featuring stacks of pamphlets and posters of a gray-haired man, nothing seemed other than ordinary.

Signs on the table told Hank to "GET INFORMATION ABOUT THE ALLIANCE HERE." It was manned by three cheerful-looking women ranging from their twenties to their forties. The youngest-looking—red-haired, trim and smiley and pretty—accosted people with handfuls of material while the other two helped lines of men and women who were lively with chatting and smiles sign up.

Was this the Alliance the NRA guy had called him about? When he passed the table on the way to the elevator, the redhead approached, gave him a sprightly smile, and said, "Excuse me, sir, I'd like to tell you about—"

He waved her off, but he smiled when he did it. The proselytizer shrugged and then advanced on a woman pulling a suitcase. He strode into an elevator and punched the button for his floor.

A brown-skinned young woman whirled through the revolving doors on the lobby's far side. She struggled to keep a torn top together—the girl from the courtyard? What the hell was she doing here?

The elevator door closed. A faint scent of gunpowder wafted from his holster, but the NRA guy shouldn't mind that.

Jewel's rush dwindled to a stop when the elevator shut its doors with her goal behind them. Robbed of purpose, she stood, unsure what to do.

The terror of the attack in the courtyard surged into her mind, and the room tilted sideways. Hands came from behind and caught her under the arms.

"Gotcha."

Jewel straightened and turned. The hands belonged to a perky redhead. Jewel said, "I'm fine, I'm okay."

Her knees sagged, Red caught her again, and Jewel told her pride to find something better to do while she let the woman help her to a chair beside a long table. Looking up into worried green eyes, Jewel said thanks.

Red's concern lightened into a smile. "You just sit till you feel better." She pointed to Jewel's gaping blouse. "I can help you with that." The woman rummaged in a box under the table and pulled out a white T-shirt. She aimed a finger at a corner of the lobby. "The women's is over there."

"Thanks again." Jewel waited a minute, and then took care standing. She was steady enough. Clutching the shirt to her chest, she hurried to the restroom. In the privacy of a stall, she took off the remains of her top and pulled the T-shirt on.

At the sink, she dampened a paper towel with cold water and wiped her face. Feeling better, she checked out her new look.

High fashion it wasn't. Her chest bore "The Alliance" in letters created with a checkerboard of pinks and tans and browns. The shirt wasn't pretty, but at least it covered her. She touched the logo with a fingertip—one spot matched the color of her skin.

Back in the lobby, the redhead asked, "Are you all right?"

Because she had been a help, Jewel smiled and said yes.

Red offered a brochure. "Maybe you'd be interested in the Alliance?"

"Sorry, I'm not buying anything, and I've got to get to work."

"Oh, we're not selling anything, just trying to, ah . . ." She shrugged and grinned. "This's gonna sound really corny, but we're trying to make the world better."

Jewel snorted. "You want to do that, start with a great big match."

Red laughed. "It's all in the brochure."

Jewel took it. A silver square reflected her face. A caption said, "You're looking at someone who can make life better." At the bottom was a smaller version of the Alliance logo.

Probably a con that promised to turn your life around quick and easy-peasy, all-you-gotta-do-is-believe-and-buy-our-salvation-program-complete-with-a-free-DVD-only $29.95.

Red handed her a slip of yellow paper. "This is about tonight's rally. I hope you'll come. It's free."

Not meaning it, but not wanting to cloud the sunny woman's enthusiasm, Jewel stuffed the note and the brochure in her purse and said, "Sure." She checked her watch. "Damn, they're gonna fire my ass."

A knock sounded on Mitch's door. He opened it, and a man dressed in jeans and a windbreaker stepped in. His gaze swept the room—Mitch sensed power coiled to spring.

What he'd been told was true; Hank Soldado did not look like someone you would want to mess with. Broad in the shoulders and thick-chested—the man looked like he'd swallowed a barrel—he was in his early thirties and had dark brown eyes, black hair, and ordinary features that Mitch thought were pleasant but not striking. But then Soldado's gaze settled on Mitch with probing intensity.

Mitch offered a handshake. "Mr. Soldado, I'm Mitch Parsons. Pleased to meet you."

Soldado's face eased as he smiled and shook hands. "Call me Hank. And let me thank you for all the things the NRA does."

Mitch held up his hand to dismiss that thought. "Well, it's not doing anything today. I'm here as a private citizen, not as a member of the NRA board, but what I want to do is in the interests of you and me—hell, of anyone who wants to hold onto their rights as an American." Mitch handed him the *Time* magazine with Noah Stone on the cover. "This man is your mission."

Hank studied the magazine. "I saw this guy on posters in the lobby. He's a Pied Piper? Charming rats?"

Anger burned in Mitch's gut. "He and his Alliance are *erasing* the Second Amendment." He took a deep breath and tried to cool down. "The reason you're here."

"And Stone . . . ?"

Mitch grabbed the magazine and threw it across the room. "The Alliance's preacher. *Time* isn't far wrong in calling him a Pied Piper. A half million people have joined the Alliance, most of them in its home state, Oregon. The politicians it backs win elections. It's stronger than the old Tea Party movement was."

"The NRA's—I mean, your interest?"

"He got Oregon to ban guns a year ago. We've challenged our asses off and the ban is still there. And it looks like it'll spread to Washington and California." He wanted to spit. "To start with."

Hank's eyebrows rose. "I think I'd have heard about a ban on guns. The NRA would have exploded, and the press wouldn't have been far behind."

Mitch waved that off. "Technically, I guess it's not a ban, but the result is the same. They slap you with an automatic felony conviction if you get caught with an illegal lethal firearm. And they confiscate them when you enter the state."

Hank said, "That's legal?"

"They think so. We've kept quiet about it because we don't want it to spread."

He scowled. "Damn. That's just wrong. We've got rights."

Mitch's insides eased. "I'm glad to hear you say that. Did you ever hear what Wayne LaPierre said back at the 2014 CPAC conference? 'There is no greater freedom than the right to survive and protect our families with all the rifles, shotguns, and handguns we want.'"

"Amen to that. I gotta hand it to you, standing up like this on your own. I'm with you."

Pleased, Mitch shrugged. "I just want to help support the people, my customers. I own a couple gun stores, do some gun shows."

"You told me there's a meeting here in Chicago where this Noah Stone is going to be?"

"He's speaking tonight at McCormick Place, a big rally for the Alliance. You can see what he's all about there." Mitch frowned. "I'm going with you, but it's gonna be hard to keep still when he spouts his crap."

"I've got some sympathy for that." Soldado strode to the magazine and picked it up. He studied the cover and then said, "So what do you want to do about this guy?"

Mitch took a deep breath. This was going okay, and Soldado was a real pro. His service as a Military Police officer in Afghanistan and an Illinois state trooper showed. "First, I want to find a legal way to take him down. For instance, a lot of our people say that his Alliance is actually a church, a religion—you know how rabid our opponents can get, so it could be true. If it is a religion, we sic the Feds on them for political participation by a nonprofit. You're an investigator, maybe you can find some evidence."

"So you just want a little private-eye work? I ask because you wanted to know if I carried." He opened his jacket, and there was the butt of a pistol sticking out of a holster.

Mitch came to the decision he'd been putting off. Only a coward would hold back from the ultimate in the defense of his country. "Well, like we used to say in the Boy Scouts, be prepared. You're a soldier, a lawman. I assume you have, ah, in the line of your duty you've, you know . . ."

Hank nodded and gazed out the window. His tone was cold and flat when he said, "There are bad guys who won't hurt anybody anymore, if that's what you're asking." He could have been talking about the weather.

We're coming, Noah Stone, we're coming at you.

3 A SHOOTER STRIKES

Jewel slipped the dictation printout into a file folder, leaned back and closed her aching eyes. She had really cranked to make up the time she'd lost at lunch, and still it had taken until—she checked at her watch—shit, almost seven o'clock to finish the deposition. The sky was darkening; the receptionist had gone. The other legal secretaries' cubes were empty and the partners' offices dark except for Mr. Reese's, the senior partner waiting for a hard copy.

She took the file to his office. He faced his big window, feet up on a credenza, leaning back in his oversized leather chair, probably thinking what a great man he was. She tapped on the door frame. "Mr. Reese? The Henderson deposition is done."

He swung around, the corners of his lips turned down like he had a bad taste in his tight little mouth. "Bring it in."

As she put the deposition on his desk, he stood and walked around to her. His slump-shouldered, potbellied body made his thousand-dollar suit look like a Kmart blue-light special. She said, "Will that be all, sir?"

"No. I need to speak to you about that"—he pointed at her chest—"that *garb* you're wearing."

"I can explain—"

"The organization you're touting there has caused serious trouble for our West Coast clientele."

Hell, their West Coast clients were always in trouble; their nails were manicured, but their hands were dirty. Although they were squeaky clean compared with the Chicago bunch.

Her boss's bunch.

She plucked at the Alliance T-shirt. "Well, it's not mine, really—"

"And you returned from lunch an hour late."

"Not a whole hour, and I was attacked by—"

"There are no acceptable excuses for either your tardiness or that . . . outfit. Completely unacceptable."

She looked at the floor so he wouldn't see her panic. She couldn't lose this job. She'd been incredibly lucky to find it; too many law firms in this city didn't see *black* and *legal secretary* as words that could go together. She said, "It won't happen again, sir."

"I know it won't. Clean out your desk."

Fear turned her stomach. Why was he doing this? Yeah, he was a jerk, but he'd never been a total ass to her. She looked up. "Please, Mr. Reese, can't I do something?"

He swept his gaze down her body and back. It felt like she was being stripped. "Well, you are a good worker . . ."

He widened his stance, put his hands on his hips, and glanced down. There was a bulge at his crotch. The letch grinned at her. "Perhaps there is something you can do."

So that's why he's doing this. Man, this was her day for dirt-bags with eager pricks. She should have known. Her looks and body had made her a target since she was twelve. Anger steamed inside her.

She smiled up at him and stepped closer until her breasts touched his chest. He rubbed against her, and she forced herself to keep her smile from collapsing.

Wait for it . . .

He said, "All right. This one time I'm willing to make an except—"

She spat in his face, wheeled, and stomped out.

He screamed, "You're fired."

"Too late. I just quit, asshole!"

She ran to her desk as he yelled, "Slut!"

She whirled to face him. He wiped at her spit with the silk hanky he kept in his breast pocket, a sick look on his face.

Looked like he was going to barf. Good. She'd sue the bastard for sexual harassment, and then . . . The silence of the office got through to her. There were no witnesses. There was no way to prove what had happened.

Knowing who the firm's clients were, she decided suing wasn't a good idea. God damn the man. She turned to her desk, her workplace for three years. She picked up her picture of Chloe. It was just a snapshot from her fourth birthday party, cake icing on her nose above the grin that always came with her giggles, but she was clearly the most beautiful child in all the world.

And now . . . with no paycheck and the pink she had to buy for Timmy's addiction, in a few weeks there wouldn't be enough in the bank to cover the rent, much less food. Fear stirred again. She denied it with the thought that she could surely find some temp work. She had good skills. No problem.

Yeah, right—she was in deep shit.

Jewel swept her gaze over her desk for things to take with her. A yellow piece of paper caught her eye; the redhead at the hotel had given it to her. It said, "Want a better life? The Alliance, McCormick Place Grand Ballroom, 8:00 p.m."

Yeah, she wanted a better life. But who'd believe anybody could really make it happen . . . Actually, the redhead at the hotel had seemed to. And she'd been pretty cool about helping a half-naked crazy Black woman.

Jewel slumped. She didn't want to go home right away, where she'd have to pretend to Chloe that everything was all right. So she'd go to this thing, kill some time, chill a little.

She called Juana and said, "I'm going to be later than I told you. Can you stay with Chloe?"

"Sure."

"You're an angel. Let me say hi to my sweetie and tell her what's happening."

Reese's hand reached past her and cut off the call. "You're not gone yet. Get out."

Holding back a sob, Jewel stuffed Chloe's picture into her bag and left to catch a bus for the Alliance rally.

Mercury-vapor lamps atop tall poles turned away night outside McCormick Place, the gigantic commercial complex near Lake Michigan. Inside the Grand Ballroom lobby, Hank and Mitch joined stragglers hurrying to enter before the Alliance program began.

Music reached Hank from speakers flanking a bank of entrance doors to the ballroom. The feel of it told him that the songwriter had smiled when he wrote the tune. And a tune it was, a sweet melody backed by foot-tapping rhythm.

Yeah, just like the old-time revivalists who used uplifting hymns to set up the sheep for a shearing as they flocked into the tent. But the people entering here didn't look sheep-like. They held their heads up and moved with vigor. They looked like people you'd call on to get things done. Hank wondered what the city would be like if it were filled with people like that.

Inside, Hank found a colorful throng pulsating with the music's beat. Banks of lights flooded a sea of seats surrounding a stage, and huge video screens hung from the ceiling. The place was packed—even the aisles were full. Everyone stood; the energy in the place was almost palpable.

Mitch said, "Jesus, look at 'em. It's a revival meeting."

Yeah, it did have a flavor of worshippers high on belief. Above the stage, the big screens showed the band. Like the music, the musicians smiled.

Hank searched for recognizable faces. And dangers.

Tension eased from Jewel as she stood at an aisle seat halfway to the stage. She couldn't remember the last time she had been stirred by the simple pleasure of music and rhythm. And the T-shirt she wore wasn't weird here; a lot of the people around her wore shirts just like it. It felt kinda like she was part of something the people around her seemed to feel pretty good about. It was catching.

She needed a lift. She'd always thought she was ready to do anything to take care of her own, but she hadn't been this day. On the other hand, she wouldn't have been too happy living in the skin of somebody who'd give an asshole a blow job to keep a paycheck coming.

The hell with that. She tuned into the music and moved with it. A worn-looking Latino guy next to her smiled at her, and damned if she didn't smile back.

Hank expected a flunky to pump up the crowd by rushing onstage and gibbering about Noah Stone's wonderfulness, but no such commotion erupted. A silver-haired, average-sized man stepped onto the stage. A spotlight followed him to the center. He stopped there and turned to scan the audience that surrounded him.

The band ended its song, and the musicians rested their instruments and faced the speaker with expectant smiles. The crowd quieted until only a murmur filled the hall.

The guy was a real showman. Hank smirked at Mitch, who nodded back.

The TV screens cut to a close-up of the man the crowd squinted to see. He appeared to be in his sixties, good-looking but not handsome. A full mustache concealed his mouth and made his face sober, serious. His dark eyes glowed with intelligence. And intensity.

Hank wondered if he was in for a fire-and-brimstone harangue. Then a smile transformed Stone's face into friendliness, and his eyes sparkled with humor. Hank resisted the pull of the man's likeability.

Stone said, "Hi."

The audience breathed a sigh.

"I'm Noah Stone, and I can't tell you how glad I am to see you. And to talk to you about joining me in the Alliance.

"The reason I want you with me is simple—I want to live a good life in the richest country in the world. But it's not material wealth I'm after, it's the things that make getting up in the morning a good thing. Shelter. Food. Good air. Good water. Safety. Work to do. Health. Community. Freedom. Is that what you want?"

The crowd muttered, "Yes" and "You bet" and "Tell me about it."

Stone frowned. "But I can't prosper with a gun held to my head. I can't prosper when courts flood the streets with criminals. I can't prosper when schools are so impoverished that they can't teach my children. I can't prosper when corruption is the standard, not the exception. In today's world, I can't prosper."

Jewel clenched a fist and murmured, "Right on." The Latino beside her whispered, "*Es verdád.*" Damn right it was the truth.

Stone moved in a circle on the stage, the overhead screens keeping his face in view. He said, "Like you, I'm willing to work hard to prosper, but I can't do it alone. You might argue, hey, we're not alone, we have government and religion to help us. The sad truth is that, despite everything governments and religions do, and sometimes *because* of what they do, we are steadily losing to a growing crush of problems.

"It doesn't even help to be rich. The rich don't have clean air. Or safety from kidnappers who take them for ransom. Or a healthy world that holds promise for their children.

"The rich don't prosper."

A woman in the third row whose husband's income was sixty thousand dollars a day pictured her youngest, his backpack oxygen tank and face mask warding off daily asthma attacks caused by toxins in the air whenever he went outdoors. She nodded.

Stone said, "It doesn't help to be religious. Yes, a church community can help you bear the burden, and perhaps you're promised something better after you die—but while you live in this world, prayer and faith are losing ground to crime, poverty, guns, and drugs.

"Even worse, faiths collide and fanaticism spawns death and destruction. Worshippers are led to murder in the name of God or Allah, and the worst of all human wrongs becomes exalted as a virtuous act.

"The religious don't prosper."

A woman who had lost her husband and her oldest child to a Palestinian suicide bomber in Tel Aviv nodded. Tears spilled as she kept her gaze fastened on Noah Stone.

Across the arena, a Palestinian-American bit down hard at the memory of his parents, slain in Gaza by an Israeli Defense Force missile.

Noah's eyes crinkled with an ironic grin. "Luckily, though, we can count on our government, can't we?"

The Palestinian joined the crowd in a bitter chuckle.

"We can count on our 'leaders' to gridlock because of sheeplike partisanship—to pander to ignorance and to fearmonger—to grasp for money and reelection—to vote according to influence, not conscience—to rule by ideology, not govern by reason.

"Back in the nineties, a Kentucky legislator introduced a bill to allow police officers to destroy confiscated guns, and the cops were all for it. But lobbyists claimed it was gun control that threatened Second Amendment rights, and the bill was changed to require the police to sell the guns and then use the money to buy bulletproof vests. Thousands of guns were put back on the street, and the cops had brand-new bulletproof vests to protect them from those weapons. *Stupid* is too nice a word for that kind of idiocy.

"Guns. Guns that kill. Lethal firearms." He gazed at the floor of the stage for a moment, and there was a sad quality to his voice when he continued. "Now *there's* cancer that robs us of our future, where murdered children and men and women cannot give us their energy, their lives, their creativity, their smiles, their songs, their laughter. Their love. For so long, it has been politically impossible to do anything to control unrestricted gun violence because of the cultural logjam nurtured by gun makers and the National Rifle Association."

Jason Schaeffer, proud member of the Mackinac Militia, bristled at the insult to the NRA. Well, he had a message for Mister High-and-Mighty. He slipped his hand into the roomy pocket of his camo pants and caressed the cool steel of his pistol. It was time to get closer to the stage.

He stepped into the aisle, said, "Excuse me," and slipped past the woman standing there.

Mitch clenched his fists. Here came another baseless attack on their rights. Oh, he sensed the lure of Stone's appeal, all right, but he had no trouble remaining detached. He observed the rapt faces around him and saw the power Stone had. This man was dangerous.

But he was just a typical gun-control nut. There were plenty of laws on the books to make sure only honest people got guns. They just needed to be enforced better. And criminals ignored laws anyway. There was really nothing new laws could do.

On the stage, Noah said, "To be fair to the NRA, the root of the problem is America's Wild West mentality—*our* Wild West mentality—that feeds the NRA's growth and influence. You see it in the militias that thrive in our nation, nourished by anti-government paranoia. The problem is not 'them,' it's us. There isn't a way to fix that anytime soon.

"But maybe there is a way to use that cowboy attitude *against* the shooters who say we'll be safer when there are *more* guns. Until now, that sounded like nonsense to me, but where I live, more guns *are* the answer.

"We're putting defensive guns into the hands of the people who are the victims, the women and men who are unarmed targets. Now, armed with nonlethal guns, they can fight attackers such as rapists, robbers, shooters, and racists." He smiled and lifted his gaze. "And they do, much to the sorrow of the bad guys."

He chuckled, and then looked out at the audience. "The other day I was asked if I was for or against guns." He grinned. "I said yes."

Hank looked at Mitch, who scowled down at the stage. "You didn't tell me about that."

Mitch shrugged. "It didn't seem important."

"But it is. The whole point of having a gun is to defend yourself." He focused on Stone again. How could the guy be against guns if he was arming people?

Mitch turned to him. "The defensive crap he's trying to sell won't protect us from tyranny by our so-called 'government.'"

Hank shook his head. "Come on, you know that's nonsense. Isn't going to happen, this is America. Our democracy is just too strong."

"You never know."

Stone's voice surged with energy and enthusiasm. "What we're doing about guns is just one example of how we, as a people, are strong and smart. We clean up after floods and hurricains and wildfires. We conquer disease. We fight famine. We defeat oppressors. Together, we work wonders. But these days we're breaking into smaller and smaller bits—cults, religions, militias, jihadists, splinters that are angrily pro this and anti that.

"We don't prosper.

"When religion separates us, when politics isolate us, when money divides us, how can we work together to change things? How do we step around our differences and understand our sameness?" Stone's voice grew quieter. "I offer you two things that can help turn us around—a promise, and a compass.

"The promise is one every Ally makes: I promise to help, the best I can." He paused, then whispered, "I promise to help, the best I can.

"That may not sound like much to you, but think about filtering everything you do through that and see what happens.

"It's a simple promise. You don't have to be a saint to keep it. Just try your best. We know there are times when our best isn't very good. When I get mad, I'm sure not likely to be helpful."

He smiled. "Kinda like you, I'll bet."

Hundreds whispered, "Yes."

"But the promise can help stop me from being hurtful. And it has."

⟳

Jason had made a promise, too, when he joined the militia—to defend the Constitution against all enemies, foreign and domestic.

Well, Noah Stone, domestic traitor, was going to get a .38-caliber dose of promise tonight. Jason's anger rose as he shoved his way through the people filling the aisle, but a sharp "Hey, be careful" from an old guy slowed him down. He didn't want to attract attention, at least not until he had Stone in his sights. He wiped a sweaty palm on his jacket and said, "Please excuse me" as he slipped closer to the stage.

Hank could never make the kind of promise Stone was talking about—police work and war sometimes called for merciless violence, the polar opposite of help. Hell, he didn't see how anybody in this world could make such a promise and keep it for more than ten minutes.

He wanted a sense of the man, not just the words and the image. He nudged Mitch with an elbow. "Going for a closer look. I'll meet you at the exit." He edged through the crowd that stood in the aisle.

Onstage, Noah Stone reached into a shirt pocket and pulled out something too small for Hank to make out.

Stone said, "The promise is our engine, but we need something to keep us on course." He raised the minuscule thing high in the air. "We need a compass."

Hank caught himself squinting hard to see. A huckster gimmick.

The view on the big screens zoomed in to show a fuzzy length of orange yarn dangling from his fingers.

"Think of this yarn as a thread." He spelled it out. "T-H-R-E-A-D. It represents an operating system for people.Not for religion. Or for business. Or for politicians. Just us people."

The picture changed to a close-up of Stone. He said, "Just you and me, one at a time." He grinned and his eyes twinkled. "Bear with me on this, I worked hard to make the letters come out right."

Hank braced for a heaping spoonful of happy horseshit. He glanced around; all faces were turned to the stage, looking eager to swallow the invisible hook at the end of that thread.

Stone said, "The *T* in THREAD is for tolerance." He smiled. "Have you ever driven past a yard littered with little statues and fountains and other yard art and thought it was dumb?"

Hank had to smile; he'd done just that.

Noah Stone said, "I used to think that way. But then I realized that the people who lived there went to a lot of effort to create that scene. They spent hard-earned dollars and their time. Then they stood back and said, 'Man, this looks great!'

"It didn't hurt me. Let it be.

"What does it matter that someone has hair you don't like, plays music you don't get, has a pierced tongue that makes you cringe, follows a religion that's alien to you, loves in ways you can't stomach, or comes in a skin color that doesn't match yours? If it doesn't harm you, let it be. Tolerate."

Just as Hank thought the next words would be *love thy neighbor*, Stone said, "Why not love instead of just tolerance? Aren't we taught to love our neighbors? Hey, if my neighbor is a nasty slob with a dog that barks all night, I'm doing a helluva job just to tolerate the guy. Don't ask me to love him—I'll fail. Requiring unconditional love guarantees failure for anybody who isn't a saint. Unearned love? I'm way too far from sainthood. Tolerance? That I can do. And so can you."

He held up the thread again. "THREAD. The *H* stands for honor. Integrity. Every unkept promise undercuts all of us. Every sloppily done job shortchanges each of us. Every bribe, every embezzlement, every corrupt act cheats us all, including the cheater."

Stone said, "THREAD. The *R* is responsibility. You do what you say you will, and you're accountable for the consequences of what you do. You steal, you pay back; you destroy, you rebuild.

"For many in our land of *caveat emptor*, the *E* in THREAD is the hardest. It stands for empathy, the opposite of 'buyer beware.'

Without concern for what others are experiencing, tolerance is a plant without water, help is a sail without wind."

⁓

Movement in the aisle caught Jewel's eye. A guy eased his way through people, heading down toward the stage. She'd seen those broad shoulders moving away from her before—it was her rescuer. She still owed him her thanks. She followed. him

Stone waved the thread. "Tolerance. Honor. Responsibility. Empathy. The *A* is for accord. As we've seen in government, partisan politics means gridlock. As we've seen in the abortion wars, uncompromising disagreement leads to misery and death. In the Alliance, we are bound to stick with it and reach accord when we disagree. Accord creates unity. And that creates strength.

"The last letter is *D*. The last word in THREAD is *do!* Make the promise and keep it. Ideals are hot air if we don't have the guts to do the hard things that need to be done. Being a good ally is hard, and to succeed, we must do!"

He raised the thread. "A tiny thing. Alone, it is weak." He broke it in two. "Weave it together with many others, and you have"—Stone plucked at his shirt—"something powerful enough to keep out the bite of cold.

"THREAD is only a word. But words have power because they bring us ideas, and ideas change human societies." His voice grew stronger. "This thread of principles weaves people into an alliance. An alliance that has power. Power to change the way things are to something better." Stone paused and surveyed the crowd.

⁓

As Hank closed to within twenty feet of the stage, he understood why Mitch was worried. The crowd responded like a thirsty man looking at a glass of cold water. Well, hell, what was there to disagree with?

But how did Noah Stone use his appeal? Or, more likely, abuse it? Hank looked for guards but saw only fans and reporters with video cameras. He spotted a familiar face, the redhead from the hotel lobby. She looked adoringly up at her leader.

Or was it master?

A man behind him yelled, "You goddamn traitor, you can't take away my rights!"

Hank spun, and a skinny man with a sweaty face pulled a pistol from his camo pants. Hank's instincts kicked in and he charged the shooter, waving his arms to distract him.

A man ahead of Jewel aimed a gun at Noah Stone. The guy who'd helped her ran straight at the shooter, his hands high, and the gunman swung the pistol toward him.

She hooked a thumb under her purse strap on her shoulder and flung the purse at the gun.

Time slowed for Hank. As if he were a spectator, he watched the man's finger tighten on the trigger. Saw the fierce, teeth-bared grin on his face. Hank planted a foot and started a shift to the right. He would never make it.

A purse whipped through the air and hit the gunman's shooting arm. His trigger finger jerked.

Alone in the silence, the pistol's report cracked.

The bullet nicked Hank's left arm between shoulder and elbow before it sledgehammered into his side. He went down.

Noah Stone dropped to the stage floor.

A news cameraman whirled and centered his viewfinder on the man with a gun.

A woman yelled, "He shot Noah!" and lunged for the gunman.

Jewel raced to the wounded man on the floor and shouted, "This man's been shot. Help!"

Noah Stone got to his feet, jumped from the stage, and hurried to her side.

The other two times Hank had been shot, he'd known immediately that the wound wasn't fatal. But not this time. He wondered how he ought to feel about death.

Close above him were Noah Stone on one side and a pretty woman on the other. The woman had a scar—the world faded away.

 **4 AN EXISTENTIAL THREAT TO LAW AND ORDER**

Marion Smith-Taylor turned from the view of cherry blossoms outside her office window and shook her head at the stacks of mail her assistant had added to the load on her desk. Surely there must be a way for the attorney general of the United States to find a law making it illegal to send said AG a gazillion memos and reports. It would save her a lot of time and Suzanne's back, too.

Her intercom buzzed, and Suzanne's husky voice came. "Can you take a call from Alexander Atkins?"

Stifling an instant "No!," Marion pushed back against the tightening in her stomach that always came with calls from the American Association for Justice's lobbyist, said yes, and picked up her phone. She didn't mean the cheery smile she hoped she projected when she said, "Alexander! How can I help you?"

"You can stop the lawlessness in Oregon, that's what you can do!"

Now what? She had big issues with what was going on in that troublesome state, but what problem could a bunch of trial lawyers have there? "Is there any particular lawlessness you have in mind?"

"Damn right. I have a client there who allegedly brought a load of pink into Oregon. Their kangaroo court system forced him to admit he drove the damned truck into the state to sell the drug. Forced him! He couldn't even plead not guilty!"

Marion planned to stop Oregon's abuse of the Fifth Amendment, but she had no desire to lighten this clown's load. Her smile was genuine this time. "I can see the problem, drug dealers having to tell the truth."

His voice pulled back to a milder, more reasonable tone. "Don't get me wrong. If he was dealing pink, he deserves everything he gets. But his Fifth Amendment rights are being trampled."

"Weren't you there to defend him?"

"I could have been, but Noah Stone's Alliance has some kind of legal support system where you don't need to hire a defense lawyer, and the guy cheaped out on me."

Aha, losing business, that's what had him worried. Marion had lost far too many cases because of deft manipulation of the law—make that distortion of the law—by defense lawyers, and she couldn't resist saying, "Gosh, that's awful, too."

Alexander sighed. He knew her opinion of him and his association. But his voice had an edge when he said, "It isn't funny. You've got to stop this legal abomination. Now."

She stiffened. In a tight voice that said don't fucking tell me what to do, she said, "I'm investigating the possibilities. Have a nice day, Alexander." She hung up on him.

He was right about one thing—Oregon's legal system had turned into an abomination when they flipped the Constitution upside down with that goddamn "Truth for Justice" initiative—led by, who else, Noah Stone and his Alliance.

Now Oregon courts forced people to testify against themselves as if the Fifth Amendment didn't exist. Hell, they were even citing the Fifth as the authority for violating the Fifth. A pal at the ACLU had told her that even they hadn't found a convincing way to challenge what was happening in Oregon.

Her anger bubbled up just thinking about it. Well, maybe Tiffany was closer to something to quash the statute. She reached for her phone, and her top legal researcher's soft voice soon answered. "Tiffany Horowitz."

"Marion here, Tiffany. How are you doing on that crazy Truth for Justice statute?"

"I don't have anything that helps us yet. My research suggests that it's actually possible to interpret the Fifth Amendment to mean that courts can require a person to testify against himself as long as there's due process of law. That actually makes sense in terms of the language of the amendment. I mean, we use the same due-process language to put people in prison, take their property, and execute them."

Marion scowled. "I don't like what I'm hearing, Tiffany. These people are undermining precedents for due process that go back to the Magna Carta."

"I'm sorry, ma'am."

Regretting her irritation, she softened her voice. "I know, I know. What else?"

"It sounds crazy, but the Alliance says its initiative is *derived* from the Magna Carta's mandate—you know, 'fundamentally rational law applied in a fundamentally fair proceeding.'"

Marion shook her head. "I still can't believe voters went for it."

"The Alliance made it sound like it would stop criminals. People liked that."

That was the trouble with initiatives—direct democracy led to rule by emotion. In this case, it was in a blue progressive state that had a tendency to steer to the left. Except, maybe, for the prison system they'd inaugurated; it sounded damn tough, and it had been a bipartisan effort. And it looked like they'd found a way to ban guns while they were pushing those new self-defense weapons—the state was like a hornet's nest that somebody had whacked.

Tiffany said, "Ah, you should know that the Alliance has started Truth for Justice initiatives in California and Washington State."

Oh, Lord. There were, what—twenty-four states that allowed initiatives? "Keep digging. We've got to find a way to stop it."

Tiffany said, "I find myself wishing . . . Never mind."

"No, what?"

"That things everywhere worked the way they do in Oregon. I mean, how rational or fair is it that so many rotten people dodge the bullet by taking the Fifth—"

"Listen to me! Oregon's new system may appear to be legal—so far—but it's not goddamn right. The Fifth Amendment is there to *protect* citizens!"

Tiffany's voice tightened. "Yes, ma'am."

Marion reined herself in. She said, "Good job, Tiffany. Keep trying."

"I'll do my best."

Marion disconnected. She shouldn't have lost it with Tiffany like that . . . but Oregon's distortion of the Constitution threatened to cripple America's judicial system. Noah Stone's Alliance was a key player. Maybe he was the key to stopping it, too. She needed to know more about the man. There must be a weakness.

Was Stone a good guy gone wrong, or did he have a nasty hidden reason for emasculating the law? Whatever he was, he was a threat, and she had the power of the Department of Justice to take him down.

She thumbed her intercom. "Suzanne, get me Joe Donovan in Oregon." One of her smartest field agents, Joe would dig out what she needed.

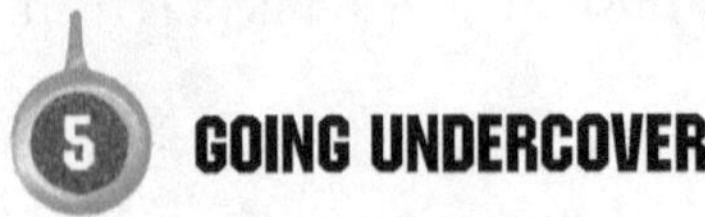

5 **GOING UNDERCOVER**

Noah Stone stepped into the hospital room where Hank Soldado lay on a hospital bed, unconscious or asleep. An attractive young Black woman stood on the far side of the bed. She looked up and said, "Mr. Stone. My name is Jewel Washington."

Noah smiled and nodded to her as he went to the bedside. Bandages wrapped Hank Soldado's torso and upper left arm. He seemed asleep, and his arms and legs twitched as if he were dreaming. "How is he?"

She shrugged. "They say he's stable."

He knew that face, those bright blue eyes. "You were there, weren't you?"

"Yeah. When he got shot."

The sound of the shot echoed in Noah's mind, and a flare of dread punched him in the belly. He shivered and fought it back. He'd been fighting it back all morning, and his stomach was in a knot. He feared that fear was winning and that years of work would shrivel and die when he became afraid do it anymore. He'd never had to think about whether his cause was worth dying for, but he did now.

He didn't want to die.

He'd learned his rescuer's name, but nothing more about the man other than that he had taken a bullet intended for Noah. He hadn't even seen what Soldado had done. Did the woman know?

"Excuse me, Miss Washington, did you see what happened?"

She shifted her gaze to him, and he was again struck by her blue eyes, unexpected in a dark-skinned face. Freckles across her nose formed a band of cocoa dots on warm brown, and a scar slashed down her cheek. More than her looks, though, there was the intensity and focus of a strong mind. She said, "Yeah. That nut was aiming his gun at you, and then this guy charged him."

"Why, I wonder."

She shrugged. "He did something like that for me yesterday morning, helped me out of a bad patch, and I'd never seen him before." She turned her gaze to Soldado. "I can tell you that he's very good with a gun."

His eyes shut, Soldado clenched his teeth and lifted his good arm until it was straight out from his body, and then he curled his index finger. His trigger finger. Shooting a gun? Tears leaked from his closed eyes. He moaned and twisted. Soldado whipped his head back and forth as if to deny something with everything he had.

Jewel reached for the call button, but Noah saw Hank's eyelids flicker. He held up a hand and said, "I think he's coming around."

Noah put his hand on Soldado's shoulder and squeezed just enough to let him know someone was there.

⌒

The lovely woman laughs and swings the beautiful child back and forth.

Words come from Hank, but he can't make them out because they are muddled and slow, as if made of molasses.

The woman frowns at him. She pulls the child close and says molasses words that make no sense. The look on her face is angry. Wild.

Insane.

The beautiful child is in danger.

He reaches for his gun, sooo slooooow . . .

His hand rises in front of him—the pistol he aims at the woman is dead steady.

She laughs and raises the child high in the air.

He pulls the trigger.

"No!"

The cry ripped out of Hank. He lunged upright in the bed.

He was holding his breath, his jaws clenched.

Again.

Why?

Pain stabbed him in the side and his arm, and he lay back in the bed. The rails of a hospital bed enclosed him. The stringent odor of antiseptic dominated the air. A vase on a tray next to his bed held a bouquet of yellow carnations.

He was alive. Good. He wasn't ready to be done yet.

Noah Stone gripped Hank's shoulder. "Mr. Soldado. You cried out."

A pretty woman on the other side of the bed took a tissue from the hospital tray and wiped at his cheeks. She said, "You hurtin'?"

The tears again. More and more, they were there when he woke up. He touched a fingertip to a wet spot on his face and then tasted. Salty? Why?

His left arm ached. Bandaging wrapped the arm and his chest from under his arms to the bottom of his rib cage. Pain pulsed in his left side. He pushed the hurt down. He had thinking to do.

The woman said, "Should I call a nurse?"

He shook his head, then licked dry lips and croaked, "Who?"

Stone poured a glass of water as the woman answered. "I'm Jewel Washington. You helped me out yesterday. You know, when that greenie and his buddy were gonna . . . were gonna . . ."

The shooting in the courtyard popped into his mind. He nodded.

She took the cup from Stone and held it for Hank as he drank cool water through the straw. She wore rings on each of her slender fingers, two on some of them. He finished, leaned his head back, and smiled his gratitude.

She said, "I couldn't thank you yesterday, so I'm here to do it now. But 'thank you' seems so . . . so nothing beside what you did for me."

There was something about her and the shooter . . . Just before the gun fired, a purse had hit the gunman. If it hadn't, he'd likely be in the morgue instead of a hospital room. He concentrated. It had been this woman's face he'd seen just before he blacked out. "The purse?"

She nodded. "I saw that gun and I just reacted."

Hank's peripheral vision caught a widening of Noah Stone's eyes. Sort of a scared look. Hank nodded to Jewel. "We're even."

She smiled. She wasn't model-pretty, but the way her looks added up—and the mind he sensed behind those bright eyes—left "pretty" running a poor second. Her business suit added to his impression of intelligence and purpose. The scar on her cheek drew his attention.

Her gaze caught his; she'd seen where his eyes were focused. She lifted her chin like a proud warrior bearing the marks of battle.

He grinned. "And thanks for the flowers."

She nodded toward Noah. "Card says they're from him."

Hank looked at his assignment. A lively mind gazed back at him from hazel eyes. Stone's expression was cool, but there were signs of tension—mouth tight, a squint to his eyes. Stone radiated the energy of a younger man, putting the lie to hair closer to white than gray. That plus not much in the way of wrinkles made his age difficult to pinpoint. Hank said, "Hello, Mr. Stone."

Stone smiled, and warmth transformed his face. "Call me Noah. I owe you considerable thanks, too, for taking that bullet for me."

Hank nodded. "Well, it wasn't something I planned on doing."

Noah said, "You don't go around saving people as a regular habit?"

Hank smiled. "Only on slow days."

Noah laughed. Jewel touched Hank's arm and said, "Listen, I gotta get to a job interview. I'm glad you're okay."

Noah said, "What's the job market like here?"

She frowned. "It would have to work hard to get up to lousy. It's a miracle when there's something decent, and I don't believe in miracles—at least I've never seen one."

Hank saw appraisal in Stone's face. Stone said, "What are you looking for?"

"Legal secretary. I'm good at it. And I've been studying at night school to be a paralegal."

Stone said, "I need good people for our legal department; our laws have been changing faster than we can keep up." He pulled out his wallet and gave her a business card. "If you ever come to Oregon, look me up."

Her eyes lit up, and then narrowed. She shook her head. "I've got a, er, sick brother I have to care for." She smiled and said, "Thanks anyway. Bye." She hurried out, tucking the card in her purse.

Noah gazed after her. "Too bad. Sharp woman." He turned to Hank. Could this man help? "Ah . . ." This was hard to talk about. "That man shooting at me . . . That was a very scary moment."

"First time?"

Noah nodded. "Never anything like it. I mean, there have been hecklers, but that comes with the job. This was—" He didn't want to think about it.

"Did the cops get the guy?"

"Yes. But where there's one—" He wished he could throw off that thought. "The offer I made to Jewel goes for you, too. I'd be pleased if you would join me. From what I've seen, and from what I've heard you did for Miss Washington, you seem like a man who could help me with security. Am I right?"

Soldado's gaze was steady. No, more than that—piercing. Soldado nodded and then said, "I hear you've got a few things going on out there."

Noah had to grin at that. "You might say we have a quiet revolution in progress."

Soldado raised his eyebrows. "Some say your operation is a cult religion."

Noah frowned. "There are . . . opponents who claim things like that. But the Alliance is totally open and free, quite the opposite of a cult, and about as secular as you can get. You'll see, if you come."

Soldado's gaze kept boring in. "I can't make that promise of yours."

Noah shrugged. "Not required."

"The way you talk about helping people, I'm not sure what I do is something the Alliance can use."

"What do you do? Something other than saving pontificators from perforation?"

Soldado smiled. "Yeah. Sometimes duty calls in harsh ways."

"Nobody does only one thing well," Noah said. "Come out and see what happens."

"All right, I will."

The fear lurking in Noah's mind took a step back. But it would return, he was sure of that. He gripped Hank's shoulder again. "I'm very pleased. I hope we can get together. Be well." He left feeling lighter and brighter than he had all morning.

Hank reached for the phone, gritting his teeth against the pain. He had it under control by the time the operator connected him with Mitch Parsons's room at the Chelsea.

He said, "I need to see you."

"What about your wound?"

"It's my ticket in. Stone and I are like blood brothers now."

"I'll be right over."

While he waited, the doc came by and told him about his injuries. The bullet had struck the holster under his jacket and stopped, leaving a cracked rib. The arm was a through-and-through flesh wound.

Hank tried to doze, but pain jabbed him awake every time his eyes closed, and he didn't want to dull his mind with painkillers. Giving up, he turned on the TV and caught a news report of the shooting. In slow motion, it showed a wisp of smoke curling from the shooter's gun barrel just before a woman slammed into him. He grinned. Not a bad body block there. Some tough women in Chicago.

The video cut to a photo of an angry-looking man, a face Hank had seen on the other side of a gun. A voice-over said, "Accused assassin Jason Schaeffer was released today into the custody of noted criminal attorney Randolph Gutierrez."

The scene cut to Schaeffer, led by a lawyer uniformed in a dark suit and a briefcase, making his way toward a limo through a crowd of reporters and cameramen on the Cook County courthouse steps. The voice-over continued.

"At his arraignment, Schaeffer pleaded not guilty. According to Gutierrez, the tape merely shows a man who took out a weapon for self-defense because a stranger in the crowd attacked him."

Gutierrez said, "It was his right to shoot his attacker. You ask me, this Soldado guy is the one ought to be under arrest."

Hank's door opened and Mitch Parsons entered. "Hey, Hank."

The news report cut to a woman who looked like a well-preserved forty-year-old Victoria's Secret model. The reporter's voice-over continued. "The alleged gunman is a member of the Mackinac Militia led by Colonel Martha Hanson." Her name appeared on the screen as she nodded to the camera.

Hank raised his eyebrows when he heard the colonel's name. She was eye candy, but on the inside, well, once a cop had stopped her for speeding and she'd shot him in the leg and driven away because she was late for a meeting. That had cost her three years in the penitentiary. It had also doubled her already significant street cred with quick-draw militia and sovereign-citizen types.

The reporter said, "Colonel, was this man following your orders to shoot Noah Stone?"

The colonel smiled. Well, it looked like a smile, but it didn't feel like one. "Now why would I want him to do that?"

"Your feelings about Stone's opposition to lethal guns are well known."

"Mr. Stone has every right to say what he wants, and I have every right to not like it." Beneath a gaze as flat as a viper's, the smile came again. "And I don't tell people to go around shooting other people." If smiles could kill . . .

Mitch grunted. When Hank glanced at him, he said, "Her eyes. You wonder if there's a . . ." He frowned. ". . . a human being in there."

Hank knew that look in her eyes. There'd been times in Afghanistan he'd felt like he was made of stone. He'd caught the same cold look on his own face reflected in a Kabul window—just before a sniper's bullet shattered the glass. He clicked the remote and Colonel Hanson disappeared.

Mitch's gaze wandered over Hank's bandages. "So, are you going to be all right?" He seemed to mean it. Sure he did. He was worried about getting some dirt on Noah Stone.

"I'll be all right. Bullet tore up some muscle and cracked a rib."

Mitch scowled. "Why'd you do it? Stop that guy."

Hank replayed his actions. There had been no thought. There was no "why." He shrugged, and it hurt. "Reflex, I guess. Years of being focused on protecting people." He gazed at Mitch. "You'd have been okay with an assassination?"

Mitch's eyes widened. "Oh, no. No. That was shocking."

"Weren't you asking me about 'being prepared' with a gun?"

"Yes. But that was theory, this was . . . reality." He shook his head. "What counts now is what happens next. How long will you be laid up?"

"I'll be mission-ready in a few days. Stone came to see me. He's grateful. I'm invited to join him out in the Oregon boonies."

Mitch nodded. "Super." He took out a business card and a pen. "Don't try taking a gun into Oregon. They check everyone flying into the state and all luggage." As he wrote, he said, "This's a gun-rights activist there who can get you a weapon." He handed the card to Hank. "Nobody but you and me and him had better ever know that password."

Hank took the card. "Like you said, be prepared."

"Good luck." Mitch turned toward the door, then stopped and faced Hank. "What did you think of Noah Stone?"

"Powerful. But to do what?"

"Change things. For the worse."

"You're right, Mitch. He needs to be stopped."

 **RUN FOR YOUR LIFE**

When Jewel's bus pulled up to Harrison Courts, the dim light of dusk did little to mask its shabbiness. She remembered all the talk when they started "renovating" the development—the mayor had said they would "cure a cancer." Yeah, right. The place swarmed with low-life squatters and gangbangers.

Slow-moving after a grinding day of job-hunting, she was the last to leave the bus. Head down, clutching a can of Mace pepper spray, she scurried across a bare dirt courtyard behind a small cluster of Blacks and Latinos. Not that she thought her Mace would do much good; the men—more often teenagers—who mugged and raped wore masks and sunglasses that blocked the worst of it. And there were usually guns in their hands.

Passing the Out of Service sign that had been taped to her elevator for a year, she trudged up four flights of stairs, breathing through her mouth to avoid the smell of urine.

When she unlocked the three deadbolts on her apartment door, Chloe's voice on the other side shouted, "Mommy!" Jewel pushed the door open, and a hurtle of little girl raced into her arms. She scooped up her daughter, a four-year-old force of nature. Juana, the twelve-year-old neighbor who looked after Chloe, lowered her pepper spray and hurried to bolt the door.

Jewel set Chloe down and took a moment to simply gaze at her. She loved looking at her girl, and not because she was her spittin' image—same milky-brown skin, same nose and big smile—but because of her innocence and bright flame of life.

"Chloe, love, you been a good child today?"

Chloe bounced on her tiptoes and chirped, "I was, Mommy. We played, and I read books." She loved to run her finger over the words when she was read a story.

Juana smiled on Chloe—they were more like sisters than neighbors. "She was fine, ma'am."

Jewel sobered. "Timmy?"

"Mostly in his bed all day. He's really hurtin'."

"Thanks, Juana." Jewel listened at the door, then unlocked it. She peered into the hall and found it empty. "Don't know if I need you tomorrow, got no interviews yet." She gave Juana two twenties and let her slip out.

Juana hurried to the next door down the hall, knocked and whispered her name. Latches clicked and she was admitted. Jewel locked up.

She tousled Chloe's hair. "Listen, honey, why don't you play while I see to Uncle Timmy?"

"He's sick again, Mommy."

"I know, sugar. I got him some medicine."

Going into her bedroom and then to the walk-in closet that served as her brother's room, she found Timmy shivering on his mattress on the floor, a sheet pulled up to his chin. The air stank of stale sweat and soiled clothes—she needed to do a cleanup.

Jewel knelt beside him and smoothed his hair. Hard to believe he was twenty-three now. He'd been her "little boy" since he was twelve and she seventeen when their mother was killed in a mugging. She loved him so much, it ached.

His jaws clenched and unclenched as he looked up at her. It broke her heart to see how hard he worked not to show his pain. She handed him a packet of pink she'd gotten from Murphy.

His eyes widened, and he flashed her a grin. "Oh, thank you, Sister, thank you." Hands quivering, he dug his dope kit out from under a pair of dirty jeans. Jewel couldn't watch, so she went to the living room and stared out a window.

Tears clouded her eyes, and she cursed the junkie chemist who had cooked up the designer drug with a hook that couldn't be removed. She'd looked for help on the internet and found out that pink was crack cocaine and freebase nicotine combined into a new drug. The nastiest part of pink was the most addictive drug known to science—nicotine in the freebase form. The crack created instant dependence, and pink's freebase nicotine created instant addiction.

"You feel like God." That's what Timmy had said at the beginning, back when he was stronger and had enough money for pink, and they hadn't believed the talk they'd heard about how bad it was. He'd do the drug and then go out for a long night, humming and snapping his fingers. He'd told her, "You're the smartest, the strongest, the sexiest. Anything is possible. And it lasts for hours and hours."

Yeah, pink gave addicts a few hours in heaven, but when it wore off, it put them on a bullet train to hell. Because it was so new, nobody'd found anything to treat the suffering and, so far, detoxing killed you. When addicts withdrew, they died in agony.

It had been just six months since pink had taken over Timmy's life because some fool at a party had slipped it into his pipe of marijuana. Now he was a condemned man.

After a dinner of fried Spam, greens, fruit salad, and a treat of Girl Scout Thin Mint cookies, Jewel snuggled Chloe close on the couch and read to her. She stayed away from stories with a father in them, because they sparked questions she didn't want to answer.

At eight o'clock, after a flurry of hugs and kisses, she tucked Chloe into bed. Timmy, now smiling and energized by a shower and clean clothes, went out to enjoy his high while it lasted. Jewel tried television, but the shows were either sex, violence, mindless crap, or all three.

Surfing channels, she caught a news report that said the guy who had tried to shoot Noah Stone was pleading not guilty. That was nuts. There was a herd of witnesses, for Christ's sake. But his lawyer would probably get him off on a technicality—she'd seen them do that a hundred times at the office.

Hank Soldado had been a hero twice in the same day. She pictured him with Stone in the hospital room. Soldado hurt but strong, Noah Stone warm and inviting, yet each had a similar edge.

She dug out the Alliance brochure. It painted a picture of life made good through work, the promise, and THREAD. She dozed in her chair and dreamed of her daughter running on green grass under a blue sky, laughing.

Free.

The next day dragged by, filled with hours of job-hunting. She found a perfect position, but they called her old boss and it went belly-up. She'd never get a job with him sinking every chance she found.

She took out her phone and checked her bank account balance. Today would have been payday, and without that things looked awfully lean. She felt as if the world was ganging up to crush the life out of her life. Noah Stone's invitation to Oregon came to mind more and more. But there was Timmy.

The following morning, while scouring want ads and having no luck, muffled whimpers from Timmy's "room" distracted her. She went back to check on him.

He lay on his mattress, shivering under a blanket, sweat rolling off his face. She knelt beside him and ran her fingers through his hair. It'd been too many hours since his last hit; he was really hurting.

He looked up at her, his eyes wet wells of pain. "Sister . . ."

"What, honey?"

"Es-s-s-steban . . ." He trailed off and shut his eyes.

So he'd been thinking about running out of pink. When Esteban Sanchez, who'd lived in the apartment below them, had run out of money for the drug he had screamed for a day and a night before he died. The story in the 'hood was that he had bitten his tongue off in convulsions.

She still had nightmares about it.

With no job, she had to stretch the time between drug buys as far as possible. She couldn't even think about what would happen when she couldn't pay for it anymore.

Timmy groped for her hand, and she took his and clutched it to her heart. He said, "I'm afraid."

"I won't let it happen," she said. Brave talk. She had maybe enough cash for another couple of weeks, and then she could start pawning her rings, which were really meant to keep her and Chloe off the street. She couldn't let that happen, she couldn't! But what else could she do?

Timmy cried out and doubled over. Jewel sighed, leaned close to kiss him on the forehead, and then left. In the kitchen, she called to see if Juana could babysit while she went to meet Murphy. She could, in a half hour. Jewel poured the last cup of coffee from the pot. Her mind kept asking her what she could do, and she kept running away from the question.

Chloe joined her with her crayons and her new *Day at the Zoo* coloring book. Jewel said, "Whatcha doin'?"

Chloe showed her. "A peacock!"

"Hey, you're stayin' in the lines great."

A muffled cry came from Timmy. Chloe glanced at the bedroom, then said, "Will Uncle Timmy always be sick?"

Jewel stroked Chloe's head. "I'm afraid so, honey."

Chloe turned to her coloring, and as Jewel gazed at her, a sinking hopelessness grew. No, Timmy would never get well. It would be this way until he died.

Thinking of the days and years ahead, Jewel had a vision of Chloe as a young woman, suffering the same way. Oh, Lord, it could happen. Living here, it could happen real easy, just the way it had with Timmy.

She couldn't deal with that now. Pushing the thoughts aside, she went to check on the state of her cash.

The Alliance brochure sat next to her purse. She opened it and stared at a photo of Alliance headquarters. It looked like a farm with a backdrop of green hills and blue sky.

Then she looked around her apartment. There were stains and dirt all her scrubbing couldn't budge. Out the window, the sky was more brown than blue.

Timmy groaned.

She paced. All right, girl, what are you gonna do about it? Leave? She had enough for bus tickets. To go where? The only place outside of Chicago she knew anything about was Oregon, and only that Noah Stone and maybe a job were there. It was so far away. Timmy would never make it. But remembering Stone's smile when they'd talked, she thought maybe she had the makings of a friend out West.

She went to the window. A boy of about ten burst into the courtyard below, running all out. Three larger boys chased him down in the center of the yard. They circled him, and then two of them pulled pistols from their sagging jeans. The boy tried to run, but they shot him in the back. After he fell, they each gave him a kick before sauntering away, laughing.

She gazed at Chloe. To stay could mean handing her child the same death sentence that boy had been under. That Timmy was under.

But she couldn't leave Timmy to die in awful pain.

And then Jewel understood what she could do to . . . to help free him.

She called Murphy to find out where he was patrolling.

Pushing through a shuffling crowd on Wabash Avenue, she saw Murphy across the street, leaning against a rusty steel beam that supported the elevated train tracks overhead. A pinkie stumbled down equally rusty steel stairs that led up to the platform where the train stopped. He went to Murphy and held out a fold of bills. The cop made no effort to hide a practiced swap for a packet of pink. Smiling, Murphy added the bills to a roll of cash damn near as big around as a baseball.

Jewel cut across the street, dodging cars like a matador with a bull charging her. Murphy scowled when she trotted up to him. Probably disappointed because she wore jeans and a T-shirt instead of a miniskirt.

She said, "You gonna give me a ticket for jaywalking, Murphy?"

"Not if you're buyin'."

She took eighty dollars from her purse. "Give me a double."

Murphy smiled, took two packets of pink from his tunic, and traded them for her money. He added her bills to the roll of cash and slipped a red rubber band around it.

Just looking at the fat son of a bitch made her mad. He was everything wrong with this city, with her life.

He smacked a wet kiss at her. She clenched her fist around the packets of pink. "I have something else for you."

The look in his glittery little eyes was greedy. "Yeah?"

She smashed her knuckles into his face. He dropped the money roll, grabbed his nose, and cried out. Blood gushed from under his hands and down his chin.

People shot glances at them and as quickly took them away.

A warm wave of satisfaction washed through her. "That's for turning your back when that punk was tearing off my clothes."

"You bitch!" he screamed. It sounded like "Ooo bib!"

A grubby man reached for the money on the sidewalk. Jewel snatched it up and glared him away.

The fat roll of cash felt damn good in her hand. It was heavy—had to be at least a thousand.

Overhead, steel wheels squealed against rails as an L train came to a stop at the platform above them.

Murphy held out a bloody hand. "Gimme." It sounded like "Gibbe."

The money was freedom. A future for Chloe.

He grabbed at her and she retreated around the track support.

"Ooo bib!" he said, and fumbled for his pistol.

Jewel bared her teeth, reached forward, and yanked the gun from his hand. She pointed it at his chest. "Thanks for the donation." She ran up the stairs to the L platform and pushed through the crowd to an open train door.

Murphy staggered onto the platform, gasping for breath. He charged her way, yelling, "Stob er! Stob er!" People turned her way, and one big guy started toward her.

Clamping the gun under her arm, she yanked the rubber band off the roll of bills and peeled off a bunch, then yelled "Money!" and threw the cash into the air. The crowd scrambled for the fluttering bills, and Murphy was shoved back. She grabbed the gun. It was black and evil in her hand. The door started to close—she dropped the gun to the tracks below the car and then backed inside. Murphy bulled his way through the money-grubbing crowd, and she gave him the finger as the doors closed and the train left him behind.

She slipped the cash into her purse and wrapped her fingers around the wad. It was real. She shook her head. Had she gone crazy? But it had felt so good when she'd— Shit. Murphy had her phone number. He'd track her down. She *had* gone crazy.

She touched the two packets of pink. It had seemed like the best thing to do, but now she didn't know if she could follow through. And would Timmy understand and take them both to—

The ring of her cell phone startled her. She dug the phone out of her purse and answered.

Murphy's voice said, "I ged oo."

She stabbed the power icon and wished the train would go faster. She had a bad feeling. This was gonna go sour.

Back home, she knelt beside Timmy's bed. His eyes watered with misery. She took him in her arms and held him close as he shivered. Tears rolled down her cheeks.

She released him, and he lay back. He said, "I'm sorry, Sister."

"So am I, honey. I love you."

Like a starving man, he said, "Did you get some?"

Oh, Lord, how could she do this?

A spasm twisted his body and he moaned.

How could she not? She held out the pink. Both packets.

"A double?" Nobody lived through a double—and Timmy knew that. He nodded and gave her a tight smile. "Thank you." He took the pink.

He reached up and stroked her cheek along the scar. "I love you, too." Then he reached for his kit.

She stood and turned away, then stopped. She couldn't do this. She started to turn back, but then left him. She had to. And Timmy was okay with it. It was what he wanted, she had seen that.

Back in the living room, she stared out the window, hoping for something to take her mind away from her pain. But there in the courtyard dirt was the bloodstain from the boy who'd been gunned down. His body was gone. It was as if he'd never existed.

She'd helped Timmy the best she could. Now it was time to take care of Chloe. And she couldn't do that when they were neck-deep in drugs and defenseless against violence and guns. And Murphy. They needed a safe place to be.

Keeping her eyes away from where Timmy was, she went to her closet, took her best clothes from the rod, and tossed them onto her bed. She pulled her big suitcase from under the bed and set it next to the clothes. She heard the rustle of his movements. Sniffling back tears, she emptied the stuff from her dresser drawers into the suitcase and folded her clothes on top.

Still avoiding Timmy, she hauled the suitcase into the living room. Chloe was working on a giraffe in her coloring book. Jewel said, "Honey, come help me do some packing."

Chloe looked up, and then her eyes widened. "Why are you crying, Mommy?"

"Uh, air pollution, makes my eyes hurt. Come on, let's round up your critters." They went to Chloe's tiny room.

Chloe collected her favorite stuffed animals and dolls while Jewel packed her library of picture books into a duffel bag. She added the animals, dolls, and Chloe's clothes, then dragged the bag into the living room. She said, "Chloe, go potty, we're going . . . away."

Afraid of what she would see, she went back to Timmy. Instead of the horror she expected, Timmy had dressed in his good clothes and arranged himself neatly on his mattress. A faint smile curved his lips, and his eyes were closed, the constant frown line between his brows gone. His chest did not move. He looked at peace.

He didn't hurt anymore.

Her fear released in a rush of sad relief. She knelt and brushed his hair, and then gathered him in her arms and held him close. He was so thin, so fragile. She whispered, "Oh, my brave Timmy."

She rocked him and murmured the lullaby she'd made up to get him to sleep when he was little. "Good night, Timmy, it's time to rest your sleepy head . . ." She let the silence take over. Tears ran down her cheeks, but she just couldn't let him go.

Chloe's voice came. "Mommy?"

Oh, God. Hoping her voice wouldn't expose her crying, she said, "Coming, sugar." Jewel laid Timmy down and wiped her cheeks. She leaned forward and kissed his forehead.

Jewel went to the living room, put her purse over her shoulder, and extended the pull handle on the suitcase. "C'mon, Chloe."

"Where we going, Mommy?"

"A better place." She hoped. Oh, Lord, she hoped.

Chloe started for the bedroom. "I want to say goodbye to Uncle Timmy."

Jewel caught her arm. "Wait. He's . . ." Chloe gazed up at her, confusion on her sweet face. "He's asleep, but you can say good-bye if you're super-quiet."

She followed Chloe into the bedroom and had to bite her lip as Chloe kissed Tommy's cheek and whispered, "Bye, Uncle Timmy." She stood and held her hand out to Jewel.

Jewel left the apartment door unlocked and stopped at Juana's for a long hug and to leave her enough of Murphy's cash to put Timmy to rest.

Hours later, as their Greyhound bus rolled westward into Iowa, Chloe slept with her head on Jewel's lap. Jewel stared out at the green, rolling country and mourned Timmy. A sensation of weightlessness from being freed of the chains of his dependence shamed her, but she knew herself, and she knew she would leave that behind. She had two tickets to Oregon, a foreign land with strange new ways and a promise of help.

7 WHAT ARE WE COMING TO?

A cold snap had hit Washington D.C. The city's famed cherry blossoms were brown and rotten on the trees. They matched Marion's mood perfectly. The humidity had returned to dismal, the new crime s+tats she'd seen on CNN this morning were disastrous, and rush-hour commuters were demented.

Four blocks from her office in the Department of Justice building on Pennsylvania Avenue, traffic slowed to a slug's pace. Finally, it crept past a parked ambulance, its lights flashing, and she saw a blanket-covered body on the pavement near the curb. Paramedics were loading a second body on a gurney into the ambulance. Two detectives interviewed people on the sidewalk.

When Marion came to a cop directing traffic, she stopped and lowered her window.

The cop, sad-faced and fiftyish, said, "Keep moving, ma'am."

"What's the problem?"

"Please keep—" He peered at her. "Oh, Ms. Smith-Taylor. Didn't recognize you. It's a drive-by. Third one this morning."

She shook her head. "What are we coming to?"

The cop sighed. "I try not to think about it."

Already weary by the time she arrived at her office, Marion collapsed into the big leather chair behind her desk. Her gaze slid across the masses of law books that covered her walls. So many laws. So many lawbreakers. She stared at stacks of files detailing vicious crimes that made her job, with one exception, depressing.

The one exception walked in and shut the door behind her. Suzanne carried a half dozen fat file folders, a handful of pink message slips, and a small Priority Mail box. Her blond hair bounced just above her shoulders as she strode to the desk and set her burdens on the one clear spot. She peered at Marion, and a look of concern shadowed her expression. She stepped behind Marion's chair, and her cool, strong fingers massaged Marion's stiff neck and shoulder muscles.

After a few minutes, Marion sighed, then swiveled and pulled Suzanne's head close to place a soft kiss on her lips. "Thanks."

Suzanne stepped to the side and studied Marion. "You're not sleeping again."

So the makeup hadn't disguised the purple bags under her eyes. She shook her head. "It was a dream about Noah Stone. First there's this nice, earnest face. Slowly, his gray hair turns brown, and his mustache darkens and gets smaller and rectangular . . . and suddenly he's Hitler, haranguing a mob."

"You think the Alliance is that bad?"

"Not on the surface." Marion turned to her computer and launched a browser. Typing in www.theallies.org, she was soon at the Alliance's home page, complete with a multicolored logo and the words *I promise to help, the best I can.*

Suzanne leaned forward to see, her hand a delightful warmth on Marion's shoulder. The faint scent of the perfume Marion had given Suzanne for Christmas brought up pleasant memories of skin on skin— No, save that for later.

Marion clicked links to flick through a series of essays written by Noah Stone and other members. "I've been through the whole site, and all they talk about is how to work together, their philosophy, and their agendas for peaceful change."

Suzanne pointed to an ad offering a free book. "There's a name I recognize." The book was *Justice Through Truth and Advocacy,* and the famous name was Edgar Aaronson, a former Supreme Court chief justice. The coauthor was Noah Stone.

Marion said, "Yeah, I want you to send for it. Aaronson was one of my heroes in law school. Maybe there's a clue there."

Suzanne made a note. "Will do."

Marion clicked on an icon of a pistol with the universal "no" circle and crossbar over it. It took her to the Alliance approach to eliminating lethal firearms and replacing them with defensive guns. "Look at this . . . when you know the facts, how can anyone argue rationally with getting rid of handguns and assault rifles?" She'd read the Alliance's ideas, but didn't see how they could really work, long-term. On the flip side, a militia "patriot" had taken a shot at Stone in Chicago, so maybe he was doing something right.

Suzanne said, "Okay, so what's so wrong with the Alliance?"

"God only knows, and She isn't telling." She thumbed through the messages and found a cluster of governors there. "And what are the leaders of California, Washington, Colorado, and Idaho up to?"

Suzanne took the top folder from the stack she'd brought in. "Well, my guess is the new FBI crime report."

Marion rolled her eyes. "They're calling to complain about Oregon again."

Opening the folder, Suzanne scanned a printout. "I bet you're right. Oregon's crime numbers are down for the fifth month in a row, and the other states' crime rates are up even more than the rest of the country." She looked up. "Do we know why?"

Marion knew half the answer. "It seems crooks are leaving Oregon and setting up business in nearby states. What do the governors want me to do, close the borders? I can't exactly call Oregon up and tell 'em to stop getting rid of their criminals." Her Noah Stone nightmare came to mind. "You know, Hitler's Germany had a really low crime rate, too."

What Marion didn't understand was why more and more crooks were slipping out of Oregon. She hit her desk with a fist. "What is it? Why's their crime rate dropping as if Superman were on patrol? The reports I get say more than a third of the citizens are already armed with those little defensive guns the state pushes, but I don't see how that explains it—all over the rest of the country there are more guns on the streets than ever, but the result is just the opposite! Every study shows that more guns mean more violence—except, now, in Oregon. It's going down."

Suzanne moved to the front of the desk, picked up the Priority Mail box, and held it out.

Marion shifted her gaze to the box and raised her eyebrows. "And that is . . ."

Suzanne's smile warmed Marion. "Something from Joe Donovan." Marion shook the box when Suzanne handed it over. It rattled.

Inside, Marion found an example of the "stopper" weapons that, according to Donovan's last report, were taking over the state. Supposedly nonlethal, the little pistol made of red plastic fit readily into her hand. It would also fit easily in a pocket or purse. Three small-bore barrels were stacked one over two. There was no trigger, though; in the place she expected to see a hammer were three buttons—one red, one white, one blue, arranged in a triangle that matched the positions of the barrels.

Three Ziploc baggies were tucked into the box. They held bullet-like objects and were labeled "nap," "tangle," and "whack." "This must be the ammunition Joe wrote about."

She slid the contents back into the box and set it in a desk drawer. "Call Cy Ligon over at the FBI and ask him to pay me a visit. He might claim he's too busy, but tell him I've got a new weapon I need analyzed. That'll get him."

Marion swiveled and gazed out the window. A siren wailed below, and an ambulance zigzagged through traffic. A quick image of a sheet-covered body flashed into her thoughts. "I passed another shooter crime scene on the way in this morning."

Suzanne said, "What are we coming to?"

"I said the same thing." Marion turned back. "Did I tell you about Charlie?"

"That cute little old security guard at your apartment house?"

"Yeah. Mugged right in my foyer. He's in the hospital with stitches and a concussion."

"And you moved to Georgetown to be safe."

"Where is safe, anymore?"

Marion returned to the Alliance website and clicked on "About Us." After skimming Noah Stone's story about the idea for the Alliance coming to him as a result of a study group in a church, she gazed at his face. Was there a religious connection? Was that what he was hiding? What were his ambitions? How did he profit from destroying constitutional protections?

When Cy Ligon arrived an hour later, she was surprised at how paunchy and graying he had become—but his eyes were as lively and intelligent as ever.

He said, "Long time since Quantico, Marion." They'd become friends when they'd gone through the FBI academy together. Though their careers had taken different paths, him staying with the Bureau and becoming a weapons expert, and her moving on to Justice after a few years as a field agent, they'd stayed in touch.

"Yeah. A little too long, I think."

"Knowing you, you didn't call me just to hash over old times."

"I've got a little puzzle I think you'll like." She led him to her desk and handed him the stopper along with the ammo.

He grinned. "Hey, a stopper."

She should have known Cy would be on top of this. As he turned the pistol over, peered into the barrels, and opened the chambers, she said, "You know about them?"

"Weapons are my life. From what I've heard, these are kinda fun and relatively harmless." He picked up a baggie and took out a cartridge, a brass casing with a paper tube in the place a slug would ordinarily be. He opened the tube and poured little balls the size of BBs into his palm. "They call this one 'nap.' These beads contain carfentanil, an opioid eight thousand times stronger than morphine. A tiny dose is sufficient to knock out a human, and the drug has a wide safety range. They break on the skin like little paint balls. A good choice for dimming someone's lights, if not knocking them out." He poured the little balls and the casing back into the nap baggie.

She said, "With so many people in Oregon using these as 'nonlethal' defensive weapons, I want to know if they can kill."

Cy's eyebrows lifted. "Interesting question." He took a tangle cartridge from a baggie, a casing with a white ball in the place of a bullet. "This's an adhesive material that expands and will bind, let's say, someone's legs or arms. You can't break or cut it. Comes off with a spray that dissolves it. Not truly lethal."

He pulled out a whack cartridge, another tube, this one with a plastic cap at one end. "Whack, here, is a mix of pepper spray and a chemical that triggers mental confusion. Your eyes clamp shut and you can't think straight. I don't see converting the whack cartridge to lethal—any killing spray can blow back on you. Tangle could kill someone if you shot enough onto their face to suffocate them, but that's pretty hit-or-miss."

He held up the baggie of nap cartridges. "This little baby, though, is all kinds of opportunity. The right poison and this can be a deadly delivery system."

"You want to see what you can do and get back to me?"

"I don't really have the time for this, Marion."

"I know, but . . ."

He smiled. "But it'll be fun." He opened his briefcase and tucked the stopper and ammo into a compartment. "What's this about?"

"The Alliance."

He nodded. "Noah Stone."

Surprised, she said, "You looking at them?"

He shrugged. "Everything we see appears clean. The way they turn out the vote, they seem to be do-gooders with muscle."

"On the surface, yeah, but what worries me is where their so-called reforms could take this country."

He shrugged. "All I know is that since they got going good our caseload in Oregon keeps dropping. I like it."

Yeah, just like Hitler's Germany.

 **8 OLD PAIN STILL HURTS**

Hank was sitting on his hospital bed when an aide came in with a tray of the stuff the hospital served in lieu of food. Hank said, "No thanks, I've been discharged and I'm leaving now."

"You can still have this."

He caught the aroma of a yellow pool of squash the consistency of soup and said, "No thanks, I'm leaving now."

The aide grinned. "Don't blame you." She left, and he went to his closet to dress. His T-shirt was snug over his bandages. His ribs were wrapped, and the dressing on his arm wasn't due to come off for a couple of days. But he felt sound enough.

He had just slipped his windbreaker over his shoulder holster when a man he'd hoped to never see again stepped into his doorway. Hank had always hated the thought of anybody tinkering with his mind, and this guy had tried his best after Amy and Marcie were— He closed the closet door.

The psychiatrist stroked his salt-and-pepper goatee, and irritation churned in Hank at the sight of the gesture. But he kept it cool. "Hello, Doc. You're a long way from the VA hospital. Run out of heads to shrink?"

Dr. Kensington grinned. "I never finished with yours. Saw the story on the news and thought I'd look in." He scanned the room. "You're out of here pretty fast."

"Got things to do."

The psychiatrist focused on Hank. "How are you feeling these days?"

Hank shrugged.

"Having any dreams about kill—"

"Nope." He wasn't about to mention tears on his cheeks when he woke up. The shrink would be all over that.

Dr. Kensington frowned. "That's not good, Hank. It's part of your PTSD. You need to—"

"I don't!" The vehemence in his voice surprised Hank . . . but the guy ought to leave well enough alone. He lowered his volume and said, "I'm fine."

The doctor studied him. "You're still troubled by it, aren't you?"

Hank lifted a fist, then uncurled it and smoothed his jacket instead. "You don't know what you're talking about. I don't have any reason to be troubled." He advanced on the doctor, forcing him to step out of the way. "Good to see you."

It felt so good to get out of the hospital that the cab ride through Chicago's muggy air was almost refreshing. Equally refreshing was the anonymity of his high-rise apartment building on North LaSalle—encounters with neighbors were few and far between, the way he wanted it. But it was nice to get a smile from Jim the doorman, a retired cop Hank liked.

In his bedroom, he glanced at the dirty clothes littering the floor and decided they were fine right there—he had enough clean stuff for his trip. Tidying for guests was no problem, because he never had them. No place to sit, for one thing. He liked things lean: one phone, one TV, one TV tray, one lamp, one table, one chair, one computer, one dresser, one nightstand, one bed.

He changed into fresh jeans and a black T-shirt and then packed a suitcase, raiding the bathroom for his anxiety meds, regretting having to leave his stash behind. Weed helped keep the PTSD triggers down. But it was legal in Oregon, so he figured he could get some there. He left his gun and holster. It felt like he was going on a mission naked.

Back in the living room, he got online, bought a plane ticket to Oregon, and reserved a room at the Ashland Springs Hotel.

When he scanned the bedroom to make sure he hadn't missed anything, he stopped at the photo of Amy on his nightstand. She gazed up at him, forever five years old, wearing her favorite flowery party dress, her black curls shining and her brown eyes alight. Her silver butterfly necklace hung draped over a corner of the frame by its delicate chain. She'd been wearing it the day she—the day she—

He turned his back . . . then he pivoted, gathered the necklace, and slipped it into the shirt pocket over his heart. Outside the window, sailboats scudding across Lake Michigan caught his eye. His focus shifted north, to where the cemetery was. Dr. Kensington said Hank's inability to remember Amy came from denying what had happened to the two people who lay at rest in that graveyard.

But he was wrong. Hank knew what had happened because he'd read the police report on what he'd done—it had been a righteous shooting. He didn't need to remember the actual event. He was done with it. He knew his failure.

When he drove out of the parking garage, he turned north instead of heading for O'Hare Airport.

At the cemetery, the two flat granite plaques lay side by side, surrounded by lawn. A surge of spring air jostled a dandelion plant that had evaded mowing and bloomed bright yellow next to the plaque engraved "Amy Lynn Soldado." Amy had loved picking dandelions gone to seed and blowing the white fluff into a breeze. She'd chase after it, all a-giggle.

One hand pressed to the necklace in his pocket, Hank knelt to pluck the dandelion flower and lay it over Amy. But he decided to leave it be—if a mower didn't get the flower, soon a breeze would waft white fluff across her grave.

His gaze turned to the stone marked "Marcella Caruso Soldado." He would never understand how things had gone so wrong with Marcie. How she could have done what the report said. How she could have thrown . . . could have thrown— Pressure grew in his mind, a sense of something surging against the inner barriers that kept him operational.

Enough. He had a plane to catch. Duty called.

 **SENDING A MESSAGE**

Martha Hanson pulled the living-room curtains aside and peeked out. Her miniature poodle joined her and stood on its hind legs, yapping to be picked up. Martha scooped her up and held her so she could see out the window, petting her head. "Shh, Sparky."

Across the street, the pushy reporter with the camera was still camped out, sitting in a lawn chair. Thank God Mackinac Island didn't allow cars or there'd have been a news van parked out there. She looked up at the sky, hoping for rain to pound the jerk, but there was nothing but blue overhead. She shut the curtains, gave Sparky a hug, and put her down. Martha went to her office and fired up her computer. She pulled up her militia website, but then just sat there and stewed, too angry to think.

She had never been so pissed off, never. The goddam media still pestered her every time she went out about dumbass Jason Schaeffer trying to shoot that asshat Noah Stone. The reason she lived on an island was to avoid exactly that! Her gaze drifted to a .22 semi-automatic rifle leaning in a corner. Maybe if she just winged the guy . . . She shook her head. That would be even dumber than what Jason had done.

On the other hand . . . She snatched up the rifle, chambered a round, and went to her front door. When she opened it and stepped out on the porch, the reporter stood and lifted his camera to his eye. He'd march across the street any second now, yelling questions at her, embarrassing her in front of her neighbors.

She snugged the rifle into her shoulder and aimed at the reporter. She was close enough to see his one visible eye widen, and he lowered the camera. At that moment she squeezed off a shot and a leg of the collapsed.

And then she almost hurt herself laughing as he ran down the sidewalk at a pretty damn good pace, holding his camera cradled to his chest. The abandoned chair sagged on the sidewalk. Her across-the-street neighbor stepped out of his front door, gave her a thumbs-up, and hauled the chair inside his house. Feeling much better, she went back to her office.

The grin on her face slid away, though, when she pulled up the *Huffpost* Crime page and there was Jason's photo with the headline "Assassin or Victim?" She clicked on the article and sure enough, her picture was there, too. Christ, she'd like to put a bullet in Jason—although she might have felt differently if he'd succeeded. Jason's bullet hadn't had Noah Stone's name on it, but someday one would.

Martha laughed. Why not now? She went into her gun room and pulled out a .44 Magnum deer rifle cartridge. Her grin came back when she rustled up a Sharpie and printed "Noah Stone" on the brass casing. From there it was a simple matter to snap a picture of it with her phone, email it to herself, and then put the image on her website. No way of knowing if Stone would ever see it, but there were plenty of folks who would get the message. She could only hope that they would do whatever they did smarter than Jason had.

10 PISTOL-PACKIN' MAMA

Chloe had been complaining about being hot and tired, so Jewel was glad when her daughter stood on the bus seat as they came into Portland and peppered her with Why this? and Why that? Jewel held Chloe close, fascinated by the pretty city with forested hills at its back and a river at its feet. Maybe it was only the pure light of early morning, but Portland seemed fresh and clean.

She wished they didn't have one more leg to go in their journey. Why did Noah Stone have to hang out in the state's bottom instead of this nice city at the top? At least they had an hour break before it was time to leave for Ashland. And they'd be on a different bus—the smell from the john in the back of this one was pretty rank.

She gazed at Chloe's downy face with a rush of adoration, ran a fingertip along a rounded cheek, which provoked a giggle and a quick kiss. Oh, if only this place would be good to her child. She wondered again if she'd done the right thing.

A freeze-frame of those punks gunning down that kid in the courtyard popped into her mind. She shook her head.

Brakes squealing the way they had at every stop for two days and two thousand miles, the bus stopped at last. The driver announced, "Welcome to Portland, folks. Since this is a port of entry, you will be checked for lethal firearms. Thanks for traveling with Greyhound."

Wondering what that was all about, Jewel led Chloe out to the parking area. The air reeked of exhaust fumes and the black smell of sunbaked asphalt, but the sky was pure blue with puffy white clouds. A breeze sighed through and took the fumes with it, replacing them with a piney scent. Jewel took a deep breath, gathered her bags, and shepherded Chloe into the bus station.

Inside, passengers formed lines leading to inspection stations like in airports, schools, and government buildings—X-ray tunnels for luggage and bags, and electromagnetic sensor gates for people to pass through. Her mouth watered when food smells drifted her way from a mini-mall on the far side of the building.

A big sign above the inspection area declared, "Possession of a lethal firearm in Oregon is an automatic felony conviction." Wow. They were serious about this.

She joined a line. Three people ahead, a passenger set a small three-barreled pistol in a basket. The security guard glanced at it and passed it through to be collected on the other side by its owner.

In the line next to hers, a scruffy young guy who'd gotten on the bus in Montana stepped through the sensor gate. It beeped, and a guard told him to empty his pockets. The man dropped a large folding knife into the basket, his eyes darting as if he expected to be busted. The guard examined it, then handed the basket around the gate. This time the alarm kept its peace when the young man went through. As he collected his knife, the guard said, "You be careful with that, son."

The next person in Jewel's line to undergo inspection, a white-bearded old dude, whipped out an automatic pistol and dropped it into a basket. The guard picked it up and ejected the magazine. Instead of bullets, it held stubby cartridges tipped with white balls. They were maybe half the length of an ordinary cartridge.

The guard shoved the magazine back into the gun and passed it on. "Nice-looking conversion."

The old fart smiled and cleared the sensor gate.

Jewel whispered into Chloe's ear, "Honey, we are way-y-y out West."

The fortyish woman in front of Jewel took a snub-nosed revolver from an attaché case. The guard popped the chamber open and found the brass-and-lead bullets Jewel expected to see. The woman held out a photo ID and said, "I have a permit to carry that, officer."

"Sorry, ma'am, nobody does in Oregon, not even cops."

She pointed at the old dude ahead and protested. "But that man had a gun."

"His weapon was re-chambered for legal defensive use. You don't have to surrender your weapon, but if you refuse I'll have to arrest you."

The woman warded him off with hands out. "Whoa! What do I do?"

"You can check your weapon and get it back when you leave the state. If you're concerned about your safety, stoppers are available for five dollars. If you're going to stay in Oregon, you can have your weapon modified."

"Stoppers?"

"Defensive weapons." The guard pulled one of the three-barreled pistols from a holster on his belt. "Like this."

The woman scowled. "I'll check my gun for now."

He placed her pistol on a conveyor belt that took it behind him to a table manned by another officer. The woman followed her weapon.

Jewel dropped her luggage and purse on the conveyor and guided Chloe through the gate. On the other side, a female security guard picked up Jewel's purse. "Whose is this?"

Now what? "Mine."

"I need to check inside, ma'am."

"Go ahead." She hoped the chunk of cash left over from Murphy's bundle wouldn't arouse suspicion.

The guard pulled out Jewel's Mace and nodded. "That's what I thought it was. Don't see it much anymore."

Jewel said, "Isn't it okay?"

"Oh, sure. New to Oregon, right?"

"Yeah."

The guard pointed toward the first storefront in the mini-mall. A sign read, "OREGON NEWCOMERS AID." "Over there"—she dropped the Mace back into the purse—"you can find out about better things than this."

"Thanks."

Jewel had no interest in the newcomer place—government and authority had never done anything for her and plenty against her. She led Chloe into the mall.

The aroma of french fries from a McDonald's set her to thinking about breakfast. She knew Chloe would be hungry soon, so she turned that way.

She passed a busy store named the Crosman Stopper Shoppe. She hated cutesy names. Its windows displayed pistols that had three barrels like the one she had seen in line, and ranged in color from bright red to ocean blue. Repulsed by the sight of so much weaponry, she moved on.

Ahead of her, the scruffy-looking young guy from the bus trailed an athletic teenage girl. She wore shorts and hiking boots, and had a big purse slung over one shoulder and a holster at her waist, a turquoise pistol grip sticking out.

A familiar tension in the man's body drew Jewel's attention. He darted quick looks at the crowd around him. Jewel did the same; there were no cops or security people in sight.

With a practiced motion he pulled out his knife, sliced through the strap of the girl's purse, snatched it, and ran.

The girl yelled, "THIEF!" as she drew the turquoise pistol from her holster. The crowd parted, clearing an opening between the girl and the running man.

Her gun gave a compressed-air cough.

A blur of something hit the thief's neck at the back of his head, but he kept running.

A grandmotherly woman, had to be eighty if she was a day, pulled a gray pistol from her bag and fired from the hip. It shot a white blob that expanded into a stringy mass and wrapped around the thief's ankles. He hit the floor hard and slid, belly down.

He rolled over and hacked at the sticky strands with his knife, and then a vacancy came into his eyes. He lay back and went limp.

The teen went to his side and retrieved her purse. The granny joined her, and the girl said, "Thank you, ma'am."

"Sure thing, honey."

A cop edged through the gathering crowd. The girl showed him the cut strap on her purse and pointed at the purse snatcher. He checked the thief's pulse, nodded, and said into a collar microphone, "Got a snatcher at the Greyhound mall. He's down with nap and tangle. I need transport."

The cop turned to face the girl with his body cam and she told him what had happened, including the granny in her story. The officer got the granny's version and then smiled and shook her hand.

Paramedics arrived with a gurney, and the curious moved on. Jewel's thoughts spun. People shooting each other down in malls, cops giving gun-toting grannies a pat on the back . . . What the hell kind of place was this? She found herself thinking that maybe this was one time she could use a little governmental guidance. She took Chloe to the Oregon Newcomers Aid office.

She found the usual tourist information—maps, a rack of brochures touting the depths of the Oregon Caves and the heights of Crater Lake.

At the store's rear, comfortable chairs, red-and-yellow floor pillows, and a low table created a reading area that included heaps of picture books and half a dozen toys. A young mother, her baby in an infant carrier on the floor beside the toys, browsed brochures.

Next to the reading area, a glass case displayed an array of hand weapons. Atop the case a sign read, "STOPPERS AVAILABLE HERE. PROTECT YOURSELF & STOP CRIME." That sounded like the place to find what she needed to know.

Chloe ran to the baby's side, dropped to her knees, and cooed baby talk.

Jewel said, "Now, Chloe, you leave that baby alone."

The mother watched Chloe for a few seconds, then smiled and said, "She's fine."

"Thanks."

Jewel gave Chloe firm instructions to stay put and play. She grinned when Chloe grabbed a stuffed bunny from the toy pile and made it dance to win a smile from the baby.

Most of the pistols in the case had three small-bore barrels in a triangular arrangement of one over two. Jewel saw no trigger. There were three buttons where the hammer would be on a revolver.

A chubby guy in his fifties, weathered skin like brown leather, stood behind the counter. She found his accent—Australian?—a little hard to understand when he said, "G'day. M'name's Tucker. New to Oregon?"

"Yeah."

"A lot of newcomers look at all these guns and wonder what the hell is going on here."

Jewel smiled—the dude was reading her mind.

"Well, all this is part o' getting rid of guns that kill ya. And a bunch of gun manufacturers helped, if you can believe that."

"Get out of here. They helped get rid of guns?"

"Spent millions."

"They did this out of the goodness of their little hearts?"

He laughed. "Hell, no. For the fatness of their big wallets." He smiled. "To be fair, at first they fought it—'twas the Oregon people who beat 'em with an initiative. The gun lobby blocked every try in the legislature, but the direct initiative to make possession of a lethal firearm an automatic felony, with some exceptions, won big, eighty percent of the vote. Seein' as how the only reason to have a lethal gun is for killing, havin' one is the same as assault with a deadly weapon. That was the stick."

"There's a carrot?"

"Yep. State offered to buy the guns or replace 'em with non-lethal defensive weapons for next to nothin'. The new nonlethal guns were, of course, sold by the gun companies at a fat profit. On top o' that, the government put on a big push for everybody to arm themselves with stoppers for self-defense. That meant a huge new market for gun makers, and fortunes were made."

He grinned. "I bought air-gun stock, myself." His eyebrows lifted. "Stoppers are pretty new here, less than a year, and I'm already seein' 'em all over the place. I think it's gonna spread to other states, an' though there's somethin' like eighty million gun owners in the U.S., there's a few hundred million folks that aren't. Imagine the money to be made sellin' a couple hundred million stoppers."

Jewel said, "Makes more sense to me just to get rid of the damn things."

"Naw. Can't just ban guns altogether, not in America. Never happen. Not practical, not feasible, and not the right thing to do, either. These days, lotta mates an' sheilas need to defend them-selves. And how 'bout hunters who maybe do have a right to hunt?"

Jewel tapped the case with one of her many rings. "These, uh, stoppers, is that right?"

"Yeah, stoppers."

"They're just defensive?"

Tucker opened the case and took out a weapon. "You'd have to work hard to kill someone with a stopper—you'd do better with a nice, heavy rock.

"Yeah, you can abuse 'em, like puttin' a loudmouth to sleep for no better reason than his mouth, an' I've been tempted, but they take away your right to carry and hit you with a stiff fine if you do. Could go to jail for assault, too."

"How come I never heard of these? I mean, you could sell a ton in Chicago."

He shrugged. "They're pretty new, and there's laws in a lotta states that won't let 'em be sold. Yet."

He handed her the gun. It was hard plastic instead of metal, and lightweight. Her hand welcomed its shape, and her thumb went easily to the red, white, and blue buttons at the top.

She said, "There's no trigger."

"That's the buttons. This's a basic stopper—got a compressed-air cartridge in the handle. You can recharge it at gun shops and gas stations. The buttons can trigger three different kinds o' rounds."

He opened the weapon and took out the top round, a casing with a paper tube. "This's nap. It shoots a quick-acting sleep drug." He took a pair of scissors from the counter, snipped off the end of the tube, and emptied what looked like miniature red BBs into his hand. "Break 'em on skin and you're asleep in a minute or so."

That explained the purse snatcher's glazed expression as he lay unresisting in the mall.

Tucker said, "Cops love nap. Nobody gets hurt, and they have a peaceful criminal ready for arrest." He took out another round, a white ball like on the bullets she'd seen earlier. "This's tangle, sticky stuff that wraps around you."

She nodded. "I saw that in the mall."

He grinned. "It takes a special chemical to dissolve it." He removed the last round, another tube, this one with plastic caps on each end. "Whack is a mix of chemicals that makes your eyes shut tight and confuses you. You can load all three kinds of rounds, or just one or two."

Jewel knew how effective just two of the stopper's loads were. Hit somebody with all three and they wouldn't be a danger—they'd be a mess.

Tucker said, "The state gave people two years to swap their lethal firearms for stoppers or have 'em re-chambered to fire nap, tangle, and whack. More'n that, there was a big ad campaign asking folks to carry defensive weapons. The state subsidizes the cost—you get a forty-dollar weapon for five bucks. You should have seen the lines. Gun makers loved it."

Jewel said, "So no more guns?"

He shook his head. "Hunters can have rifles or shotguns with three-round magazines. Can't do much mass murdering with those. Or they can trade illegal rifles in for long-range tranquilizer guns, or the state will pay to re-chamber their rifles for tranquilizer darts. With nonlethal guns, a hunter has to work a little harder to bring down his game, can't blast 'em from hundreds o' yards out, but heck, it's supposed to be a sport, in't it? Y'got a choice when you bring down your game, too—either finish it off or let it go. And wounded animals don't run away to die slow and painful. Even shotguns work with a load of tangle. Funny thing is, a lot of hunters are changin' over voluntarily 'cause they like the sport of it."

"Do a lot of people carry stoppers?"

"I hear one out of three and growing. The bad guys are way outgunned."

She thought of the quick action in the mall and the crowd's casual attitude. They hadn't been afraid when the thief struck. Jewel flashed on how different it might have been if she'd had a stopper when those shitheads grabbed her in Chicago.

She hefted the pistol and said, "How do I . . ."

He smiled. "You register, do a little trainin', and pass a test." He tapped the counter. "Y'can take care of it right here."

She was torn. She'd hated guns all her life and had been teaching Chloe how wrong they were. Yet here she stood, a gun in her hand and a desire to have it. Being attacked in Chicago came back to her, only this time she imagined it was Chloe instead. She nodded. "I'll do it."

Tucker got a senior woman who worked the front of the store to look after Chloe and took Jewel to a small target range in the back. Training was simple: a video on how to use the weapon and what to expect from its capabilities, instruction from Tucker on how to aim and use each of its rounds, and a short session of shooting at a target.

She learned she wasn't cut out to be a gunslinger, but the stopper was "point-and-shoot" easy for hitting a close-up target. Tucker stressed that it was a weapon to take seriously, and that she couldn't use it on someone except to prevent harm or stop a crime.

After Jewel passed her test, Tucker encoded her Social Security number into a chip in the forest-green stopper she chose. "This way, if you ever lose the gun or it's stolen, when it's recovered it can get back to you. It's also a way to identify people who abuse their weapons."

He grinned. "I'll tell ya, it was pretty wild here for the first month or two, people put to sleep and whacked all over the place just because somebody got pissed off. A couple people did die—"

"C'mon, how nasty can you get with something this harmless?"

"You can pump nap into somebody until an overdose shuts down breathing. The shooters who did that kind of stuff were soon nabbed, and things settled down. Durin' the same time, gun deaths dropped by eighty percent."

She paid five dollars for the stopper. At Tucker's suggestion, she also bought a package of extra nap rounds—they came in a tube that looked a lot like a tampon package.

Jewel found Chloe cuddled up next to the senior woman, happily absorbed in *The Little Engine That Could*. The second Chloe noticed Jewel, she stopped repeating "I think I can, I think I can," wriggled off the chair, and ran to her. "Mommy, I'm hungry."

"Okay, honey, we'll get breakfast."

She thanked the woman and followed Chloe's skipping exit from the store. There was a comfort in having her new stopper in her purse. Now to get a Mickey Dee's breakfast into her daughter before they got on the bus for the last part of their trip to . . . what?

11 LOOKING INTO A GUN BARREL

Noah slowed his car as he neared the turnoff for the Alliance campus, now seeing its openness filtered through his new paranoia about people stalking him with guns. Anyone could walk right in.

It had been a mistake to take a look at the Mackinac Militia website. There had been three articles by Colonel Martha Hanson about Noah Stone, each one railing about the "enemy of freedom" and the traitorous damage he was doing to the fundamental rights of Americans. Oh, she hadn't said anything directly about shooting him, but after telling her minions that Noah Stone was coming to take away their guns, she had asked, "What are you going to do about it? Are you going to stand and fight?"

And then there'd been a photo of a hunting-rifle cartridge with his name written on it.

That night the colonel's soulless eyes had invaded his dreams, and he still hadn't shaken the fear that had awaited him when he woke up. Militias were networked; in southern Oregon, even here in Ashland, Noah knew that the Rogue Valley had its own troop.

Just ahead, three cars and a pickup were parked alongside the road, and a dozen or so men and women blocked the driveway to the campus. Two held signs that said, "Give back our guns." He'd seen those before. A stocky man held a revolver across his chest as if he were a soldier of some kind. Noah tightened his grip on the steering wheel.

When he stopped in front of them, he recognized about half of the protesters, including Sam Gleason, whose hardware store accounted for a lot of Noah's credit card debt. Sam had his ten-year-old son with him. Sam started a chant. "Free-dom. Free-dom. Free-dom."

Noah unbuckled his seat belt, checked to see that his stopper was holstered, then opened the door and got out. He raised his hands and said, "Can we talk?"

The chant went on for a few more *freedoms,* and then Sam signaled for quiet. When the chant petered out, he said, "The Supreme Court says we have a right to carry guns."

"You mean like that guy who wanted to shoot me in Chicago?"

Sam glanced down as if embarrassed, and then looked Noah in the eye. "We want 'em for self-defense against guys like that."

"You've just expressed the paradox," Noah said. "The only reason to carry a lethal firearm is other lethal firearms. If they weren't there, then we wouldn't have a need for them." He patted his stopper. "And stoppers would be plenty of self-defense."

Sam said, "That's no defense against somebody armed with automatic weapons. We aren't safe." He pulled his son closer to him. "Our schools aren't safe."

"You want his teachers armed with guns?"

The woman spoke up. "There's a school district in Texas did that."

Noah said to her, "Do you have a child in school?" When she shook her head, he turned back to Sam. "So, do you want your son's teacher carrying a gun?"

Sam nodded. "Crazy people see signs that say 'Gun-Free Zone' and attack schools, and we need to defend them. It wouldn't happen if everybody knew teachers were packing."

After a chorus of "Yeah" and "Damn straight" died down, Noah said, "But what if your son's teacher is the one who goes crazy?"

"Oh, she wouldn't—"

"She could. What if a bad day in class pushes her over the top and she takes the lethal weapon that you want her to carry and shoots your son dead?"

"She wouldn't—"

"She could. Some other teacher at your school could. What do you do then? Shoot her? And then go to your son's funeral?" Sam's son's eyes widened, and he looked up at his dad. Noah hated talking this way in front of the boy, but there wasn't really much choice, was there?

He unholstered his stopper and held it up for all to see. "Now, what if that teacher has a stopper instead? If a crazy guy with a lethal weapon attacks, she has a chance to stop him. If the teacher goes nuts, it'll be darned hard for her to wipe out a classroom full of kids with a stopper . . . or a knife . . . or just about any weapon other than a gun."

Noah scanned each face. "I know many of you, and you're good citizens, good people. I also know that if you step back and really think about it, you'll get it."

He was getting louder, but this was important. Still, yelling never convinced anybody, so he softened his voice. "This isn't about the right to bear arms—we shouldn't even need to carry any kind of gun. It's not like the British are invading and we have to fight them off with our muskets."

Their expressions were hard and cold. How could he connect with them? "Look, I like guns. I love to shoot targets, and I used to love to hunt." Until he'd shot a rabbit and it had screamed like a mortally wounded child. "If targets and hunting were all guns were used for, you wouldn't be hearing from me. But guns kill innocent people every day. You see it on the news, right?"

A couple of the men glanced at each other, then turned back to listening; they seemed interested now, not so hostile.

Will Stevens stepped forward. He carried one of the signs. He was also the county chairman of the president's party. "There are plenty of laws against crooks and nuts owning guns. All we need to do is enforce 'em."

"The cops do enforce them, but there are too many loopholes like buying guns at gun shows, and too many millions of guns out there with no way to find them. Guns used in crimes don't turn up until the crime happens."

He heard a rustle of clothing and movement beside him. A man's voice said, "You won't have any trouble finding this one."

The speaker was the guy with the pistol, and he aimed it at Noah's head. The muzzle was no more than two feet away. It was a big gun, maybe a .44 Magnum. Noah had seen the man around town, but had no name for him.

Sam provided it. "Mark, put that down."

"Why should I? I'm an American with inalienable rights, and I want my gun rights back. I think I've got the answer in my sights."

He wouldn't really pull the trigger, would he? Right here in front of all these witnesses? But his eyes were wide and staring, and he didn't blink. Noah's stomach clenched. One nervous jerk of that trigger . . .

Noah pointed at the gun barrel aimed at him. "Mark, there are two kinds of guns here in Oregon. There's yours, which will kill or wound me . . ." He held up his stopper. "And this one, which is for defending me . . ."

He put his stopper's muzzle in the bore of the pistol barrel and pressed the button for tangle. His gun hissed, and white goop oozed from the pistol's muzzle. If the shooter pulled the trigger, the gun would blow up in his face.

Noah finished, ". . . without hurting anybody."

Mark lowered his weapon and examined it. "Shit. It'll take forever to get that crap out of there."

"Why don't you have the gunsmith re-chamber your gun for stopper ammo when he works on it? You don't want to go to the Keep, do you?"

Mark raised the gun high, holding it like a club, and Noah aimed his stopper at the man's face. Sam stepped between them. Mark lowered the gun and said, "Screw you." He stomped to a car. Two others scrambled to get in, and he tore away, his tires spraying the group with gravel.

Noah's knees wanted to give out, so he leaned against his car for support and turned his gaze back to Sam.

Sam stared after the car for a moment and then turned to Noah. His face had paled, and he didn't look so determined anymore.

Noah said, "Do I need to say that that's why we need to get lethal firearms off the streets?"

Sam swallowed hard. "I'd never seen . . . never been that close to . . ." He trailed off and looked down at his son. "C'mon, buddy, we've got some thinking to do."

Sam and his boy headed for the pickup, and the rest of the crowd broke up and went to their cars. Some threw brief glances Noah's way. Each time he caught one, the person looked away. He thought they were a little afraid.

He didn't blame them.

He was a lot afraid.

 **A SAFE HAVEN?**

Jewel's day-long trip from Portland to southern Oregon was a restful cruise through a sea of green. Most everybody she knew would have found miles of emerald fields boring, but she drank them in as if they were a remedy for what ailed her. The highway cut through the broad Willamette Valley, and then it climbed into mountains.

The bus went up mountains, around mountains, down mountains. Jewel loved how small waterfalls tumbled from cliffs near the road, the clear water a miracle—all she knew about water outdoors was nasty Lake Michigan and the brown, soupy Chicago River. And it delighted her to go through clouds that touched the earth. This land was magic.

At last the highway dropped into a big valley and headed south for Ashland. Chloe curled in the seat beside her, asleep. A growing sense of safety had relaxed Jewel when she and Chloe got off the bus to stretch their legs at stops, a remarkable feeling to have around bus terminals. Oh, men still looked at her as though she were their favorite candy, but now she had a stopper.

Yeah, being a pistol-packin' mama wasn't all bad. Whether the guys with hungry eyes wanted to do anything or not, in this state they knew she could be holding. No wonder they called 'em "stoppers."

She flashed on Green-Stripe in Chicago jamming a gun under her chin. What if they'd had stoppers in Illinois? He'd be in jail now—or would he even have attacked her?

She shook off that nasty memory and let the valley embrace her. Rolling hills to the east were green with grass and clusters of trees. To the west, forested foothills rose to a mountain standing tall over them, its cap of snow white against clear blue sky. Close by the highway, tidy orchards and vineyards covered much of the valley floor. Cattle grazed in acres of meadows.

Scattered homes thickened among the pines and oaks on the foothills and turned into a narrow little town strung along the slopes. Ashland looked like it ought to be framed and hung on a wall.

They left the highway, and she ran her fingers through Chloe's hair to wake her. Her head felt hot, like the time she'd spiked a fever and had to go to the hospital. And her cheeks were red. They weren't just flushed—they looked as though she had been slapped.

Jewel sat her up and discovered a rash on Chloe's chubby arms. Jewel had seen fevers before, but this was strange. An image of her dead brother popped into her mind. Oh, no, don't let anything happen to Chloe.

Panic knotting her belly, she scooped Chloe into her arms and rushed to the front of the bus. The driver told her to be seated, and she snapped, "She's sick. Get us there."

The instant the bus stopped and the door opened, she bolted out. Inside the station, she ran to the ticket window and pushed her way to the front of the line. The clerk, a tired-looking woman whose face looked like it wore every irritation she'd ever had, said, "You gotta wait your turn."

Jewel tried to be cool, but Chloe's cheeks were so red! Her voice shook. "My little girl is sick! Where's the closest clinic?"

The clerk shook her head. "Next."

The seventyish man Jewel had cut in front of leaned around her. "Help the lady out. I got time."

Her face still pinched and sour, the clerk pointed and said, "About a mile that way."

"Where can I get a cab?"

The clerk glared at her; the old man tapped Jewel on the shoulder and pointed at double glass doors that opened onto the street. "Sometimes one's out there."

Jewel ran for the door.

To one side of the bus station was a motel, on the other a convenience store. Across the street a bunch of buildings looked like a college campus. No cabs were in sight. Just her luck to land in a one-horse town.

A van pulled away from the convenience store and revealed a taxicab parked there. The driver, a big soft drink cup in his hand, was getting into the cab. Holding Chloe close, she ran toward it.

The cab backed out and turned to enter the street. Gripping Chloe to her with one arm, she stepped into its way and waved. The cab veered around her and accelerated.

As it passed, she kicked the rear fender and yelled, "Hey!" The driver slammed on his brakes.

She ran to the cab and jumped into the rear seat. "Take me to the nearest clinic! Please hurry."

The cabbie, a bulky guy in his twenties with a bushy brown beard and a ponytail held with a rubber band, gazed at her in the rearview mirror. With his plaid flannel shirt, he looked as though he'd just come down off a mountain after trapping beaver. His face was haggard, his eyes droopy with purplish hollows beneath them. The only life in his face was a glare of irritation.

Even his voice sounded tired. "Sorry, lady, I ain't gonna do it. I'm on my way home, I been drivin' twenty hours, and the closest clinic is in the wrong direction."

"But you stopped! You have to take me!"

"I stopped 'cause you kicked my cab. And I don't have to. Get out."

"My little girl's sick. Please."

"Lady, I'm beat. Out. Unless you want to go home with me."

He put his cab in gear.

She took out her stopper and pressed the barrels against his neck. "I'll shoot you."

"Sure, lady, fire away. Hit me with nap, I'll go to sleep. Tangle, I'll sit here locked to the steering wheel. Zap me with whack, I'll drive in circles with my eyes shut." He shrugged. "And then you'll go to jail."

Fury choked Jewel. "You son of a bitch!"

He rolled the cab forward.

"Let me out!"

He stopped and stared at her in the rearview mirror with all the emotion of a lizard. Fighting back tears, she struggled out and kicked the door shut.

The cab pulled away.

When it was about ten feet from her, the cabbie yelled, "THREAD!" The cab screeched to a stop. It idled for long seconds, then its tires shrilled as it raced backward and rocked to a stop next to her. The cabbie leaned toward her and said, "Okay, let's go."

She got in, and the cab sped down the street. The cabbie glanced in the rearview mirror. He didn't look so angry anymore.

"I'm sorry, lady." He held up his right hand to show a ring of many colors. One of them blended with the driver's skin. She'd seen the same ring on a lot of hands during her travel through Oregon. Come to think of it, the old man she'd cut in front of at the Ashland bus station had worn one.

He said, "I'm new at this Alliance thing, just did the promise a week ago, and I ain't used to trying hard with people."

Grateful for the ride, she said, "That's okay."

"Name's Franklin."

"Yeah." She stroked Chloe's brow, afraid to touch her cheeks.

Five minutes later, Franklin wheeled his cab into a half-circle drive in front of an old, three-story brick home that had been converted into the Alliance Free Clinic. He eased to a stop. "That's six eighty, ma'am."

Jewel shoved a ten at him and ran, clutching Chloe to her chest.

Half an hour later, she walked out of the clinic, Chloe cradled in her arms. A gentle nurse practitioner had diagnosed a mild viral infection called fifth disease, which she said was also known as "slapped cheek disease." Since a rash had appeared, Chloe was no longer contagious, and the nurse expected the redness to fade in a few days. She gave ibuprofen to Chloe and a double dose of calm to Jewel. The only cost had been a promise to do two hours of community service. Jewel had a list of places that needed help.

She stopped when she saw a yellow cab with a familiar-looking figure standing beside it. Hadn't what's-his-name told her he was beat and on the way home?

The cabbie opened the rear door and gestured toward the seat, an I'm-being-pleasant smile peeking through his beard. His body language still read exhausted, but his expression had new energy.

She ambled toward him. She figured it was up to him to start this ball rolling, so she held her silence.

His gaze dropped to the ground, shifted back to her face, then settled on Chloe. "How's your little girl?"

"She'll be okay. You waited to ask me that?"

He didn't rise to the hostile edge in her voice. "Kinda. Wanted to see if I could help."

Okay, here it came. Why couldn't guys just leave her be? If this kept up, she was going to have to gain fifty pounds and wear sacks. She played the game. "I don't see how."

"How about a free ride to where you're going next?"

That sounded good. "Why?"

He said, "It's the Alliance promise to help I made. I couldn't stop thinking how you must have felt, scared for your little girl like you were and me actin' like a total asshole."

She couldn't help but crack a smile. "Total."

He nodded. "So I didn't want to leave it like that. Where can I take you?"

"A motel, I guess. No, the bus station. I left our bags."

"Let's go."

She stepped past him and sat on the rear seat. She thought about how much cash she had. "You know a cheap place we can stay?"

He nodded. "I've got a spare room you can use, too."

She frowned and started to get out. "Yeah, right. Guys are all the same."

He laughed and held up his hand to stop her. "I'm not thinkin' what you're thinkin' I'm thinkin'. My cousin lives with me"—he smiled—"and he'd think it was a hoot, the idea of me hittin' on a woman, even one pretty as you."

It took her a few moments to realize he'd just told her he was gay. She had to get a grip. She couldn't go around thinking all every man wanted was her brown ass. She sank back into the seat and the cabbie shut the door. She said, "Thank you, uh . . ."

"Franklin Emerson."

"Thanks, Frank."

"Franklin."

She laughed. "Right. Chloe, this's Franklin, our new friend."

Chloe peeked up and dimpled a little smile.

"And I'm Jewel." She took a closer look at the guy. Go to his house? Well, she kinda liked him. He was working hard on the promise thing. As she watched, his knees sagged ever so slightly. Man was beat. On top of that, she had her stopper. She could handle him.

She smiled and said, "So let's go get our bags." Franklin got behind the wheel and started out.

Jewel cuddled Chloe close, relaxed, and felt a rush of gratitude that she was okay; there was nothing like danger to your baby to remind you what was important.

Franklin's home looked like an old farmhouse plunked down on a residential street. It sported touches of gingerbread, and a broad porch wrapped the front and one side. Jewel especially liked the porch swing hung from chains, partly screened from the street by a wisteria vine that grew across the front. Tall maples and oaks shaded the house and yard.

Jewel felt right at home in the living room, mostly because the furniture was early Goodwill like hers had been. She wondered what had happened to it. She should have told Juana to take whatever her family could use.

Franklin helped her and Chloe get their bags in. A hallway led to four bedrooms: a tidy one that Franklin said was his, one with a musky scent coming from it—his cousin Earl's—and two unused but clean rooms with single beds and small dressers. Franklin said, "Sometimes I rent rooms to actors in town to do a play."

Jewel was quick to say, "Let me know what, I'll pay."

"You get a couple days to look around." He grinned and tousled Chloe's hair. "And squirts stay for free. Don't take up much space. Make yourself at home." He pointed to his room. "I'm takin' a nap."

After Chloe and her rubber ducky had enjoyed a playful bath in an old-fashioned tub with feet, Jewel tucked her into bed in the smallest bedroom for a nap. Then she surrendered to exhaustion and collapsed on the porch swing. A quiet hour went by, and then Franklin joined her, two beers in hand. She accepted one, and they sat in restful silence.

The rumble of a busted muffler interrupted the quiet when a red pickup truck pulled into the driveway and stopped behind Franklin's cab. A shirtless, blond young man, tan, lean, and muscled, bounded out of the truck and trotted up to the porch.

Franklin smiled. "Jewel Washington, meet my cousin Earl."

Earl hopped onto the porch and took Jewel's hand. His blue-eyed gaze flicked to her scar and then took in the rest of her, then came back to look her in the eye. He smiled. "A pleasure."

Jewel was surprised to find herself liking the way Earl looked at her. She said, "Me, too."

Franklin said, "Beer?"

"Like to, but I got a meeting."

Franklin said, "Where you heading?"

Earl glanced at Franklin. "You know." He rushed into the house.

Franklin scowled. "I don't like that militia crap. It's trouble."

Earl burst out the door, pulling a white T-shirt over his head and trotting to the truck.

Nice butt. Lordy, it'd been so long since she'd had a little lovin' from a decent man. She was lonely for some sweet company.

He jumped into the pickup, then leaned out the window and said to her, "Will I see you later?"

Franklin said, "She's staying with us for a while."

Beaming, Earl said, "Franklin, you have just made my day."

He roared out of the driveway.

"Your cousin seems nice."

"He's one of the world's great people, except for the militia thing. He's a set designer for the Shakespeare Festival, got a real artist's eye."

"What's the militia thing?"

Franklin gazed after the departing truck. "I just don't understand it. Earl's a liberal guy most ways—hell, he couldn't care less that I'm gay. But his daddy was real paranoid about the government, especially gun control, and I guess he passed on a pretty serious case of it." He glanced at her. "Don't let on I said anything, okay?"

Jewel sat back and swigged her beer. "I won't. Ah, how's he feel about women?"

Franklin grinned. "I think you're gonna like that side of Earl."

Ashland was lookin' good.

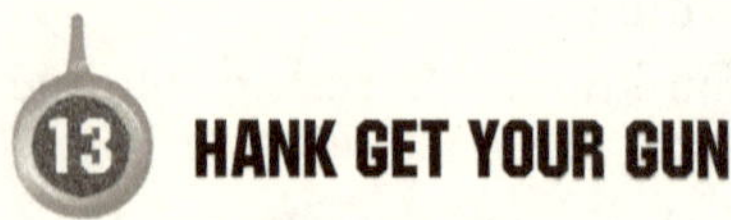

HANK GET YOUR GUN

As Hank's plane descended to the Medford, Oregon, airport, he marveled at the contrast between the green Rogue Valley and the flat, gray-brown mess of Chicago. Oh, Chicago was a great city, but it sure didn't come close to mountains surrounding a pretty valley when it came to being easy on the eyes.

When he went to claim his suitcase, he found incoming luggage being X-rayed and some bags searched—he was glad Mitch had warned him about trying to pack a gun.

He rented a four-wheel-drive SUV and sped south on Interstate 5. In twenty minutes he took the first Ashland exit and soon drove along the city's main drag, if *city* was the right word for two primary streets lined with tidy little buildings that housed shops and restaurants. He parked on Main Street and left his car to get a feel for the place.

The physical pleasure of just being there surprised him. The mountain air was crisp and fresh. It felt good to breathe. The late-afternoon sun warmed his skin, and a breeze brushed his face with a softness unlike Chicago's heavy air.

On lampposts hung crimson banners with a golden lion rampant, celebrating what Wikipedia said was the town's most famous institution, the Oregon Shakespeare Festival. Who'd have thought a tiny town way out West would have theater that could win a Tony Award?

Tree-shaded sidewalks were lively with tourists. There were long-haired young men and tattoos aplenty on colorful people, a mix of young and geriatric, all lively and busy. No gangbangers swaggered with pistols in their hands.

But there were guns. Brightly colored pistol grips stuck out of small holsters on a half dozen strollers, mostly women. Maybe these were the nonlethal guns Noah Stone talked about in his speech. The absence of two and a half pounds of Colt .45 under his jacket reminded Hank that he had no weapon.

He pulled out his wallet and fished for the card Mitch had given him. A call from his cell phone and the password got him directions to an address. Now impatient with strolling tourists and their chipper mood, he hurried to his car.

The address on Kent Street was an ordinary ranch house in an orderly row of middle-class homes. Grade-school children played in the driveway next door, and a blond, lean woman in her twenties walking a beagle came toward him. She gave him a nice smile, which he was happy to return.

When he stepped onto the porch of his contact's house, he heard a man shout, "Goddamn it, we gotta take Stone out!"

Hank peeked in a narrow window beside the door. Two men sat in a cramped living room, drinking beer from cans. He waited a moment, but nothing more was said. A scrawny cat appeared from under a bush and wound around his legs. He gave it a scratch on the head and then knocked.

A short, beer-bellied man opened the door. A woolly black Fu Manchu mustache framed his down-turned mouth, and bushy muttonchops decorated his fleshy jaws. "Yeah?"

Hank said, "I called. You Hatch?"

Rick Hatch nodded, his manner cautious but welcoming. "Yeah. I got word from Mitch you might be coming around." He pushed the door open and stepped out. After careful looks up and down the street, he said, "Ah, you got an ID?"

After Hank showed his driver's license, Hatch backed into the house and said, "Come on in."

When Hank entered, Hatch waved a hand at the other man: clean-shaven, good-looking with a lean body, blond hair, and a tan. He sat forward on a plaid couch, a framed velvet painting of dogs playing poker on the wall above it.

Hatch said, "This's Earl Emerson."

Earl smiled and said, "Howdy." His voice was the one that had shouted the threat to Noah Stone.

Hank nodded.

Hatch eyed him. "What can I do for you?"

"I need a handgun."

The fat guy raised his eyebrows and smirked. "Hey, you can get a stopper at a buncha stores. Five bucks."

"You call those handguns?"

Hatch snorted. "I call 'em pee shooters 'cause they're about as useful as pissin' into the wind." He led Hank down a narrow hall to a closet in a small bedroom. He pulled on the hanger rod, chock-full of clothes, and it swung toward him and out of the way. Reaching up, he hauled on a slim rope and drew down an attic stair. The odor of gun oil spilled from a dark hole above. Hatch led the way up, turning on a light at the top.

Hank could stand straight only in the center of the attic room. Racks filled with shotguns, rifles, and assault weapons lined one wall. A table at the end of the space displayed a dozen handguns and holsters, plus boxes of ammunition.

Hatch smiled and said, "Welcome to the right to bear arms. What's your preference?"

Hank picked up a .45 automatic like his own—yeah, the Colt was an old design, but he trusted it, and it fit his hand just right. He racked the slide, then ejected the magazine; the weapon was clean and well cared for. But there was a red square bonded to the frame that didn't belong. "What's this?"

"A counterfeit ID chip to make it look like it's been modified. So you can carry it in public. Just don't let a cop check it with a detector."

Hank now saw that most of the guns, even the rifles and shot-guns, had similar red squares. The assault weapons didn't. "I need to know more."

Hatch picked up a 9 mm Glock. "This's a legal weapon, been converted for use in Oregon. I hated to do it, but I needed a model to work from." He pointed to the red chip on the legal gun. "State puts these little microchips on legal gunpowder weapons. Stick a police detector next to it, you get a beep for okay. No beep, it's illegal. Trouble is, nobody's been able to copy the chip's circuits."

He ejected the magazine. Instead of full-sized bullets, it held short, stubby cartridges with a white, plastic-like slug at the front instead of lead. "I got tangle loaded in this one." He pulled back the slide and showed Hank the gun's guts.

Part of the chamber was plugged with steel—a normal bullet wouldn't fit. Hatch said, "Only things'll go in here are little nap, tangle, and whack rounds. The microchip connects to the chamber; you try to modify it, you destroy the chip."

Hank shook his head. "Are all guns in Oregon like this?"

"Pretty much. 'Cept for legit hunting weapons, ain't a real gun that's legal, not target, not nothin'. Even hunters have to go through the hassle of showing a gun license to buy ammo." The light of a zealot shone in Hatch's eyes. "We fought 'em, by God, we fought 'em. What made it so hard was the state sold the idea that they weren't taking guns away, just making 'em safer. And they paid to change 'em over. And they teamed up with the Alliance to come up with those stinkin' little stoppers for five bucks a pop. Usin' my tax dollars!

"With all that safety runnin' around, guns that killed didn't have a chance. Hell, we couldn't even argue they were takin' away our Second Amendment rights 'cause we could carry those little popguns for self-defense. We got shafted and couldn't do a thing about it."

Hank sympathized; no way did he want to live without the weight of a pistol against his ribs. He looked at the guns on the racks. "I don't see red chips on the assault weapons."

"Well, since they don't have any legitimate civilian use, not hunting or nothing, they're just flat banned. I gotta admit, they are weapons of war—if you're a hunter, the real thing is sure better than an assault rifle. You want something heavy, too?"

"No." He hefted the pistol. "I need a shoulder holster and a box of shells. How much?"

"A thousand."

Hank lifted his eyebrows.

Hatch answered. "It's the risk. You get caught with just one lethal firearm, let alone a whole roomful, you go to the Keep. Automatic. No appeal, no nothin'. I get caught with this many, I'm doomed for sure."

Hank dug cash from his jeans and peeled off a thousand. "The Keep?"

"Hell on earth." Hatch handed Hank a holster and cartridges and led him out of the gun "shop."

Back in the living room, Hatch settled on a chair and said, "Earl, tell him about the Keep."

Earl's sunny disposition went behind a cloud. "It's where they send you for a violent crime if you don't let 'em brainwash you."

Next to being without a weapon, Hank hated being caged. It had taken him three months to escape from an Afghan prison, and that was the only time he'd come close to losing it. He still had flashbacks. "I won't let that happen."

Earl said, "You go into the Keep, you don't come out unless you're pickled."

"Pickled?"

Earl scowled out the window as if feeling an old hurt and said, "Yeah. They call it deep therapy, but it's brainwashing." He turned his gaze on Hank. "We don't exactly know what they do to you. The guys who've had it just smile and say it's the best thing ever happened to them. They're robots." He frowned. "We lost two friends that way."

Hatch said, "Yeah. They were good guys, believed all the right things, fought for the right to carry. Now they're a couple of law-abiding pansies. One's a kindergarten teacher, the other one works for the devil himself."

"For Stone?"

Earl nodded, then looked a question at Hatch.

Hatch told him, "Go ahead. Mitch says he's a good guy."

Earl stared into Hank's eyes. "We're going to take Stone out so things can go back to the way they ought to be."

"Who's we?"

"The Rogue Valley Militia." He glanced at Hatch. "Me."

"You think killing Stone will do what you want?"

Earl said, "It started with him, it'll end with him."

Hank saw a deep hatred in Earl. It was personal. "When?"

Hatch shrugged.

Eyes wide, Earl said, "It's gotta be at some event so the faithful see their hero's nothing but a sack of meat like everybody else."

This guy was not rowing with both oars. But he wasn't Hank's problem.

Hatch gazed at Hank for a long moment. "Parsons said you're on our side. You want to help us out?"

Earl frowned. "We don't need any outside help, Rick."

Hatch looked to Hank, the question still on the table.

"No thanks." He turned his gaze on Earl. "I'm on the side of the law. But I won't rat on you, either."

Earl shrugged.

Hank checked his watch. There were a couple of hours before sunset, and his ribs ached. He wanted some time off and a leisurely supper. Noah Stone could wait.

Maybe he should ask these guys for a good place to eat. He glanced at the dogs-playing-poker painting.

"Thanks," he said to Hatch, and left.

 **HELL COMES TO GEORGETOWN**

Marion slipped into baggy sweats as soon as she got home from the office, poured a glass of wine, and then sank into the deep cushions of the leather easy chair that had been her dad's. She could still smell his scent, a blend of pipe tobacco and the faint mustiness of the law libraries in which he'd spent so much of his life. She missed him. And she missed the legal mind of a premier defense attorney. She needed his wise perspective on what to do about the Alliance.

She sipped her wine, enjoying the smooth, husky taste of a California chardonnay. Gazing into the wine's golden depths, she thought of the California valley from which it came, a valley now coming under the influence of the Alliance. She didn't like what was happening.

The doorbell sounded low chimes, and she wished whoever it was would go away. But no, they rang again. She pushed out of the chair and pressed the intercom button by her door. She made no effort to conceal her irritation. "Yes?"

Suzanne said, "It's me."

Marion regretted the edge in her voice. "Oh."

"Did I get it wrong? Didn't you say seven o'clock?"

Oh, shit, she and Suzanne had agreed to a quiet dinner at her place. Guilty because she'd let her petulance spill over onto Suzanne, she hurried to say, "Oh, I'm just tired. I'm glad you're here."

"I brought Chinese, so— HEY! What're you— Oh God, oh no—"

A scream shrieked from the intercom, then cut off.

Marion slammed out her door and raced down the stairs. Through the glass foyer door she saw Suzanne slumped against a wall, a sack of take-out cartons spilled at her feet. She clutched her neck; blood ran from under her hand. A man looked up at Marion, Suzanne's purse in one hand, a knife in the other.

He wore grubby gray overalls like mechanics wear, but his had a spray of red across the chest. A Washington Commanders cap shadowed a face that could have been normal, even nice—except his showed a mix of rage, lust, and fear.

He pushed the foyer's outer door open just as Marion burst through the inside door. She lunged, shoved him in the back with both hands, and propelled him out. He hurtled through the air, hit hard on his belly, tumbled down a half dozen concrete steps, and lay still on the sidewalk.

She spun and saw Suzanne sliding down the wall. Heart thudding, Marion caught her and eased her to a sitting position. Suzanne's eyes were wide. Blood spread red on her white shirt. Marion tried to pull Suzanne's hand away to see the wound in her neck, but Suzanne held tight. Yet the blood flowed.

Marion sobbed. "Suzanne. Suzanne, love."

Suzanne's gaze darted helter-skelter. Marion tried to keep the fright out of her voice. "I'll call an ambulance, you'll be okay." She started to rise, but Suzanne gripped her arm.

Suzanne breathed, "I—"

Marion freed her arm from supporting Suzanne. "I've got to call—"

Suzanne's eyes glazed. Her chest stilled.

Panic flooding through her, Marion gripped Suzanne's shoulders. "No! You've got to hang on! You've got to—"

Suzanne's hand dropped from her neck into her lap. No longer driven by a beating heart, blood oozed from a deep slash across her throat.

Marion crushed Suzanne to her, and the empty-sack vacancy of a lifeless body sent a shuddering moan through her.

The man, the man who did it—she twisted and saw him struggling to his feet.

Rage swamped her grief. She lurched up and ran out, plunged down the steps, and crashed her six feet of solid muscle into him. He tumbled into one of the huge maples that lined her street, rebounded, and sprawled on the grass.

Marion hit the sidewalk on her shoulder and rolled to a stop. She sprang to her feet, grabbed his shirt, pulled him up, and slammed him against the tree trunk. She stepped back and kicked him in the testicles with all the leverage that years of martial arts training had taught her.

Screaming, the man fell to the ground, clutching his groin.

Raging, crying, she kicked and kicked wherever she could land her foot until arms wrapped her from behind in a bear hug, lifted her away, and a man said, "Easy now, easy. I'm a cop."

She fought the grasp, but he was a big man; he held her until she stopped struggling.

A vestige of sanity returned, and she thought of Suzanne. With new strength, she shoved the cop's arms apart. Pointing at her building, she said, "She's hurt. Hurry!" and raced up the stoop and into the foyer.

Marion gathered Suzanne in her arms, and then the cop knelt and checked Suzanne's pulse. His glance at Marion confirmed what she already knew. He radioed in a homicide and then asked Marion if she was hurt.

She was, but in no place that bled. Even though it was useless, she rode in the ambulance with Suzanne, holding her hand.

At three in the morning, a dream took her once more out her door in answer to Suzanne's cry. She saw the killer again, the blood on his overalls, the knife in his hand.

Then his face morphed into . . . hers! Her body filled the jumpsuit, her hand held the knife.

She woke to her own scream.

Sleepless hours later, Marion stared at her television while the morning news reported that Suzanne's killer, a convicted felon named Roy Pennington, had been released early from his sentence for assault and rape because of prison overcrowding. He hadn't been able to get a job because of his record. He had died of shock and massive internal hemorrhaging before the ambulance got to the emergency room.

Marion felt no guilt for having killed the man. There was only fury numbed by exhaustion and unrelenting grief. She dressed for work and then put her tear-soaked pillowcase and sweat-drenched sheets in to wash. In the bathroom, not even repeated drenching with Visine could get the red out of her eyes.

When at last she thought she was ready to go to the office and endure the flood of sympathy and questions that would swamp her, she aimed the remote at the television to shut it up. But not soon enough.

The announcement of a commentary titled "Our Failing Justice System" blared at her. Bruce Ball, wearing his most sober face, intoned, "Where are we safe anymore?"

Her instant answer took her by surprise. "Nowhere." She sank onto the couch. It was true. The proof was the bloodstains in the crime scene that had been her foyer. She wasn't sure she had the will to walk past the yellow crime tape that blocked off the corner where Suzanne had— Suzanne had—

Bruce Ball said from the television, "What are we coming to? A return to the Old West? Or the heyday of the Capone mob era? Will Attorney General Marion Smith-Taylor, tragically affected by the murder of her assistant yesterday—" He paused, and Marion felt that he was staring at her. "Will she have the muscle to do anything about the violence that rules our streets? Or will it be law enforcement as usual, our courts unable to move against criminals and our police outgunned?"

Marion stabbed the power button to send him to blankness and then threw the remote across the room. Damn him! Damn them all. She did her best. It wasn't her fault.

It wasn't.

It was.

⑮ THE PROTECTOR

She laughs and raises the child high in the air.

He pulls the trigger.

The bullet hits the woman in the side. The force of it staggers her. Her eyes straight at his, she throws the screaming child over the edge of the roof.

A gasp pulled Hank out of sleep and sent his hand groping for the gun on his nightstand. He rolled out of bed into a fighting crouch, but the hotel room was empty. Morning sunlight cast a bright rectangle on unfamiliar gray carpet.

It had been his voice. He'd been dreaming again. About . . . about . . . Amy? He glanced at his daughter's necklace, its chain curled on his dresser. He couldn't bring the dream back, though there was a sense of pressure in his head.

He decided that going back to sleep was impossible. That was okay, he had work to do. He ordered breakfast from room service and showered.

He spent the day familiarizing himself with Ashland, cruising through neighborhoods in bright sunshine with his car windows open, fresh air swirling, getting a layout of the town in his mind and making sure he had a "back door" for escape into the mountains in case he needed one.

Late in the afternoon, Hank stood in the Alliance campus parking lot and did a slow turn, taking in foothills and mountains to the west, hills to the east, and rolling valley spotted by homes to the north and south.

A red barn was the largest building on the campus. Chickens, goats, and pigs wandered freely. Two grade-school boys pursued a small spotted pig, their giggles music in the air.

Other structures looked newer but designed to carry on a farm theme. Curving sidewalks connected buildings; people of all ages and colors strolled or hustled along them. He saw women in sweeping Indian saris and Chinese men in suits mixing with denim-clad Americans.

Satisfied that the place seemed peaceful and fortified by the pistol under his windbreaker, Hank headed for the main building. It looked new, built in Victorian style, with gingerbread and odd wings and angles to it. Two stories tall, it had a three-story, round tower on one corner.

The place was so rustic, he wouldn't have been surprised to find a gingham-clad receptionist in a lobby of Early American furniture. But the reception area was a mix of modern, antique, and happenstance—a blue neon sculpture of a bird in flight complemented an antique oak sideboard; a glossy black Oriental desk sat on a Navajo rug.

The receptionist, a barefoot young woman working at a file cabinet on one side of the room, wore a denim miniskirt and a black T-shirt with a diagonal orange line wandering across the front. Her olive skin and black hair suggested Hispanic heritage, and her accent confirmed it when she asked if she could help him.

He said, "I'm here to see Noah Stone."

"Do you have an appointment?"

"No. Name's Hank Soldado."

She brightened. "Really? Super!" She came to him with a hand outstretched and a smile beaming. The orange line on her shirt turned out to be a hugely magnified photo of a yarn thread like the one Stone had used in his Chicago speech.

"We're so grateful for you saving Noah. We'd be lost without him."

He took her hand, struck by the size of her emotion and what it said about Noah Stone. "So, is he in?"

She pointed at a spiral staircase at the round tower's base. "He's at the top. I'll let him know you're coming."

As Hank passed the second floor, Noah Stone called down. "Hank Soldado! I hoped, but I didn't really think you'd come."

Hank reached the top and Noah greeted him with a broad smile and a strong handshake. The intensity of Noah's welcome came at him like a warm breeze; the man held nothing back.

Or was it just the practiced glad-handing of a slick salesman?

Noah said, "Are you all right?"

Hank nodded. "Almost good as new." He took in the room. Windows encircled it, giving a 360-degree view of the valley and mountains. At the rear of the house, a field sloped down to a tree-lined creek three hundred yards away. Those trees could conceal a sniper's approach; a marksman could easily take out someone in the room. The scene was beautiful, the exposure dangerous.

Stone's built-in desk occupied eight feet of the curved wall. It held two computers, both monitors turned on. A chaos of papers and books covered the remaining surface. A drawing board created one of the few uncluttered spots, a pencil sketch of a beach scene taped to its surface.

In the room's center sat a round coffee table, complete with coffee thermos; around it were a half dozen comfortable-looking directors chairs.

Noah said, "Coffee?"

Hank nodded. "Black."

Stone took a chair at the round table. He wore a small holster on his belt, a pistol butt sticking out of it.

As Noah poured, he said, "I inquired about you. I now understand why our promise wasn't something you feel comfortable with. But I still think you can help me."

Hank sat next to him. "You look like you've got all the help you need."

"The attack in Chicago scared me, Hank. Badly. I went to that militia's website, and would you believe they have a picture of a bullet with my name on it? And that woman, Colonel Hanson . . ." His eyes widened. "It's like she's asking people to shoot me."

"Yeah, she's a piece of work." Not to mention a certified psycho.

Noah pointed at the road leading into the campus. "Then the other day, right out there, a man aimed a gun at my head." He told Hank about the incident.

Hank studied Noah. Mouth tight. Eyes tight. Body tense. The man was terrified. And Hank couldn't blame him. But Noah's move to stop that shooter showed guts. He gestured at Noah's gun. "Stopper?"

Noah handed the pistol to Hank. "Chicago started me carrying it, thank God."

After Noah took him through its capabilities, Hank said, "Looks like a good idea." It wasn't. Once Hank had his Colt in his hand, nothing the stopper could do would be fast enough to stop him. He gave the gun back to Noah. A water pistol would do as much good.

Noah said, "The whole time, I wanted to run. I felt like a coward."

Hank had seen the expression on Noah's face before, on men so crippled by deep fear that it broke them. "It's not cowardly to run when someone wants to shoot you." That triggered the beginnings of a flashback to an ambush in Afghanistan, heat and scrub brush and shots—Hank fought it back and offered a smile. "I've sure done it." He was going to have to find a marijuana dispensary this evening.

Noah didn't smile back. His face was drawn, and he seemed older. "I used to feel safe here, but now . . ." He gazed out the window. "I don't know if I can do it without the help of someone like you. Hell, I don't even know if I can do it at all anymore."

Would Stone's dread take him out? It seemed likely. If there were another incident, a man untrained in combat couldn't keep playing the role of a target in a shooting gallery without cracking. Maybe if Hank got closer to Noah, he could now and then give the guy a little push toward quitting. "When do you want me to start?"

Stone turned to him. His rigidity left him with a sigh and a slump of his shoulders. He smiled. "Now would be good."

Hank nodded, and then gave his first little push. "Then you should have bulletproof glass in those windows."

Stone seemed shocked. "Oh, no one would ever—" He broke off and scanned the windows.

"They could." Hank stood and walked to a window and pointed. "And they can, from that creek." He swiveled. "Or those houses over there."

Noah joined him. "Way over there?"

"I know a dozen men who would call it an easy shot."

Noah's eyes widened, and he stepped back from the window. "What else?"

Hank pointed at the stairs. "There's no security in your lobby. The receptionist just sent me right on up, no ID check, nothing."

Noah shook his head. "I have a hard time ascribing evil intentions to people. But you're right." He turned to Hank. "I'm glad you're on my side."

The man's open trust invited—no, demanded—honesty. "I'm not on your side when it comes to taking away gun rights guaranteed in the Constitution. I never will be."

"You know the argument is that the Second Amendment refers to militias, not individuals." Before Hank could protest, Noah held up a hand. "I know. Nobody's going to win that one the way things are now. That's why we sorta did an end run with stoppers."

"Seems to me that banning guns is an overreaction. Why not work to control them?"

"The easy answer to that is the politicization of the issue. Nothing's going to get through Congress that would amount to any meaningful control." Noah looked him in the eyes.

Hank knew that was the truth. Nothing would happen. "Yeah, but still—"

"Hank, the real answer is that there are three hundred million guns out there. Do you think controlling them is remotely possible?"

Okay, not when you put it that way. He shrugged. "Why you?"

Noah gazed out the window at the mountains. He sighed. "Remember that school shooting in California a couple of years ago? The kindergarten class?"

He did. "It haunted me for weeks." They all haunted him. Guns gone wrong hurt everyone.

Noah turned to Hank. His eyes glimmered with moisture, and he wiped at them. "My niece was one of the children slaughtered by that madman. She was five."

A wave of emotion gripped Hank's throat, and he saw Amy's picture, back home on his dresser. Forever five. He wanted to remember his daughter clearly, but his mind blocked the memories, the doc said to protect him. He swallowed to get the lump to go away. It didn't. It would fade, but it was never far from the surface, a giant sorrow waiting to drown him.

Noah's mouth hardened, his gaze intensified, a force of its own. "I will do everything in my power to clean this land of this terminal malignancy that kills thousands of innocents every year."

Hank had nothing to say to that. He had to admit that if all those guns weren't out there, he might not feel like he had to carry one. But the only world he could deal with was the real one.

Noah breathed out and relaxed. "Sorry, Hank, I get a little worked up. But doing something about guns is what led to the Alliance. I promise that I won't proselytize to you about what we advocate, even though we need you and I think you need us. All I ask is that you listen and learn with an open mind."

"Doing that is a necessary part of my job, sir." The "sir" that popped out of Hank surprised him. But there was an uprightness to the man that merited respect.

Noah clapped Hank on the shoulder and said, "Let me give you a quick tour."

Outside, Hank heard pride in Noah's voice as he pointed out buildings. "That cottage houses our public relations and advertising group. They do promotion, set up press speeches and conferences, that stuff."

He pointed at a building that looked like a stable. "In there is our legal department, with advocates who help people in court inquiries and researchers looking for better laws. We had something to do with getting the gun laws changed in Oregon."

"I heard you're out to ban guns."

"If I could, but that'll never happen." He patted the stopper holstered on his belt. "We were behind the effort to get these adopted by the state. What I'm against are weapons that are designed to kill people."

"But what about our rights—"

"*Your* rights?" Noah scowled, and his voice rose. "What about *this?* 'We hold these truths to be self-evident, that all men are created equal, that they are endowed by their Creator with certain unalienable Rights, that among these are Life, Liberty and the pursuit of Happiness.'" Noah's gaze seemed to bore into Hank when he said, "Is it a denial of *your* rights for me to try to stop you from opening fire and extinguishing *my* right to life?"

Hank opened his mouth to argue, but a good counter didn't come to mind. "Well, I'm sure not against your right to life."

Noah's voice turned rough. "You aren't, but there are plenty who are. For example, that guy in Chicago. If he hadn't been able to have a gun, you wouldn't be here."

Hank raised his hands in surrender. They'd have to agree to disagree. He said, "What's the round building?"

Noah eased his body. "That's our commons. It has a hall for gathers, a cafeteria, a library, recreational stuff, and a workout room."

Hank said, "Who comes to these gathers?"

"Alliance members and nonmembers who are interested in us. We've taken heat from several churches because some of their people stopped going to church and started coming to gathers, even though we're careful to schedule around church service times."

This sounded like what Mitch had been talking about. "So you've got a religion going here?"

Noah laughed. "No, no. But our gathers do fill a need for community. We have our rituals, and a speaker gives a talk. I guess you could label the promise our dogma, but that's ridiculous."

It sure sounded like a church to Hank. If it waddles like a duck . . .

"Actually, the idea of the Alliance started with a religious studies class I took at the Unitarian church."

And quacks like a duck . . .

"That sounds religious to me." Hank wished he were wired; this could be useful to Mitch.

"It wasn't so much religion that insp;ired me as a book I learned about in that class. *The Chalice and the Blade* showed how different the world was ages ago in societies where men and women operated as equals instead of as masters and subjects. It traced many social problems to the breakdown of that ancient partnership.

"That book set me to thinking on what we could do if we all worked in partnership. It gave me an organizing principle for something that could start small. It's like trying to write a novel— conceiving the whole thing at once is an impossible task, but writing one page isn't so hard."

He stopped and gazed at Hank. Noah's passion burrowed into him. Noah said, "If I talk with you and persuade you to make the promise because you see the good it can do, then you'll talk to someone else, and they'll talk to someone else."

The man's charisma tugged at Hank, and he shook it off. It was clear that Noah had the power to head one of those mind-bending cults that shaped people to fit his "vision."

"So how does all that come around to taking away . . . restricting guns?"

"After I read that book, I had the idea that people could partner together in an alliance. The promise is about how to do it. As for guns, when you think about a peaceful society such as ours, lethal firearms in the hands of criminals and killers is just wrong. Out of sync with who we have become as a people, a society of laws. It's logical that protecting people from being gunned down is a big way to implement the promise—and to protect our right to life."

They came to a cluster of bungalows around a central fountain. A bell rang, and teens, middle-aged people, and seniors bustled from one building to another. Hank said, "You've got a school?"

"Sort of. Must be time to change classes. We've taken a page from the Mormons. This's a training school for people who volunteer to spread the word."

And has feathers like a duck . . .

"Missionaries?" For the Apostle Noah?

"Advocates. I look at it this way: the quicker we get the word out and the better we are at doing it, the quicker things can change."

Mitch had to hear about this.

A lean, dark-skinned man with a bushy black mustache, his head swathed in a kaffiyeh just like the checkered headgear that Yasser Arafat had once worn, hurried up to Noah. "Mr. Stone, Mr. Stone!"

Noah smiled. "Hank Soldado, meet Faruq Al-Kadri. Faruq is the lead Ally in Palestine. He's here with a group of trainees."

Al-Kadri absently shook Hank's hand, his gaze darting to Hank's face and away. "My pleasure. Mr. Soldado—"

"Hank is my new head of security."

Now Al-Kadri focused on Hank. His regard was shrewd. "I am most glad to see this happen. After Chicago, well, the movement cannot lose Mr. Stone."

Stone said to Al-Kadri, "I wish you'd call me Noah."

Al-Kadri twitched a smile. "It would not be respectful. The American casual attitude does not work so well when we are trying to establish you in my country as a revered world leader."

Hank looked at Noah. Revered world leader? There was more to this man and his movement than Mitch had let on. Or did he know?

Noah raised a hand in denial. "Faruq, it's the promise that will bring your people to peace, not some foreigner you shove down their throats as a 'leader.'"

Al-Kadri scowled and ran a hand over his mustache. "No, Mr. Stone, you do not understand. In my culture, there has to be a central figure, a strong leader we can follow."

Noah's scowl matched Al-Kadri's for fierceness. "I've told you no on that, Faruq, time and again!"

The Arab stood his ground. "It must be."

Hank could see Stone struggle with what to say next. Would he pull rank on the guy? Instead, Noah grinned and then said, "Your training is going well?"

At last the man smiled. "Ah, yes! The teachings of the Alliance are not so different from parts of the Koran." He frowned. "Though one hopes not so easily distorted by fundamentalists." His smile returned. "How do you misrepresent a promise to help? My young ones, how is it said, swallow it down?"

Noah laughed. "I think you mean 'eat it up.'"

Another bell rang and Al-Kadri startled, then checked his watch. "Time for the brainstorming on THREAD. We are trying to find a good Arabic word to use in its place." He hurried to a bungalow and disappeared inside.

Hank said, "The man has energy."

Noah laughed. "A half hour with Faruq is like drinking four cups of coffee. But he's working wonders in Palestine. Their issues are different from ours here, but the solution is the same—a community bound by the promise."

"So you guys are international?"

"Getting there." A burst of laughter rose from a cluster of four fair-skinned people who ranged in age from a teen girl to a man in his sixties. Noah pointed. "Some of our Brits. Their branch of the Alliance is growing, and one of their people just won a seat in Parliament."

He swept the valley with his hand. "I started out just wanting to help what's here. But these days, everywhere is 'here.' The details change—guns in this place, terror in that one—but the fundamental causes are the same. Fractured societies, greed, corruption, poverty, all the ills brought on when people don't do what people should do—help each other. What hurts us most is no sense of community across—"

An electronic chirp interrupted; Noah checked his phone. "I've got a conference call to Moscow, if you can believe it. Make yourself at home. I'll catch you later."

He hustled toward the central building. Hank strolled.

After circling the grounds, sauntering along the creek and past a housing development, Hank knew the place could never be properly secure. But it didn't have to be an open invitation to an attack he thought was certain to come. Stone threatened too many people. Too many angry, frightened people with guns who knew how to use them.

Near the barn he stopped and gave Mitch a call to fill him in on Stone's growing fear and his reaction to the bullet with Noah's name on it at Martha Hanson's website. Mitch seemed encouraged, and Hank felt the same way. Although he did feel bad about seeing Stone . . . Noah . . . hurting.

As he pocketed his phone, a cab pulled up beside the main house. A slender woman and a little girl got out, and the woman stood for a moment, probably getting her bearings just as he had. The cab's engine died, and the big man driving leaned back and closed his eyes.

The child took off running toward the spotted pig. Her brown legs flashed, and then both she and the pig squealed, she with delight, the pig with fright. The sight of the child stirred something inside him that felt good. It was delight.

On a sunny spring day at a playground, he rides with Amy on a merry-go-round, holding onto her to make sure she couldn't fall off, to keep her safe—

Pain stabbed him in the temple. The memory vanished.

The little girl tripped and crashed on her belly. She lay limp and still.

Hank launched into a run, but the woman beat him to her side. She rolled the child over, and a loud wail sirened when the girl's breathing kicked in. The mother cradled the child and crooned, "You're okay. Okay. You just got the wind knocked out of you. Hey, where did that silly pig go?"

Ah, the old distraction trick. The little girl sniffled, then got up to look for the pig. Her mother stood. With thoughtless trust, the child leaned against her mother's legs as she peered around the yard.

Hank said, "She all right?"

The mother looked to him and her eyes widened. "Mr. Soldado?"

Her scarred beauty was unforgettable. Chicago. The sexual assault, his shooting, then her visit to the hospital. He dredged up her name. "Jewel Washington?"

 **TEARS, AGAIN**

Hank Soldado wasn't the larger-than-life strongman she remembered coming out of nowhere to save her in Chicago. He was—dark. Carrying a weight. But still she was glad to see him. "Yeah, it's me. How are you?"

"Fine."

"You here to see Mr. Stone?"

"Already did. You?"

"I'm hoping he meant what he said about jobs out here."

Soldado's look eased into a smile. "I think this is one guy who means what he says." His gaze left her to go to Chloe; it softened with an odd, almost sweet look of pain. "This your little girl?"

"One hundred percent."

He sank to one knee and put himself at eye level with Chloe. His voice was gentle. "You okay?"

Chloe said, "Yes." She studied him, then stuck out her hand. "I'm Chloe Washington."

Soldado took her tiny hand in his and said, "Hi, I'm Hank Soldado."

Chloe spotted the pig. She sped away, calling, "Here, piggy, piggy, piggy!"

Soldado stood and watched after her. Jewel scrutinized him. His face was composed, but there was tension—

"Mommy!"

Jewel spun to see Chloe racing for her, a pint-sized goat trotting in pursuit, fear on her daughter's face. When Chloe reached her, Jewel caught her under the arms, laughed, and swung her high into the air. "You're okay, sweetie." She lowered her into a hug.

Chloe wrapped her arms around Jewel's neck and her legs around her waist, and Jewel held her close. When she turned back to Soldado, her words died on her lips.

Tears streamed down his cheeks.

"Mr. Soldado?"

Chloe peered at him and said, "Mommy, the man is crying."

Soldado's eyebrows lifted, and then he touched a finger to a cheek. He stared at his fingertip, and his eyes widened as if he were surprised that it was wet. "I'm sorry, I . . . I . . ."

Jewel backed away a step. Normal people didn't go from a conversation to tears for no reason. "Ah, we gotta get going." When she passed him, he didn't even glance at her. After she figured they were far enough away so he couldn't hear, she whispered to Chloe, "I guess he's sad."

"I hope he feels better. He's nice."

Maybe he was. But maybe something was seriously wrong with him, too. She glanced back. He hadn't turned to look after her; he stood, his head now bowed.

When Jewel entered the old-timey building, she found a receptionist chatting on a phone at her desk. Jewel set Chloe down and said, "Now you stay by me."

She smoothed her pleated blue skirt. What if Noah Stone didn't remember her? What if there were no jobs in this little town?

The girl hung up, scribbled a quick note, and then said, "Hi, I'm Becky. How can I help you?" She smiled when Jewel asked for Noah, and directed her upstairs. As Jewel turned to go, Becky held out the note and asked, "Will you give this to Noah? We can have the newcomers meeting at Lithia Park where he wanted it."

Jewel took the note. Hand in hand, she and Chloe climbed the spiral staircase. When they reached the top, a flutter of joy at the sight of Noah Stone surprised her. His smile warmed her, just as she remembered. She let out a breath she hadn't realized she had been holding.

Noah came to her, his hand outstretched. "This is my day for surprises from Chicago! Welcome." He took her hand. "You see Hank Soldado outside?"

The weird incident in the yard flashed in her mind; an impulse followed to tell Noah about it. But she put it away. No matter how wacko Soldado was, she owed him. She just nodded and said, "Yes."

Noah's gaze dropped to Chloe, and his smile grew even warmer. He squatted, held out his hand, and said, "Hi, I'm Noah."

Chloe put her hand in Stone's. "I'm Chloe Washington." Jewel smiled at her daughter's grown-up manners.

"Happy to meet you, Chloe Washington. Come look at this." He led her to a window seat and lifted the top to reveal a stash of children's books. "See anything you like?"

Her eyes as bright as if he had revealed a trove of candy, Chloe dug in and came up with three books, topped by *The Little Engine That Could*. She hopped onto the seat and plunged into the book, reciting the story as she studied the pictures.

Noah gestured Jewel toward a chair and then took one for himself. "Coffee?"

She shook her head. "I haven't got long. My ride's waiting for me, and I have to see about school for Chloe." She took her résumé from her purse and held it out to him. "I just came to see if you meant what you said about work here."

"I always try to mean what I say. You're—a legal secretary?" He took the résumé and scanned it.

Pleased that he remembered, she nodded.

"I'll give this to Benson Spencer. He's in the Legal Building. It's, ah . . ." He turned to the windows and pointed at the stable. "Over there. The courts are crammed, and I'm sure he can use help in our advocacy program." He looked back to her. "He's out of town until Friday; can you wait until then?"

She smiled hard enough to make her cheeks ache. "No problem. Thank you, Mr. Stone. You won't regret it."

"I already don't. Maybe you'd like to come to this month's newcomers meeting and learn a little about the Alliance. But I don't know where—"

"Oh!" She held out the receptionist's note. "At some park."

He took the note and smiled. "Ah, back in the outdoors. Come to the band shell in Lithia Park Thursday evening, five-thirty. I think you'll enjoy it."

"I'll be there." She waved to Chloe. "Come on, honey, put the books down and let's go."

Chloe's lower lip stuck out in her I-don't-wanna pout. Jewel said, "I'll read to you when we get home."

Chloe clutched the books to her chest.

Noah laughed and said to Jewel, "Take those with you. You'll be back soon, right?"

"Right."

Stone walked to a window. "Before you go, will you come here for a minute?"

She went to his side. Below, Hank Soldado walked toward a car in the parking area.

Noah turned to her. "What happened out there?"

So he'd seen. Of course he had; he wasn't the type to miss anything. Including a lie by omission.

She shook her head. "I don't know, really. We were talking, and suddenly he . . . he had tears running down his face." Noah questioned her with a look. "I don't know why, and I don't think he did either. It was a little scary."

Noah gazed out at Soldado. "Yes, he can be scary. There's tension in him—like a time bomb. The question is"—he looked back to her—"who, or what, is he going to blow up?"

That evening, Jewel sat on Franklin's porch swing, her mind whirling with excitement about the chance for a job with the

Alliance and worry about the Hank Soldado thing. Here she was in a nice place, a job on the way—and a man she thought was a good guy had freaked out on her. She hadn't realized how much she'd been counting on finding safety at last, but now? Bewildered, she sank into a black mood.

Chloe dashed out, and Jewel flinched at the slam of the door behind her. Chloe plopped a book that "Uncle Noah" had lent them in her lap and said, "Read, Mommy?"

Jewel snapped, "Leave me alone!" When Chloe wilted and turned away, Jewel's guilt made her feel even worse.

Then Earl arrived home, whistling, for God's sake. When his smile bounced off her gloom, he took a long look at her, then hurried into the house and came back with a goblet of red wine. Chloe trailed him, her book still wrapped in her arms.

Jewel accepted the wine, but with a scowl, not meeting his gaze.

Earl scooped up Chloe and carried her upside down and giggling into the house. He bellowed, "Franklin!"

Franklin's voice came. "What you got there, Earl? It's upside down and making strange noises."

"I hereby appoint you Chief Story Reader and Distractor. I've got dinner to do."

More giggles came when Franklin said, "Yes, sir. But it isn't going to be easy, reading upside down."

A grin tried to make an appearance on Jewel's face, but she batted it away with bad mood.

Classical music started up, sending soft strains of violins through the window behind her.

Thanks to the wine and music, she had mellowed some by the time Earl reappeared and set up TV trays, complete with cloth napkins and floral place mats.

"Is Madam enjoying her evening on the veranda?" His smile was so appealing that she almost said yes. She sipped her wine instead and looked away. Damn it, people should leave foul moods alone. She wasn't done with hers yet.

Minutes later, he reappeared with dishes of a tasty stir-fried something. The warm smell of it roused hunger in her. He refilled her wine, and Franklin came out with Chloe on his shoulders. When Franklin set her on a chair in front of a TV tray, Earl handed her a glass of sparkling cider in a wineglass.

Eyes wide, Chloe looked at Jewel and said, "I can have wine, too, Mommy?"

That did it. She smiled and said, "You can have some of that special 'wine.' Be sure to say thank you to Earl."

Chloe said thank you and sipped. "It tickles!"

Franklin and Earl chuckled and settled into seats, Earl parking himself on the porch swing next to Jewel. Like an oddly crafted family, the four of them dined to the music as they watched the sunset color the world rosy.

By the end of supper, Jewel's mood had done a one-eighty. She'd never heard much classical music, but she loved the way it soared and, though it had no drums, stirred powerful rhythms within her. Soon Earl had the stereo cranked up, and she and Chloe danced in the front yard to Mozart and the applause of their audience of two.

She insisted on doing the dishes and felt better for it. At the end of the evening, after putting a tired and happy Chloe to bed, she and Earl sat in the porch swing to enjoy a glass of wine. Franklin plopped into a chair and popped a beer.

She shivered in the cool night air, and Earl put an arm around her shoulders. She liked his warmth.

Earl said, "So you're working for Noah Stone, the Alliance's grand high Pooh-Bah."

She laughed at the title. "Not exactly, and I don't really have the job yet. It's in their legal office, I think, something about advocacy."

"But you'll be there, at the headquarters?"

"Yeah."

Earl gazed out at the gathering darkness. "I'd sure like to meet up with Mr. Stone."

"Maybe you can at this newcomers meeting he wants me to come to. It's at some park Thursday night."

His voice sharpened. "Lithia Park?"

"That was it."

"Yeah, that sounds good. I'll take you."

"Okay." She looked to Franklin. "Franklin?"

"Naw, I'm already an Ally. But I'll sit on Chloe for you."

She smiled at Earl. "It's a date."

Earl looked toward town and said, "Yeah. It's a date."

Hanks PTSD had hit him like a tsunami when Jewel and her daughter left him. After a drive back from the Alliance headquarters that he didn't remember and a dinner he hadn't tasted, Hank entered the bathroom in his hotel room. He splashed cold water on his face, hoping to wash away the cotton that had blanketed his mind since she picked up her daughter and his tears had poured.

What was wrong with him? He remembered only a rush of panic when the woman raised the child high in the air. He wished he'd looked for a marijuana dispensary. And a bottle of whiskey.

He studied his eyes in the mirror. They were tired and sad.

Hank thought of Chloe's little hand in his, so remarkably tiny, as fragile as a glass figurine, yet warm and soft. He hadn't felt the warmth of friendly flesh since—he couldn't remember when.

He missed that touch.

There was no one to give it to him.

It was harder than usual to go to sleep.

The bullet hits the woman in the side. The force of it staggers her. Her eyes straight at his, she throws the screaming child over the edge of the roof.

Hank pulls the trigger again.

Again the woman staggers. Then she dives off the flat rooftop after the little girl, her muffled laughter falling away.

He runs to the—

The night was deep when his cry shocked him from sleep and convulsed him upright. His chest heaved, but his mind was blank. A breeze from his window brushed his face. Something on his face was cool. He touched under his eyes, and his finger came away wet.

17 DEEPER AND DEEPER

Troubled by the previous day's fugue, Hank sought relief in work. He spent the morning at the library, researching the Alliance and its role in Oregon. In the afternoon, he strolled around the town, visiting art galleries and reading the menus posted on the windows of a host of nice-looking restaurants.

A stop by a local marijuana shop gave him what he needed to dull the triggers that let his PTSD loose. By evening he felt his mind was working as sharply as ever.

That night, he went to the ballet, but not for the dancing. In anticipation of Noah Stone appearing at the Alliance newcomers meeting the next evening, Hank wanted to check out the park, and the *Rogue Valley Times* had said a dance school was putting on a free performance there as a fund-raiser.

A band shell, its stage no more than a ground-level concrete slab, sat at the bottom of a grassy slope below a street that curved through Lithia Park. On the far side of the street, more lawn slanted upward through a grove of trees laid out in orderly rows.

Behind the band shell, Ashland Creek burbled down from the mountains and through a wooded area that offered picnicking, hiking, and a wide trail where families strolled and joggers puffed.

As time for the ballet performance drew near, couples and families spread blankets on the lawn before the band shell, the first row as close as ten feet in front of the stage area. From there, an attack on Noah could be swift and deadly.

People opened picnic baskets and munched meals. By the time the ballet master strode onto the stage to introduce the program, the audience had filled the lawn, humming with conversation punctuated with laughter, tolerant of children racing between blankets and leaping over outstretched legs.

The PA system blared classical music, and the ballet troupe's dancing had bucolic charm. To Hank's eye, a few of the ballerinas were a little heftyer than acceptable in big-city circles, but a couple of beauties showed real grace. Children in the audience imitated the dancers' movements on tippy-toe.

Satisfied that he knew how to handle Stone's arrival the next night, Hank turned to leave, but then he glimpsed a pair of eyes on the far side of the audience focused on him instead of on the dancers. He stopped but didn't turn that way, instead gazing out at the crowd, keeping the watcher in his peripheral vision.

It was a dark-haired woman in jeans and a T-shirt, and she was definitely watching him. He flicked his gaze to her, and her stare flinched away. He edged up the slope and around the audience to come down behind her. As he neared her position, she received a call on her cell phone. She nodded and spoke a few words, ended her call, stood, stretched, and strolled away from the lawn.

Her face nagged at him. He'd seen it before. Something wasn't right about this. He followed.

She ambled up a path that led through trees and bushes. He trailed her as she passed a stone building shrouded with greenery—it housed restrooms. She turned at a corner ahead and disappeared from sight. He glanced back. No one could see him from the lawn, and he rushed to close on her.

When he rounded the corner, she was waiting, facing him. She'd known he was coming. And that meant—

Two big hands grabbed Hank's wrists from behind and yanked his arms painfully back, a foot swept his feet out from under him, and he crashed, his face in the dirt.

He twisted and saw the woman whip a pair of handcuffs from her jacket pocket. When she got close, he kicked, catching her in the stomach. She stumbled back against a wall.

A fist clubbed his temple in just the right spot with just the right force. Things went dim, and he didn't feel like doing anything anymore. He was aware of hands lifting him to his feet and his wrists being cuffed behind his back. They helped him to an isolated picnic table screened by bushes.

When his head had cleared, Hank studied them. A Black man who looked like he could be a pro linebacker and the woman sat across from him, calm and relaxed, their hands at ease on the table, although a stopper sat within easy reach of the man's right hand. Each wore a ring made up of bands of pinks, tans, and browns.

Hank's wallet lay open in front of the man, his driver's license and retired officer ID cards on the table. So was his .45.

He said, "Well?"

The woman said, "I'm Sally Arnold, and this's Joe Donovan. We're Department of Justice." She took a slim wallet from her pocket and showed him an ID.

Joe tapped the .45 and frowned. "You've been frequenting a man who sells illegal guns."

Hank flashed back to the blond who'd been walking a dog in front of Hatch's house, and he studied Sally. Her blond wig gone, her lean face intense now, she wasn't the pleasant neighbor she'd been posing as. "The pretty neighbor."

She smiled. "Yeah. We've been staking out Rick Hatch, who not only deals guns but is a member of a particularly wacky militia bunch. We like to see who comes to visit him."

Joe said, "Gives us all kinds of leads into lowlifes around town." He studied Hank and then fingered his ID cards. "You don't appear to be a lowlife."

Hank shook his head. "I'm not."

Donovan spun the .45. "You weren't visiting Hatch to pick up this illegal cannon?"

"I have a job to do that requires a weapon."

Sally glanced at Joe, and then said to Hank, "And that job is?"

"Security for Noah Stone."

Sally raised her eyebrows. "We haven't seen you around before."

"Just got here."

Donovan added, "ID says Chicago."

Hank relaxed. These weren't local cops; maybe he was okay. "Where we met up."

Sally's eyes widened. "The attack?"

Hank nodded.

Donovan frowned at Hank. "You the one who stopped a bullet for Stone?"

"Yeah."

"And you're helping him with security?"

"I think I can make him safer." Except from Hank Soldado.

Donovan smiled. "Well, why are you sitting there wearing bracelets?"

Hank grinned. "You don't think they're 'me'?"

Sally hurried to unlock the cuffs; Hank stretched cramped muscles. "Nice work, the way you caught me."

Donovan pushed Hank's ID and gun back to him. "I think we were lucky."

Sally leaned forward, taut with intensity. "How long you been here?"

"A couple days."

"Wait till you've spent some time. They're really onto something." She smiled. "I'm moving my folks out from Ohio."

"The prosperity thing?"

Donovan smiled. "Damn right. And we're gonna help it get better."

Sally took up the story. "We're working with local cops, helping clean up the place."

Donovan smiled. "Though business is gettin' a little slow."

The crime business sure wasn't taking it easy where Hank lived. "Slow?"

Donovan nodded. "Real crooks, the ones who make a living out of it, are clearing out. I think it's the stoppers." He tapped the little gun. "Here, if somebody with a stopper catches somebody doing wrong, the bad guy knows he's likely to be hit with nap and wake up lookin' into a cop's baby blues. Anyplace else, even if a cop comes along, a perp with a gun has a chance to take him out, grab a hostage, do something to get away. But not with nap, tangle, and whack."

"Stoppers work that well?"

Sally nodded and picked up the stopper. "I was in a liquor store Saturday night when this guy tried to stick it up. The second he pulled out his piece, whap, a shopper hit him with nap. The robber made the mistake of takin' a shot at the dude, and half the people in the store whipped out stoppers and gave him a nap shower plus wads of tangle. The nap overdose killed him."

"Yeah, but nap isn't instantaneous, is it?"

"Less than a minute."

"So he could have done more damage?"

Donovan said, "Here's the damage—he didn't rob or kill, and the next day two more shady types headed south for California."

Hank let that sink in. "You mind if I go now?"

Joe exchanged glances with Sally and then nodded. "See you around."

Hank got up and, to the strains of *Swan Lake* filtering through pine trees, left them. They were good people.

He hoped they wouldn't get in his way.

⌒⌒

It was late in the evening when Jewel rose with the rest of the audience in the Oregon Cabaret Theater to give the singers a standing ovation. She flashed a smile at Earl and got one in return. The performance of "My Way," a musical tribute to Frank Sinatra, had been one rush of delight after another. "That Old Black Magic" was so good it had given her shivers.

When the applause died out and the audience began leaving, Earl said, "Want to meet the cast?"

"Oh, yes!" What a treat—the perfect dessert since she sure didn't have any room left in her belly for more food. She'd never eaten anything as good as her coconut cashew chicken, although a taste of Earl's pan-fried catfish had run a close second.

On the way down from the tier that held their table for two, she once again marveled at how an old church had been transformed into a theater. Even the stained-glass windows somehow blended perfectly with the huge crystal chandelier that Earl said had come from an old movie palace.

As they approached the stage, a long-haired man with a swishy way of walking rushed at Earl. With a big smile, he shook Earl's hand and said, "Your set is great! The actors love working it."

Jewel turned to Earl. "You didn't tell me you did the set."

He shrugged. "It's in the program."

The long-haired man eyed Jewel and said, "Please tell me that you dance, sing, or act."

Jewel laughed. "Nope, not a stitch of talent."

With an exaggerated sigh he said, "Too bad."

Earl said, "Wesley, don't you ever stop being a director? Meet my friend Jewel. We're on our way backstage."

Wesley shook her hand. "Please come again."

After meeting the cast and wondering how such regular-seeming people could do such amazing things, Jewel stepped from the theater into a cool evening. Even though it was ten o'clock, trickles of conversations and sprinkles of laughter came from other theatergoers sauntering down the sidewalk. A sense of belonging settled on her.

Partly because of the wine they had shared at dinner, but mostly because of the show and Earl's company, Jewel's spirits were high, relaxed, and easy. A breeze caressed her face, and they walked in silence.

A pretty blond woman came up to Earl. She hit Jewel with a chilly glance, then lavished a warm smile on him. "Earl! Haven't seen you for a while."

Resenting the invasion, Jewel edged closer to Earl. It pleased her when he didn't stop to talk. He said, "Been real busy, Stephanie. See you around."

As they strolled, Earl reached for her hand, and she welcomed the feeling of his skin on hers.

"Thank you, Earl, for everything. It was a wonderful evening."

"My pleasure."

A black SUV drove past as they waited to cross Main Street. Hank Soldado was at the wheel. Jewel shivered.

Earl said, "You cold?"

She shook off a dark feeling. "No. I'm fine."

"You might want to bring a sweatshirt or something to the Alliance meeting tomorrow. It gets cool in the park when the breeze comes down off the mountain."

"I will. I saw Noah speak in Chicago. He's good."

"Yeah?" A streetlight put a gleam in his eyes. "Should be interesting."

 **TIME TO BEARD THE LION**

Marion's intercom buzzed. "There's a Mr. Cy Ligon here to see you. He didn't have an appointment, but—"

"Send him in."

The FBI agent hurried in and plopped his briefcase on her desk. "Sorry to drop in on you, but I just got urgent marching orders, gotta help identify some assault rifles down in Alabama, a KKK rally got out of hand and some good ol' boys shot up a kindergarten in a Black community." At her look, he added, "Nobody was hurt."

Ligon took out the red stopper she had given him and said, "I wanted to give you my results on this before I left."

He opened the stopper and took out a nap cartridge. "Notice any difference?"

She examined it. "Looks the same."

He slipped it back into the weapon and pointed to the three-round chamber. "I loaded these first two nap rounds with the liquid form of VX gas. It's a lethal nerve agent Saddam Hussein used on the Iranians. Hit somebody with this, they're dead real fast."

"You actually did it."

"Yeah." He snapped the weapon shut. "This little gadget can be deadly, but you have to get close."

She said, "Thanks, Cy."

"My pleasure." He handed the stopper to her. "Be very careful with that." He rushed away.

So Noah Stone's little world wasn't so perfect after all. The little gun felt good in her hand, though. It did seem like it would be good to have handy for protection. She decided she'd reload the gun with the real ammo and keep it in her apartment. She slipped the stopper and the little case of cartridges into her purse.

She buzzed her secretary. "Samantha, get me on a flight to Ashland, Oregon. Today."

It was time she saw the Constitution-killer in person.

⑲ DEATH IN A PARK

On the evening of Noah's speech in the park, Hank drove to the Alliance campus to take him to the meeting. Light illuminated Noah's tower room. From the parking lot he could see Noah at his desk, and so could a gunman. If he were really doing a security job, he'd have to introduce the man to the concept of window coverings. That Earl guy he'd met at Hatch's place could be creeping around with a rifle . . . No, the militia boys said they wanted Noah's killing to be public.

Like at tonight's event.

He parked and jogged inside. He climbed the spiral staircase unimpeded. Why wasn't there an electronic lock on the front door for after-hours?

Noah was shaking something granular from a jar onto a small piece of paper. Hank caught the distinctive aroma of high-resin marijuana.

Noah glanced up and smiled. "Hey, Hank. Just a minute." Hank watched as he crafted an expert joint. Hank read heavy tension in the man's eyes and a tightness in his face.

Noah lifted the joint. "For after the meeting. I never do this stuff when I have to use my brain for anything more complicated than walking. But you're driving, and a toke after a night like tonight takes the edge off." He smiled. "It's nice living in a civilized state with legal weed." He slipped the joint into a wooden case.

Noah stood and took a deep breath. "I hate this."

"You hate what?"

Noah waved a hand toward the town lights.

"Meetings?"

"Speeches. Sometimes it makes my guts cramp up for hours before. And it's worse now." He looked to Hank. "That attack in Chicago and then having a pistol pointed at my head here, where I live . . ." Noah gazed out a window, then turned back to Hank. "Tonight is a test. I don't know if I can do this anymore."

"You do what you have to do."

Noah took a deep breath. "Let's go."

Yeah, you do what you have to do. Hank wondered if he would have to do anything to Noah Stone. The man had courage.

Clusters of pedestrians strolled in the street that led to the band shell, slowing the drive to the parking area closest to the stage. Hank spotted the barefoot receptionist, Becky, waving from a parking place he'd sent her to hold. She carried a hand-printed sign that read, "Noah's Spot."

When Noah saw her, he frowned at Hank. "I don't want any privileges."

"Security. The shorter the walk, the less the exposure." He had to do something to make Stone think he had a new security man.

Noah sighed. "I guess you're right."

As soon as Noah stepped out, a dozen people swarmed around him with greetings and questions. Instinctively, Hank put his hand on the pistol inside his windbreaker and moved toward Noah.

Noah lifted his hands high. The voices silenced. He smiled widely. "I'd love to talk with each of you, but as you can see, there may be one or two too many."

The crowd chuckled. Hank relaxed and let go of the gun butt.

"If you have questions, ask them during my talk. If you want to visit, come see me during office hours. Okay?"

Hank braced himself to force a way through the throng, but the people surprised him by dispersing and hurrying to find places on the lawn in front of the band shell.

As he led Noah toward the stage, a cop approached. Noah said, "Hey, Tom."

Tom nodded and said, "Hey, Mr. Stone. Crowd seems okay." His gaze shifted to Hank, and his eyes narrowed. "I don't know you."

Noah said, "Tom Stevens, meet Hank Soldado. He's helping me with security."

Tom put his hand out for a shake, and Hank took it. "Glad to have you, Mr. Soldado." The officer smiled at Noah and then strolled away, his gaze sweeping the crowd. Hank liked his alert manner.

Noah mounted the stage and accepted a cordless microphone from the bearded guy Hank had seen running sound for the ballet. At the stage's rear, two young men and two young women wielded guitars, a keyboard, and drums to make the happy music Hank had heard at the Alliance rally in Chicago.

Hank surveyed the crowd—maybe sixty or seventy people filled the sloping lawn in front of the stage in talky clumps, clustering on blankets or sitting in low folding chairs.

They were young and old, white and yellow and brown and black. Clean and upbeat, they reminded him of the people he had seen at the Alliance rally in Chicago.

And they were too close to the stage for decent security.

But Noah's security wasn't really Hank's problem, was it? On the other hand, he had taken the job, hadn't he? He was on alert and couldn't have shut down even if he'd wanted to. Duty was duty.

*

At the fringe of the crowd, Marion sat on her jacket and leaned back on her hands. Even though she was on a mission, it was hard to avoid feeling at ease when you sat on soft green grass surrounded by trees, blue sky overhead, and people having a good time.

Despite her feelings about Noah Stone's policies, she found herself wanting to hear more from him. That could come soon—he had left a sharp-eyed, sturdy-looking guy who had to be security and strolled onto the stage.

One thing marred the peaceful scene, though—little guns in holsters on belts, the stoppers she'd had Cy Ligon look into. They were supposed to be nonlethal, but Cy had put the lie to that. She studied Stone's security guy. She focused and spotted the telltale bulge of a shoulder holster under his jacket, a lump far too big to be a stopper. So even though Stone advocated against real guns, his staff carried them. Sorta hypocritical.

Whatever. She shifted her gaze to a young woman helping her baby stand. No one paid Marion any attention, and she felt like a regular person. It was nice.

Hank did the swift, look-for-inconsistencies scan that had become second nature to him. About a third of the audience wore stoppers in plain sight. He didn't see the little weapons as dangerous. Or particularly useful. Hank liked the reassuring weight of his .45, snug in its shoulder holster, loaded with good old lead slugs.

At the top of the slope, Joe Donovan and Sally Arnold stood on each side of the audience. Good to see them there. He caught Joe's eye and got the faintest of nods. Guy was sharp. Interesting that pros like him and Sally were in Stone's camp.

He glimpsed a beauty he recognized; Jewel Washington sat on a blanket, concentrating her gaze on Noah. Next to her, s itting with his legs crossed Indian-style, was Earl Emerson. Hank couldn't see a weapon, but Emerson wore a denim shirt open over a T-shirt, tails out.

He seemed as absorbed as Jewel. But Hank had seen the rage behind Earl's pleasant facade at Rick Hatch's house. Was he here to take his shot? Scouting for a future attempt? Or just courting Jewel?

Jewel couldn't remember feeling this relaxed in years. The crowd's mood was part of it—she'd been greeted with smiles when she'd spread a blanket borrowed from Franklin on the grass. All of it— the surrounding green of trees and the cool, clean air laced with the scent of pine—felt like the way people ought to live.

Noah Stone stopped to chat with the musicians, so she let her gaze wander. It came across Hank Soldado, prowling along the edge of the crowd like a stalking wolf.

She glanced at Earl, who looked serious as he stared at Noah. He'd been so comforting after her experience with Soldado, the way he'd made all the bad things go away. She laid her hand on his thigh.

He startled, and then lifted her hand and ran a finger over her rings. He leaned and gave her a brief, soft kiss on the lips. She could see developing a case of like for this guy.

Turning his gaze to her hand, he said, "I never saw so many rings." All but one of the rings held precious stones. The standout was a plain gold circle on her little finger.

"My savings account. A creep can snatch a purse, but it's a lot harder to take money off your fingers."

He wiggled the plain ring.

She said, "I got that from Chloe's father. Right after he gave me this . . ." She traced the scar on her cheek. "The ring used to be in his nose."

"Ouch."

"He was high on crank and meth and PCP and God-knows-what when he did it." She shook her head at the memory. "Hell, he didn't even feel my ripping it out for a good five minutes. Should have seen him yell when he did. He pinked a long time ago."

The mention of pink brought to mind the brother she'd left dead in a closet. Tears rose in her eyes.

She leaned against Earl and things were better.

The music ended, and enthusiastic applause started when Noah strolled to center stage, then died when he raised the microphone to speak. Smiling, he said, "Are all you people interested in the Alliance?"

"Yes," the crowd answered, its tone cheerful.

He laughed. "Okay, here's what you'll be doing as an Ally. Working for prosperity. I don't mean the money-in-the-bank kind, but the good-stuff-of-life kind. Shelter. Food. Good air. Good water. Safety. Health. Community. Work. Freedom. Is that what you're looking for?"

"Yes!" said the audience.

Noah continued. "If you join us, we are enriched by your talent, your intelligence, your sweat, your support. But what do you get from the Alliance? A chance for prosperity? Yes, but as Allies make life better for each of us, we make life better for all of us, and here in Oregon you enjoy many rewards of the Alliance's work without doing a thing. So why should you join us?"

Jewel wasn't about to give up her independence, so she was glad she got the good stuff without having to make any promises. But she was willing to work for what she got, so it wasn't like she was a freeloader.

"Because you won't be alone anymore, that's why. With an Ally, you know the promise has been made, that he's committed to acting in your interest. An Ally is someone I would buy a used car from."

People around Jewel chuckled. She smiled. She'd have to remember that when she went to buy a car.

"An Ally, even if a stranger, is a friend in need. Can you say that of any stranger you meet? Or even some of your friends? Or some of your family?"

The promise sounded good to Jewel—but promises were made to be broken.

Hank shook his head. Hell, after breaking down and bawling in front of Jewel Washington for no good reason, he couldn't even trust himself.

He focused on Earl, who leaned forward, arms wrapped around his knees, revealing the bulge of a gun butt under his shirt at the small of his back. It looked too big to be a stopper—had to be a lethal cannon from Rick Hatch's arsenal. His gut tensed.

❧

Jewel looked to Earl; his face was knotted in a fierce scowl. She touched his hand, and he flinched. Then he switched on a smile that didn't ring true. She said, "Something wrong?"

"No. He's great, isn't he?" Earl went back to watching.

She turned back to Noah.

Stone stepped closer to the stage's front edge. "I've done this long enough to know you have questions. So let me stop jawing and hear from you."

A young woman in threadbare clothes, her face wan but her eyes bright, raised a hand. Noah pointed her out and she stood. "What does it cost to join? I ain't got a lot."

Noah nodded. "You will have to spend some of yourself. We ask a tithe of your time, your effort, your skills. Minds are a far more valuable resource than dollars, and each of us has something to contribute. To receive, we give. To earn, we work."

The girl smiled. "I got the time, all you want, and I'm a good worker."

"I look forward to it, then."

❧

Caught up in Noah's words, Hank shook his head to break away and refocus on his job. Earl still sat, leaning forward. Was he here to do something, or was he just stalking his prey?

A twentysomething Latino man stood. Cheeks pocked with acne scars, hair long and black, mustache dark and fierce, to Hank the man was a picture of a racial stereotype. In a high, clear voice colored with a Mexican accent, he said, "What about people like me?"

Noah smiled. "What do you mean, 'like you'? Male? Black-haired? Standing up?"

The crowd chuckled, but the Latino scowled. "No, man, Chicano."

Noah raised his hand to the audience. On it was a ring. "You've seen rings with many colors on Alliance members. You've seen the colors on Alliance T-shirts. They are skin colors." He lowered his hand. "The more colorful the threads woven into our tapestry, the richer, stronger, and more interesting it is. There is only one race, the human one. We're all people like you. Anybody who doesn't see that doesn't have the sense God gave a carrot."

The Latino thought that over and then smiled. "Gracias." He sat and put his arm around a Latina who was breast-feeding a baby.

A twentysomething woman rose, her bushy hair black, her nose a proud beak. "I've heard that the Alliance is against religion."

Hank tuned back in. Some said the Alliance was against religion? Not according to Mitch. How could a church be against religion? Although, now that he thought of it, many religions were against *other* religions.

Noah frowned and then said, "Here's the truth: the Alliance respects any religious belief so long as it does not teach, advocate, or incite harm to human beings. Does that sound antireligious to you?"

The young woman said, "No."

"We also respect the right to *not* have a religious belief. The Alliance is a place where all people can gather for common cause, regardless of faith. Or lack of it."

This was no church, not even close. Hank wondered where Mitch had gotten the idea.

Noah said, "In the Alliance, whether you are a true believer or an atheist *cannot* make a difference in how you are treated. To allow that would be immoral."

He sent his gaze across the audience and then shook his head. "You see so-called Christians blindly attack people of the Muslim faith, painting them all with a terrorist brush. You see radicalized Muslims rationalize murdering innocent Christians because they are 'infidels.' I wish those people would recognize how un-Christian, un-Muslim, inhuman, and immoral what they do is.

"Without morals, we are not complete human beings. So, in the Alliance, we think hard about the moralities of living together, and we work hard at uprooting cultural cancers that set one person against another."

The woman raised her hand. "But what about faith? Don't we need faith?"

Noah said, "It so happens I'm not inclined toward what most people think of as faith. I have a theory that some folks are genetically disposed toward believing in religion and others are not."

Stone shifted his gaze to the distance for a moment, and then back to the woman. "But I do have a belief, and perhaps that's a kind of faith.

"I believe that human beings can do right by each other. I believe you and I can join together to ally despite our differences and prosper together. That's my faith."

The black-haired woman said, "Thank you" and sat on the lawn.

Hank scanned the audience. The faces were rapt, all turned toward the stage. He didn't blame them. When did you hear that kind of honesty from a public figure?

Earl Emerson leaned forward. His body looked taut. His right hand clenched and unclenched, over and over.

A middle-aged woman waved her hand frantically. Noah pointed to her. "The woman who's about to levitate."

She smiled and stood, and then her face sobered. "Does that go for gays? LBGTQ people? The old OCA is trying to come back—is the Alliance like them?"

Noah's gaze turned black. "We don't have anything to do with the Oregon Citizens Alliance. It's a fraud because it represents only some citizens while it persecutes others, especially gays. Good people were led down a terrible road by the OCA in the nineties, pushed by ignorance and bigotry."

Marion marveled at how such a rational, reasonable, personable man could be leading a movement to eviscerate the Constitution. Maybe she needed to sit down with Tiffany when she got back and review her findings. There had to be a way to counter the Alliance.

But still, she couldn't find a thing wrong with what he'd said so far. It was difficult to consolidate such fair-mindedness with advocating taking away the fundamental fairness of Fifth Amendment protections. Why couldn't Stone see the contradiction?

Jewel thought all this sounded a little too good to be true. Be nice if it was . . . but no, in her experience people just didn't act like Noah talked. As for him, it could all be an act. But she hoped it wasn't.

Noah said, "Many come to the Alliance shackled by powerful prejudices created by their culture, their families, their peers. We help cut those chains with deprogramming, for programming is what prejudice is—we aren't born with it. Like a cavity in a tooth, bigotry is a rot that poisons the whole system. Dig it out and replace it with a strong, healthy filling and you're the sound, sane person you were meant to be."

A man who looked to be in his sixties said, "Who decides what that filling is?"

"You do. Therapy is based on the principles of THREAD. You either agree to that or keep your cavities. It's your choice, and you're in charge all the way. It's counseling and discussion with a very specific goal."

The man said, "What about crime? I heard you don't believe in punishment."

Noah said, "You read the papers. Do you think punishment works?"

After a moment's reflection, the man said, "Doesn't seem to, not for the real crooks."

Hank had to agree. Prison was often a finishing school for criminals.

Noah nodded. "Fear of punishment doesn't stop people who are intent on doing harm, and it doesn't do anything for victims.

"If you steal a thousand dollars from me, which rights the wrong—putting you in jail or you paying back my thousand dollars? Which is more likely to prevent you from stealing again—jail time or therapy that changes the way you think about stealing and maybe even helps you find a job?

"Here, no one goes to jail for 'property crimes.' They make restitution and go through therapy."

An angry edge came into Noah's voice. "But violence . . ." If wrath had a face, it would have looked like his.

"Violence cannot be made good by restitution. It cannot be prevented by the threat of punishment, because too many people don't think about consequences when they commit a violent act.

"Violence is not tolerated by the Alliance. That's why we consider the simple possession of a lethal firearm to be an act of violence, and Oregon law agrees. Lethal firearms have no place, no reason, no *use* in a modern democratic society, because they are useful only to maim and kill."

He scanned the audience. "To maim and kill—so owning one is by definition the first step of assault with deadly force."

Earl Emerson sprang to his feet and stood at attention as if he were a soldier.

Hank tensed. Then he eased into a "ready" mode and narrowed his focus until it seemed like Earl was the only one in the audience. He slipped his hand inside his jacket and gripped his pistol.

Noah smiled. "I'm sorry, I get carried away. You have a question?"

Earl's voice was tight. "Isn't Oregon still a part of the United States?"

Noah's brow wrinkled. "Yes, of course it is."

"Still under the Constitution?"

Noah nodded. "I see where you're going."

Earl's voice rose. "We have a right to bear arms."

"But that doesn't make it right to—"

Earl swept his right hand under his shirt and brought out a gun. He cried, "You goddamn Commie, we want our guns back!" His left hand joined the other to steady the pistol.

Time slowed as adrenaline slammed Hank into action. A split second after Earl grabbed for his gun, Hank pulled his out. A man behind Earl reached for a stopper in a belt holster. But it would never stop Earl from blowing Noah away.

His mission for Mitch was gone from Hank's mind. His only thought—not even a thought, more of a primal reaction—was that Earl was about to do a terrible wrong and an innocent man would be killed.

Hank's gun came up, oh . . . so . . . slowly. Honed reflexes aimed and triggered his lethal firearm.

The bullet struck Earl in the temple.

Blood, bits of skull, and brain matter blasted out the opposite side of his head.

Gore spattered Jewel's upturned face.

Earl triggered his shot, but the force of Hank's bullet had twisted his body—Noah Stone grabbed his shoulder, then fell to the stage floor.

Earl's body sprawled beside Jewel.

Hank wheeled to see if there were other attackers.

Tom the cop ran at him at full speed, his stopper pointed Hank's way. Tom shouted, "Drop it! Drop the gun!"

Something hit the side of Hank's neck. He touched it and found moisture.

He turned toward its source; Jewel Washington stood, red with blood, her legs straddling Earl Emerson's body, her stopper aimed at Hank.

Tears washed trails through the blood on her face, and she stabbed another button on the stopper. A streak of tangle hit his chest and arm, its sticky wrapping immobilizing his gun.

Drowsiness started his eyelids lowering. His knees gave way, and he fell facedown.

The cop's knee smashed into his back and crushed him onto the ground.

The last thing he saw before he passed out, his cheek jammed into the cool grass, was Noah Stone. Hank's vision seemed to telescope in to Stone's face. He saw horror. Fear. And regret.

Long after the shooting, after the arrest, after the crowd had been interviewed and dispersed, after Noah Stone had been whisked away in an ambulance, after the gunman's body had been carted off in a coroner's van, after the shooter was handcuffed and shoved into a police car, Marion sat on the lawn.

She sat surprised by the emotion that had flashed through her when she realized that the assassin's shot had not killed Noah Stone.

Relief. No, it was more. She would have been relieved if anyone had been spared an assassin's bullet. This was joy.

Was she falling under Noah Stone's spell? She shook that silly thought away. She was just in a kind of mental shock.

But she was no longer thinking about Noah Stone as the enemy. If only he weren't behind the constitutional heresy that—

A police officer stopped beside her. "You okay? Need any help?"

She did, but not the kind a cop could give. She smiled, extended her hand, and said, "Maybe a hand getting up." The officer nodded, pulled her to her feet, and strolled on.

At the hotel that night, thoughts hammered at her until three glasses of scotch silenced them and she slept.

A cop drove Jewel to Franklin's house after taking her statement. Franklin rose from the porch swing, then cried out when he saw her bloody clothes. She had to relive the shooting to tell Franklin about it.

She didn't tell him people said Earl had tried to kill Noah Stone. That had to be a mistake—she was sure there was a good reason Earl had had a gun. After all, he'd been talking about the right to carry one.

Franklin stared into the night, struck dumb.

Shock still damming up her emotions, Jewel stumbled into the house—so quiet without Earl's classical music, so dark without his smile. She found Chloe safely asleep. She showered, scrubbing until it hurt to get Earl's blood off, and then threw her bloody clothes into the garbage.

In her bed and still awake when Franklin passed by on the way to his bedroom, her dry eyes focused on the ceiling, his sobs pierced her. His tears opened the valve that had closed hers off.

She cried into her pillow.

HELLO, HOOSEGOW

In the limbo before becoming fully awake, images flickered through Hank's mind. Earl Emerson aiming his pistol at Noah. Drawing his own gun and firing. Earl collapsing. Jewel shooting him with that silly excuse for a weapon. His helpless fall to the ground—

He opened his eyes to a sunrise framed by a barred window in a gray concrete-block wall.

He sat up and discovered that he was on a bunk in a cell. His hands were free of tangle. His mind seemed clear. He called out, "Hey, anybody there?"

The door opened and Tom, the cop from the park, came in. His manner was stiff and formal. "Yes, Mr. Soldado."

"What am I doing in here?"

"Being held for the inquiry."

"Into what?

"You don't remember?"

Hank stifled a rush of irritation. "I remember just fine. And I don't remember doing anything that would put me in a cell."

"You killed a man—"

"Who was about to kill the heart and soul of the Alliance."

Tom finished, "—with an illegal firearm."

"Yeah, but there was no time—"

The cop held his hand up. "Save it for the inquiry."

Hank wasn't going to get an ounce more out of this guy. "Do I get a phone call? Can I have a lawyer?"

"Sure. All the calls you want. And the Alliance will make sure you have an advocate, or you can hire your own lawyer if you'd rather do that." He unclipped a cell phone from his belt and passed it through the bars. "I'll be back."

Hank searched his memory for Mitch's number and dialed.

"Mitch Parsons here, how can I help you?"

"This is Hank. I'm about to explore the workings of Oregon's justice system from the wrong side of the bars, and I thought you should know what's going on."

"I saw the story on the news. Jesus, what a mess. You okay?"

"Physically, yeah. There's some kind of inquiry, and they say the Alliance will help by providing what they call an advocate. I guess that's a defense lawyer."

"Can I do anything to help?"

"Just stay tuned, I may need something along the way."

"You got it."

Hank ended the call. He gripped the bars that enclosed him. God, he hated being caged.

He eyed the room and studied the bars, doors, windows, looking for anything that could lead to escape.

Jewel faced the bathroom mirror, dried her eyes, and started putting on her mascara for the second time. She'd been doing okay until Franklin flicked on the TV news.

She'd gone into the living room just as the local reporter said, "Police believe last night's assassination attempt on Noah Stone would have been successful if it hadn't been for the quick, heroic actions of a newcomer to the Alliance organization, Hank Soldado."

Franklin had turned to her, shock on his face. "Assassination?"

"No way, that's wrong."

The reporter continued, "According to authorities, the gunman, a local set designer, was also an expert marksman. The gun he used was a lethal firearm, which wounded Stone in the shoulder."

Franklin groaned. "Oh, no-o-o."

Jewel went to him and wrapped her arms around him. "It's a mistake, I just know it is."

The TV picture had widened to show the reporter with another man behind the news desk. The reporter said, "With us is legal reporter Jim Bosley. Jim, can you tell us why Hank Soldado is in jail even though he is being hailed as a hero? Isn't what he did a form of self-defense?"

"Well, there are technicalities about the weapon he used to stop the attacker."

Jewel had slammed off the television, tears spreading mascara streaks. She said, "He kills a man and it's just 'technicalities'? God, this sucks."

Jewel's journey in Franklin's cab to interview for the job at the Alliance was sad and silent. She rode in front with him, Chloe between them. She thanked him with a weak smile and hugged Chloe. "I think you'll like school."

At the Alliance Legal Building, a pink-cheeked receptionist who looked hardly old enough to be out of high school greeted her with a smile. Jewel said, "Is Benson Spencer in? I'm Jewel Washington."

"You bet, Ms. Washington, he's expecting you." The receptionist touched a button on her phone and said, "Ms. Washington is here."

Jewel checked her image in a mirror on the wall and saw that at least she looked businesslike in her gray suit. She hid her grief behind the blank expression she'd cultivated for whenever she didn't want her feelings to show.

She'd stood in her depression for maybe fifteen seconds before a short, round, bald man dressed in jeans, loafers, and a red polo

shirt bounded down the stairs next to the reception desk. He hurtled at her and skidded to a stop just short of a collision.

Radiating energy like heat from a stove, he grabbed her hand
and shook it. "Welcome, welcome, Miss Washington, Jewel," he
said, smiling. He held up her résumé. "Noah told me all about you,
this looks great, as far as I'm concerned you're hired, come on up,
we've got a lot to do, come-come-come!"

He jogged up the stairs. His energy had weakened her depression, and her interest kindled as she double-timed after him.

Upstairs, individual offices took up the outside walls and an
open central area held a secretary's station, a lounge with cushy
chairs and couches, and a law library. The chubby, sixtyish secretary, looking comfy in shorts and an orange-thread T-shirt, sat at
her desk, fingers attacking a keyboard. A youngish man in jeans
and a knit shirt with the tail out searched through thick volumes
spread over a table. He glanced up, gave Jewel a quick nod, and
went back to his work. This was like no law office she'd ever seen.

Benson waved a hand at the woman as he zoomed past.
"This's Marge, she knows everything, you need something, don't
ask me, I'd just have to ask her." Marge raised a hand and a smile
to Jewel. As they passed the young man at the table, Benson said,
"Mike Potts, associate advocate."

Benson slid to a halt beside an office and gestured her into it.
Jewel stepped past him into her new world.

It was utilitarian but comfortable: an oak computer station,
the computer already turned on; a work table; two forest-green
side chairs; a bookcase stocked with reference books.

Benson followed her in. "So you were a legal secretary in Chicago."

"Yessir."

"Noah said working on paralegal?"

"Yessir."

"Excellent. We can help you with that. Here your title is associate advocate. This is your office, mine's next door."

He picked up a manila folder and a paperback book from her desk. "Come see me in twenty minutes and we'll get into salary and that stuff, but first I want you to do some prep for a hot case." He eyed her. "I expect you'll have questions, and we can do all that at the same time."

He handed her the file folder. It was labeled "Henry Soldado." "You're going to assist me on this case." Then he offered the book: *Justice Through Truth and Advocacy.* "Most of what you need to know about how we work is in here. It's a lot different from the adversarial system you're accustomed to. Sort of a kinder, gentler justice."

Surprised, she said, "Soldado's actually in trouble?"

"Most certainly."

Jewel couldn't keep the bitterness out of her voice. "How? I mean, the TV says he's a big hero. Says he saved Noah's life for the second time."

"How he did it is the problem."

"What's that mean?"

"He killed a man and used a lethal firearm. Both of those things are against the law."

Yeah, sure, the "law" is gonna do right, gonna get the he-ro. "What do I have to do?"

"Assist me in being his advocate, do research, get his story."

"I can't." She held the folder out to him. "I don't think Earl did what they say. I think this man's a murderer."

"Emerson a friend of yours?"

"He . . . was."

Benson's gaze softened. "I'm sorry about what happened to your friend, but Noah requested that you be assigned to this case, and we take Noah's requests seriously."

"You mind if I ask Mr. Stone about this?"

He smiled. "Heck no, you want to tackle the gorilla in his tree, go ahead." He hurtled out the door and around the corner into his office, calling, "Marge! Marge! I need you!"

When Jewel stepped from her office, she was almost run down by Marge.

In Noah's office, an attack of nerves hit Jewel while she waited for him to end a phone call. It didn't help that his arm was in a sling from being accidentally shot by Earl. She sure needed the job— but how could she possibly make herself defend that monster?

Noah hung up and eyed the folder she gripped. His stern expression didn't make her feel any better. He said, "That was Benson. So we've got a problem?"

She took a shaky breath to start her protest; he raised a hand to silence her. "I won't force you to take that case, but I want you to." He smiled away his somber expression. "By the way, good morning, and welcome to our team."

The smile relaxed her. "Thanks. But I don't see how I can do a good job, the way I feel."

"I understand you had a relationship with the young man, and I'm sorry for you and for him. But we have to go beyond feelings at times. Even if you don't join the Alliance, everyone who works here has to abide by our principles—especially legal advocates."

He held out a hand for the folder and opened it on his desk. Skimming through its pages, he said, "If there was ever a man who needed empathy, it's Hank Soldado." He lifted his gaze to her. "He did help you in Chicago, didn't he?"

"Yes. But it wasn't really me he was saving; he was just stopping a crime. Coulda been anybody."

"That's just it. It could have been anybody. I think Mr. Soldado is a highly principled man. Important things could come from him." He held the folder out to her. "It would help me if you took this. And it might help you, too."

How could she say no? This man was one of the good guys. All she'd had to do was show up and he had given her a job. But—

Noah said, "You want to see justice done, don't you?"

"Sure." But she wasn't going to hold her breath, not after what she'd heard on the news.

Noah studied her. "What is it?"

"Nothin'."

He gazed into her eyes as if he could read her thoughts. "If you can't be honest with me, Jewel, this isn't going to work out."

A little embarrassed by being such a coward, she said, "Yessir. After everything I've seen on the news about him being a hero . . . It's just that I haven't seen much justice in this world, especially not from the law."

He again offered her the folder. "You will here."

If that was true, she did want to see Soldado get what he deserved. "But I have to help him?"

"No, what you have to do is help discover the truth."

"Whatever it is? I mean, they say this guy saved your life."

"Whatever it is."

"And you're good with that?"

He nodded. Now it was her turn to study Noah. He meant it, didn't he? She reached for the folder. "Okay."

Back in her office after meeting with Benson about job details, Jewel decided to avoid the folder's contents as long as she could. She opened the book instead. It started with "America's system of justice has taken it far. But that system has become emasculated by technicalities and crippled by its adversarial nature, and justice is too often not its result or even its goal. What do Americans do when a system fails? We replace it with a better one."

One author of *Justice Through Truth and Advocacy* was Noah Stone in collaboration with a Supreme Court justice. She read on.

Two hours later, what she had read made sense, but the conclusions shook her; they seemed to violate everything she knew about the way American justice worked.

Or, as the book pointed out, didn't work.

Jaw clenched, she tackled the folder. After she read the reports and learned about the death of Soldado's family, she felt a touch of sympathy for the man, but she was a long way from empathy. The rest of his background made it clear that he was a dangerous man. The idea of spending hours with him in meetings and courtrooms unnerved her.

But she found the book's notions on how to make justice really take place fascinating. Could they work? If her job as Hank Soldado's advocate was to go for the truth, she could do that. In this case, it sure as hell needed to be heard.

And if there was justice here, you could stick a fork in the son of a bitch, 'cause he was done.

21 JUDGMENT DAY

At ten o'clock on a Monday morning, three days after the shooting of Earl Emerson, Hank sat at a table in a courtroom. Benson Spencer flanked him. Beside Benson sat a woman he recognized and sure as hell hadn't expected to see on his side, the attorney general of the United States. On the other side of Marion Smith-Taylor, Jewel Washington studied notes. So far she had avoided looking at him. He didn't blame her.

It wasn't a good omen that Noah Stone sat with the state's advocate—the prosecutor.

Hank scanned the room for the security he would have to deal with if this went south on him. He was not going back to that cell, not for doing nothing wrong. He'd been on the side of the law his whole life, but he could make an exception if he was railroaded.

Only a guard at the door wore a stopper. Hank saw no stoppers on the citizens and reporters who thronged the room. That made sense; even though the state promoted them, they wouldn't allow weapons in a courtroom.

Except there was another gun in the room. His Colt sat on a table in the center of the room. It could come in handy.

A man entered from a door at the rear of the room and said, "All rise."

At the state's table, the people's advocate, Jenny Sochanski, sat next to Noah. He smiled when the honorable judge Edith Crabtree entered the courtroom with her usual chin-up dignity. As she eased her heavy body into the chair behind the tall judicial desk, Noah scanned the most crowded courtroom he'd seen in thirty years. "Be seated," the judge said.

Every seat was taken. He recognized half a dozen prominent citizens, a reporter from the local press, and famous faces from the networks, including Bruce Ball. A network-pool TV camera stood in a corner.

After a quick session of *voir dire,* the jury of six had been seated in the jury box. He knew Tim, who owned the paint store, and there was the young woman who jogged with her dog on his street. The rest looked reasonably alert.

In the center of the room, Don Wyngate, the court's chief investigator, stood ready in front of the evidence table. Noah thought maybe he'd trimmed his beard, probably on account of the TV cameras. The table held an ugly-looking pistol and a laptop computer.

A railing separated visitors from the court area and the long table for the accused and the advocates. Hank Soldado sat with Benson and Jewel, her navy blue suit and serious expression quite lawyerly. She didn't look happy, but she did look determined. He liked her toughness.

Most of Hank's Alliance advocate team was as expected; far from usual, though, was the presence of Attorney General Marion Smith-Taylor. Noah was struck by the weariness he saw in her face. Dark bags swelled under her eyes, and a deep frown creased her brow.

Opposite the jury box sat the witness chair and, in front of it, a table with a computer monitor and the verifier's headgear, a headband with sensors mounted on a front-to-back strap across the top. From it wires trailed out the back and led to the verifier computer. Other monitors displayed output from the computer to the judge, the jury, and the advocates.

Even though Noah had seen the verifier's brain fingerprinting technology in action for a year now, he still marveled at how it revealed the truth of testimony. It didn't exactly detect lies, but it sure let you know if the truth was being told.

He'd tried it, just to test it, and testified that he'd skipped lunch when he hadn't. The question had triggered his memory in his brain of lunch at The Breadboard, and the verifier had instantly detected the knowledge, which let his lie be known. And it had lost him a twenty-dollar wager. He wouldn't bet against it again.

Judge Edith rapped her gavel. "Court is in session." She turned to the court clerk. "Mr. Ferris?"

The clerk intoned, "The people of Oregon inquire into the shooting death of Earl James Emerson, said to be caused by Henry Steven Soldado, and into the possession of a lethal firearm by the accused."

The judge said, "Are the advocates ready?"

Jenny answered affirmatively for the people. Benson stood and said, "Yes, Your Honor. And I would like to introduce my new associate advocate, Jewel Washington."

Jewel stood and nodded. "Your Honor."

Edith smiled. "Welcome, Ms. Washington." She nodded toward the advocates' table. "I see we have guests. Ms. Smith-Taylor, Mr. Stone."

Noah and Marion stood. Marion smiled at the judge. "If it pleases Your Honor, I'm here as a friend to the court."

Noah said, "The same goes for me, Edith."

Judge Edith leveled a judicial gaze at him.

He hastened to add "Your Honor."

"We are privileged to have such weighty friends. Welcome."

They took their seats.

She turned to the chief investigator. "Mr. Wyngate, the evidence?"

"Ready, Judge." He indicated a laptop computer on his table. "I'd like to start with a video of the shooting."

After entering the video into evidence, the investigator said, "Call Lea Shoop to the stand." A guard opened a side door and a plump teenage girl entered, her steps quick and stiff-legged. Her wide eyes looked scared.

Wyngate escorted her to the witness chair and placed the verifier headband on her head. On computer screens around the room, an ever-changing graph of her brain activity appeared. At the screen's bottom was a dull green circle. If a witness said something that triggered a memory, the green light glowed. If there was no memory of that *specific* event, then it did not come on.

Judge Edith turned to the jury. "I remind the jury that you may ask questions, but you must be recognized by me before you do so." She nodded to the investigator. "Go ahead, Mr. Wyngate."

"Miss Shoop, did you shoot video with your phone at the Alliance newcomers meeting on the night of the sixth?"

She nodded.

The monitor screen showed a spike in one brain activity graph line. The green circle glowed brightly below it and then dimmed. Her answer had been confirmed by activity in her brain, a memory that coincided with her affirmation.

Judge Edith's voice was kindly. "You'll have to speak up a little, Lea."

Lea's cheeks flushed red. "Sorry, ma'am. Yes, I did. Shoot a video. I did."

Wyngate turned the laptop so that she could see the screen and tapped a key. The screen showed the audience in front of the Lithia Park band shell. Noah Stone stood on the stage. Other computer monitors in the courtroom showed the same image. "Is this from your video?"

"Yes, sir. That's what you got off my phone."

The green light glowed.

Marion raised her hand. "Your Honor?"

Edith nodded and Marion rose. "Ah, aren't witnesses usually sworn in?"

"We don't require that anymore, not since the verifier became part of our process. And, as you well know, if a person intends to lie, the swearing-in has no meaning anyway."

"That may be true, Your Honor, but lie detectors have no legal standing in court. The oath is the only defense against perjury."

With the calm patience of a parent explaining something to a child, Judge Edith said, "We do not use a lie detector, Ms. Smith-Taylor." She aimed a hand at the witness stand. "This is brain fingerprinting. I'm sure you're aware of the technology."

At least Smith-Taylor had the grace to blush. "Yes, ma'am, but we have not accepted it in federal courts."

The judge's voice sharpened. "We accept it here, as have other state courts in the United States, Ms. Smith-Taylor. The machine has proven accurate time and again. The science is valid. The machine detects an uncontrollable recognition response in the brain when something a person holds in memory is mentioned." She took a deep breath. "It works. Is that clear?"

Smith-Taylor dropped her gaze to the tabletop. "Thank you, Your Honor." She sat.

Wyngate said to the witness, "Please tell us how you came to have this video, Miss Shoop."

"Uh, I was recording Mr. Stone's speech when this guy stood up in front of me and then pulled out a gun." She swallowed. "Then his head kind of blew up and I swung around to where I'd heard the shot come from." She pointed at Soldado. "And that man was . . . he was . . ."

Wyngate said, "That's fine, Miss Shoop. We'll let the video tell the rest of the story." He tapped a key and the video started. "The action begins just before the shooting."

The courtroom grew hushed. The footage was jerky, but clear. At the moment Earl Emerson aimed his gun, his face twisted, his hand tightening his finger on the trigger, Noah heard a gasp from Jewel beside him. He glanced at her; she covered her mouth with a hand, her expression one of horror.

Then the monitor showed Earl's head explode. The image blurred as the camera phone swung. It stopped at Hank Soldado aiming his gun at the victim. Other people in the scene held stoppers, but no one else had a lethal firearm. Heads in the audience turned toward Soldado. Wyngate stopped the playback and turned to his witness. "Miss Shoop, is that the video you shot in the park?"

Tears ran down the girl's cheeks. She nodded, glanced at Judge Crabtree, and said, "Yessir. It was horrible."

"That's all, Miss Shoop, thank you." The girl slipped the headgear off before Wyngate could help her and scuttled out. He turned to Hank. "Mr. Soldado, please take a seat on the witness stand."

Soldado went to the chair; his face could have been chiseled from granite. Wyngate put the verifier headgear on him. Noah hated to see this happening to a man he'd liked and trusted.

The tension was almost tangible. The investigator began. "Mr. Soldado, did you shoot a man named Earl Emerson on the evening of the sixth?"

Marion stood. "Objection, Your Honor. He cannot be compelled to testify against himself."

Judge Edith said, "In our state, Ms. Smith-Taylor, every citizen is required by law to help determine the truth regarding a matter under inquiry. He will answer the question."

Marion lifted her chin. "I respectfully submit, Your Honor, that to force him to testify violates his rights under the Fifth Amendment to the Constitution of the United States, which specifically states that 'No person shall be compelled in any criminal case to be a witness against himself.'"

Irritation soured the judge's voice. "Partially true, Ms. Smith-Taylor. If you wish to quote the Constitution, please quote the entire relevant clause. In this case, it says, 'No person shall be compelled in any criminal case to be a witness against himself, nor be deprived of life, liberty, or property, without due process of law.'

"Because Oregon has a compelling state interest in securing justice for its citizens, the state interprets this clause to mean that, just as we can deprive persons of life, liberty, and property with due process of law, so can we compel someone to testify if there is due process of law, even if to do so is contrary to his desire to be declared innocent. In this state, we have established that due process, and you're holding it up."

Marion thought for a moment, then said, "I must reiterate my objection. The American adversarial system was created to reach the truth, and protections for the accused have been built into the law."

Noah raised his hand. "If I may, Your Honor?"

"Please, Mr. Stone. Perhaps you can help the court head off further interruptions."

Noah rose and addressed Marion. "In principle, the adversarial system seeks the truth. I think you'll agree, however, that in practice each side seeks victory and truth often has little to do with the cases presented by the defense and the prosecution."

The attorney general's jaws clenched. "We have a due process of law."

Noah said, "Do we? *Vaughn versus Tennessee* said, 'Aside from all else, due process means fundamental fairness and substantial justice.' Where is fundamental fairness when thousands of criminals are acquitted because they get away with a lie? And where is justice when thousands of innocent people are convicted because 'the system' is too crude an instrument to reveal the truth?

"Under the modern adversarial system, a robber arrested coming from a bank with a sack of stolen money in his hand will plead not guilty, and then the system will attempt to prove that the robber did what a bank full of people and the robber himself know he did. No one is surprised when he lies about his culpability.

"And, in a courtroom, no matter what oath he swears to tell the truth, it is expected that he will plead not guilty, which is often a lie. It is 'the system.'

"Worse, a small procedural error can get the crook off altogether on a technicality—even though all, including the judge and the prosecutor, know that he did the deed.

"William Kunstler, a top defense lawyer, is reported to have said, 'Screw the law. You get the guy off any way you can.' Defense lawyers distort the truth in order to free known criminals. Prosecution lawyers do the same in pursuit of conviction. Lawyers seek to discredit opposition witnesses, not to glean the truth from them. The adversarial system is about winning, not justice."

He paused and gazed at Smith-Taylor's calm exterior. "Have I mischaracterized the adversarial system?"

Her voice thick with emotion, she said, "Whatever its shortcomings, the American legal system has served the people since our nation was founded."

Noah stifled a rush of irritation and kept his voice calm. "How well does a system serve the people when it permits, no, *encourages* the flagrant, premeditated freeing of criminals because it is forced by convoluted technicalities to respect lies as if they were truths?"

She offered no answer.

"An entire industry of criminal defense lawyers dedicates enormous intelligence and resources to win freedom for people who have committed vile wrongs. That's a crime against society, and here we have done something about it.

"A lie should not be allowed to set a wrongdoer free or imprison an innocent. Real justice cannot transpire until the truth is known. Here, where the aim of our legal system is truth instead of victory, the adversarial system has been changed to one of advocacy."

He gestured toward Benson and Jenny. "We have two advocates, one that looks after the rights of the accused and one that looks after the rights of the people. They are both required by law to seek the truth."

He pointed at the verifier. "We use science to verify a statement as true or false with ninety-nine percent accuracy. When you add in the testimony of witnesses and physical evidence, our ability to determine the truth is as close to one hundred percent accurate as any human system can get.

"In our system, the famous O. J. Simpson murder trial wouldn't have taken a year of time and millions of dollars. Within days, the jurors would have known whether the police had tampered with evidence. Jurors would have heard from O. J.'s lips the truth of what he had or hadn't done. The truth—"

He stopped and grinned at Edith. "I'm sorry, Your Honor, I get fired up about this subject." He couldn't stop a feeling of pride at seeing the justice system he'd dreamed of in action. He sat.

"That's fine, Mr. Stone, I do too, and it doesn't hurt to be reminded. Now, Ms. Smith-Taylor, are you clear on how things are going to work in this courtroom?"

Smith-Taylor's face had paled beyond exhaustion. In flat tones that revealed her effort at control, she said, "Yes, Your Honor. Nonetheless, for the record, I object to the coercion of this defendant."

Judge Edith tapped her gavel. "So noted."

"With all due respect, Your Honor, if this man is convicted on the basis of his forced testimony, I will be appealing this case."

The judge nodded. "You'll have to get in line. A fellow who drove a truck of that nasty pink drug into the state plans to take his conviction to the Supreme Court. Maybe you can join his case." She shifted her gaze to Hank Soldado. "Please answer the question. Did you shoot Earl Emerson?"

All eyes turned toward Hank.

22 LIFE ON THE LINE

Hank straightened in the witness chair. He wasn't about to do this the easy way. And Smith-Taylor might find grounds for an appeal if he put up a fight.

"No," he said.

A line in his graph spiked. The green light glowed. His brain had betrayed him by acknowledging a memory of shooting Earl when he'd denied it.

The judge sighed. "Mr. Soldado, please tell the truth as you know it. You will stay in that seat until you do."

Marion Smith-Taylor stood, and Edith held up a hand. "And, before your friend of the court protests, this is not coercion. To lie is a conscious decision. And so you shall sit there until the truth as you believe it to be is heard."

The attorney general sat.

Hank shrugged and said, "Yes. I shot him to stop him from killing Noah Stone." The green light glowed.

Don Wyngate said, "You are in the employ of the Alliance?"

"Yes. To provide security."

The investigator held up Hank's forty-five. "Is this your weapon?"

"Yes." Green light.

"Were you aware that it is a lethal firearm—" he ejected the magazine, still filled with ammunition, and held it out for the jurors to see "—and that it was loaded with high-powered bul-lets?"

Legal proceedings were so tedious. He resisted an impulse to say "Duh." He said, "Yes." Green light.

Wyngate set the pistol and the clip on the evidence table. "Did you know that possession of such a firearm is against the law in this state?"

"Yes, but I needed it to do my job."

"You did not think a stopper would work?"

"No. Nap would have taken too long. Emerson would have had plenty of time to kill Mr. Stone because he was using a lethal firearm."

A hand went up in the jury from a thirtysomething man.

Judge Edith nodded to him. "You have a question?"

"More of an observation, ma'am."

"Can't have observations from the jury, sir, just questions."

He thought, then asked, "Mr. Soldado, didn't you know a spray of whack would have shut his eyes instantly and stopped him just as quickly as a bullet could kill him?"

Hank started to shake his head, but then remembered that Noah had described it to him. But he hadn't really known for sure it would do that, so he said, "No, I didn't." The green light remained unlit to show no belief of what whack could actually do.

The investigator followed up. "If what the juror said is true, sir, could a stopper have prevented the attack without loss of life?"

They had him there. He said, "If true, it might have." He gazed at the jury. "If, that is, someone had shot it in time. As it was, I was the only one quick enough to react."

"Are you certain of that?"

Hank thought of the shooting. He'd been so focused on Earl that he hadn't seen anything else. "No." The green circle stayed dim. No knowledge of that.

The people's advocate, Jenny, raised her hand, and Edith nodded for her to speak. Jenny said, "Mr. Soldado, did you have reason to believe that Earl Emerson had deadly intent toward Mr. Stone?"

He didn't see a need to get into the conversation with Hatch and Emerson. "No."

The green light flared. Busted again.

Hank sighed. The thing was good. Trying to lie would only make him look guilty to the jury. He said, "Actually, I had previously heard him threaten Mr. Stone's life." The green light lit again.

"So you felt certain that murder was his intent?"

"I knew it was."

Jewel, her voice businesslike, asked, "Mr. Soldado, do you feel that you were justified in killing Earl Emerson?"

Soldado looked her squarely in the eyes. "Absolutely."

The green light glowed.

"Any remorse?"

What kind of question was that? The guy was set on murder. He shrugged. "None." Green again.

The judge turned her gaze on the advocates. "I think we have all the information we need, unless the advocates or the accused wish to call other witnesses."

Benson stood. "Not here, ma'am. The facts are clear."

Jenny rose and said, "The people's advocate agrees."

Judge Edith addressed Hank. "Mr. Soldado, we also inquire into extenuating circumstances that may modify the consequences of your wrongdoing, so I have a couple of questions. Because we understand that people who are angry are not wholly rational, I want to know if you were angry with Earl Emerson at the time you shot him."

Hank said no, and the verifier reflected no memory of anger toward Earl.

"Mr. Soldado, do you have anything to add?"

Hank removed the verifier headgear and turned to the jury. "This seems simple to me. Yes, I shot a man and killed him. But I did it to prevent the murder of an innocent man. As an officer of the law, I've done the same before. I had only seconds to stop him, and there was no time to debate the niceties of which weapon should be used." He dropped the verifier gear on the table in front of him. "I believe I'm guilty only of saving a life."

The judge said, "I'm sure Mr. Stone is especially appreciative of your good intentions. The jury may consider your purpose, but I must warn you, the state of Oregon is determined to end gun violence, and it is your behavior that the law must deal with."

She turned to Benson. "Mr. Spencer, do you have evidence or witnesses in regard to any extenuating aspects of Mr. Soldado's mental state or competency at the time of the shooting?"

Benson said, "No, Your Honor, there is no reason to doubt his sanity or competency."

Judge Edith turned to the jury. "It has been established that the accused, Henry Soldado, did knowingly possess a lethal firearm, and that he did shoot and kill Earl Emerson with it. Unless the jury wishes to modify the statutory consequences for these wrongs, Mr. Soldado will receive the following: for the possession of a lethal firearm, a choice of separation from society for a period of ten years or therapy; and for the killing of Earl Emerson, a choice of separation from society for life or therapy to a level of satisfaction that he is rehabilitated. The jury will go to the polling room and either approve those consequences or recommend alternatives."

The jury filed out.

Judge Edith focused on Hank. "Our juries don't ordinarily take long, Mr. Soldado, because they know the truth. I customarily take this time to explain a few facts to the accused.

"There is a contract between society and the individuals who live in it. Society provides things an individual cannot—roads, electricity, hospitals, medicines, the internet—the many, many things that make up modern life. In return, the individual does not damage society by inflicting harm upon its citizens and property.

"Once a wrongdoer breaks that contract, he no longer has a right to the things society provides. Furthermore, society has the right, if not an obligation, to exclude the wrongdoer so that he or she can no longer harm its citizens or property.

"In our state, Mr. Soldado, we recognize two basic wrongs against society: crimes against property and crimes of violence against persons. We desire justice and, as would anyone who analyzes crime and punishment, we have learned that punishment is not justice. Punishment works to teach small children and to assuage desires for revenge, but has little to do with the righteous resolution of wrongs.

"For property wrongs, restitution is justice. To allow a property loss to stand while the wrongdoer sits in a cell, meals and shelter provided and paid for in part by his victim's taxes, provides no justice, and very little punishment.

"But you have wrought violence, Mr. Soldado. There is no restitution for a lost life. There are two alternatives open to you. One is separation from the rest of us by confining you for—if the jury agrees—the rest of your natural life unless therapy can be effective. In the interests of full disclosure, the fact that life expectancy in the Keep averages two years could affect your decision."

Marion rose. "Your Honor?"

The judge nodded.

"I find a life expectancy of two years shocking. I must object. The Eighth Amendment protects us from cruel and unusual punishment."

Judge Edith gazed at Marion. "Yes, it does. However, there is no punishment involved. We simply separate criminals from society, and we offer therapy as a way for them to redeem themselves and rejoin us. Prisoners are provided with adequate food, clothing, and shelter, and then we leave them alone. There's nothing cruel about that. Confining prisoners to a prison is neither cruel nor unusual. And it is not punishment.

"The Keep has no bars, no cages—personally, I believe that locking a prisoner up in a six-by-ten cell for twenty-three or more hours a day is quite cruel. The short life expectancy in the Keep may be due to the violent nature of the prisoners. They are free to be nonviolent if they wish. And free to seek therapy and release."

She turned back to Hank. "The alternative to confinement is therapy, a rigorous, sometimes invasive treatment designed to avert your commission of unjustified violence. Your advocates will explain this option thoroughly, and you will have adequate time to consider your choice."

He'd die before he let them mess with his mind.

A green light beside the polling room door went on and she said, "Mr. Ferris, please reseat the jury."

The jurors filed in and took their seats. The foreman handed a slip of paper to the clerk, who delivered it to Edith.

She read the words and addressed Hank. "Mr. Soldado, the jury finds that you have committed the wrongs under inquiry and sees no extenuating circumstances calling for reduction of consequences."

She turned to the foreman. "Is your verdict unanimous?"

"Yes, Your Honor. Uh, we'd like to add something."

"Go ahead."

The foreman stood and addressed Hank. "This wasn't easy. You did save a life, no doubt about that. But what we couldn't get past was the fact that you could have done it with a nonlethal weapon. Most of us wished we could set you free, but it just wasn't right."

Hank risked a glance at the evidence table. His gun and the magazine were only a half dozen feet away. He schooled himself to show no emotion that would alert a guard. He nodded to the foreman.

Judge Edith said to Hank, "Mr. Soldado, you have twenty-four hours to choose which course you wish to pursue, and you will remain in the custody of the police."

Marion stood, her expression a blaze of fury. Her voice was heated when she said, "That's it? You call this a trial?"

"We call it an inquiry, Ms. Smith-Taylor. And we have learned the truth. There's nothing more to do."

"An appeal. I want to file an appeal."

Judge Edith shook her head. "That's your right, but do you doubt that you have heard the truth? You would appeal *truth*? You represent the Department of *Justice*, do you not?"

Marion's silence was answer enough.

The judge banged her gavel. "Case closed."

The guard beside the table moved toward Hank.

Hank leaped from his chair, shoved the investigator into the guard, scooped up his pistol, slammed the magazine home, and yanked the slide to seat a bullet in the chamber. Okay, he was armed, but he was in a building packed with cops. He needed a hostage.

Three long strides to the advocate table—Jewel was closest, and he grabbed her hair. He pulled her out of her chair and pressed the muzzle of the gun into the soft flesh under her jaw. She cried out, a sob filled with pain and fear.

He hated doing this to her, but it was his life at risk, not hers.

The guard at the door slapped his hand on his stopper; Hank turned his prisoner to face him.

"You do anything, she's dead."

The guard lifted his hand away from his weapon.

Noah stood. "Please don't do this."

"Sorry, sir, but I'm not going to prison for doing nothing wrong, and I will never allow my mind to be destroyed."

Hank moved, steering Jewel ahead of him by her hair. She grabbed her purse as they left the table.

It surprised Marion that she trembled. Despite her years in law enforcement, she'd never been so close to the threat she had seen in Hank Soldado's deadly gaze. She'd felt like a bug about to be squashed.

After Soldado and his hostage left, the crowd surged toward the door. The TV reporter, Bruce Ball, beat them to it.

He opened the door and poked his head out.

A shot boomed and he jerked back in. The crowd backpedaled and settled into making calls and messaging with cell phones. The investigator and a guard dashed out a rear door. The judge looked pale.

Marion sat. Scenes from the trial flashed through her mind. Hank Soldado denying the reality of what he had been videotaped doing, trying to beat the system just as Noah Stone had said. The way the verifier revealed falsehoods. The lack of swearing in, even though she couldn't deny that it was functionally useless.

Noah Stone's words attacked her. "How well does a system serve the people when it permits, no, encourages the flagrant, premeditated freeing of criminals because it is forced by convoluted technicalities to respect lies as if they were truths?"

She'd had no answer because the truth was more than she'd been willing to admit to. The system hadn't served Suzanne, had it, when it turned her killer loose? Shaking started in her hands, and then a chill took over her body. How many other thousands had been victimized by the system that she served? What could she do about it?

 **RUNNING**

Hank figured he had only minutes before the place boiled with cops, so he was relieved to see a pickup pull into a parking spot. He forced Jewel toward the truck as the driver opened his door. When the man saw the Colt's muzzle in his face, he scrambled out the other side.

Two cops ran toward them from the courthouse, stoppers aimed. One yelled, "Halt!" Hank snapped a shot over their heads, and they ducked behind parked cars. He shoved Jewel into the cab and jumped behind the wheel.

She scrabbled for the opposite door, but stopped when he jammed the pistol barrel into her back.

He said, "I've killed one person with this, you don't want me to kill another."

She let go of the handle and slumped back, her eyes wide.

He was a bastard for doing this to her, but he pushed the feeling down. "Buckle your seat belt." That would slow her if she made another attempt to escape.

The cops charged the truck and he rolled up his window. They fired their stoppers, and the rounds bounced off. So much for "stoppers." He floored the gas pedal and fishtailed out of the parking lot.

In town, he parked in an alley, took Jewel's arm, and they strolled like tourists to his SUV in the lot behind the Ashland Springs Hotel. A block away, a siren raced past on Main Street.

He drove up-slope toward Mount Ashland, winding through quiet neighborhoods until he connected with Ashland Loop Road, a narrow track into the mountains—his "back door."

Jewel broke her silence. "Look, just let me out. You're not going to be needin' me anymore. I won't tell where you went."

"Sure you will, and I don't know that I don't need you." He glanced at her. The fear in her expression reached him. "Listen, I have no intention of hurting you."

Tears came to her eyes and her voice quivered. "It's my little girl. She's only four."

Damn. He'd forgotten about her child. "Where is she now?"

"At school."

Okay, so she wasn't alone. "Somebody'll take care of her. I get the feeling this is that kind of town."

"But she'll be so scared."

He snapped at her. "So am I, lady." Then he thought of Chloe crying and hated what he saw. "You have anyone you can call?"

"Franklin."

"Got a cell phone?"

She nodded. "Okay, call him, but that's it. Then stay put and enjoy the scenery. I can tie you up, but I'd rather not take the time."

The road twisted through tall pines into a world of cool silence. The police would block all entrances to Interstate 5 and put another roadblock at the California border, only twenty miles away. Helicopters would likely search other roads into California. No, his way out was to the west, across the Siskiyou Mountains to Gold Beach, a fishing town on the Oregon coast. There he could find a boat to take him to California or Washington.

∿

After a series of roads wound past Mount Ashland—Jewel was amazed at how much snow still covered the ground and trees even though it was spring—they hooked up with logging roads that weren't much wider than the car. On one hairpin curve, Jewel found herself leaning away from the sheer edge, closer to Soldado. She'd never been so scared. He had the nerve to smile at her, so she forced herself to sit straight.

"What happens if a car comes up this road?"

"Somebody has to back up."

She shuddered and tightened her seat belt. They drove deeper into endless mountains along a network of narrow roads that scored the sides of steep slopes.

After what felt like an eternity of bouncing, dusk came, and Jewel was glad to hear Soldado say it was time to get under cover. He turned onto tire tracks that wound between trees and led up a forested slope. They got lucky—the trail ended at a deserted shack made out of beat-up old planks and tree limbs, but it had four walls, one window, a roof that didn't look like it'd stop much rain, and two doorless doorways. The snow was sparse here, but it was chilly.

Inside, two battered kitchen chairs and a rickety card table tilted on a dirt floor, and a raggedy canvas cot sagged next to a wall. A rope suspended a kerosene lantern from the low ceiling, and the builders had cut a hole in the roof above a stone pit that held ashes and bits of charred wood.

Soldado lit the lantern and then towed her by the hand to search outside. He had the car keys, so she wondered where he thought she was gonna go. He found a stash of canned food and a baggie of marijuana under a cairn of rocks. Behind the shack, a pine tree shielded a crude latrine. Beyond that was a small patch of cleared ground, likely an old grow operation gone bust when Oregon legalized pot.

Jewel was starved. She hadn't eaten since breakfast, and not much then. Too nervous about her first try at being an advocate. That wasn't going real good so far, either.

Cans of cold corned beef and peaches later, they sat in silence. The quiet was enormous. She couldn't think of anything to say. But she thought of something to do.

Picking up her purse, she said, "Gotta go potty," and headed for the rear door.

As smoothly as a cat, Soldado blocked her way and extended a hand for her purse.

She gripped it with both hands. "I need it."

A wiggle of his fingers insisted.

"It's my time of the month, and you better let me take it if you don't want me leaking all over the place."

He waited, hand out.

She gave the purse over.

He opened it, then raised his gaze to hers as he took out her stopper.

She shrugged and stuck out her hand. "I still need a tampon."

He tucked the stopper into a pocket, rummaged through the purse, then handed it back and said, "Go ahead."

Outside, she went to the latrine. She really needed to pee, anyway. As she did, she opened her purse and pulled out the tube of nap reloads for her stopper. As she'd hoped, he hadn't paid any attention to her spare ammunition. He probably didn't know what it looked like, and besides, the case really did look a lot like it held a tampon.

A bullet without a gun was no more a threat than a rock. But not with stoppers. She picked at the crimped paper end of the nap cartridge with her fingernail until the beads were exposed. Amazing how such tiny things could knock a grown man out. The trick was to not knock herself out, too.

She dug through her purse and discovered a foil-wrapped cough drop left over from winter. When she unwrapped it, the inside was sticky. Perfect. Careful not to break any of the little BBs, she emptied them onto the foil. They stuck nicely. She folded the edges of the wrapper into an open cup that contained the beads but let her grip the bottom. She tucked her hand into her suit coat pocket. If she had a chance, she'd hit him with a nap.

When the sun went down, so did the temperature. Soldado used the marijuana as kindling to start a fire built with wood he tore from a fallen pine. His hands shook just enough to notice, and he inhaled deeply of the smoke from the pot. His hands stilled, and he seemed to relax.

He pulled the cot near the fire and gestured her to it. She'd have liked to ignore it, but she was too cold. Keeping the hand with nap in her pocket, she lay on the cot and he sat on a chair, close to the fire.

After staring at the flames for long minutes, she shifted her gaze to Soldado. He seemed lost in the fire. His history and the things she'd seen him do tumbled in her mind.

His dossier said he'd been a top cop in the MPs and then a decorated deputy in Illinois. He had resigned after the tragedy that struck his wife and daughter. He had PTSD.

And he had cared enough to save her in Chicago. And Noah Stone, twice. And when he wasn't taking her hostage, he had been gentle with her and Chloe.

His dark eyes suddenly shifted and his gaze locked with hers. His intensity reminded her of Noah Stone's penetrating look. He broke the stillness. "I'm sorry about your little girl. I'll set you free tomorrow afternoon."

Jewel realized she wasn't crazy with worry about Chloe. "I think she's okay. Franklin will look after her."

He turned back to the fire.

She wanted to hate him, but couldn't. A memory of Green-Stripe in Chicago flashed; she could see him ripping her blouse open and then falling to the pavement, dead. A corner of her felt gratitude for her rescue.

Her mini-movie of the attack gave way to a replay of Soldado's bullet exploding Earl's brains all over her; another corner of her hated him.

Then she pictured the sling that supported Noah Stone's injured arm, and the video of the shooting. Another corner felt indebted for his saving of Noah, because Earl had meant to kill him—she'd seen the look on Earl's face before half of it had burst into . . . into—

And then Soldado had stuck his gun under her chin just like Green-Stripe had.

Shit, she'd run out of corners in her mind at this rate. And, if she was going to escape, she had to get Soldado off guard.

She tried a little fake sympathy. "You look really tired." Once she said the words, she realized that her tone wasn't all that fake.

❧

She was up to something; Hank knew her interest wasn't sincere, but he wished it were. He was weary of being on guard all the time. "I am."

He stood, slipped off his belt, and stepped next to the cot.

She shrank back from him.

He said, "Please lie down and put your hands by your sides."

She jammed her free hand into her coat pockets and glared at him.

"Please, I just want to rest. I'm only going to secure you for a few hours. You can rest, too."

Her gaze held his as she slipped her hands out of her pockets. When he leaned down to loop the belt around her and under the cot, she jammed something against the side of his neck. He knocked her hand away and touched his skin. It was wet.

She sat up and said, "I think you have a nap coming on."

"Nice work, Ms. Washington." He knew what would happen, so he dropped the belt, eased himself to the floor next to the fire, and surrendered to unconsciousness.

❧

Jewel shuddered with relief and reaction. She dug into his pockets for the car keys and ran to the SUV, her only thought to get back to Chloe. But the dark was like black ink, a threatening nothingness to a city girl who had never known a night without the glow of a million lights. And she hadn't driven more than a half dozen times in her life. She dug her cell phone out of her purse. No bars.

She'd never find her way through all those branching logging roads in the darkness, and she could drive over a cliff or run into a bear or something, so she returned to the shack. Soldado lay unconscious and helpless. Jewel took down the rope holding the kerosene lantern and used it to tie his feet tight to the post, and then put his hands behind his back and cinched them together with the belt.

Retrieving her stopper from his pocket and his pistol from where he'd tucked it in his belt, she moved the cot to the opposite side of the fire from him, added wood, and settled into a restless sleep, stopper in hand.

Deep in the night a rustling sound woke her. She bolted up and raised her stopper, hoping some wild animal wasn't in the shack. It was cold, and the fire was down to embers.

It was Soldado, struggling to get out of the belt that bound his hands. With a grim kind of satisfaction, she hit him with a shot of nap. She reloaded the empty chamber, then piled wood on the embers and fell asleep watching flames grow.

Morning sunlight woke Jewel. Stiff from her night on the cot, she turned to find Soldado's intense gaze on her from across the dead fire. Startled, she sat up and aimed her stopper at him. His gaze was steady. "You've got me."

He was still tightly bound. She relaxed. "Yeah, I have." She stood and walked to the door.

"You going to leave me here?"

She started to say yes, but wondered if he'd be safe. There might be wolves or something. Or, considering what she knew of him, he'd escape. Leaving him could be letting a killer get away. "I guess not." She went to him and aimed the stopper at the base of his neck, where his shirt opened.

He said, "You don't have to do that. I'll even drive, if you want. You've got the guns."

Seeing the alertness in his eyes and knowing how quickly he could move, she pressed the button for nap. He winced when it struck his neck, then shrugged and closed his eyes.

She worked up a sweat dragging him to the car and buckling him into the backseat, cussing herself for not making him get in the car before she turned out his lights. Taking no chances, she used a shot of tangle on his bound hands.

As she followed the GPS and drove back through the mountains, she struggled with whether to go home first or to the police station. It wasn't much of a fight; she wanted her baby in her arms. As it turned out, a cop car was at Franklin's house when she slammed to a stop. She ran past a startled officer and yelled, "He's in the car."

Chloe burst out the front door and flew to Jewel, and they held each other for a long time.

Franklin appeared. His hug felt awfully good, too. They watched as a police van arrived and the officers freed Soldado of his tangle and took him away. Jewel held Chloe on her hip and felt a moment's weakness in her knees as she realized that it was over.

She sat on the porch swing, Chloe in her lap. No way she was gonna go to work, and she didn't want to be more than a couple of inches away from Chloe for a while. She stroked Chloe's hair and said, "Hey, how about a picnic in the park?"

Chloe said, "Can I make peanut-butter-and-jelly sandwiches?"

"You bet, honey."

Chloe said, "Yippee!" and slipped off Jewel's lap to dash into the house.

Jewel smiled up at Franklin. "Thanks for looking after her."

"Hell, you don't need to thank me. My pleasure."

Jewel and Chloe spent the afternoon in Lithia Park, swinging and sliding at the playground and playing catch with an old tennis ball they found near a pair of courts.

Her daughter's giggles pushed back the terrors of the last day and night. Hank Soldado was out of her life.

But his weary smile drifted through her mind now and then.

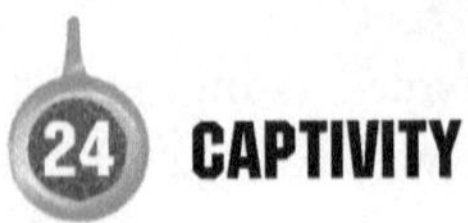 **CAPTIVITY**

For the second time, Hank woke in a cell after overindulging in nap. Figuring he wasn't going anywhere, he lay quietly and gazed at the bars while his mind cleared.

He hated being caged.

He pictured the fierce determination on Jewel Washington's face when she got him with the nap. One helluva woman.

The door opened and Benson Spencer entered, accompanied by a guard who looked like a senior citizen. The guard carried an orange jumpsuit. He glared at Hank as he limped to the cell, opened the door for Benson, and dropped the jumpsuit on the floor. "You'll need to change into that."

"I don't know. It's not really my style."

"Your choice. We've got some big guys who would love to help you." Hank picked up the jumpsuit, stripped, and put it on.

Pointing at a ceiling camera, the guard told Benson, "Just signal when you want out." He closed Benson in the cell and limped away.

Hank said, "Hello, advocate."

Benson wasn't his usually jolly self. "You're not an easy man to side with, Hank. I can't decide whether you're a good guy or a bad guy."

"Hey, I had to run. You didn't do much of a job defending me."

"Defending you wasn't my job. My job was to find the truth and to make sure you weren't screwed. The truth is, you did kill Earl, and you did it with an illegal firearm."

Something had flickered in Benson's eyes when he mentioned Earl. Hank said, "You knew him, didn't you?"

Benson's gaze dropped to the floor. "He was once a friend."

"You're one of the guys they told me got pickled."

Benson looked up and laughed. "Pickled! Man, if you knew the sweat I wasted being afraid of therapy. That's what I'm here about—your alternative to the Keep."

"Some alternatives: prison or a pickle jar."

Benson's tone sharpened. "Do you know anything about either one of them?"

"No."

"How about some facts before you draw conclusions?"

"So tell me."

"The Keep is to Oregon what Australia was to Britain in the 1700s. Every violent criminal in Oregon is sent there. There are two Keeps, a big one for men, a smaller one for women."

"Where is it?" When he escaped, Hank wanted to know where he could run to.

"Southeastern Oregon, out where there's nothing but sagebrush and high desert."

He'd better pack a lunch.

Benson said, "Like the judge explained, you lose the things society creates. No television, no mail, no medicine, no air-conditioning, no weight rooms, no basketball courts, no extras.

"The state provides the basics: shelter, food, water, and clothing. There are no guards, no pastors, no doctors. No cells and no bars. Just violent people."

Hank said, "I can see why the life expectancy is only two years."

"The Keep was built to handle five thousand. Four years ago it was nearly full, but we estimate there aren't more than three thousand now.

"The alternative to the Keep is therapy in a small hospital the docs call the Repair Shop."

"Cute. Better than Butcher Shop, I guess."

Benson rolled his eyes. "First they analyze you. As Noah says, you are what you think. They isolate the things that drive the behavior that got you in trouble. Then they help you change 'em."

Hank snorted. "Brainwashing!"

"No. They start with noninvasive techniques such as deprogramming, which can work on problems like racial bigotry."

"Noninvasive. So there are 'invasive' techniques, too? What, lobotomy?"

Benson shook his head. "They use neurosurgery, and the decision is completely up to you. It's voluntary. You don't want to do it, they'll try other approaches."

"They operate on your brain? Why?"

"Think of it as having an abscess—the infection poisons your whole body. A doctor uses invasive techniques to clean it out, and your body returns to a healthy state."

"That's what they did to you?"

Benson nodded. "I wanted it. Like the rest of the men in my family, I had a fanatical belief that I had an unrestricted right to own any kind of gun, and that anyone who said different was a traitor. My belief was bulletproof, and there was no way to reason me out of it. Earl thought the same way."

The old Benson would have been a man after Hank's own heart. He'd grown up believing the same thing, mostly because it was true, but, he had to admit, his family had a lot to do with it.

Benson said, "At the Repair Shop they took out the basic belief, which left me with no opinion at all. Since then I've studied what the National Rifle Association says and the Supreme Court's decisions, and decided I don't have an unlimited right to carry any kind of gun. More than that, I'm convinced that states have the right to control guns. At least that part's been upheld by the Supreme Court. There was no brainwashing, no attempt to convince me one way or the other."

"That you know of."

Benson threw up his hands. "It's not like that!"

Hank watched Benson for signs of . . . of what? What did a washed brain act like? There didn't seem to be anything wrong, but . . . "So that got you out of the Repair Shop?"

"When the stuff that causes the problems is gone, then so is the wrongdoer. You're considered a different person. The idea is to help people, not punish them."

"How could you let them do it to you?"

Benson gazed at Hank for a long moment. His voice was soft when he said, "There came a time when I had to trust."

Hank shuddered inwardly. "I'm not going to let anybody carve up my mind and trust that they won't screw with it while they do." His mind was who he was!

Benson said, "They don't do anything you don't agree to, and you have a medical advocate who makes sure that's all they do."

"Sure, they tell you that."

"I'm the same guy who went in, I just don't think the same way about guns."

Yeah, he *thought* he was the same guy.

Leaning forward, Benson said, "Hank, choose the therapy."

"No thanks. I don't care how lousy the Keep is, at least I'll still be me."

"Maybe the you that you are isn't the best you can be."

"That's a risk I'm willing to take."

Benson stood. "That's it, then. You'll be transferred tomorrow. But you can change your mind anytime." He waved at the camera.

Hank asked, "How's Jewel? I feel bad about her. She just happened to be in the wrong place at the wrong time."

"She'll recover. Strong woman."

"You're telling me."

The gimpy guard returned, unlocked the cell door, and stood well back with his stopper ready. As Benson stepped out, Hank said, "Let her know I'm sorry. It wasn't personal."

Benson studied him. "You don't get it, do you? Violence is always personal. It was her personal chin you jammed that gun barrel into."

"Just tell her?"

Benson's energy bubbled back up. He beamed and said, "Will do."

Motioning Hank to back up, the guard scooped up Hank's clothes, locked the cell door, and limped away.

After they'd ended the visit, Hank stretched out on his bunk. Into his mind came the image of Jewel's indomitable face as she hit him with nap. Beautiful, and he wasn't thinking of appearance.

25 TEACH YOUR CHILDREN WELL

Mitch's office was quiet. Too quiet. He turned away from the Smith & Wesson order he needed to get shipped. He couldn't concentrate. Hank Soldado's report of Noah Stone's fear of guns kept popping into his mind—maybe there was a way to use it to scare Stone off, especially now that Hank was out of the game.

Mitch couldn't blame Stone for how he felt after the shooting in Chicago. Speaking of scary, there was Hank's report on the Mackinac Militia website. Yeah, Colonel Hanson was one spooky woman. He got on the internet, Googled the militia, and went to the site.

Jesus, there really was a bullet with Noah Stone's name on it. If only— No, better be careful what you wish for. Don't go there.

Still, Hank had said Stone looked primed to break. Too bad Hank had ended up convicted of murder. Mitch didn't know what he should do now.

His daughter appeared in the workshop doorway. Carrie said, "Is it time, Daddy?"

That sparked a smile, and he shut the computer down. They had a date to introduce her to the Cricket .22 rifle he'd gotten for her ninth birthday. He figured she was smart enough and responsible enough to have her own gun—as long as she was properly trained, of course, and that was why they were going to the shooting range.

Mitch beamed with pride as he escorted Carrie to the shooting range in the basement of NRA headquarters. He held her new rifle cradled in one arm, and a big grin stretched her face. He took her to a firing station and laid the rifle on the counter. She reached for it, but he stopped her with a hand over hers. "What's our first rule about guns?"

"Never point one at a person."

He gave her his serious look. "What if it's not loaded? Is it okay then?"

She shook her head and then said, "Never assume a gun isn't loaded." Her smile said she knew she'd nailed it.

He grinned and patted her on the head. "Good girl. Now, I know this gun isn't loaded, but you shouldn't take my word for it, check it yourself. Once you do that, it's okay for you to handle it here. Get used to it, practice aiming down there where that old target is while I go get a fresh one."

When he went for a new target in the storage room, he noticed a flash of red from a crumpled target on the floor. Wishing people would clean up their messes, he picked it up. There was something familiar about the shiny red paper taped to its front—he smoothed it out and found the *Time* magazine cover of Noah Stone, riddled with bullet holes.

It gave him a shudder and made him a little embarrassed that he'd had thoughts about putting holes in Stone's face, even though it was just a finger doing the shooting. Creepy. He wadded the thing up and tossed it into a wastebasket.

After rigging Carrie's target and sending it out a short distance, he took his time introducing her to her Cricket rifle, a scaled-down version of an adult weapon. Although it was just a .22 caliber, it could kill, and he intended to drill her on safety. He ignored her sighs of impatience as he took her through the rules. At last he let her load the gun and take aim at the target.

He stepped back and said, "Remember, pull it in tight to your shoulder and squeeze the trigger, don't jerk it." Although a .22 didn't make much noise, he insisted she put on earmuffs before shooting.

His cell phone rang. It was Hank Soldado. "Hey, Hank, how are things going?" He'd seen the story on the internet of Hank's failed kidnapping of that woman.

Carrie looked back at him. He stepped away and gestured for her to keep going, keeping an eye on how she handled the rifle.

Hank said, "Well, my day in court didn't work out too well."

Mitch said, "I saw. I know you weren't guilty. I'm sorry you couldn't get away."

He heard a smile in Hank's voice when he said, "I just chose the wrong person for a hostage." Strange.

Carrie squeezed off a shot and hit the ring next to the bull's-eye. She looked back at him and he gave her a thumbs-up. He said to Hank, "You saved Stone's life when you shot that guy. Why'd you do it?"

"I don't know. Just reacted, I guess."

A considerable pause came along. Then Mitch said, "Maybe I wish you hadn't."

"You want him dead?"

He pictured the bullet holes in the *Time* cover. "Oh, no! It's just the problem would be gone. I don't know what to do now."

Hank said, "How about getting an appeal going for me?"

"Yeah! I know a couple good lawyers." Mitch laughed. "Well, except they haven't been having much luck in Oregon courts. But I'll do what I can."

"Thanks. I'll keep you informed. What'll you do about Stone?"

He'd been stewing over that. "I don't know. I just don't. But I feel the pressure building. We need to do something, and soon, while Stone is shaky."

"Luck." Hank ended the call.

Yeah, luck. He could use some of that. He stepped on a loose cartridge case as he moved closer to the shooting station. It was from a hunting rifle.

A hunting rifle. A bullet like the one Colonel Martha Hanson had on her website. The one that scared Noah Stone.

26 THE KEEP

Now outfitted in an orange jumpsuit, Hank was stretching after breakfast when the gimpy guard banged the cellblock door open and Joe Donovan and Sally Arnold entered. Donovan lifted a set of shackles and said, "Time to go."

Sally said, "Guess we ought to thank you for taking Emerson out the way you did. The Alliance offered us your job, and now we're looking after Noah Stone."

Relief popped into Hank's mind. Well, he did like the guy.

She said to Hank, "The Ashland police deputized us to get you to the Keep." She aimed her stopper at him as Donovan opened the door. "You got away from them a little too easily."

Donovan said, "Grab some bars."

Hank gripped two bars up high with both hands and spread his feet. Donovan entered, slipped the shackles onto Hank's ankles, then handcuffed his hands in front of him. "Sorry about this, Soldado."

Hank straightened, angered by the cuffs. "How do you feel about what they're doing to me, Donovan?"

"I think you're getting screwed, in a way, but I also think you screwed up. Around here, they like to make sure screw-ups have consequences. The bad guys, and I'm not saying you're one, don't get away with much."

Hank glanced at Sally's stopper. "You think I could have stopped Emerson with one of those toys?"

"Hell, they've stopped you a couple of times, haven't they?"

He couldn't deny the truth of that.

Sally said, "Tell him about the kidnapping charges."

Donovan grinned. "Yeah. You should know that Noah talked the cops out of nailing you for kidnapping Jewel Washington, and she went along with it."

Sally swung the cell door open. "You'd have gone from being in deep shit to completely flushed."

"I wish I could thank him."

"You'll get your chance." Sally led the way out, and Donovan followed Hank. Outside the cellblock, she passed an open door and halted at the far side. Donovan stopped Hank with a tug on his sleeve. "In there."

Noah Stone waited inside, his arm in a sling. He frowned at the shackles, then gazed into Hank's eyes. "Hank."

"Noah." Hank nodded at the sling. "How's the arm?"

"It'll be okay. Since I do most of my work with my mouth, it doesn't slow me down much." His eyes twinkled with irrepressible humor. "Hey, the doctor said the physical therapy might even improve my backhand."

Dutifully, Hank smiled. A silence settled between them. Hank broke it. "I hear you quashed a kidnapping charge."

"I was sure you never meant any harm, and Jewel confirmed it." He gazed into Hank's eyes, and emotion thickened his voice. "I owe you my life again."

Hank lifted a foot and rattled his chains. "Could you do something about this?"

"Probably."

"Probably?"

"But I won't." He went to the window and gazed at the mountains. Turning back to Hank, he said, "Violent crime here has dropped significantly since two things went into operation—an effective move against lethal firearms, and arming citizens with defensive weapons. And more criminals are off the streets now that the courts can get to the truth. I won't do anything to corrupt the strength of what we've accomplished." He gazed at Hank. "I think you understand that."

Hank nodded. "I'd do the same. So I guess that's it, then."

"No, it's not. Take the therapy."

Just the thought of strangers poking around in his mind unsettled Hank. "That I can't do."

Noah's gaze bored in on him. "I sense a connection between us, Hank. You're a good man, a strong man, and you could be a force with the Alliance."

Hank rattled his handcuffs. "I can't believe you want to recruit me."

"Since I met you, I've seen possibilities in what I could do that weren't there before, a chance to do my work with someone who can be a true partner." He pleaded with his eyes. "Haven't you felt something?"

Hank thought about it. Yeah, he guessed he had, but even though there were good things about what Noah was doing, he could never help take guns away from Americans. He shrugged.

Disappointment registered in Noah's expression. "All right. For your own sake, please take the therapy. The Keep will kill you."

Hank smiled. "If you knew how many have tried to do that, you wouldn't think so." On the way out, he paused to look back at Noah. Noah again gazed out at the valley, his expression sad.

Had Hank been wrong about this guy?

After a brief trip in a police van out Route 66 to the tiny Ashland Municipal Airport, Hank, Donovan, and a shackled big man named Dalrymple boarded a police helicopter. The other prisoner also wore an orange jumpsuit.

Dalrymple was thick through the chest and had shoulders like a swimmer, and even thicker through the waist like a swimmer gone soft. The man swaggered, his expression smug. After locking leg shackles to steel floor rings, Donovan buckled into a seat beside Hank.

Hank nodded toward Dalrymple. "What's he in for?"

"Rape. A twelve-year-old."

The chopper took off for a place where, if all Hank had heard was correct, he was likely to finish his life.

Hank was dozing when Donovan shook him and gestured toward a window. Hank peered out; it was time to start working on his escape. Dalrymple stared out a window of his own.

Below spread arid, flat emptiness speckled with sagebrush and occasionally gouged by a ravine or pimpled by a rock out-cropping. Miles away, mountains defined the distance. If there ever was a middle of nowhere, this was it.

A flat-topped butte came into view, isolated in barren desert. Sheer rock walls rose for hundreds of feet.

Donovan took up a microphone and spoke on the PA system. "This is your new home."

A white structure dominated the butte's top. Its shape reminded Hank of a three-bladed propeller from an old-fash-ioned airplane, with a round center connecting long extensions. The helicopter dropped.

The "blades" of the propeller became huge, rounded struc-tures that looked like giant white medicine capsules lying on their sides, half buried in the desert. Hank estimated the buildings at eighty feet high. Indentations crisscrossed their surfaces, giving them a quilted look.

Attached to the end of the "capsule" that reached the butte's edge was a featureless, one-story concrete building, maybe twenty feet square. From it, a windowless shaft dropped down the side of the butte, like an exterior elevator shaft on a fancy hotel. Some hotel. The shaft ended at a similar building at the butte's base. There, greenery surrounded a cluster of houses and a two-story building.

Donovan said, "The square building at the top is where you'll be inserted into the Keep."

Dalrymple said, "What the hell are those big white things?"

"Air structures. Teflon-coated fabric is held up by air pressure and down by steel cables. They're usually used for indoor sports like tennis. There's even a small golf course inside one back East."

Hank spotted two human figures lying prone on a mound fifty yards outside one building. Black lumps moved around them. As the chopper passed over, the lumps turned into buzzards that flapped up and away. The human figures didn't move.

Hank looked to Donovan, who said, "We call that Bone Hill. The inmates don't have shovels."

"Harsh."

"Hey, they had a choice. Just like you."

The chopper flew over a tall fence that outlined the rim. Donovan said into the microphone, "Note the fence, gents. It is twenty feet tall, angles inward at thirty degrees, and is covered with more razor-sharp spikes than a hedgehog from hell."

Hank studied the fence. There was no way in hell he could climb it. Maybe he could go under it.

Every fifty yards along the fence were forty-foot poles. "On top of those poles are video cameras, motion detectors, and infrared cameras. Pretty sensitive, too—they've spotted snakes going under the fence."

Okay, scratch the tunnel. The helicopter banked away from the top of the butte and dropped so fast that Hank's stomach complained.

Three uniformed men armed with stoppers greeted the helicopter when it settled onto a landing pad at the base of the butte. On another pad, cardboard cartons were unloaded from a cargo chopper and moved on a conveyor belt into the small building at the bottom of the shaft that ran up to the Keep. Two guards aimed stoppers at the opening into the building.

Donovan gathered two fat manila envelopes and stood. "It's home sweet home, gentlemen."

Hank said, "What're those?"

"Your personal effects, in case you're released."

Standing, Hank said, "I'd like to have something from mine."

"Against the rules." Then he gazed at Hank. "What?"

"Little necklace. Was my . . . my daughter's."

Donovan opened an envelope, pawed through the contents, then came up with Amy's necklace. "This?"

Hank watched it dangle. The last of a life once worth living. He couldn't leave it behind. "Yeah." He reached out, palm up. "Can I . . . ?"

Donovan shrugged. "Can't see any harm in it. It sure as hell isn't a weapon." He handed the necklace over, and Hank stuffed it into a pants pocket.

Dalrymple stood. "Hey, I had some pictures I want."

"We burned that filth." Donovan gestured. "Let's go."

He led his prisoners down a sidewalk through a lush lawn. A half dozen cottages clustered around a central plaza, complete with a fountain. A park provided picnic tables, a tennis court, a basketball court, and a small swimming pool. A hard-fought four-on-four basketball game thumped on the court.

Donovan said, "Medical and security staff are quartered here. They say it's pretty boring duty, but easy."

He herded them past a white two-story structure with barred windows. "This's the Repair Shop. If you decide to do therapy, you go here instead of up to the Keep."

Hank concentrated on the small windowless building at the base of the shaft. When they reached it, a guard entered a code in a keypad beside a steel door. The door slid sideways.

Inside, a middle-aged man rose from a computer workstation in the center of the room. He was steady-eyed and looked Asian.

Donovan said, "Got some new fish for the pond, Arnie."

Arnie nodded. "We'll send 'em up." He shook hands with Donovan. "Been a while."

"Business is slow."

"The slower, the better."

Hank eyed a row of barred holding cells along one wall—five feet wide and seven long, with a cot and a toilet in each. They looked secure. Well, if he couldn't find a physical weakness, there was sure to be a human one. Steel shelves along another wall were piled with blankets, clothing, DVD players, books, and other sundries.

On the butte side of the room, a double wall of bars formed a cell around elevator doors. A chair and a verifier headset sat next to the elevator.

Hank gave no resistance when a guard put him in a cell, removed his shackles, and locked him in. Dalrymple bitched about it but complied.

Arnie rattled doors as if to make sure they were secure, and then addressed them. "You'll go into the Keep in the morning. I suggest you get as much rest as possible. I'll bring food later, water now if you need it."

He crossed to the shelves. "Before you go in, I'll give you supplies." He took two sets of thick pamphlets and DVD players. "You get these now. They're the only reading or viewing material allowed inside the Keep, and they concern therapy. I suggest you look through them—you may want to change your mind about going to the Repair Shop. It's never too late."

He handed each man a pamphlet and a DVD player. Dalrymple dropped his on the floor. Hank held onto his.

Donovan stuck his hand through Hank's bars. "Good luck."

Warmed by the gesture, Hank shook hands. "Same to you."

After Donovan and the guards left, Hank settled on his bunk and checked out the video. It portrayed what some Alliance PR hack viewed as a prosperous life by showing a picnic on the Applegate River, day trips to Crater Lake and the Oregon Caves, a stroll on a Pacific beach at Bandon-by-the-Sea, the ballet in Eugene, and a gathering at an Alliance center.

He examined the pamphlet. The title was "Your Door to Freedom." His bullshit detector went to high alert.

The first section offered case histories of three men who had chosen therapy. They happened to be a murderer, a man caught with a lethal firearm, and a rapist.

The pamphlet reported that after therapy, the rapist ended up happily married and a good father to three little girls. The weapons charge went to work for the Alliance—that had to be Benson Spencer. The murderer became a police chief in a suburb of Portland. The text said that with deep therapy, you were certifiably better adjusted than ninety-nine percent of the population, which was just fine with prospective employers.

That was crap. They liked 'em because people with lobotomies didn't cause trouble.

The second section explained the treatment at the Deep Therapy Center. It jibed with what Benson had said. But what weren't they telling?

No, he was better off figuring out a way to get out of the Keep. With his mind intact.

 A MOST DEADLY WOMAN

As the ferry closed in on the dock at Mackinac Island, Mitch was a little surprised to realize that his palms were sweaty. Nerves about meeting Colonel Martha Hanson? He'd researched her, and there'd been a rape in her history with a gruesome outcome. A burglar had attacked her in her home when she was in high school. Afterward, she'd grabbed a pistol from her daddy's gun cabinet, shot the rapist in the kneecaps, tied him spread-eagle on her bed, and castrated him. The prosecutor had not pressed charges against her.

Okay, so she was tough and violent. More than that, though, she was outside his understanding. Oh, he understood being a patriot, but to believe that your little militia was key to saving the United States from a dreaded government takeover didn't seem quite rational to him. Nonetheless, he hoped she could be useful.

It was too cold to walk, and with cars not allowed on the island, there were no regular cabs. He took a horse-drawn buggy to the colonel's two-story Victorian house, pink, complete with white gingerbread and a wraparound porch that overlooked the harbor.

When she opened the door, the visceral appeal of her beauty was far greater than he'd anticipated. He'd seen photos and knew that she was a looker, but he hadn't counted on dark lashes rimming hazel eyes that commanded his attention. She was smaller than he'd anticipated, too, no more than five curvy feet tall, her figure still drawing his eye even though she wore a flannel shirt and khaki pants. Her black hair waved out from her head and over her shoulders. It was hard for him to believe that she was a hard-line military leader.

Martha Hanson said, "Hello, Mr. Parsons. Please come in."

When he stepped inside the foyer, a tiny little dog yapped up at him. She scooped it up and kissed the top of its head. "Now, Sparky, be nice to our visitor. He's come a long way to see us."

"You are a little out of the way here. Don't you feel isolated?"

"It's easier to defend an island. Except maybe in the winter, when you can walk to Michigan, although a snowmobile across the ice is a lot faster." She gave the dog another kiss and baby-talked. "Isn't it, Sparky?" She led Mitch into a parlor.

When he had seen the pink house, he'd wondered if the warrior talk on her website was fiction, but the AR-15 mounted over the fireplace mantel, flanked by American flags, showed how wrong he'd been. Not only was the weapon very real, but the wear on the stock said it had seen plenty of use.

He turned to her. "I appreciate your letting me visit, Colonel."

"Please, make it 'Martha.'" She sat in a leather chair and nodded at a love seat on the other side of a coffee table. "Sit."

The love seat looked antique, and he took care when he lowered himself onto it. The room could have been a lady's parlor from the 1800s, with lace doilies on the lamp tables and chair backs—except there were also guns displayed on every wall, plus a bow and a crossbow. A mounted elk head stared at him from above her chair. He pointed and said, "Did you—"

"Crossbow." Settling her little dog into her lap, she said, "But you didn't come here to admire my hunting prowess."

"Maybe I did. You've been going after Noah Stone."

She scowled. "That bastard. I wouldn't mind having him in my sights."

"Maybe you should. I'd like for you to." Her eyes widened, and he realized how she might interpret his words. "I don't mean literally . . . Well, in a way I do, but not like your elk friend."

She set the little dog on the floor and stood. "Cappuccino? It sounds like this could take a while."

As she worked on the coffee in the kitchen, he studied photos that decorated the fireplace mantel along with a plaque displaying a bronze star—just like his grandfather's. The name on the plaque was Martha Summers Hanson. Most of the photos were of military men, and one grainy photo looked like it could be from World War I. "All these soldiers family?"

She called from the kitchen, "My family has been fighting for freedom since the revolution." The hiss of an espresso machine frothing milk came from the kitchen, and then she appeared with two cups. "I did a turn in the army, then got Purple-Hearted out."

He'd found that online, too: she'd been injured while rescuing a fellow soldier from enemy fire. The bronze star was for that action. Whatever else she was, she had courage.

She brought him his cup, and he sipped. Despite the addition of steamed milk, the cappuccino was strong enough to climb out of the cup if he wasn't careful.

She said, "What do you mean, getting Noah Stone in my sights?"

"You've already had him there once—the shooting in Chicago? That was one of your militia, right?"

"I issued no orders for any kind of shooting."

"But your website incites—"

She stopped him with a raised hand. "You can take it that way if you want to, but nothing on my site advocates violence. Believe me, I know the games the government plays to take out people like me, and I'm very careful."

"How about that photo of a bullet with Noah Stone's name on it?"

Her eyebrows lifted. "Just a picture, free speech and perfectly legal."

"Well, Stone has seen it, and it scares the shit out of him. I have good information that he's on the edge of quitting." He told her about Stone's confrontation with the gun owner in Ashland and how he'd said he wanted to run.

Martha smiled. Her face would have been lovely and bright except there was no warmth in her eyes. "And you think I can push him over?"

"I was thinking that maybe if we added fear of you to his fear of being shot, he'd quit."

She gazed at him. "You want me to attack him?"

"Not for real. He gives a lot of speeches. If you were to show up and aim a gun at him . . ."

She went to a gun cabinet and took out an automatic pistol. "You mean something like this?" She racked the slide and aimed between his eyes.

With her stony eyes behind the pistol, he wanted to put his hands up in surrender. He had no doubt about the effect it would have on Noah Stone. "Yeah. Exactly like that."

She stepped closer, keeping the gun aimed at his forehead. Her eyes widened. And they glittered. "You think just scaring the guy will work?"

It was sure working on him. "Oh, yeah." He stood and was glad when she lowered the gun. "So you'll do it?"

She touched one of the U.S. flags on the mantel. "He needs to be stopped." She turned to him. "I'll need a donation."

"Agreed. I'll send you a check."

"When? Where?"

He'd had time to think about this on the ferry ride. "It has to be public. The impact will be greater, and it will weaken his influence."

She paced, twice dry-firing at the elk head. She stopped. "Got it. I know Rick Hatch in the Rogue Militia there, and he'll know what's going on, and when."

"I know Rick. A good man. He'll have the gun you need, too. It has to look real."

Her smile made him think of a timber rattlesnake he'd shot back home. She said, "Oh, it'll be real enough to take Noah Stone down a bunch of notches." She put the pistol back in the gun case, took something out, and turned to him. "Think I should send him this, put a little extra pressure on?" She handed him a rifle cartridge.

It was the one with Stone's name on it. It was disturbing, but he wanted Stone out of action. "Do it."

She took the bullet back and then said, "You want to stay for supper?"

Her smile was warm this time, but he nonetheless felt like a chicken being invited to step into a pot. "That would be great, but I need to get back. Call me when you go to Oregon. I want to be there to see the guy crumble."

On the ferry back to Mackinaw City, Mitch decided to be hopeful. This was going to work. Colonel Hanson was clearly a woman who knew how to carry out a mission. He was sorry it couldn't be Hank, but they had Stone unbalanced right now, and they couldn't wait to give him a shove.

 **A DEBT TO PAY**

To Jewel it felt like coming home when Franklin pulled into his driveway after picking her up from work. She and Chloe slid out of the backseat, but he didn't shut off the engine.

Jewel leaned into the front passenger window and said, "You're not stopping? I think there's a cold beer with your name on it."

"Evening's the best time for picking up fares—folks going out to dinner before theater and then going to the theater. I'll come back for a dinner break then and go back out when performances end."

Disappointed, she said, "Yeah, I know." Franklin was starting to feel like family.

He smiled. "Save me that beer." With a wave, he backed away.

On the way into the house, Chloe asked, "Is Franklin my uncle like Uncle Timmy?"

Jewel tried to ignore the tug on her heart. How would she ever tell Chloe what had happened to Timmy? She hid her thoughts behind a smile. "It's not the same, honey, but close."

"I miss Uncle Timmy."

An image of Timmy's smile before pink got him popped into Jewel's mind. Her sweet boy. "I do, too, sugar, I do, too." Had Juana been able to take care of his . . . last needs?

While Chloe played with a Raggedy Ann doll Franklin had given her for an "unbirthday" present, Jewel took her cell phone from her purse. She'd kept it pretty much off since leaving Chicago, but Murphy was long gone now. Wandering onto the front porch, she punched in Juana's number.

Juana answered and said, "Jewel! How are you? How's Chloe?"

Jewel smiled. "I'm fine, she's great. I wanted to ask how things went—"

"A cop came. Right after you left. The officer—he had a hurt nose—he found Timmy."

Murphy. She'd gotten out just in time. Anger brewed in Jewel. "What'd he do?"

"He came banging on my door. He was mucho angry, very scary. I say I don' know nothing. Don' know where you are. And then they took Timmy."

Oh, Lord.

Juana sobbed. "I'm so sorry! I didn't take care of him like you say."

"You couldn't help it. That's okay."

A silence, then Juana said, "I didn't use the money you left for . . . you know."

Jewel knew how much she needed it. "That's all right. I want you to have it."

Juana's voice carried a grin. "Oh, *gracias, mil gracias!*"

"Hey, I gotta go. You take care."

"Si. Give Chloe big kisses for me."

"I will." She disconnected. That bastard Murphy. A black flower of pain opened in her gut. She doubled over, wrapping her arms around her middle. With a long o-o-o-o-o-h, the grief she'd held at bay finally took her. Sobs tore loose and spilled into the air.

At nine o'clock that evening, after reading *The Runaway Bunny* to Chloe and tucking her in for the night, Jewel poured a glass of chardonnay and collapsed into a living room chair. She wanted to talk about her day at the Alliance, but with Franklin out cabbing, there was no ear to listen.

Franklin was easy to talk to, so accepting. The people at work were nice enough, but something in her stopped her from connecting. At lunch, Benson Spencer had been talking about the trouble his neighbor was having keeping the Alliance promise. Hell, she couldn't imagine herself even making the promise. It *sounded* good, but if you lived it you had to leave yourself wide open to being shafted. Like a sitting duck. And sitting ducks ended up being somebody's dinner. But still . . . it felt like she was missing out.

Enough of that. She turned on the television to search for something worth watching and came across Bruce Ball on *Headline News*. Next to an inset picture of picketers carrying signs that read "Free Hank Soldado," Ball was saying, ". . . protesters today in Ashland, Oregon, picketed the headquarters of the Alliance, demanding freedom for convicted killer Hank Soldado." Jewel had walked through the picketers to get to work. They'd been loud, but not violent.

The picture cut to a woman about Jewel's age. The woman said, "He saved the life of a great man. He should be getting a medal, not a prison sentence!"

Bruce Ball returned. "*Headline News* tried to contact Noah Stone, the man whose life was spared when Hank Soldado gunned down an assassin. A representative told us that the Alliance leader was unavailable, but that he completely supports the Oregon system of justice. More on that from our legal correspondent, Kate Sellers, after this." The picture dissolved into a commercial for a retirement home.

Jewel clicked off the television. The *Rogue Valley Times* had been swamped with letters to the editor defending and condemning the verdict in about equal numbers. She wished the whole thing would go away—there was something about what had happened to Soldado that troubled her, but she'd been unwilling to dig it out.

She picked up a mystery novel, but her eyes were tired from researching online all day, and her head throbbed.

A check on Chloe found her tangled in her top sheet, deeply asleep. After straightening her out, Jewel let her weariness take over. Undressing and putting on an oversized T-shirt, she turned on the classical music radio station and stretched out on her bed. She drifted . . . drifted . . .

The tall blond punk with a green stripe in his hair grabs her arm and whips her around. Behind him, Murphy watches, gloating.

She spins away, but there is another, identical Green-Stripe facing her. And an identical Murphy behind him, complete with smirk. She turns in a circle—she's surrounded by sets of Green-Stripes and Murphys, and more are arriving, all of them the same.

The closest punk rips her blouse open.

Behind her, a hand yanks it completely from her. She huddles, arms crossed over her breasts.

The Green-Stripes unzip their pants and reach inside. She screams, but no sound comes out.

Suddenly the head of the Green-Stripe in front of her explodes, showering her with blood. One by one, each of her attackers suffers the same fate, each collapsing to the sidewalk.

Beyond them, Hank Soldado stands in a marksman's stance, his pistol aimed her way. The Murphys run away.

She steps over a body and walks toward Soldado to thank him. Jewel extends her hand for a shake. Suddenly her hand holds a pistol. She squeezes the trigger and Soldado's head explodes.

She cries out. "No!"

"Mommy, Mommy . . ."

Jewel jerked awake. Chloe stood beside her bed, tugging on Jewel's T-shirt. Her daughter's eyes were wide with fright.

"Mommy, are you hurt?"

Jewel shuddered and wrapped Chloe in her arms. "No, honey, it was just a bad dream."

"I was scared."

"It's all right, baby. Hey, why don't you climb in with me so neither one of us will be scared?"

Chloe crawled under the sheet and snuggled close.

Jewel tried to relax, but the dream rose into her thoughts. It had told the truth—she had killed Hank Soldado. The Keep was a death sentence, and she had stopped him from escaping. She had betrayed the man who had rescued her. And had saved Noah Stone's life.

And Hank would die for what? For preventing the killing of an innocent man. Where was the justice in that?

Sleep refused to come. After Chloe's breathing eased into the easy rhythm of slumber, Jewel left the bed to sit in the living room and wrestle with the horror of her dream—and what she had done to Hank Soldado.

As she struggled with what she might have done, should have done, she realized that Noah Stone was a part of it, too. The laws that had doomed Soldado came from Stone and his Alliance.

Soldado had rescued Noah from Earl's bullet, and in return Noah and his Alliance had tossed Hank Soldado into a deathtrap.

Noah Stone, the guy who kept promising to help.

So what was she gonna do about that?

29 CONFRONTING EVIL

Marion shook her head. Focus! Her thoughts had been so fractured since Suzanne— Focus! She took the top manila folder on the morning stack and removed the papers. Wishing they'd fix the air-conditioning in her office, Marion fanned herself with the folder.

She called Tiffany Horowitz. "How are you doing on the so-called 'inquiry' that put Hank Soldado in prison?"

"Appears legal. It can be appealed, but you know how long that takes. Ah, I reviewed that book you sent for, too."

"Book?"

"*Justice Through Truth and Advocacy.* The one by Noah Stone and the chief justice? Their ideas about advocacy instead of adversity are starting to make sense to me."

It bothered Marion that they were starting to make sense to her, too. But she had a job to do and a Constitution to defend. "I've seen their ideas railroad a man into prison without a proper defense. It's your job to find a way to stop them." Yes, Hank Soldado was guilty, but he was entitled to a defense. The oh-so-agreeable process of the Alliance's advocates had hardly been a rigorous defense.

Wasn't he entitled to that? Even if he was admittedly guilty?

Even though she had seen them reveal the truth?

Sounding as though she'd been scolded, Tiffany muttered, "Yes, ma'am."

Marion hung up, opened a desk drawer, and took out a bottle of scotch. She half-filled a coffee mug and sipped. Her gaze went to the chair where Suzanne had sat to talk so many times. The knot of grief that seemed permanently stuck in her throat threatened to swell and cause more tears. She numbed it with a swallow of scotch.

She toggled her intercom. "No interruptions."

If she and Suzanne had lived in Oregon, the man who had killed Suzanne would be in the Keep because of his earlier crimes, and most likely dead. And even if he hadn't been, Suzanne could have defended herself with a stopper. Her attacker would have known that and maybe not even tried.

Anger rose. Where were Noah Stone's grand ideas when Suzanne had needed them? He should have saved her!

She shook her head. That was crazy; Noah Stone had nothing to do with Suzanne's death. Her killer was on the street because of a broken-down legal system.

Marion was the nation's chief law officer.

Wasn't Suzanne's death her fault?

Her phone rang, the direct line. "Yes?"

"This is Joe Donovan, ma'am."

Damn, she should have made sure to see him in Ashland. "Glad you called, Joe. I was going to call you and Sally—"

"This is a courtesy call, Ms. Smith-Taylor. Our resignations are in the mail to you, but I thought it was only right to let you know that we're going to work for Noah Stone."

"But why . . . Oh. Now that Soldado is gone, he's scared."

"With good reason, ma'am. He's been shot at twice."

She stood and paced to work off her anger. "He's got a lot of nerve, stealing my agents."

"It was us who went to him. We like what he's doing."

Okay, live with it. "I understand. Do me a favor and keep me informed?"

"We owe you that much. Stone will be okay."

Why was she concerned? Stone was the guy ripping holes in the Constitution.

But he was making things work better out there, wasn't he? People were safer.

It was time she had a conversation with Noah Stone. He didn't seem like a fanatic. Maybe she could get him to see how wrong it was to subvert the Constitution no matter how worthy his goals. Maybe there was a way to work with him for change without destruction. She checked her schedule. She could go there in two days.

After asking her new secretary to get her to Ashland, she took out a notepad and started organizing her arguments.

An hour later, she realized that she was feeling like the defense on a losing case, not the prosecution of a successful one. Marion called for coffee and went back to work.

 **30**   INTO THE BELLY OF THE BEAST

It was a few minutes before a clock on the wall reached nine o'clock in the morning when Arnie, flanked by two stopper-carrying guards, gave each prisoner a long look and said, "I urge you one last time to do the therapy."

Trying to sleep on a jail cot made Hank contrary. He'd have probably said no even if he'd wanted to do it. He yawned. Dalrymple didn't take Arnie up on the offer, either.

Arnie said, "As you wish." He held out a hand, one finger decorated with a multicolored Alliance ring. "Now put one arm through the bars. If you're right-handed, make it your left arm, left-handed, make it the right."

Hank did as told, and Dalrymple followed suit. A guard slipped a cold band of dull gray metal around his wrist and clicked it shut. It was a tight fit, and where the ends met there was only a hairline crack; no way he'd be prying it apart. There'd be no sliding it over his hand, either, unless every bone was pulverized.

Arnie said, "Your wristband carries a transmitter that sends a signal unique to you. We have receivers located over a two-hundred-mile radius.

"The band is titanium alloy, and nothing in the Keep can cut it—the hardest metal inside is the aluminum trays in mess kits. The bracelet also monitors your body temperature. If it falls low enough for long enough, we'll know that you're either dead or the band is no longer on you, which would mean that your hand has been cut off or crushed to a pulp to take the band off. With no medical care in the Keep, that probably means you're dead. It has happened."

Hank started to hate the band.

"If you get past the fence and survive the climb to the desert floor, there are no public roads or other human habitations for a hundred miles in any direction. Or water, or shelter. There is, however, a population of rattlesnakes and scorpions. Even if you make it that far, helicopters will still track you down through the wristband."

Damn.

The other guard put two neat stacks of supplies on a table outside the barred elevator area. Arnie pointed. "Blankets, another coverall, underwear, socks, a toothbrush and toothpaste, needle and thread, soap and towel. You have the pamphlet and the video.

"The elevator takes you to the release room on the top of the butte, which looks like this . . ." He swiveled a monitor on his desk so they could see the picture. Hank made out a bare room with a metal door in the far wall. Arnie tapped the screen and said, "This door takes you into the exit chamber. Because of the air pressure needed to hold up the prisoner buildings, the chamber is an airlock with two doors."

The view cut to a smaller room with another door. Arnie tapped the screen and indicated a panel beside the door. "You push this button. Be sure you're clear when the doors close— they're powered by hydraulics at ten tons of pressure per square inch. When the first door is closed behind you, and only then, you can open the outer door into the Keep. If you're lucky, nobody will be waiting."

Hank asked, "What if we don't want to go out?"

"I guess you won't be eating. You'll get pretty thirsty, too."

"What if somebody stays in the elevator?"

Arnie shrugged. "It sits there until it's empty; we've got the time."

"Outside the exit chamber?"

"You're on your own. You find a bed for yourself, get your own food, force somebody to get it for you, whatever—there's plenty, all ready-to-eat. There are more clothing and sundries, tables, beds, and chairs." He grinned. "All the necessities are provided to everyone, equally. Each building has toilet facilities and showers. You can stay in the building attached to the exit room or go to another one. A conveyor delivers food to the supply area in the first building."

He tossed a set of keys to the short, wide guard. "All right, Mannie, let's start with Mr. Dalrymple."

The guard opened Dalrymple's cell door. Dalrymple didn't move. The guard reached in and hauled him out by an arm.

Looking for any angle that could be turned into an escape, Hank said, "Let's say I decide to do the therapy after I'm up there. How do I get back out?"

Arnie grimaced. "Shit, I'm sorry, I left out the most important part."

Mannie and Dalrymple paused. Arnie walked to a Plexiglas plate in a metal frame affixed to the bars outside the elevator. "By the exit chamber door inside the Keep there's a panel like this. Hold your wristband up to it; a detector reads your code and the door opens for fifteen seconds. Once you're inside the room, we'll talk. The door won't open again for twenty-four hours unless I trigger it to let you back out."

The guard escorted Dalrymple to his supplies. Arnie pushed a button on his desk, the double-barred door opened, and Mannie guided Dalrymple into the elevator and then returned for Hank.

The second guard stood with his stopper ready.

Now was the time. Up in the Keep, there wouldn't be a key to take the wristband off, and there was that fence and a hundred miles of nowhere. Down here, there was a nice helicopter that Hank knew how to fly.

When Mannie reached for him, Hank grabbed his wrist and yanked. When the guard stumbled forward, Hank clubbed him on the side of the head with a fist. Mannie dropped, and Hank wrenched the stopper from his holster. He turned it on the other guard.

Hank didn't know which button did what, so he pressed the first and second. Nap beads shot out, followed by a stream of mist that hit the guard's face. The guard twitched and staggered, his eyes clamped shut.

As Hank swung his weapon toward Arnie, tangle from Arnie's stopper pinned his gun hand to his side.

Arnie smiled. "Drop it. Unless you'd like to go into the Keep napped."

Hank opened his hand as best he could. The stopper fell through a gap in the tangle web.

Pressing a button on his desk, Arnie said, "I need help in here."

Two guards entered, stoppers drawn. Arnie pointed. "Jimmy, cover these guys, especially the troublemaker."

Arnie checked Mannie's pulse. He sighed and said to one of the new guards, "Better get a gurney over here from the Repair Shop. He's going to need a little treatment." He opened the barred door to the elevator area and signaled Hank to enter. "In."

Hank applied all his strength to break the bonds of the tangle. It gave slightly, then no more. "Like this?"

"You're a lot less trouble that way."

"Up there, I'm in trouble this way."

At Hank's feet, Mannie stirred and moaned. Arnie knelt and put a hand on his shoulder. Mannie's eyes cracked open. Arnie said, "You okay?" Mannie nodded, then winced.

Arnie stood and considered Hank. "You're the guy who saved Noah Stone's life?"

"That's what I'm in here for."

Arnie gazed at Hank, then took an aerosol can from a drawer. "Don't use this much—hope it's still good."

He sprayed the tangle; it sagged and fell away.

"Thanks." Hank fetched his supplies, went to the elevator, and joined Dalrymple. Arnie pushed a button, the doors closed, motors whined, and the elevator rose.

When it stopped and opened, they edged into the room, spreading to create space between them. The elevator shut behind them.

The steel door into the exit chamber was set in a steel frame cemented into concrete block walls. Hank tapped the button on the panel and the door rumbled open. It revealed a bare room four feet square, with a steel door and control panel on the opposite wall. Hank led the way into the room. Behind them, the door closed.

In grisly testimony to the force behind the doors, just inside the outer door lay a mummified hand, the rusty brown of dried blood staining the floor under it. A spider skittered away from the bones. Hank tsked; apparently there was no maid service up here.

Dalrymple said, "You gonna open the door?"

Hank didn't want to be first out in a prison filled with thousands of the state's most violent men. He said, "Help yourself."

Dalrymple snorted and swaggered forward to stab the button. This door lifted straight up. Instead of being squared off, the bottom edge was wedge-shaped, and the doorjamb in the floor was shaped to receive it. With ten tons of pressure behind it, the door would cut through anything in its way. Nasty.

Hank's ears and skin sensed the increased air pressure that supported the huge fabric roof. Foul air flowed in, carrying an eye-watering stench of unwashed men and God knew what else. Men waited outside the door.

One of them coughed. Dalrymple retreated a step.

Arnie's voice said, "I need to shut that door. Please step out." Hank spotted a tiny camera in a corner of the ceiling.

Hank stepped to the doorway. A semicircle of beefy, unkempt men waited for them. Sure they did; they'd seen the police helicopter arrive and had expected new fish to be delivered. Seeing nothing to gain by waiting, Hank moved out. Dalrymple came after. The second he cleared the door, it slammed home like a giant guillotine blade. Very nasty.

There were five in the reception committee, all bearded and, judging by the odor that drifted to Hank, unwashed for entirely too long. Two wore their hair pulled back in ponytails, three let it bush out. Of course, there were no scissors or razors in the Keep. A crude tattoo of a skull and crossbones decorated each man's forehead.

The air structure stretched before them; it still reminded Hank of a giant pill, long and rounded. The ceiling arched eighty feet over a half acre of concrete. King-size lighting fixtures hung from the roof. Scattered through the space were chairs, tables, and beds, some clustered together, others isolated. Pieces of clothing littered the floor along with occasional piles of what looked like trash. It was a gray scene, the only color hundreds of orange jumpsuits. Men lounged on beds and chairs. A couple of card games were in progress. On the far side, two men fought inside a circle of cheering prisoners.

Twenty yards from the door, a row of metal pipes ending in showerheads stuck up through the floor. Nearby, a couple dozen urinals decorated a low concrete wall, and toilets occupied a row of half-wall stalls. Fifty feet past the "bathroom" stood a thirty-foot square formed by what looked like walls of fabric. It appeared to be a tent without a roof, and was flanked by a smaller square, maybe ten feet to a side. Hefty men stood guard at the big square's entrance.

Hank noted that none of the five men waiting for them had made a move to get inside the exit chamber. He figured that was a sure sign he could rule it out as an escape route.

Each man carried a stout club about two feet long, one end tapered to a point sharp enough to put a serious hole in someone's belly; a fist-sized rock tied to the other end looked good for bashing.

The biggest man said, "Take it."

The other four stepped forward and grabbed the supplies the new arrivals carried. Hank let his stuff go without protest, but Dalrymple hung on, saying "Hey, that's mine!"

One thug stepped behind Dalrymple and smashed his fist into a kidney. The rapist dropped his bundle, and his assailants grabbed their loot and rejoined the semicircle. The leader aimed his club at the topless tent. "We're going there. You give us a problem, well . . ." He slapped his club head into a palm. "Did they show you Bone Hill on the way in?"

Hank nodded.

The leader said, "Let's go."

FUNDAMENTALLY RATIONAL AND FAIR

Jewel closed the folder on the Armstrong file, done at last, and sooner than she'd thought. She was getting the hang of the Alliance system. She leaned back and sipped her coffee—bleh, it was cold. Can't have that. Just as she stood to go for a fresh cup, her cell phone dinged. A text message. She checked the screen.

It was from Murphy's number. It said, "Gotcha."

Fear clenched her. No . . . She didn't know what to do, where to turn.

Benson appeared in her doorway, papers in his hand. Good, he'd know what . . . Why was his always cheerful face so down? A uniformed police officer appeared behind him. It was Tom, the nice cop she'd seen around town.

Tom said, "Ms. Washington, I—"

Benson said, "Let me, Tom." He held up the papers. "Jewel, Tom is here to take you into custody. The State of Illinois has a warrant for your arrest." He squared his shoulders and took a breath. "The charge is murder. And there's an officer here to extradite you."

This was crazy. "Who did I murder?"

Benson read from a sheet of paper. "Timothy Washington."

She dropped into her chair, sucker-punched by his words. "My brother? I didn't— Who said—"

Benson said, "The charging officer is John Murphy."

"That lying bastard!"

Tom stepped into the office and took a pair of handcuffs from his belt. "Sorry, ma'am. I gotta do this."

She stood and backed away, hands out in protest. "This is all wrong."

"Please don't make this any tougher."

Benson said, "I'm on this, Jewel. Just stay calm."

The cop clicked the cuffs on her—cold, heavy, scary—and he said, "You have the right to . . ."

Four hours later, Jewel sat in a jail cell, still wracking her brains to figure out what to do. She thought about Hank Soldado sitting there and understood why he had tried so hard to escape. She felt so—*trapped*, as helpless as a newborn.

The cellblock door opened and Benson hustled in, a file folder in his hands. The jailer followed, keys in hand. Benson said, "Hi, Jewel. You okay?"

"Yes. No. I'm so damn scared for Chloe."

"I checked. Franklin's taking care of her. Ah, if it's all right with you, I'd like to act as your advocate."

"Oh, yes, but I don't get why I need one. I didn't do what they said." It struck her that Hank hadn't thought he'd done anything wrong, either.

The jailer opened the cell door and swung it back. Benson said, "Come on. We've got an inquiry to go to."

"So fast?"

Benson reddened. "Uh, I asked for a favor." Now that was something, Mr. Letter-of-the-Law asking for special consideration.

A pulse of fear struck. She shrank back from him. "Oh, God, Benson, I don't want to go to the Keep."

"Did you do what they say?"

Not trusting her voice, she shook her head.

He said, "Then you've got nothing to worry about. Come on, let's get this done."

She held her arms out for handcuffs.

Benson said, "No need for that. Come on."

When they stepped into the courtroom, another shock greeted her—Murphy sat by the state's advocate, Jenny. He looked different . . . His nose veered to the side. The creep smiled at her like an executioner who enjoyed his work. It was a Black woman's word against a white Chicago cop's. She was in deep shit.

The only other people in the courtroom were the jury panel and the court clerk. Just as she and Benson got settled at the advocate's table, Judge Edith Crabtree strode into the chambers and took her place behind her desk. The judge rapped her gavel, peered over her reading glasses at Murphy, and said, "Well, what can we do for the great state of Illinois?"

Jenny rose. "Your honor, Officer Murphy seeks extradition of Jewel Washington on a charge of first-degree homicide committed in Cook County, Illinois." She held up a folder. "He has provided the appropriate paperwork."

The judge considered Jewel. "Ms. Washington? Aren't you with the Alliance advocate team?"

Jewel stood. "Yes, ma'am, Your Honor."

Murphy stood. "That doesn't matter, what she is here. It's what she did there that counts."

Judge Crabtree leveled her gaze at Murphy. "You are absolutely correct, Officer."

"Then let me have her and I'll be on my way."

"Ah, but here in Oregon we like to inquire into the facts of 'what she did there' before making judgments."

Murphy protested. "She poisoned Timothy Washington."

Anger flared in Jewel. The son of a bitch. She opened her mouth to protest, but Benson stopped her by saying, "Your Honor, the accused is ready to proceed with the inquiry."

Murphy sputtered, "I got all the paperwork. The Chicago D.A. said just pick her up. What kinda deal is this?"

"The 'deal,' Officer, is to get at the truth. Please be seated." As Murphy lowered himself into his chair, the judge turned to Jewel. "Please take the witness chair, Ms. Washington."

Again Jewel thought of Hank as she walked to the chair and had the verifier headset placed on her head. He'd been convinced he was innocent, yet he had been sentenced to sure death. And now she was in the grip of the same system. Going back to Chicago would be as bad as being sent to the Keep.

Benson started the questioning. "Ms. Washington, do you know a Timothy Washington?"

"Yes. He's . . . he was my brother." The verifier light glowed green.

"Let's get right to it, Ms. Washington. Did you poison your brother?"

"No, sir." The green circle remained unlit. There was no memory in her of doing anything like that.

"When did you last see him?"

"The day I left for Oregon, 'bout a month ago."

"Was he alive when you left him?"

She pictured Timmy, lying dead on the closet floor. Tears filled her eyes. She said, "No." The light flickered green.

Benson said, "But you did nothing to harm him."

Oh, God, what was the truth? She'd bought pink for him, time and again. But what could she have done differently? She shook her head and the green circle stayed dim. Mercifully, the judge didn't ask for her answer out loud; she wasn't sure she could hold the tears back.

Benson turned to the judge and said, "That should be enough, Your Honor. We recommend denying the order for extradition as Ms. Washington is clearly not guilty of the crime she is accused of."

The judge said, "Jenny, does the state have any questions?"

Murphy shot to his feet. "I sure as hell do!"

The judge scowled and her voice boomed. "You will watch your language in this courtroom."

Murphy shrank a little and then muttered, "Yes, ma'am." He straightened. "But that's not all there is to it. Let me ask her some questions."

"Of course. We are, after all, here for the truth."

Murphy swaggered over to stand in front of Jewel. The bitter reek of old sweat struck her. He said, "Let's see if you tell the truth about this."

The judge said, "Please get on with it, Officer."

"Did you give your brother the drug known as pink?"

Oh, shit. But she had to answer. "Yes." The light greened.

"Did you give him a lethal dose?"

"Yes."

"Did you know that he would take it?"

She shuddered. Timmy's *Thank you* whispered in her mind. She nodded; the light glowed green. "Yes, I knew he would take it." Jewel lifted her chin. "I *hoped* he would."

Murphy faced the judge. "At the least, Your Honor, this is a case of assisted suicide, if not manslaughter, and you have to allow the extradition so justice can be served." He returned to the advocate table and sat.

Judge Edith said, "You have a point. The circumstances seem to call for further investigation."

A member of the jury panel raised her hand. She was in her thirties, and her eyes were moist. The judge said, "You have a question?"

"Yes, Your Honor."

"Proceed."

She addressed Jewel. "Had your brother been addicted for long?"

"A year. It seemed like forever."

"Did you care for him?"

"Every day."

"Did you buy drugs for him?"

"Every day I could afford to."

A tear rolled down the woman's cheek; it was mirrored by one from Jewel's eye. The woman said, "Why?"

Jewel gazed at the judge. "To stop the pain." The green verifier light turned on. "And withdrawal would kill him."

"But the pain always came back, didn't it?"

Jewel took a breath and tried to harden herself. "Yes."

"Why did you provide him with a lethal dose?"

Jewel cried out, "To stop the pain!"

The woman said, "Yes." She turned to the judge. "My husband died of this evil drug." She shuddered. "I still hear the screams."

Benson asked Jewel, "Was the supply of this drug plentiful?"

"Oh, yes."

"Then why didn't your brother go get it himself?"

"No money, and he was so weak." She glared straight at Murphy. "And I had the connection."

Benson was quick to pick up her meaning. "And who was that connection, Miss Washington?"

She pointed at Murphy. "That scumbag."

The verifier light glowed green.

Murphy jumped up. "That's a lie!"

Judge Crabtree said, "Well, we can't have that, Officer. Would you like to take the stand and answer a few questions?" Her smooth tone didn't hide the venom underneath.

Murphy glanced at the verifier monitors. "I have to wear that thing?"

"Yes. All you have to do is tell the truth. It will know when you do."

Murphy paled. "Uh, no, no, I don't think I ought to do that. Uh, testify, I mean." He sat.

The judge rapped her gavel. "Considering the evidence before us, I see no reason to honor this request for extradition. But we have our process, our *due* process." She turned to the jury. "Does the panel need to adjourn to take a vote?"

The jurors shook their heads. The woman whose husband died of pink raised her hand.

The judge said, "Yes?"

The woman stood. "I think it's clear, Your Honor, that there's no justification for the extradition. However that man died, this woman didn't do it. But is there any way to arrest the—" She pointed at Murphy. "Scumbag?"

The tiniest of smiles appeared at the corners of Judge Crabtree's mouth. "I'm afraid there's no way we can detain the scu—ah, officer. But we will be in communication with our peers in the Cook County justice system."

If Murphy had looked pale before, he now looked bleached. He threw a look at Jewel hard enough to make her flinch.

The judge banged her gavel. "This inquiry is closed. Miss Washington, please return to your life, and enjoy every minute of it."

Jewel took the headset off, relief bringing a wide smile. "Oh, yes, Your Honor. Thank you."

The judge pointed to the back of the courtroom. "It's not me you thank. It's the people who made truth the goal of our system."

Jewel turned, and there was Noah. He nodded and then slipped out the door.

Benson shook her hand and said, "Well, do you think our system is so bad now?"

Jewel, still quivery inside with the fear that had filled her for hours, said, "Maybe it worked for me. But one right doesn't fix a wrong. Hell, Soldado could be dead by now because he *saved* a life."

Benson shook his head. "And took one."

"Righteously."

"But not rightfully."

Jewel shook her head. "You're never going to sell me that."

Benson scowled. "Then maybe you don't belong here."

32 THE BEAST IS HUNGRY

Hank headed for the fabric structure, followed by Dalrymple. Two men fell in on each side, their clubs ready, and the leader took up the rear.

Hank passed a barrier fence of bed frames turned on their sides and tied together three-high that extended from the side of the concrete elevator building. The makeshift fence enclosed an area stacked high with cardboard boxes, leaving only a narrow opening guarded by big guys with tattoos on their foreheads. A ramp sloped down into the area from an opening high in a side wall.

As they passed, a cardboard carton arrived and slid down toward a mound of goods. A line of inmates formed at the opening to the enclosure. The tattooed guys handed out packages that Hank guessed were food.

A straw-thin man stumbled to the opening. A guard said, "You're still on Doc's shit list." He shoved and sent the skinny guy sprawling.

When Hank drew near the cloth square, he discovered that it was made of sheets stitched together. At the entrance, tattooed guards stepped aside to admit them.

Inside, blankets had been sewn together to form a dirty beige carpet. Hanging sheets partitioned off an area to the rear. In the center of the main area, a three-foot mound covered with blankets had a chair on its peak—a throne?

To one side, three small tables tied together formed a banquet table with wooden chairs all around. Two portly men, each with a tattoo on his forehead, lounged in chairs near the throne. They gazed dead-eyed at the arrivals.

A pretty young man stepped out from the partition, saw them, and ducked back in. When they reached the foot of the mound, a burly, red-bearded man stepped from the rear quarters. At his appearance, the pudgy men snapped to attention.

Medium tall but thick, moving with power, Red-Beard strode to the mound and sat on the throne. His jumpsuit was clean and new, and he carried a wooden stiletto. He wore no tattoo on his forehead, and his eyes flashed with intelligence. Hank thought he also saw the glint of madness.

The man eyed them. "I'm Doc. I control the food for the Keep, and I'm also the only doctor in the house." He grinned. "I wasn't always, but I am now. This is my world."

Hank came up with an old news report: this was the Portland surgeon who had rid himself of three wives the inexpensive way. The only medical man here would have power.

Doc aimed his gaze at Hank and said, "What're you in for?"

Hank saw no sense in pissing off a bunch of big nasties with weapons, so he kept his voice mild when he said, "Killed a man."

"Maybe you'll become one of my bonemen." He looked to Dalrymple. "You?"

Dalrymple sent his gaze to the floor. "Armed robbery."

Hank snorted. When Doc raised his eyebrows, Hank said, "Raped a little girl."

Doc rubbed his beard and grinned. He nodded at Dalrymple, and then said to the big guy who'd brought them to the tent, "Nick, take the new pussy to the whorehouse."

Dalrymple backed up a step, hands up in protest. "Now, wait a minute—"

He shut up when one of the fat guys stepped close and rested the sharpened point of his club handle in the hollow at the base of Dalrymple's throat.

Doc laughed and said to Nick, "Take that thing away." Two bonemen grabbed Dalrymple by the arms and escorted him out. Doc yelled, "Food!" He stepped down from his throne and studied Hank. "Is there a possibility of intelligence here?"

Hank shrugged.

Doc laughed and commanded his minions. "For two!" An imperious wave of his hand signaled Hank to follow.

The portly men scrambled into action. One scurried to a table in a far corner, scooped up two packages, and rushed them to the banquet table. The other hurried to a plastic bucket by the corner table, grabbed plastic tumblers from a stack, dipped into the container to fill them with water, and rushed them into position beside the packages. The first stooge stood behind the head chair, and when Doc got there, the chair was pulled out for him with elaborate courtesy.

The packages were . . . MREs! Meals-ready-to-eat, concocted for the military. God, if they were the only thing to eat—wasn't there some law against cruel and unusual punishment?

Doc frowned at the package. "Goddamn MREs. I'd kill for a hot breakfast; it gets harder and harder to choke down this room-temperature mystery muck. Have a seat."

Hank took the chair by the other MRE. He ripped the heavy plastic open and stared at the contents for a long moment.

Doc nodded. "Yeah." He opened his MRE. "So," he said, "what's happening out there? Are the Allies still big dog in the street?"

After a half hour of Doc ranting about the evil Alliance, one of his hangers-on had just taken away their empty MRE containers and another had provided finger bowls and towels when a skeletally thin man hurtled through the tent door, his arms windmilling to regain his balance. He fell on his front with a grunt of pain, rolled over on his back, and lay there. A bloody mess had replaced his face, but there was something familiar about him . . . It was the skinny guy who'd been thrown out of the food line.

Nick, his knuckles red with blood, sauntered through the door.

Doc said, "What's this?"

"Tried to steal food."

Doc went to the skinny man. He prodded him with a toe, and the man whimpered. Doc turned to Hank and said, "Come here."

Hank did as told.

Doc held out the wooden stiletto. "Kill him."

Hank took the weapon, its point honed to an ice-pick-sharp tip. The blackened wood felt hard; they'd used fire to temper it.

He looked down at the man, whose eyes were clenched shut.

Hank glanced at Doc's face, and then Nick's. If he didn't do as told, he would suffer the same fate. He knelt and poised the stiletto over the man's heart.

The man's hands grabbed the shaft. Poor bastard still wanted to live.

Although Hank had killed people, he wasn't a murderer. The Alliance promise whispered into his thoughts. To help, the best you can. Hank stood and handed the stiletto to Doc. "I don't think so." Nick brought his club up and Hank braced for an attack, but Doc held up a hand.

Doc shrugged. "Your loss. You could have been one of my men."

"Thanks for the breakfast." The hair on the back of Hank's neck prickled when he turned away. As soon as he cleared the tent door, he shifted into a ground-covering stride and headed for the exit at the far end of the building.

The place was a zoo packed with uncaged beasts. He passed hundreds of dirty, long-haired men. Each eyed him as if he were a threat or a potential victim.

As he closed on the connecting building, he looked back. Forty yards behind him Nick, flanked by three weighty men, marched toward him. Prisoners hurried to clear a path for them, and an occasional laggard received a shove that sent him crashing into others.

Nick grinned at Hank and thumped his club into his palm.

Hank slammed through the door into the round center and ran through a door to another building.

This air structure was less crowded, and the men seemed thinner, less vigorous. Many lay on beds and stared at nothing.

There was no place to hide. The floor under the fabric contained only furniture, the bathroom area, and men.

He looked up. Outside, though, the roof should support a man. He ran to an exit door.

The desert air was cool, and he could see for miles. All desolate.

He'd kill for a gun. He smiled at the thought, but took the impulse seriously. He stuffed four stones, each about the size of an egg and heavy, into his jumpsuit pockets.

He pushed against the building fabric; it gave only slightly. It was slick, too—Donovan had said Teflon. Half-inch steel cables, anchored to a concrete foundation with steel rings about six feet apart, angled across the fabric at forty-five degrees. He jammed a toe against the fabric above a cable and reached overhead for another.

He inched his way up. Sweat popped out and quickly evaporated. The wall was pretty much vertical at the start, but soon the slope allowed him to lean his body against the structure for support.

Three quarters of the way up, he looked back at a nasty slide to the desert floor. From the top it wouldn't be much different from a fall from eight stories up.

The curvature of the structure prevented him from seeing the base. He liked that because it kept anyone on the ground from seeing him unless they went a ways out. He'd bet he couldn't be seen once he was on top.

Just as he had the thought, one of Nick's men trotted into view, headed away from the building. He turned and spotted Hank. He pointed and shouted, "Up there!"

Hank climbed.

On top of the air structure, Hank knelt, a rock in each hand. Wait till you see the whites of their eyes, he thought; kneeling would make them have to climb higher before his position was revealed.

A head appeared to his right . . . one of the guys who'd taken poor old Dalrymple to get screwed. He faced away from Hank's position.

He was not a lucky man.

Hank sprang to his feet, wound up just like when he pitched at college, and let fly.

The stone took his target square on the temple. He fell backward and disappeared down the eighty-foot slide to the ground.

Hank murmured, "Still got the old high hard one."

Two other men puffed their way to the top, one twenty feet to Hank's right, the other fifteen to his left. He took another rock from his pocket.

No sign of Nick.

Doc's men were in no hurry—where could he go? Aerobic workouts were apparently not a part of their lifestyle; they gulped air, hands on knees for support.

Hank let fly a rock at the nearest man. As soon as he released it, he shifted the other rock to his throwing hand and went into a windup.

His target twisted right, the rock missed by inches.

This time, Hank aimed to anticipate the move.

The man laughed when he turned back toward Hank, only to see the finish of Hank's second throw. He twisted to the right again . . . into the path of the rock.

It crunched into his elbow with a meaty smack; in the quiet of the desert the crack of bone breaking came loud and clear.

The guy howled and clutched his arm. "Goddamn, he broke it. How'm I gonna get down with a broke arm?"

Hank heard the slap of feet on fabric and wheeled to see the other man charging. The boneman roared, club held high, other arm spread wide. He was big. And fierce.

And easy.

Hank faked toward the club arm, and the attacker reflexively extended his other arm to block. Hank grabbed his hand, fell back, planted a foot in the dummy's belly, and put momentum to work.

The man flipped through the air, landed on his back, and slid helplessly on the slick fabric.

Hank got to his feet and watched as the man went straight at Broken-Arm, who tried to sidestep. He slipped as well.

They collided and spun away from the roof's center, a tangle of legs and arms.

Down the slope they went, grabbing at cables. Their screams faded when they disappeared beyond the curve of the roof.

Hank stared at the point where the two had vanished.

Their screams cut off. Three down.

Something smashed into the back of his head, the world turned gray, and he pitched forward onto his belly, grasping for a handhold—

33 A RIGHTEOUS PLAN

Martha slipped her electronic earmuffs back on after reloading the clip in her .45 caliber Glock 21. As good as the sound baffles were in her basement shooting range, she knew too many militia members who said "Huh?" a lot because they were too cool to use the muffs. Macho idiots. She taped a printout of the Alliance logo onto her target and ran it out for her last run.

Thirteen rounds later the *A* in *Alliance* was just a hole. She inhaled the scent of gunpowder and smiled, set her muffs on the workbench, and cleaned the gun.

Sparky was waiting for her when she emerged into the kitchen, her tiny claws clicking on the linoleum as she danced and hopped and yipped a greeting. You'd think Martha had been gone for days.

She picked Sparky up and cuddled her. "I'm sorry to shut you out, honey, but you know the noise hurts your little ears." She rustled up a Teenie Greenie dog treat, and Sparky trotted off to enjoy it in her little bed.

Her palm still tingling pleasurably from the Glock's recoil, Martha headed for her office. An email from Rick Hatch awaited her. She'd followed the disappointing reports of the Rogue Militia's failure to take Noah Stone out, so she needed to know more than ever when she could meet up with the bastard. The message was simply "How about this?" and a link.

The link led to a *Rogue Valley Times* notice. Noah Stone would give the dedication speech for a new university building in two days.

Excitement stirred in her belly. This was gonna be big. She was gonna make the son of a bitch shit his pants in front of his followers. She wondered if there would be TV cameras.

Woo-hoo.

She dialed Mitch Parsons.

Mitch pushed his desk chair back. He couldn't sit still, so he paced. Nothing was happening to stop Stone. A new poll out West had close to a majority of voters in California and Washington agreeing with gun laws modeled on Oregon's. It was happening, and with Hank Soldado out of action, Mitch couldn't do shit. He fished out a mini Tootsie Roll, his fourth in a row, but the hell with his stomach.

He stopped beside his grandfather's Colt .45 automatic, hanging on pegs at the bottom of the bronze star plaque above the fireplace mantel. It was exactly like the one Colonel Hanson had. Mitch used his sleeve to polish away a fingerprint on the plaque and then lifted the gun. Holding it, he felt stronger, more sure of himself.

His cell phone rang. He hung the pistol back on its pegs and answered.

It was Martha Hanson. She said, "Pack your bags."

"What?"

"Be in Ashland in two days. Wire me a thousand dollars today, and you need to arrange for that tool that we talked about that you want me to show your Oregon friend."

Oh, God. Excitement fluttered in him, fear on its heels. "What's, ah, where—"

"It'll be at a speech he's making at the college. I'll send the info. Are we on?"

With a sense that he was locking the safety bar on a roller coaster car, he said, "Yes. I'll be there. I'll get the, er, tool then."

The call ended. First thing he had to do was round up the cash. His gaze went to his grandfather's gun, and then he thought about how it had felt when Hanson had aimed a pistol barrel between his eyes. He had a feeling Stone would be retiring soon.

Mitch whistled as he went to his computer to book a flight.

 **34 SURRENDERING TO WIN**

Pain flared red in Hank's closed eyes. Awareness came with it, and more pain flashed when a foot landed a kick to his ribs. Nick's deep laugh sounded above him.

"Wake up, you son of a bitch. I ain't got all day and I want to see your face when you go."

Hank opened his eyes. The sun was hot on his face.

"Ah, there you are." Nick drew back his foot to kick again. "Good-bye."

Hank twisted, but not quickly enough. The kick caught him in the shoulder blade and sent him rolling toward the fast way down.

He scrambled with hands and knees and feet and managed to stick a toe onto one cable and snag fingers on another to stop, belly down, ten feet frolm Nick.

He looked up at the boneman. "Hello, Nick."

Nick nodded. He stood still as if inviting Hank to get up.

Hank was happy to oblige. He crawled and pulled himself to the top of the roof. Nick waited. Hank had nothing to fight with . . . Wait, that lump pressing into his right leg was his fourth rock, still in his pocket.

Hank sat up with his right side hidden from Nick.

Nick held his club ready. His smile was white in the midst of his black beard.

Hank got up on hands and one knee, his left foot on the roof, his right knee down to position his pocket out of Nick's view.

"Why didn't you just roll me off while I was out?"

"And miss the best part?"

"Maybe you ought to slide down and sell tickets first." He slipped his hand into his pocket and gripped the stone.

Moving to get up, he faked weakness, stopped a fall with his left hand on the roof. The move concealed his right hand taking the rock from his pocket.

Nick laughed.

Hank staggered to his feet and poured everything he had into a burst of speed. He twisted his shoulders away from Nick, slid his left foot forward and planted it. With a growling roar, he uncoiled and fired the rock as hard as he could.

The rock slammed into Nick's diaphragm. Nick doubled over, his breathing paralyzed.

Hank lunged forward and kicked him in the face, straightening his body and knocking him onto his back.

Hank stamped on Nick's wrist, wrenched the club from his hand, and raised it to deliver a killing blow.

But Nick was out. Hank slipped a toe under Nick's side and edged him toward the long slide down.

He stopped. He didn't feel right about this. Although Nick was a brutal thug, it would be murder. But he needed to be eliminated.

Hank figured he just needed to rest. Nick wasn't going to give him any trouble for a while. He sat near Nick's head, ready to club him if need be. If Nick attacked, then Hank could give him a fatal shove and it would be self-defense.

Concentrating on catching his breath and ignoring his pain, he looked out at the desert. The quiet was so complete that it seemed like a vast, empty sound. He saw no sign of human existence.

There was life out there, but what? Lizards, snakes, spiders, scorpions, and sagebrush, maybe a mangy coyote or two and whatever they hunted.

His life had become a desert filled with vermin.

He had no friends. No family, his parents gone. Hank had been going through the motions: eating, sleeping, working. A hollow man. Only his work as a lawman had kept him going, and he didn't have even that anymore.

Scenes from the Alliance video came into his mind. People at play and work. Families. Images of laughter and affection took him to Noah Stone's playful grin. Hank missed Noah's intensity and the warmth of the friendship he offered.

Then there was Jewel, working her hardest to survive in a nasty world, but still deep-down decent. A bright future was hers to have—as long as the Alliance kept doing their thing. But Hank was sure Mitch wouldn't stop just because Hank was out of action. If he took Noah out, without Stone's leadership Hank doubted the Alliance could stand up to the heavy enemies it was making. Too late, he wished he'd warned Noah Stone that they were coming after him.

But now Hank had a new life. He could survive in the Keep, maybe take Doc down and become King of the Scum. Or he could try to escape. In his professional opinion, escape was not possible. Even if he could escape, what for? Was life out there any different from in here?

Okay, they kept pushing the therapy thing. Noah had told him to do it, and Hank thought maybe he could trust him. But Noah had never had it done to him.

Benson Spencer had gone through it, and was supposed to be—no, was—Hank's advocate. He seemed okay.

A breeze tugged at Hank's hair; it stirred in his mind an image of a puff of wind wafting a strand of brown hair across a little girl's face. He saw her bright smile and happy brown eyes— Reflex jerked his mind away before pain could strike, but there was an ache underneath. He dug into his pocket and took out Amy's necklace. It was hard to look at.

He lifted his gaze to the emptiness of the desert.

He did feel one thing.

Alone.

So. Completely. Alone.

Something gave way in his mind. Up welled a longing for peace, and friendship, and love. He'd had those things before. Maybe he could again. Through the therapy.

Okay. He stood.

Fear rose with him. *But they'll mess with your mind,* it said. *You won't be you.*

Being him wasn't all that terrific.

Yeah, but it's still you.

But staying in the Keep would be worse than death. To survive, he'd have to become more of an animal than they were.

Maybe, the fearful side of him said, *it'll be easier to escape from the Repair Shop.*

True. It wasn't hundreds of feet up in the air and surrounded by huge fences. Hank could find tools to get rid of the tracking band on his wrist and then break out. He'd deal with the quality of his life on his own, a whole man.

Sounded good. He looked down at Nick, still stone cold out, a shove away from being another threat gone forever.

He gripped Nick's hands and lifted.

A half hour later, Hank's bloody fingertips slipped on a cable; he forced them to dig in and hold. Sweat dripped from his face, and his back ached. His searching toe found good old ground instead of another cable. He let go and toppled backward. He lay there for long minutes as the pain of his effort eased from his body.

At last, strength and will returning, he untied the strip of shirt that had kept Nick's arms around his neck.

Hank stood. Nick lay on his back, unconscious. Whatever. He had a chance, and Hank had no more to give. Anyway, Hank would soon be down in the Repair Shop, working on escape.

He went to Doc's building and, figuring that the red-bearded dictator wouldn't be happy about Hank leaving before he was beaten to a bloody mess, joined the line leading to the supply area to blend in. As he passed Doc's little cloth castle, Dalrymple emerged from the smaller square—must be the whorehouse. Walking with short, wincing steps, his gaze on the ground, he joined the line a few places behind Hank.

The door to the elevator down was forty feet from the supplies pickup point. No one paid any attention to the door. Why should they? Newcomers weren't inserted unless a helicopter announced their arrival, and it wasn't an escape route.

At the shower area a hundred feet away, someone was bathing, concealed by blankets held by two pudgy men and a couple of bonemen—Doc's men. Hank kept his face turned away from the showers, bowed his back, and slumped his shoulders to imitate the body language of the inmates around him.

He shuffled forward and received his MRE.

The shower shut off, and one of Doc's attendants handed a towel in.

Hank slouched toward the sensor panel that opened the door to the elevator room.

Doc emerged from the shower, wrapped in his towel, and stood surveying his subjects, a satisfied smile on his face.

Dalrymple, his high-pitched voice carrying, yelled, "Soldado? That you?"

Hank continued to walk toward the door.

Dalrymple said, "Soldado? Hey, wait a minute."

Out of the corner of his eye, Hank saw Doc's attention turn his way. The sensor panel was a dozen feet ahead. Hank dropped his MRE and sprinted for it.

Doc shouted, "Stop that man!" His men ran toward Hank, clubs raised.

Hank held his wristband up to the sensor panel. Nothing happened.

Of course, the computer below needed time to process. Or maybe Arnie was asleep.

Hobbling as though it were painful to run, Dalrymple hurried toward Hank. "Hey, take me too."

The nearest of Doc's men threw his club. It cracked the Plexiglas panel. Damn, don't break the thing.

Dalrymple lumbered into a clumsy run. "Wait!"

The heavy steel door lifted, the wedge-shaped cutting edge on the bottom rising above Hank's head. He had fifteen seconds. He stood in front of the doorway, faced the charging men, and silently counted time. One-thousand-one.

The first of Doc's men dived at Hank.

Hank sidestepped, added a shove to the man's momentum, and slammed his head into the concrete wall. The boneman sprawled on his back, out. One down.

One-thousand-three.

Hank backed through the doorway.

One-thousand-four. Dalrymple was almost there when a man tackled him.

One-thousand-six.

Dalrymple stretched a hand toward Hank, his face pure pain. "They raped me."

One-thousand-nine.

The man's anguish reached Hank. He kicked Dalrymple's attacker in the face, and the boneman rolled away, screaming, hands to his nose.

Hank grabbed Dalrymple's hand and hauled.

One-thousand-eleven.

As Dalrymple's arm came through the door, a second man landed on his legs and stopped his slide toward the door. Hank couldn't step out; he'd be trapped in the Keep for another twenty-four hours.

One-thousand-fifteen.

The door sliced down.

Hank held Dalrymple's left hand and most of his arm.

The steel door muted Dalrymple's scream, but not enough.

Arnie's voice whispered, "Jesus Christ."

Shuddering with horror, Hank dropped the arm and faced the camera. After a deep breath, he said, "You going to let me in?"

"You want to do the therapy?"

"Yes."

The inner door rumbled open and he stepped through.

When Hank came out of the elevator, Arnie awaited him outside the double-walled containment cell, Mannie the guard beside him. Both trained stoppers on him.

Arnie said, "Didn't take you long."

"I've got better things to do with my life." Hank headed for the door.

Arnie held up a hand to stop him. "This might surprise you, but some guys get the idea they can escape from the Repair Shop because it doesn't look so tough."

Hank grinned. "Imagine that."

Arnie grinned right back at him. "So I've got the verifier all warmed up. Just take a seat."

Hank concealed his disquiet. "I've already done that."

"Ah, but you see, you don't get past these bars unless I'm convinced you're sincere about therapy. Saves a lot of trouble. You don't pass, you just go back."

Hank sat, thoughts speeding, looking for an out. There wasn't one. He'd have to beat the machine.

"Please put the headset on."

He sat and put it on.

Arnie and Mannie stared at the monitor on Arnie's desk as Arnie asked, "Hank Soldado, did you decide to undergo therapy?"

All he could do was try. "Yes."

Arnie made a sound like a game show buzzer. "Wrong answer. Back you go."

Hank said, "Wait."

"It won't do any good."

"Just give me a minute. This is my life here!"

Arnie shrugged. "Sure. I'm gettin' paid for it."

Hank thought of the desert, a symbol of his life. Of waking up with tears on his face. Of the hole where his heart used to be. That was the life he had. It wasn't good enough anymore. But how could he surrender his mind?

Benson Spencer's words came to him. "There came a time when I had to trust."

He fished Amy's necklace from his pocket. A memory surfaced. Amy blew on a dandelion and giggled at the stream of white fluff. He could see her! Hank took a deep breath. "Ask me again."

Shaking his head, Arnie said, "Hank Soldado, do you want to undergo therapy?"

He kept his mind's eye on Amy as he said, "Yes."

Arnie looked up from the monitor in surprise. "Is it your intent to escape?"

Hank conjured up Jewel Washington's fierce expression when she fought him with nothing more than tiny nap beads. "No."

Arnie smiled. "I'll be damned. Never seen that." Relief eased Hank's mind and body. Arnie unlocked the cell door. "Come on out. I'll escort you to the Repair Shop personally."

When Hank stepped from the cell, Arnie stuck out a hand. "Welcome back."

As Hank took the hand, emotion surged in his throat and made it hard to say "Thanks." He felt as though he had conquered a mortal enemy.

 ## WHERE IS THE JUSTICE?

Jewel smiled at the murmur of Chloe's singing coming from the backyard. She stood at the kitchen stove, frying up a batch of chicken for Friday supper, enjoying the domestic sizzle of hot oil, trying to relax. She'd been edgy since Murphy had tried to get her. No one knew if he had left the area, though he had checked out of his motel. Now there was somebody who belonged in the Keep.

But not Hank Soldado. She just couldn't shake her anger at what she saw as criminally unjust.

Franklin's deep voice joined Chloe's, and Jewel could make out the words of the song, sung with a simple singsong melody: "I've got T-H-R-E-A-D, I've got good deeds in my head . . ."

Jewel scowled. Couldn't the damned Alliance propaganda leave her alone in her home? She turned the flame down under the chicken and went to the back door.

Franklin was pushing Chloe in a tire swing he'd hung for her from a branch of an oak tree. They sang, "T-H-R-E-A-D, green and yellow and blue and red . . ."

Jewel called out, "Could you guys stop singing that?"

They stopped and looked at her. Franklin said, "It's just a little song about—"

"I know what it's about, and I don't want to hear it."

Franklin opened his mouth, paused, then said to Chloe, "You ready for a spinner?"

Chloe giggled. "Wind me up!"

Jewel watched while Franklin turned the tire 'round and 'round, twisting the rope tighter and tighter until he let go and Chloe spun, yelling, "Wheeeeeeee . . ."

Jewel stepped back into the kitchen to get the chicken cooking again. Franklin came in, took a beer from the refrigerator, and twisted off the cap. "What's the matter?"

"I just don't like them brainwashing my child."

"Hey, it was me who made up that song."

She adjusted the flame under the skillet. "Well, I don't like you doing it, either."

He sat at the kitchen table. "Why not? THREAD is a good thing."

"So everybody says, but I don't believe it."

He held up his hand with the Alliance ring on it and wriggled his fingers. "It did you some good when you got here."

She didn't have an answer for that, so she concentrated on turning the chicken.

Franklin said, "Why haven't you joined the Alliance? You work for 'em."

"It's just not right for me."

"Why not? Does a lot for me and a whole bunch of folks."

Okay, that was hard to argue with. She and Chloe had both been helped by the changes the Alliance had made. If it weren't for their advocacy system, she'd be back in Chicago with Murphy gloating at her through cell bars. She thought about it while she took three potatoes from the sack in the pantry and washed them.

Okay, why couldn't she sign up, make the promise? Something in her resisted, something that expected . . . betrayal. Like her mama said, "Ain't nobody there for you but you."

Jewel turned to face Franklin. "I don't trust it."

"What did the Alliance ever do to you?"

Nothing, but she wasn't about to give Franklin the satisfaction. "You want mashed or baked?"

"Baked sounds good."

As she put the potatoes in the microwave and set the timer, Franklin said, "So why are you so down on the Alliance?"

He'd push at her until he got an answer, so she turned to him. "It's that goddamn promise Noah Stone keeps yapping about."

"What's wrong with it?"

"You make a promise, you live up to it. Stone didn't."

"Aw, you're not talking about—"

Her anger flared. "Damn right I am. Noah said, 'I'll try my best to help,' but he didn't lift one finger to help Hank Soldado."

"He couldn't."

She yelled, "He could have done something!"

"You mean use his influence to get around the law?"

She pushed her face right at his. "Goddamn it, the man stood up for Noah, and then Noah didn't stand up for him! How's he expect anybody to trust him when he turns on you like that?"

Franklin's voice rose, just a little. She was getting to him. "The way I see it, Noah did stand up for Hank, and for me, and for you when he wouldn't make an exception."

She snorted. "No way it's for me, 'cause I don't agree!"

"I thought you hated Hank Soldado."

"It doesn't matter what I hate, I'm talkin' about right and wrong. Don't you try to change the subject."

Franklin sat, silent. Jewel grew embarrassed about losing control. "I'm sorry, Franklin. It's not you."

He rose and went to the kitchen window. Looking out at Chloe on the tire swing, he said, his voice gentle again, "But it is, Jewel, it is me. And a lot of people in this town. If you're going to live here"—he turned to her—"and if Chloe is going to grow up here, you need to get this straightened out."

He was right. And despite all that had happened, she liked it in Ashland. She had a future in this place. "I don't know how."

"Go to the source."

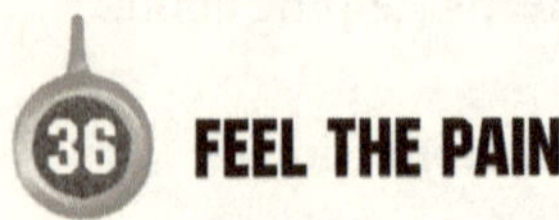

36 FEEL THE PAIN

Hank awoke refreshed the next morning in a Repair Shop room, maybe even looking forward to the day a little. The plain white room, furnished with a hospital bed and a small dresser, was no Holiday Inn, but he thought it was a fine place to be. He tried the door. Locked. Well, that made sense. He'd had the idea of escaping. Who wouldn't?

There was a sink and medicine cabinet, and he discovered a razor there. As he shaved, wondering what was next, doubt slithered into his thoughts. What would they do to his mind? Afterward, would he recognize the face in the mirror? Fear prodded him to escape, to keep his mind intact even if he had to live on the run. But he wanted more from life, not less. He dressed in a white T-shirt and white cotton pants he found on the dresser. He was gonna do it.

He got a little surprise when it was Arnie who unlocked his door. "Good morning, Hank," he said. "You look better."

Hank looked down at his white clothes. "I feel like an ice-cream man." He grinned. "But I guess it's better than looking like a giant Cheeto."

After a friendly breakfast, Arnie escorted him to the doctor and introduced him to Dr. Gladys Moore. Her office reminded Hank of a cozy study. Bookshelves framed a console that held a computer. A sofa, a recliner, and a rocking chair bracketed a glass coffee table on a burgundy Oriental rug. A pitcher of water, glasses, and a pill bottle sat on the table.

Dr. Moore looked relaxed in the rocking chair, a file folder open in her lap. Some would label the plump, fortyish woman with a long face "horsey," but intelligence gleamed in the doctor's gaze, and her warm smile made her attractive.

"Take a seat." She indicated the recliner, and he eased into it. After a brief how-do-you-feel chat, she said, "The first thing I need to do is rummage around in your head a little. We'll use hypnosis."

His stomach clenched. But he had to, didn't he? "Okay."

"Good. Recline the chair for me, will you?" As he tilted back, Dr. Moore pulled a low stool from behind the recliner and sat beside him. Using a soft, low voice, she urged him to think of a pleasant place, something comforting. He couldn't think of anything. He tried, but there was a knot in his belly that wouldn't unclench. No way was he going to be able to let go.

After five minutes of her suggesting relaxation, he was as tight as ever. She stopped and said, "We may have to use sodium pentothal, though a natural hypnotic state is much more effective."

Hank had a thought. He took Amy's necklace out of his pocket and held it in his hand. He closed his eyes and visualized her photo on his nightstand. "Try again."

As the doc crooned, Hank went to a place where a little girl laughed in bright sunshine . . .

Dr. Moore's gentle voice said, "Wake."

Hank opened his eyes and gazed at her as she settled into her rocker. It seemed as if no time had passed, but his back was stiff. He stretched as she said, "I've isolated three factors harming you. First, the circumstances around the deaths of your wife and child have you locked in a cycle of depression, and it contributes a great deal to your PTSD."

He frowned. He didn't want to hear about that.

"You and I can deal with that by using hypnosis to make conscious what happened, and then helping you accept it."

"Okay, but that's personal stuff. What about the trouble that got me in here? The way I see it, I was wrongly convicted, at least wrongly sentenced to the Keep." She raised her eyebrows, and he added, "Well, yeah, I did have a gun. But I wasn't wrong there, either. I have a right to one. We all have that right. And I did kill a thug, but it was justified."

"I won't argue the right and wrong of your positions, although I disagree. It was your powerful sense of duty that led you to shoot that man in defense of another. But that leads me to something that is a problem, your absence of feeling when you killed him. You have lost a sense of the value of human life that most people carry.

"We also need to do something about your convictions regarding your right to a gun. Or, to be more specific to Oregon law, to a lethal firearm."

A sinking hit his stomach. Here it came, the part where they fucked with his mind. "What I believe is not uncommon. There are a lot of folks like me. Hell, it's the Constitution of the United States. You're not going to get me to go against that."

She nodded. "I won't ask you to. But that doesn't excuse you from breaking the law. The solution that will get you released from here is to change those beliefs and, perhaps, open your mind to the legality of the gun control Oregon has implemented. And I know where the core belief comes from."

Dr. Moore sat back and gazed at him. "Your pro-gun programming is profound, going back to your childhood, and strongly associated with your family."

That was no surprise. "Yeah. They taught me. So what?"

She nodded. "I see it as more or less benign, not rabid like so many others, but it still limits your thinking. However, we—you—can get rid of it."

That didn't sound like something he wanted to do.

She said, "I'll show you later. I think we can take care of the stone killer part of you at the same time." She made a note in her file and looked back up at him. "That part will be tougher."

"But first . . ." Dr. Moore put the folder on the coffee table and moved to the stool beside his chair. "Let's work on the deaths of your wife and child. It'll strengthen you for handling the other issues."

His gut tightened. His old shrink had been right; he was afraid. "Okay."

"Good. Relax now . . ."

His mind opened, ready. The doctor's gentle voice said, "We're going back to the day your wife and daughter died, the twelfth of September. You were working—where were you?"

"In my car, in Chicago."

"What were you doing?"

"Watching a building."

"Why?"

"A suspected murderer lived there, and I was detailed to surveillance."

She said, "You're going to relive what happened now."

Memory became reality.

Hank stretched and stared out his car window at the house across the street. He imagined the suspect charging out, spewing bullets from an assault rifle. Anything to break up the boredom—in Hank's business, drowsy equaled dead.

His cell phone vibrated in his pocket. He keyed it open— damn, Amy's nanny. She wasn't supposed to call him on the job except in case of— "What's wrong?"

Gretchen's whisper shook. "Your wife—she's here."

Impossible. "How?"

"I don't know. The doorbell rang, and there she was."

Dear God. "Does she have Amy?"

"I tried to stop her, Mr. Soldado, I tried."

He started his car. "I'm coming. Call 911 now!" He disconnected, slammed into gear, and floored the gas. How could Marcie be out of the hospital? With her postpartum psychosis still raging five years after she'd beaten their baby girl, he couldn't even mention Amy's name to her.

As he raced south on Lake Shore Drive, he called home. "How . . . how is Amy?"

Gretchen said, "I tried to grab her away, but your wife screamed she would kill her if I came closer. Amy was crying. They went upstairs, and I don't . . . I don't hear her anymore."

"Stay away from them." He rounded a corner and screeched to a stop in front of his brownstone. The afternoon sun dappled its walls with the shade of trees lining the street. It couldn't have seemed more peaceful.

He yanked out his gun and raced for the front door. It swung open before he got to it.

Gretchen pointed. "There!"

He ran up the stairs and into Amy's bedroom. Toys and books cluttered the floor. Her window stood open; a breeze stirred the chintz curtains. His wife's laugh came from outside. He scrambled through the window and thundered up the iron fire escape.

At the edge of the flat roof, Marcie, as slender as ever, her long brown hair swirling in the breeze, held Amy over the parapet. Amy hung like a rag doll, her eyes closed, her body sagging, limp. Marcie laughed as she swung Amy back and forth. Amy's head lolled with the motion. Her butterfly necklace glittered at her neck.

When she'd asked to wear her necklace that morning, he'd said it was just for special days. And Amy had said, "Maybe today is special, and we just don't know it yet."

He had smiled and helped her put it on.

Hank's steps crunched on the roof's graveled surface and Marcie looked around.

She smiled. "Hi, honey, I'm home."

His heart ached at the madness in her eyes. "Please put Amy down, Marcie."

She frowned. "You like her better than me."

"No, honey, no way. You're the best. Just put her down."

Marcie brightened. "But she won't hurt me anymore." She hugged Amy's limp form to her. "I fixed that."

He prayed that Amy was only unconscious. "Lay her down, Marcie, and step away from her."

She scowled at him. "No." She swung Amy back out over the parapet. "We're playing."

He aimed his gun. "Put her down."

She laughed and lifted Amy high in the air and smiled up at her. "Isn't this fun, honey?"

She brought Amy back inside the parapet, safe from the long fall—he pulled the trigger. The bullet took Marcie below the ribs. Blood reddened an air-conditioning tower behind her, and she staggered back against it.

Marcie screamed at him, "Fuck you!" She threw Amy over the edge of the roof.

Too late, he pulled the trigger again.

The bullet spun Marcie to face him. Her expression softened. Her eyes cleared, and the woman he loved looked out at him. "I'm so sorry."

She staggered to the edge and then dived over.

Hank ran to the parapet. Their bodies lay side by side in the alley. It looked as if they were holding hands.

His heart locked up.

Dr. Moore's voice said, "Three . . . two . . . one . . . wake."

He opened his eyes; the shift from Marcie and Amy lying broken in an alley to the doctor's caring eyes disoriented him. She said, "That's what really happened, Hank. Amy was already dead by the time you reached the roof." She placed her hand over his. "You're not to blame."

Sorrow filled him like water pouring into an empty glass. Tears welled in his eyes.

"Go ahead," Dr. Moore said. "I'm here if you need me."

His chest seized as if a giant fist squeezed it. He couldn't breathe. Pain coiled in his lungs, and he tried to gasp. Then it smashed out in a long moan. He turned his face away from Dr. Moore, crossed his arms over his chest, and fought to hold the pain back. But he couldn't. He lay his head back onto the recliner and wept.

 **CAN'T GET THERE FROM HERE**

It was almost noon when Jewel poked her head into Noah Stone's office—it had taken most of the morning to work up the gumption to do this. Franklin was right, she was never gonna have a life here until she worked out her problems with Stone's way of doing things. He stood at a window, coffee cup in hand, gazing at the valley.

Damn, she didn't want to do this. But she had to. "Excuse me, Noah . . . " she said.

He turned to her and smiled. "Jewel! Come in, please. Coffee?"

Coffee on this stomach was begging for heartburn. "No, thanks. I, uh, need to talk?"

"About the Hank Soldado thing?"

"How did you—"

"I've seen you frowning for days now, and Benson has told me about your feelings. Have a seat."

Feeling that he was somehow an opponent, she said, "No thanks."

His smile faded. "So what's on your mind?"

She blurted, "Why didn't you do something to save him?"

"I tried to persuade him to go through therapy. He could have saved himself."

"You could have stopped him from being sent to the Keep."

"I couldn't."

Who was he trying to kid? "I don't believe that. You've got the power."

He gazed at her. At last he sighed. "I guess, from your way of thinking, I could have 'arranged' something." He shook his head. "But I had a promise to keep."

"That's keeping your promise? How can anybody trust you to help if you turn your back on a man who saved your life?!"

"Because you can trust me to keep my promise."

"Trust you? How? You promised to help, and you didn't do shit."

His eyes saddened, and he looked older. As though suddenly fragile, he eased into a chair by the coffee table. "Jewel, you don't know how tempted I was to help him." He looked up at her. His face looked like something hurt inside. "I wanted desperately to save Hank from the Keep. I thought there was so much we could do together . . ."

His emotion cooled her anger. He seemed sincere, but . . . "Why didn't you do anything?"

He gazed at the mountains outside, and then turned to her. His eyes were brighter, determined. "To use my influence to circumvent the court's ruling would have corrupted the system I've worked so hard to see become a reality."

His voice took on an edge. "Think it through. If I'd gotten Hank off, that would say it's okay to break the gun law if you think you have a good-enough reason or a good-enough contact. So somebody else would, I guarantee you, think they can get away with the same thing. Corrupted, the system would break down."

She thought he was probably right about that. Still, Soldado had saved his life. "But—"

He held up his hand and she waited for the rest. He said, "To undermine the system that holds the capacity for real justice would be breaking my promise to all, including Hank Soldado. And you. He got justice, and so did you when that awful man from Illinois came after you."

She shook her head. "That's all theory. This is a man's life."

His gaze became as hard as his last name. "They are the same."

She didn't know what to think. You could trust Noah Stone to keep to the rules. But you couldn't trust him to do everything he could for you. Defeated, she said, "I guess maybe I'll never understand."

His expression softened. "I'm sorry."

"I am, too."

 **38   GOING UNDER THE KNIFE**

After the morning session with Dr. Moore, Hank had a lunch of hardly anything—it was difficult to look at a plate of food when your mind was filled with a slide show of a dead life. Blocked memories poured in. Marcie in her wedding gown, him a grinning idiot beside her. An April stroll along Lake Michigan with Marcie, so into each other that the chill spring wind could have saved its breath. Him when he first held Amy in the delivery room.

And then Marcie throwing Amy's body off the roof. All the good memories turned to ashes. Hoping for relief, Hank arrived at Dr. Moore's office early.

She said, "How're you doing?"

He shrugged.

"Memories, right?"

He nodded and knew he hadn't kept his grief from his expression.

She said, "The good ones will get stronger and stronger and the bad ones will fade. I promise. Take a seat and let's get started on your other problems. We're going to revisit some things I found in our first session. One is pleasant, the other—" She shook her head. "Isn't."

He reclined, and her voice soon stilled his thoughts. Into his mental quiet, she said, "Go back in time, back to when you were ten years old. You're standing with your uncle Walt in the backyard of the farm you lived on and you've been playing cowboys and Indians with your toy gun."

His mind's eye looked up from a ten-year-old height at his uncle, a husky man with a handlebar mustache and a twinkle in his eyes that Little Hank loved. His uncle pointed at him. "Mighty nice six-shooter you've got there, cowboy."

Little Hank settled his hand on the butt of the cap gun holstered on his hip. He smiled. It was a gift from his mom. He said, "Yep. It shoots straight, too."

"What do you shoot?"

"Bad guys."

His uncle leaned forward. "You know, I think I'd like to have a gun like that. Maybe I'll just take it."

Hank backed away a step. "No, you won't."

"Oh yeah? I'm a lot bigger than you."

Hank drew and aimed at his uncle. "You better not."

"You're going to shoot me?"

"That's what you do to bad guys."

His uncle grabbed for the gun, and Hank pulled the trigger. A cap banged, and his uncle grabbed his chest and fell to the ground. And then started the deep belly laugh that was so funny. "Got me!"

Little Hank holstered his gun and leaped onto his uncle, and was wrapped in a mighty hug.

Dr. Moore's voice intruded. "Now you're fifteen. It's your birthday, and your uncle has a present for you."

His birthday cake waiting on the dining room table, Uncle Walt came up to him, one hand behind his back, and said, "Got somethin' for you. It's the most valuable thing there is." He held out a gleaming new .22 rifle.

A rush of pleasure zoomed through Hank as he took the weapon. He brought it to his shoulder and sighted out a window, imagining drawing a bead on the rabbit that kept invading the truck garden. "Oh, man! Wow, Uncle Walt."

Hank lowered the barrel to point at the floor. Walt said, "This gift might look like a gun to you, but it's a lot more than that."

Hank studied the rifle and saw nothing extra about it. "I don't get it."

His uncle said, "It's freedom. Your freedom." He tapped Hank's chest. "Hold on to it, son. It's your God-given right, handed down to us by our forefathers to defend ourselves from tyranny." He gave Hank a hearty clap on the shoulder and said, "Now I gotta find me a cold beer."

Hank cradled the rifle to his chest and felt a surge of pride.

Dr. Moore soft voice came. "Hank, you will now return to the present. You will remember what happened. Three. Two. One. Wake."

Hank opened his eyes and stared at the memories that replayed in his head. They felt warm and good. He smiled.

The doctor nodded at his reaction. "The incident with the cap gun became your core 'teaching' about guns. Add to that many years of very positive events with your Uncle Walt. Your feelings about guns run deep."

She was attacking his very roots. "So? I feel what I feel, and I can't help that."

Her smile eased his mind. "Oh, there are many good things that stem from your relationship with your uncle—I think he's where your strong sense of honor comes from."

"So what's the point?"

"Those feelings fuel your conviction that all Americans have the right to own guns, all kinds of guns. But it doesn't have to be that way, if you agree to change."

His gut tightened. Was this what his fear had warned him about? "Change how?"

"Let us isolate that belief in your brain and eliminate it so you can consider the issues without being mentally handcuffed."

This was what Benson Spencer had let them do. And he was out of the Keep. He had a life. And he seemed just fine.

But there was more, wasn't there? "And the other part? You said I was a 'stone killer,' but I don't think I am."

"How did you feel about killing that man who attacked Noah Stone?"

He shrugged. "It was . . . necessary."

"But what did you feel?"

"Nothing much."

"What about the two men who attacked Ms. Washington in Chicago?"

"You know about that?"

She smiled. "I told you I was going to rummage around in your mind."

He shrugged again. "It was necessary."

"No regret? No remorse?"

"Why?"

She leaned forward. "That's what I'm getting at. Those people were human beings."

He scowled. "They were animals out to hurt people. Like rabid dogs. You put them down."

"Animals. That fits with what I learned from your memories."

He flashed on carrying Nick from the top of the Keep. "But it's not always that way. I didn't kill a man in the Keep who was pretty much an animal. And he attacked me. I could have killed him, but I didn't."

She nodded. "There's conflict between two models of right and wrong in your mind. One is rational and humane, but there's a deeper, antisocial model that trumps it." She gazed at him. "It is profound. Do you remember much of your childhood experiences with your father?"

He never thought about his father. Never. Then he understood. "He did this to me?"

"Sadly, he did. I found many incidents of . . . well, let's call it deep programming. To defeat it will, I'm afraid, take more than psychotherapy."

"What's 'more than psychotherapy'?"

"The same technique we'd use to eliminate your conviction about guns. Neurosurgery."

Now they were into the scary part. "You carve up my brain?"

She laughed. "Hardly. For one thing, we don't cut at all—we do stereotactic radiosurgery using a CyberKnife to ablate a tiny spot in your brain that we identify by using MEG, MRI, and fMRI."

"When did we stop speaking English?"

She laughed again. "Sorry. Stereotactic is a way to locate a precise point within your brain, and radiosurgery projects radiation into that location from outside—the CyberKnife is a robotic surgical instrument that's accurate to half a millimeter. Because it's noninvasive, you're ready to go the next day.

"MEG is magnetoencephalography, which identifies neural pathways and locations inside your brain. And fMRI is functional magnetic resonance imaging that also locates neural activity. Before surgery, we use hypnosis to stimulate the activity we want to locate and then we create a precise picture of its location. We use radiosurgery to eliminate it."

"Eliminate? Eliminate what? I don't think so."

"We've talked about your beliefs about guns. Even more harmful, though, is the way you dehumanize certain people."

What the hell was she talking about? He didn't dehumanize people, he protected them.

"Let me show you. I think you'll agree once you remember."

He had to will himself to relax into the recliner, but he managed. Her voice soon stilled his thoughts. Into his mental quiet, she said, "Go back in time, back to when you were six years old. You're walking along a street in downtown Peoria with your father. Can you see him?"

His mind's eye looked up from a six-year-old size at his father. A shabby John Deere cap shadowed his father's face, but Little Hank knew there was a frown there. His focus went to the part of his father's face that stood out most—his down-turned, sour mouth.

The doctor's gentle voice intruded. "Now you see Bernie Allen coming toward you."

Little Hank looked ahead and there was Bernie, walking toward them. Bernie was a funny guy who went to high school. Little Hank liked him.

His father said, "Look at the way the queer walks, Hank."

Little Hank wasn't sure what a queer was, but he'd felt the belt too many times in his six years to ignore an order. So he looked. Bernie kinda wiggled when he walked, but that was just the way he was.

Bernie smiled at him. "Hey there, Hank." Little Hank enjoyed the musical sound of his voice.

Before Little Hank could answer, his father lunged and grabbed Bernie's shirt with both hands.

"Keep away from my boy, faggot!" He slugged Bernie in the gut. When Bernie doubled over, Little Hank's father kneed him in the face, sending him crashing into a garbage can. Bernie sprawled on the sidewalk, gasping for breath and bleeding from his nose.

Grabbing Little Hank by an ear, his father forced him to stand over Bernie. His dad leaned close to Little Hank's face and glared with mean eyes. "That is an animal, boy, an animal that breaks God's law, rutting with other beasts who profane the Word of God."

He kicked Bernie in the head. "Animals that break God's law ought to be put down. Not just the queers and niggers and spics and Jews whose very existence is an insult to the Lord." Spittle flew from his father's mouth. "The thieves and fornicators, too, and those who visit violence on others, they are all animals, all doomed to the fires of Hell."

His dad stopped and knelt in front of Little Hank, his scowl triggering a wave of trembling in him. "There's real human beings, God-fearing righteous people like you and me, and then there's the animals. This world would be a whole lot better off without 'em, and don't you forget it."

Holding back tears, Little Hank nodded.

"What'd I say they were?"

Little Hank whispered, "Animals . . ."

"I don't hear you!" his dad screamed into his face.

Little Hank wailed, "They're animals."

"Wipe up them faggy tears."

His dad released Little Hank's ear and strode off. Little Hank trotted to keep up, trying to hold back a sniffle.

Dr. Moore's voice intruded. "Hank, you will now return to the present. You will remember what happened. Three. Two. One. Wake."

Hank opened his eyes and stared at the memory that replayed in his head. It sickened him. But it rang true. And there were scores like it echoing through his mind.

The doctor said, "That incident was just one of many times you saw your father use bigotry and brutality to dehumanize those he hated, and apparently he hated just about everyone. Those we can dehumanize, we can kill without feeling; it's the syndrome that enabled Nazi soldiers to take Jewish babies by the feet and smash their skulls against walls.

"I want to take away your ability to dehumanize people." She rested a hand on his forearm. "The question is, may we do it? Your medical advocate will make sure we do what we say."

His old fear of the government screwing with his mind whispered. *Escape. You can do it from here, easy. Right now. All you have to do is make your move.*

Then he thought of the desert he'd seen from the top of the

Keep, the desert that was just like his life. Escape wouldn't change that. He didn't want to live in a desert anymore.

"What if I don't do the surgery?"

"Psychotherapy is the only alternative. It could take months, a year, but I think we can get it done that way, too."

"You 'think'?"

"It's not as precise or definitive as the surgery."

They could cut out the part of him that was a monster? Life was too short for psychotherapy. And they were coming after Noah. "Let's take the shortcut."

She stuck out a hand to shake. "A man of action. I like that. Tomorrow?"

He shook her hand. "Tomorrow."

The next morning, Hank met his advocate, Dr. Oliver, another surgeon/shrink, a wise-looking man in his fifties with a face like a basset hound. Hank liked Dr. Oliver and thought he'd see the job done right.

After a session in the MRI tunnel and the MSR (which he'd learned meant "magnetically shielded room") for the MEG, Hank lay on an operating room table. A snootful of Valium made the room a pleasant place. Dr. Oliver, his hound-dog eyes easy to recognize above his mask, stood ready beside Dr. Moore. Hank gazed up at the doctors. Above his head, a white robotic arm whirred as it positioned itself.

Hank smiled. "It feels like I'm a new car on an assembly line."

Dr. Moore positioned his head with her hands and tightened a strap across his forehead that held it in place. "Just relax and hold still now. This will take only a few minutes."

A few minutes to change a lifetime. Hoping that he would wake up as himself, Hank closed his eyes and concentrated on Amy's necklace.

He woke on a hospital bed in a recovery room. Memory of what he'd been through surfaced. His mind was clear and sharp. As he listened to his thoughts, the mental "voice" inside his head sounded the same. His kinesthetic sense of body said that all was as it should be. As far as he could tell, he was the same.

As far as he could tell.

But his mind was not at rest. Unbidden, a memory of killing Earl Emerson appeared. If only Hank hadn't been contemptuous of stoppers—and Earl's right to live—Earl could be alive now, and maybe even well.

Earl faded away, and the two punks Hank had killed in Chicago came to mind. If Illinois had treated guns like Oregon, he could have just stopped them. Hell, Jewel could have stopped them. And maybe therapy could have started them on the road to becoming decent human beings. How many rapes and assaults could be prevented if people could defend themselves with weapons like stoppers? But he'd used a gun. To kill. Not to disable.

To put them down.

Marcie's anguished face appeared. In the world Noah Stone was creating, his wife might be alive now, well and loving him. But he'd used a gun.

Oh, how he missed her touches.

The haunts at last left him alone. He drifted off.

When Hank woke in his room the next morning, he lay still, eyes closed, searching inside to see if he was truly himself. Nothing seemed wrong or alien, but there was one change. He sensed the low, deep ache of his sorrow for Marcie and Amy waiting to come again.

But other than that he was . . . empty. His thoughts seemed to echo in a void, uncushioned by the presence of anyone else in his life. He'd once had a life—he could now summon memories of laughter and love.

He rose to ready himself for his last session with Dr. Moore. Along with the envelope of his belongings, his clothes were on the dresser, the same jeans and black T-shirt he'd worn when he arrived—and when he'd killed Earl Emerson in the park. Ah, if only . . . He shook off a sense of regret. Regret changed nothing.

But now he felt something.

Just as he finished dressing, a knock came and Dr. Moore's voice said, "Okay if I come in?"

Hey, the door must be unlocked. He opened it and tried a grin. "It's your hospital."

She closed the door behind her. "Let's see how we did."

He reclined on his bed and held Amy's butterfly necklace in his hand. Fear that it hadn't worked and he'd be sent back to the Keep crept into his mind. Well, apparently he wasn't completely empty.

She said, "I'm going to search for the memories and conditioning that supported your feelings about guns and human life."

In seconds, he went under.

It seemed like only a moment had passed when she woke him and said, "We've done it, Hank. I'll order up a police helicopter to give you a lift out of here. You can pick up your life where you left off."

He wondered where that was. "Doctor, I can't thank you enough."

"Hey, you're the one who made the tough decisions, I'm just the mechanic. Where will you go now?"

He blanked. Go? Where did an empty man go to be filled? There was nothing in Chicago except bad weather and bad memories. Ashland? He'd pretty much destroyed any welcome he had there. Hell, he wouldn't want someone around who killed and kidnapped people.

An image of sunlit waves crashing onto a beach popped into his mind. "In that video Arnie gave me, there was a place, something about the sea . . ."

She smiled. "Bandon-by-the-Sea. I love it there."

"Good spot to think?"

"Yeah. Look for a place called the Windermere. It's a funky old 1950s motel a stone's throw from the prettiest beaches you'll ever see." She gazed at him and then nodded. "You'll be okay. That's what I told Noah this morning."

"Noah Stone?"

"How many Noahs do you know? He called to ask about you yesterday. He was very pleased to hear you were doing therapy."

The information warmed Hank, and he wondered how anybody could be that . . . big? He slid off the bed.

"So where to?"

After the Keep, freedom and lazing on a beach sounded mighty good. But Noah was maybe the only friend he had in the world, and he didn't know people were out to get him. He said, "Ashland."

She grinned and then said "What the hell" and hugged him. He hugged back.

39 PRELUDE TO FEAR

As Mitch watched for his suitcase at a Medford airport baggage carousel, a woman's voice said, "Fancy seeing you here."

Colonel Hanson's eyes—beautiful and cold—greeted him. Her flannel shirt and pants had become a gray business suit and spike heels, her wavy black hair pulled back in a bun. He looked around to see if anyone was watching. No one appeared to be, but her standing next to him made him nervous. What if someone recognized her?

She solved his problem by reaching in front of him for a floral suitcase. As she extended the tow handle, she said, "I'm at the Ashland Springs Hotel under the name of Betsy Ross. Bring me the gun there." She looked him up and down. "And I don't socialize when I'm working."

Somehow, he was glad to hear that. She headed for the car rental counter, and he went back to watching for his bag.

At Rick Hatch's house, Mitch sat on the patio in the backyard, a cold beer in his hand. "I hear you've had your differences with Noah Stone," he said.

"That's for damn sure."

"I'm here on a mission to stop him. I need a gun."

Hatch shifted his gaze to the green hills across the valley for a time. "I don't think I want to do that."

Mitch sucked in a breath. "For God's sake, why not?"

Hatch looked to him. "I'll be straight with you. Even though I hate what he's done to our right to bear arms, things are gettin' better around here. My window-cleaning business is growing more than my gun business has dropped off. The more money comes into the valley, the more people can afford to have me do their windows." He glanced at the house; inside, his wife hummed as she worked in the kitchen. "And Betty tells me she feels safer these days." He chuckled. "She carries one of them pee shooters."

Mitch said, "You don't sound like a militia man, Rick."

"Times change." Hatch took a long pull on his beer. "No, I think I'm better off lettin' Noah Stone keep on."

Mitch sipped beer and took a moment to calm himself. "In your militia, didn't you take an oath to defend our country? The Constitution?"

Hatch stiffened. "Yeah."

"Then live up to it. Which one of your rights do you think Stone will take away next? Free speech?"

Hatch studied him. "This's a matter of principle for you, ain't it? Well, I'd be the last one to say you don't have a right to fight for what you believe in."

Mitch smiled and took an easygoing tone. "I'm not going to hurt him, Rick. Just scare him so he stops doing what he's doing."

Hatch said, "Well, I figure Stone's already done the hard part. I guess things'd be okay if he was, uh, out of the picture." He pushed up from his chair. "You just set there a minute." He shambled inside.

Mitch gazed at the hills across the valley but didn't really see them. If Noah Stone's new world could sway the likes of Rick Hatch . . . well, the country was in for a world of hurt if they didn't stop him.

The screen door swung open and Hatch stepped out holding a revolver. "Like I said, it's a matter of principle, and I got to respect that. I'm with anybody who wants to fight for the American way." He handed the gun to Mitch. "That's fifty bucks. Got five rounds in it. You gonna need more?"

The gun was heavy and cold. It felt deadly. He gave Hatfch fifty and said, "This ought to do." He stood and offered a hand to shake. "Thank you, Rick, for your service to our country."

Hatch took it. He blushed. "Yessir. I mean, you're welcome."

"It's too bad that no one else can ever know, but I will."

Hatch straightened and pulled in his paunch. "Duty's duty, I always say."

As Mitch drove to his motel, he thought about that. Yes, duty was duty, and it had to be done.

40 WHAT'S THE RIGHT OF IT?

In the Alliance lobby, Marion asked the pretty Hispanic girl if she could see Noah Stone.

"He's in a meeting..." The young woman squinted at Marion. "Don't I know you? Mister Soldado's trial, maybe?"

When Marion identified herself as the attorney general, the receptionist said, "Oh, I better let him know." After a brief phone call, she pointed to a spiral staircase and said, "Please go on up."

As Marion neared the top, a man's voice boomed, "This is crazy, Stone. Worse, it's socialism."

Another voice said, "Oh, come on, Adam. Socialism? That's such a tired old horse."

She stepped into the room and found Noah Stone and a stocky man sitting across from each other at a round coffee table. She said, "Mr. Stone?"

Stone stood and came to her with a smile and his hand out. "Madam Attorney General, it's good to see you." She shook his hand and was warmed by his welcome.

"I don't want to interrupt—"

"I think my friend Adam and I have reached an impasse." He took her elbow and guided her to the sitting area. The other man stood and Stone said, "Marion Smith-Taylor, meet Adam Jordan. He's your party chairman here in Oregon."

Jordan got to his feet and smiled. "I hope you'll have better luck than I did. This man is stubborn as a rock."

"Adam is upset about a bill we're working up to tie free health care to voting."

"It's social—"

"—ism," Stone finished. "I know what you think." He gestured to the coffeepot on the table. "A little heart-starter?"

Marion sat and poured a cup while Jordan said, "Noah, you can't force people to vote, no matter how good your intentions."

Marion said, "I don't know about that. Citizens in Australia are required by law to vote and fined if they don't. Did you know that ninety-five percent of citizens vote in Australia? Think of it. Ninety-five percent."

Jordan scowled. "This isn't Australia."

Stone sat next to Marion. "And we're not going to force anybody. What I propose is voluntary."

Jordan said, "It's bribery."

That got Marion's attention. "Bribery? With health care?"

"The idea," Stone said, "is to provide free health care to every citizen who votes—the state will pay their health insurance premiums. Their kids will be covered, too. A carrot instead of a stick."

"And if they don't vote?"

"Then they can buy insurance from a private company or through Obamacare."

Jordan jabbed a big finger at Stone. "Tell her about the forced exercise part."

Stone lifted his eyebrows as if to say "Spare me." "There's one other little requirement for the free coverage—you have to do a minimum of three hours of exercise a week."

Jordan folded his arms across his chest. "Kids, too!"

Marion said, "You have to exercise?" That sounded smart.

Stone stood and paced as he talked, passion in his voice. "Yes. We know that exercise makes you healthier. The healthier you are, the less medical care you'll need, the less money it costs you and the state. It's a win-win."

Jordan waved that away. "Unenforceable."

"I'd like to give the honor system a try."

Marion said, "Why require voting?" Then it struck her. "This isn't about health coverage."

Noah smiled. "You're good." He went to a window. "Out there, people are cut off from the whole of us, swamped by the struggles of daily life, turned off by powerlessness, adrift. You've heard people say their votes don't count."

He faced her. "During elections, we're so swamped with political babble that it's almost impossible to pay close attention, and too many of us let ideologues take over governing until it is too late. I believe that if you have to vote, you will think about issues, at least just a little. You'll be less likely to be a 'low-information' voter controlled by buzzwords and hate speech. If we all have a hand in what happens, that could bring us closer together."

Like everything Noah Stone advocated, it seemed to make sense, both socially and economically. She had to say, "I'd need to study the details, but I don't think there's anything legally wrong with your plan."

Stone turned to Jordan. "So, Adam, can I count on your support in the Senate?"

Jordan said, "My party would kill me."

Stone winked. "And your voters will love you."

Jordan grinned at that. "I'll think on it. That's all I can promise." He nodded at Marion. "Pleasure to meet you." He glanced at Stone. "Good luck with the mule." He gave her a wink, and he left.

Stone gazed at her. "I'm sure you didn't just drop by to learn about local politics."

Local politics? If this idea clicked, it could become national. She sipped her coffee and then said, "I want to understand why we're on opposite sides and maybe move toward a resolution."

"I don't see that we are on opposite sides."

She set her mug on the table. She couldn't talk about this without using her hands. "Let me be blunt. You are perverting the rule of law."

"I see myself as supporting the rule of justice."

"They're the same."

He shook his head. "Not at all. It was once the rule of law that you could enslave human beings." He pointed at her. "It was once the rule of law that women couldn't vote. Where's the justice in that?"

Trapped. She raised her hands in surrender. "Yes, there are bad laws. But we change them."

He clapped his hands. "Exactly! If the law isn't working to bring justice, then we change the law so that it does. We use the law to seek justice, not to make rules."

"But the Constitution—"

"—should be a living set of rules. Interpretation should stem from now, not the 1700s."

Marion couldn't disagree with that. Her quiver was empty. She stood. "I don't like to lose an argument, so I'm going to retire to my corner to lick my wounds and give this some thought."

He smiled. "You would make a great Ally." He strode to his desk. "But before you go, I want to ask you about this." He took something from a drawer and handed it to her.

It was a deer rifle bullet. On the brass case "Noah Stone" was printed. She looked up at Noah.

"It came in the mail. And I've seen it before." He went to his computer and clicked on a bookmark. A page that declared itself to be the Mackinac Militia site came up. Noah clicked a link, and there was a photo of the bullet she held in her hand, or at least one identical to it.

She said, "The Mackinac Militia? Is that the one headed by—"

"Colonel Martha Hanson." He clicked an "About Us" link and there was Martha Hanson staring out, grim-faced against a background of an American flag.

Noah turned to her. "Is this illegal? Can the law go after them?"

She weighed the bullet in her hand. "This was all that came? No threatening note?"

"That was it. I can't even prove it came from her. Except for the fact that there it is, on her website."

"I'll have to check it out," Marion said. "Can I keep this?"

"I sure don't want it." He turned to the computer screen. "That woman . . . I don't like to think about why she sent that bullet."

"Probably just a scare tactic."

His usual lively face seemed to sink in upon itself, and his shoulders sagged. "Well, it's working." He clicked away from the site and turned to her. He put on a smile and said, "Hey, you coming to my speech at the university tonight?"

Marion wanted to learn all she could about Stone. "I'll be there."

Joe Donovan knocked on the doorframe and stepped in. "Pardon the interruption, but . . ."

Marion said, "I'm finished. Thank you, Mr. Stone." She turned to leave, but Donovan's words stopped her.

"Dr. Moore called. Hank was released from the Keep. He's on his way here."

She turned back. "Is he . . . different?"

Noah said, "He has to be, or they wouldn't have freed him. But who knows how different? Or in what way."

Marion shook her head. As far as she could see, the guy was trouble.

It was afternoon when Hank pulled into the driveway to the Alliance campus. It paralleled a pasture where a couple of cows and a pony grazed. He saw a world far different from his earlier visits, not because it had changed, but because he had. He tapped his foot to the rhythm of Sheryl Crow's "Every Day Is a Winding Road" on the radio. Yeah, it was long and winding. But now he wanted to travel it.

The pony ambled to a fresh clump of grass, and he thought of how Amy would have delighted in it. If only Marcie hadn't been sick, there could have been so much joy in their lives. He was glad to find that the love he'd felt for Marcie was still there. She could be at rest now, in his mind.

He drove on toward the campus. A sense of arrival after a long journey energized him. And added a prickle of anxiety. What if Noah Stone didn't want him around? Well, he'd deliver his information and then go.

As he pulled into a parking space, he recognized a slender figure striding toward the Alliance legal department. Jewel Washington. He turned his head to avoid detection. Was he hiding from her? Yeah, he was. He'd done her wrong, and it wasn't easy to own up. He owed her. He owed Benson Spencer, too.

He watched her move on. He had to smile—what a fighter. In his new world, he'd like to get to know her. He grinned; he just might have totally screwed that up by killing her boyfriend and kidnapping her.

A line of dark clouds boiled over the mountains to the west, dimming the day. A gust of wind played with her skirt, and she hurried to enter the building. It was time to get his ass in gear. He got out and headed for the administration building. Hank didn't know if he had a place here, but he knew he didn't have one in Chicago. He'd never thought much about "belonging," but now he had a sense of missing out on something.

When he was a few yards from the door, Noah Stone burst out, trailed by Joe Donovan. Donovan was saying, "Noah, I need to talk to you about security for tonight's event."

Noah checked his watch. "You handle it. I'm late for an Alliance board meeting downtown."

"I can't brief you if you're not here."

"The ceremony's not until tonight. Catch me later."

Hank stopped and waited to be noticed. What would Noah do? How bad an idea was this?

Noah's gaze settled on him, and then he smiled. Tension Hank hadn't known was there slipped from his shoulders.

"Hank!" Noah strode to him and shook his hand. "Damn, I'm glad to see you!"

Feeling like a little kid whose favorite teacher had just given him a gold star, Hank said, "Yeah. Me, too."

Donovan stuck out a hand for a shake, and Hank took it. Donovan said, "Good to see you."

Noah's gaze appraised Hank. "You okay?"

Hank smiled. "Actually, never better."

"No hard feelings?"

"Quite the opposite."

Noah clapped him on the arm. "Damn, that's good to hear." He started down the walk and pulled Hank with him; Donovan followed. "You're coming back with us, right? Say yes."

Hank hesitated. "Well . . . I need to have a talk with you."

Noah's eyes seemed to twinkle with energy. "Great. There's a lot I want to talk with you about."

"This is about trouble. A man named Mitch Parsons is coming after you." At Noah's blank expression, Hank said, "He says it's just him, but he's NRA."

Noah shrugged. "So what's new?" They reached a fork in the walk. He paused and probed Hank with his gaze, then laughed. "We've got a future ahead of us, Hank, I promise you that."

Hank raised a hand. "Now, I told you when we met that I couldn't make that promise of yours."

"We'll see." He gripped Hank's shoulder. "Man, it's a great day!" He hustled away to the parking lot.

Donovan looked to Hank. "I can use your help with security tonight. Come on, I've got a meeting about it with the legal folks."

In the Legal Building, Hank recognized some of the people gathered in the second-floor lounge—Sally Arnold was there, and Benson Spencer. He didn't know a youngish man, or an older woman putting doughnuts and coffee on a table.

Donovan smiled as he announced, "Look who's back with us!"

Benson sped to Hank and pumped his hand. "Hank, Hank, Hank!"

Hank grinned, and then he sobered. "I owe you, Benson."

"What for?"

"You gave me the key." In response to Benson's puzzled expression, he clapped him on the shoulder and said, "Another time, over a beer or five."

Benson beamed. "I'd like that."

Sally said, "Good to see you."

Hank was liking this. "Yeah."

Donovan introduced Mike Potts and the secretary, Marge, then said, "Is Jewel going to help?"

In answer, Benson called, "Jewel! Time!"

Jewel emerged from an office with a frown on her face. "Sorry, I needed to get ready for—" Her eyes widened when she saw Hank.

He nodded.

She averted her gaze and took a chair.

Donovan poured a cup of coffee. "I've asked you folks here because we need people to help out at Noah's speech tonight."

Benson asked, "Help do what?"

"Just be extra eyes for us and let us know if anything looks suspicious."

Hank said, "Something is up?"

Joe said, "A top NRA guy named Mitch Parsons just flew in from the East Coast and then paid a visit to Rick Hatch, and the only reason we can think of to visit him is to get a gun." He gestured at Hank. "And Hank tells us he's after Noah. On top of that, Marion Smith-Taylor is here, too."

Sally cocked an eyebrow at Hank. "How'd you know about Parsons?"

Hank said, "He contacted me back in Chicago about working with him, but I went with Noah. The good thing is I'll know him when I see him." It was time to get off this topic. "What about the attorney general?"

"She's a puzzle," Joe said. "She came to see Noah, and he says he had a good conversation with her." He frowned. "But she still worries me. I talked to friends in the Justice Department, and the word is she wants to come after the Alliance but doesn't have legal grounds, and she's pretty pissed about it."

Mitch hadn't wanted to take action himself before, so why was he here? He seemed like a decent guy, and definitely not the type to shoot somebody. Hank wished he could call Mitch right then, but it would have to wait.

Joe asked the group, "Are you familiar with these people?"

Jewel said, "I met her, but not this Parsons guy." The others nodded.

Joe said, "Okay. Can you help us out?"

Benson said, "Sure," and everyone but Jewel said yes. She glanced at Hank, then said, "I . . . I don't know if I can get a sitter."

Donovan said, "Come if you can, but with Hank here I think we have enough. We'll meet at seven inside Daggett Hall at the university to assign positions. Many thanks."

Benson clapped his hands. "Back to it, people—we have that robbery to deal with."

Jewel hurried to her office. Hank followed and stood in her doorway. He said, his voice soft and low, "I want to say that I understand—no, more than that, I feel deeply how wrong what I did to you and Earl was. And I'm sorry."

She stared up at him. Her face could have been carved from mahogany.

He felt disappointment, then chided himself. What did he expect, a big hug?

She looked down at the papers in front of her.

He left. Downstairs, he called Mitch's cell phone number.

Mitch answered on the first ring. Hank said, "Hey, Mitch. I'm out and free."

"That's great! Too bad you're pretty much done with Noah Stone."

"Actually, no. I'm back in Ashland and helping him out."

Mitch's voice tightened, got a little higher in pitch. "Ashland? Really."

"Yeah. Same as you, I hear."

Silence. Then, "After I lost you, I wanted to see the enemy in person, you know, maybe get a better handle on what to do."

So he wasn't going to say anything about his visit to Rick Hatch. Had he gone there for a gun? "Listen, I'm going to be at a speech Stone is giving tonight, and—"

"Yeah, the dedication at the university. Hey, I'll just see you there."

Well, Mitch didn't seem to be hiding anything.

 **THE STORM HITS**

Jewel said to Chloe, "Forks go on the left, honey." Chloe placed a fork next to a plate and Jewel smiled. "The other left, sweetie."

Setting two more plates around the table, a twinge of sadness stirred when she passed the chair that had been Earl's regular spot. She called out to the kitchen. "It was creepy, Franklin, Soldado walking around free as a bird, nobody paying him no never-mind."

"I thought you wanted him out of the Keep."

"I just thought he got screwed. The guy's a fire lookin' for a place to start." Why the hell did he have to come back to her town?

She went to the window and gazed out. Rain clouds had gathered, but the neighborhood was peaceful. "I sure don't want him around here. Not after . . . you know. I mean, how would you feel if he got into your cab?"

Franklin looked up from pouring pancake batter into an electric skillet. They were having Chloe's favorite supper. "Weird. But he's done the therapy, and he's different now."

She returned to setting the table. "So they say. But I'm not!"

"You got to let that go."

"I can't." She set the last spoon in place and told Chloe, "Get yourself some milk, honey."

Chloe skipped into the kitchen and climbed onto a step stool to get a glass from a cabinet; Jewel followed and leaned in the doorway. "I can't feel for people the way the Alliance says."

Franklin flipped pancakes and then glanced at Jewel. "Maybe you could use a little therapy."

She gave him a glare. "There isn't anything wrong with me. But I don't know if I can work there if he's gonna be around. Donovan asked us for help at the speech tonight, but I felt weird about Soldado bein' part of it."

"Help with what?"

"Donovan seems to think Noah might be . . . there could be trouble."

Franklin turned and grinned at her. "So you a secret agent now?"

She smiled. "My girl-of-action days are over. They just wanted people to watch out."

"Just as well you didn't want to go. I got an audition that'll take 'til about eight."

Thunder rumbled through the house. She moved to the dining room window and watched sprinkles dot the glass. She pictured Hank Soldado. That afternoon he'd been . . . looser. "Soldado did seem different today. He even tried to apologize. But when I look at him, all I see is grief."

A flash of lightning flared. Thunder cracked. Raindrops spattered the window and then came hard.

Hank was surprised to see so many come out in a heavy rain to attend the dedication of Daggett Hall on the Southern Oregon University campus. There was even a camera crew from a Medford television station. Noah Stone had a lot of pull in this town. At ten minutes to eight, the auditorium swarmed with rain-soaked students and citizens. The crowd was happy, swirling, laughing, handshaking, smiling. Its hubbub roared up to the balcony where Donovan and Hank observed.

Hank had seen familiar faces—Judge Crabtree stopped by and welcomed him back, though she did scold him about what he'd done in her courtroom. But he'd spotted no one with a hint of the telltale tension that meant an attack. He hoped the therapy hadn't cost him his edge.

He touched the holster clipped to his belt, and then took out the stopper Donovan had given him. It hadn't taken but a few minutes to learn how to use it. He still had doubts about how useful it could be, though.

He stood beside Donovan in the upper tier; below them a broad aisle ran across the auditorium. From it, two aisles ran down to the stage, splitting the audience into three parts. Donovan had somebody from Legal at the two exit doors on either side of the stage. Sally Arnold, slim and attractive in a rare dress—a powder blue that went well with her eyes—swept her gaze back and forth from her position on the near side of the stage.

Donovan said, "Everybody's in place except Jewel. I guess she couldn't make it."

Hank pointed toward a back corner of the hall on the far side from where they stood. "Our esteemed attorney general." Marion stood near an entrance, scanning the crowd. He hoped she was going to leave Noah alone.

Then Mitch Parsons entered on the near side. He scanned the hall, and Hank gave him a little wave when they made eye contact. Hank said to Donovan, "There's Parsons. I'll go see if I can find out what he's up to."

Marion shivered and crossed her arms over her chest. It wasn't cold, it was the doubt that had been growing in her since her conversation with Noah Stone. Were the rules of law and justice not the same?

When she was a law student, she and her classmates had ridiculed professors whose minds had ossified into rigid views of the law and who would have no truck with the changes modern society demanded. Had her reflexive reverence for the rule of law led her to become as hardened as those professors? Noah Stone was right: slavery had once been the law, but it was hardly justice.

She spotted Hank Soldado moving toward the entrance on the other side of the auditorium. How could he be out of prison so soon? She'd fought the Oregon system that had put him there, but even though it wasn't the same rule of law she advocated, she'd come to admit that it had been justice.

Advocated. She had to give Noah Stone the win on that issue, too. His advocacy approach had gotten justice for Hank Soldado far better than the adversarial system she loved and hated could have.

What would her father say? As a defense attorney, he had relied on the protections of the Fifth Amendment for his clients. Yet he had been an honorable man, and she knew that the times his defense had freed a client who he knew was guilty had brought him sleepless nights.

Marion lifted her chin. All right, she'd see what Noah Stone had to say tonight. Maybe she did need to change. But what would the consequences be?

Jewel paced on Franklin's front porch. Rain poured down. Every time headlights appeared, she squinted into the darkness, hoping it was Franklin. Come on, come on, rehearsal had to be over by now!

The violence that seemed to explode around Hank Soldado had nagged at her, and she'd gone from uneasiness into a sure feeling that trouble was coming. Whatever she thought of the Alliance's promise, she cared about Noah Stone. She needed to be there tonight.

A car pulled up across the street and doused its lights. It sat there for a couple of long minutes, and then a big man got out and took a step in her direction. Franklin's cab swung around the corner and cut him off, and the man got back into his car.

Franklin pulled into the driveway, and she yelled into the house, "Chloe! Come on!"

Chloe ran out, ready in a hooded yellow slicker and rain boots. Jewel grabbed her purse off the porch swing and they ran for the cab, Chloe squealing as she splashed through puddles.

When Franklin opened his door to get out, Jewel shouted, "Take me to the campus?"

"Sure."

As they climbed into the cab, Jewel said, "Daggett Hall. Fast."

Franklin turned to her. "What's wrong?"

"I got a bad feeling."

✺

"And now," the dean said from the lectern on the stage, "a man who has devoted great time and energy to helping raise funds for this magnificent new facility, Noah Stone."

Hank reached Mitch. "Hey. Good to see you." He saw no tell-tale bulge of a holstered weapon under Mitch's jacket. He looked clean.

Mitch's response was less than enthusiastic. "Yeah. You, too." His voice was tight. So were his eyes, his body. Good ole Mitch was stressed about something. A murmur rose in the audience, and they turned to the stage.

Noah entered from the wings to applause that blossomed into a standing ovation. He greeted it with a smile. At the lectern, he held up his arms for quiet, and the audience returned to their seats. After his trademark pause, he said, "You honor me, and I thank you. But the honor truly belongs to thousands of others who have had the courage to change themselves and our world."

He gazed at the audience. "I'm known to be something of a Johnny-One-Note, so it may surprise you that I'm not here to recruit you for the Alliance." That earned him chuckles. "I'm here to thank you. Through your hard work and generous donations, the university has a new language arts center." He brought his hands together and applauded, and the audience joined him.

When the applause quieted, he said, "Although I'm not on a recruiting mission, I do have a few words for the students here. As you begin your adult lives, I ask you to do one thing.

"There are good people in this world who are having a tough time. They do the best they can, they work hard, often at more than one job, but things just don't get better. They need help to live a decent life, and they're not getting it in a world that's more against them than for them.

"So what I ask you to do is this: for their sake, and for yours, make the promise. Before you leave tonight, say and mean these words: I promise to help, the best I can."

He chuckled. "Now, I've been a youth, and I read Ayn Rand in college. I know that right now a bunch of you are thinking that the promise sounds like some kind of mushy altruism of the most virulent kind. Ayn Rand would have thrown up at the words of the promise."

Answering chuckles pattered up from the audience.

"But the truth is, and what Ayn Rand missed about the nature of a helping hand, that making this promise is just about the most blatant exercise of self-interest imaginable. It is this simple: when I make your life better, mine becomes better, too."

Franklin's cab splashed to a stop on Siskiyou Boulevard. He pointed into the darkness and said, "Daggett Hall's the big building on the left."

Jewel peered through the darkness and rain. A curving sidewalk led to the building twenty yards away—what the hell did she think she was doing here, anyway? Lightning flashed, and the boom of thunder prodded her to open the cab door. She gave Chloe a quick hug and said, "You go on home with Franklin, and I'm sure he'll read you some stories."

Franklin said, "You bet, Munchkin." His brow furrowed, and he looked to Jewel. "Hope everything's okay."

She tried for a reassuring smile. "I'm sure I'm just being weird. Prob'ly PMS. I'll call you when it's over." She stepped out and he pulled away, quickly gone into the rain and darkness. She trotted toward Daggett Hall.

Headlights hit her. A car bounced over the curb and slid to a stop on the lawn in front of her.

She dodged around it, but the driver's door was flung open and a bulky figure rushed her, arms outstretched. Floodlights from Daggett Hall gleamed off of Murphy's fat face, an ugly snarl warping his mouth.

Panic hit her. She spun to run across the lawn toward the building. Murphy plowed into her and sent her tumbling to the grass. She rolled onto her back and looked up.

Puffing, Murphy stood over her. He grinned. "Gotcha, bitch."

Rain stinging her face, Jewel stared up at him. Her stopper! She scrambled for her purse, snapped it open—

Murphy grabbed her wrist and yanked her arm up. The purse dropped, spilling its contents onto wet grass. Her stopper bounced to a puddle an arm's reach away. He snapped a handcuff around her wrist and hauled her to her feet. "You're goin' with me. Now."

He grabbed her other wrist and started bending her arm behind her. She fought, but his strength was too much. Chloe flashed into her mind, Chloe all alone. She wrenched, and her rain-slick skin slipped from his grip. She whirled, swinging her fist, but he stiff-armed her in the chest with both hands and knocked her onto her back.

He dove onto her, and her breath smashed out. She crashed her forehead into his nose. She heard the crunch of breaking cartilage. Murphy howled, rolled off of her, and grabbed for his face.

Jewel twisted, rolled to her stopper, and snatched it. Taking deep breaths to get her wind back, she stood.

Murphy staggered to his feet and turned toward her.

She mashed a button. A spray of whack hit him in the eyes, his howl turned into a shriek, and his hands went to his face.

Jewel's knees wanted to give way, but she steadied herself. As she backed away from Murphy, he wiped at his eyes. Squinting at her with one eye, he pulled a big black pistol from under his coat. It was no stopper.

She took careful aim and pressed the tangle button. The white, sticky stuff expanded and wrapped Murphy's hands and the gun, locking them together. Blinking against the rain and the sting of whack, he lifted the gun and swung it in her direction. A shot blasted, and she felt the bullet whip past her face.

Jewel lunged at him, her arm straight out. When her stopper was inches away, she pressed the last button. A dose of nap broke on the dry skin under his chin. She dodged back as he lifted his gun, and then kicked his hands away. His knees sagged. He dropped to the grass, then rolled onto his side and was still.

Jewel went to him. She shoved his shoulder with a foot to roll him onto his back. She knew he couldn't hear her, but she said, "I'll be callin' the cops." With that lethal firearm trapped in his hands, she knew he was going to be in a world of hurt—and then the Keep. She drew back a foot and kicked him in the balls with everything she had. A grunt whooshed from him, followed by a low groan. Let the hurtin' start now.

Lightning flashed and snapped her back to her mission. She grabbed up her stuff from the ground and jammed it and the empty stopper into her purse. Handcuffs dangling from one wrist, she ran for the entrance to Daggett Hall.

THE TRIGGER IS PULLED

Marion mouthed the words as Noah said them. I promise to help, the best I can. They touched her with . . . was it hope?

Noah said, "If you make the promise, you'll need the courage to change yourself." He grinned. "Man, do I know how hard that is."

The audience chuckled. Noah sobered. "In me, in you, in each of us are chains that bind us to old lessons and old reflexes. They can cripple our ability to move forward, to embrace the change we need. You can break them."

Noah's gaze came to Marion and he said, "I know you can break them."

Deep within her, Noah Stone's words resonated as true. There were times when chains—and rules—needed to be broken.

Mitch leaned close to Hank and said, "He's what I want to see broken." He scanned the crowd around them, and then glanced at the entrance on the far side.

When he turned back, there was a tiny smile in the corner of his mouth. Hank said, "What are you up to?"

On the stage, Noah said, "I have a little announcement for you tonight before we get to the punch and cookies."

Students said "Awwwwww" and the audience laughed.

Mitch's smile disappeared. "Just glad you're free again."

Hank's cop instincts twitched. A lie.

Marion stepped forward to get a better look. She collided with a woman hurrying toward the aisle that led to the stage. Marion stepped back and said, "Excuse me. I'm sorry."

The black-haired woman, a foot shorter than Marion, glanced up at her with a hard-eyed stare as though Marion were the smaller person. She moved on and turned down the aisle. Those eyes . . .

Marion knew those eyes.

Noah said, "This new center is named after Raymond Daggett, the storied political science professor who raised eyebrows during his entire career at SOU because of the way he spoke out for the people. In his honor, then, I have a political announcement to make.

"As you know, we're in the heat of a presidential campaign, and I've been asked over and over who I'm for. The Alliance board has met, and we have an endorsement."

Those eyes— The militia woman. Colonel Hanson. Marion had seen her on Noah Stone's computer monitor that morning. Along with a bullet that had his name on it.

The woman's eyes looked just like those of the guy who'd killed Suzanne.

And she was pulling a pistol from her purse as she marched toward the stage.

Not this time! Marion ran down the aisle after Hanson.

Hank decided to get next to Noah, because the endorsement he was about to make would cause an uproar. He headed across the space in front of the stage.

He was halfway to Noah when a woman in the far aisle called out, "Noah Stone!" She raised a pistol above her head. "We want our rights back!"

It was Colonel Hanson—crazy Colonel Hanson. Hank yelled "CLEAR!" at people milling in front of him and sprinted toward her aisle. He pulled his stopper from his holster, but people jumping to their feet blocked his shot.

She fired into the air. He lowered his head and ran harder.

⌘

Mitch flinched at the gunshot and then laughed. That ought to do it. Noah Stone would run screaming from the stage. Mitch clapped his hands. He'd done it!

⌘

The sound of the shot struck Noah like a fist. He searched for the source—there, in the aisle, it was that militia woman! Fear ripped into him and he started to back away, and then the screams of the audience broke through. People could be hurt in a stampede.

He stepped forward, spread his arms out, palms down, and called out to the audience, "Be calm. Help is on the way."

⌘

Marion cried, "No-o-o-o-o-o!"

Colonel Hanson glanced back at her, then faced Noah and aimed the gun at the stage.

Marion ran as hard as she could, knowing that she was too late.

⌘

Hank closed on the aisle . . . two more strides . . . he leaped upward with all of his strength. As he turned in the air, rising in front of Noah, he looked up the aisle and down the barrel of Hanson's pistol. She wouldn't miss. Above the gun barrel her eyes glittered just like those of the guy in Chicago when he went for Noah. They glittered, they narrowed . . . She pulled the trigger.

The bullet hit his left shoulder and spun him.

Hank hit the floor on his belly, and his right hand smashed down. His stopper spun away, out of reach. Hanson didn't even look his way. The tendons on the back of her hand stood out as she squeezed the trigger again.

Noah stared at the gun centering on him. The crowd noise dimmed, and calm settled into him. He shifted his gaze to Colonel Hanson's hard eyes. To her he said, "I promise to help, the best I can."

Hanson screamed, a full-throated primal blast of fury, and pulled the trigger.

There was a bang, a hammer slammed him in the chest, and he fell backward.

Mitch gasped. That wasn't supposed to happen! He shook his head as if he could deny what he'd just seen, but that didn't stop horror from flooding his mind.

Hank surged to his feet, his shoulder a blaze of pain, but he could use the arm. He dove onto the stage and crawled to Noah.

Noah still breathed. Hank ripped Noah's shirt open and stared at a bloody hole in his chest, way too close to his heart. Blood pumped out. Hank raised his head and roared, "I need a doctor!"

A man somewhere shouted, "Here!"

Hank leaned close. "A doctor's coming. You'll be okay."

Noah's gaze went to the blood on Hank's shoulder and then to Hank. He smiled. "We have just *got* to stop meeting like this."

There was no smile in Hank, but he tried. "I will if you will."

Noah looked into Hank's eyes, deep sadness filling his own. He said, "There's so much left to do. Help me." He gasped and then stopped breathing.

Hank started CPR.

⁂

Jewel smashed through people at the top of the aisle. Hank knelt beside a man on the stage . . . He was doing CPR. Noah!

Ahead of her, Marion Smith-Taylor flew down the aisle toward the stage—toward a small woman who held a gun. Jewel raced after Marion.

⁂

Marion screamed. The woman turned toward her and shot.

The bullet slammed into Marion's neck—

⁂

It seemed to Mitch that the woman running at Hanson fell in slow motion. This couldn't be real.

He ran to the aisle.

⁂

After a check of pulse and a look into Noah's eyes, the doctor looked up at Hank, his expression stricken. "He's dead."

A young woman screamed, "Noah's dead!" More screams spread through the audience alongside bellows of anger. Men raised their fists but had no one to hit.

Jewel jumped over Marion's body, dove for the shooter, and crashed into her.

They fell, Jewel on top, gripping the woman's wrist to force the gun against the floor. It fell from her hand, and Jewel stared into wide, insane eyes.

43 FURY

Loss swept through Hank. It emptied him, and then rage filled his mind. He stood and looked up the aisle. People had backed into the rows of seats, leaving the aisle clear. Mitch Parsons ran down from the top toward a woman who lay on her back in the aisle. It was Marion Smith-Taylor.

The shooter sprawled on the floor, pinned by Jewel Washington, the pistol beside them.

Hank vaulted from the stage and bolted toward them as Jewel pulled Colonel Hanson to her feet. The violence Hanson had begun flared into a storm of fury. The crowd roared.

He tore Hanson from Jewel's grasp and spun her to face him. Her wide eyes narrowed, and she stared at him with a flat, cold gaze. He closed his hands around her throat. She grabbed his wrists with her little hands. He was going to crush her larynx with his thumbs. He wanted her to suffer—he squeezed, but slowly.

Around him, faces were masks of loathing; fists clenched and unclenched, eager to crush something, anything. Mouths opened and shut. Hank heard only the pounding of his pulse in his ears.

Jewel yelled something that got through. "Kill her!"

He would do that. Hanson's pistol lay on the floor. Yes. That would be justice. Gripping Hanson's neck with one hand, he stretched down and picked it up.

Hank shoved the barrel deep into the soft flesh under her chin. Her eyes widened with what looked like the first hint of fear he'd seen from her. He tightened his finger on the trigger.

Noah's dying words whispered inside his head. "Help me."

A killer couldn't do that.

The screaming faces around him were like those he'd seen in the Keep—bestial. But these were the people Noah had asked to make a promise to help. Hank's rage ebbed. What would Noah do now?

He'd try to help them, wouldn't he?

Suddenly, as though a switch had been turned on, the cries of the crowd crashed in on him. Jewel's scream hit him full force. "Kill the bitch!"

Shouts came from all around. "Shoot!" "Shoot!" "Shoot!"

One hand still on Hanson's throat, Hank lowered the pistol and stared at it. He'd loved guns and all the good things that came from them his entire life. But this thing in his hand was no more and no less than a metal tool made for killing.

He threw the gun as hard as he could, and it slid across the stage to dark recesses at the back. Hanson was safe. From him, at least.

Jewel screamed at him, "What are you waiting for?" She forced her body between Hank and Hanson and reached for her throat.

Hank grabbed Jewel's wrist, yanked her away, and twisted her to face him. "That's not the way!"

She screamed into his face, "It's my way!"

"It's wrong!"

"Not by me!"

Hank released her and pointed at the stage. "It is by him!"

Jewel stared at Noah's body, the doctor kneeling beside him. The rictus of hatred contorting her face collapsed into confusion.

⌇

No words came to Jewel. No words to deny what had happened. No words to call back her insane craving to kill Hanson. Had there been a gun in her hand, Hanson would be dead. Why hadn't she picked up the pistol?

Jewel didn't feel that killing Hanson would have been wrong. But she knew what the man who lay dead on the stage would say. And he would be right.

She watched as Hank gripped Hanson's arm and towed her toward steps that led onto the stage. People lunged for her with hands like claws, but Hank put his body between her and her attackers and stiff-armed them away.

On the stage, he led her to the lectern. The audience roared its bloodlust, and Hanson faced it, head high, defiant. Jewel stood mute, void of rage . . . and everything else.

Hank raised one hand; it took minutes, but the audience quieted. He spoke into the microphone on the lectern. His voice low, he said, "This . . ." He glanced at Hanson, and his expression softened. To the audience, he said, "This human being—"

The audience bellowed denial that she was one of them. But Jewel knew she was. She knew what it felt like to want to kill. She gazed at Hank as he waited for quiet. His face seemed calm, but how could that be?

When the crowd wound itself down, he said, "This human being has just killed"—he pointed to Noah's body—"that beloved—" His voice choked off, and now his face revealed his anguish. The crowd remained mute.

His sorrow touched Jewel, deep, deep down. Her throat tightened. This was not the man who had killed Earl.

After a long moment, Hank finished. ". . . killed that beloved and benevolent man."

Hanson turned to Hank, her expression hard and icy. Then the corner of her mouth ticked up in a tiny grin. Jewel saw Hank's fist clench, and she hoped he would smash Hanson in the face.

A white-haired man screamed, "Hang the bitch!" Others echoed his cry. Yes!

Hank relaxed his fist and raised his hand high. Quiet returned. He stood straight, two glistening trails of tears down his cheeks. He said into the stillness, "I promise . . . to help . . . the best I can."

Jewel stared. How could he do that? Where did he find the strength?

She'd once said she'd never seen a miracle. But this . . .

The silence deepened as if the audience held its breath.

Jewel gazed up at Hank, and tears flowed from her eyes. She had felt the wrath in him when he held Hanson's throat and had shared it, had wanted him to crush the life out of the woman. But somehow he had conquered it. If he could do that . . .

Her mama's advice surfaced. "You got to be hard. Ain't nobody there for you but you." But Noah Stone had been there for her. And Franklin. And Hank Soldado.

Hank's gaze found her. He said again, this time to her, "I promise . . . to help . . . the best I can."

The promise. Oh, if only the promise could be true! A knot inside her loosened, opening the way for his words to reach her. Hank had it right. Noah had it right. Jewel strode to the stage, vaulted up, and went to Hank's side.

He turned to her. Through his sadness, he smiled. Then he turned back to the audience. Jewel lifted her chin, faced the silent crowd, and added her voice to Hank's. "I promise . . . to help . . . the best I can."

Footsteps thudded on the stage, and Donovan and Sally added their voices to the chorus. The doctor stood and said the words.

Judge Edith Crabtree, streaks of tears glistening on her cheeks, made her heavy way onto the stage and joined Hank on his other side. She said the litany.

The woman whose husband had shouted, "Hang the bitch!" said the promise. She tugged on her husband's shirt until he joined her.

Singly, and then in twos and threes, and then by the score, the members of the audience said the words.

Mitch knelt in the aisle, cradling the woman's head in his hands. Her eyes were shut, and her neck poured blood. He tried to stop it with his fingers, but . . . He leaned close and said, "Ma'am? Ma'am?"

The woman's eyes flickered open. Her gaze lifted past him and looked far away. She whispered "Oh, Suzanne" and smiled.

And then she stopped breathing.

Around him, people chorused something, but it was just a blur of noise. He stared at the woman.

The color seemed to fade from her face. Her eyes stared up, vacant now.

He laid her head down and gazed at his hands. Her blood dripped from them.

He looked up at the dead man who lay on the stage.

Jesus, what had he done?

He tried to wipe the blood off on the floor. He rubbed. And rubbed.

What had he done?

 **KEEPING THE PROMISE**

Alone in his hotel room, Hank flicked on the TV to catch the afternoon news. Maybe it would take his mind off the bone-deep ache in his shoulder. The pain meds were too tempting—he'd seen a lot of guys live through a hit and die from the dope. Speaking of dope . . . he loaded a pipe with a bud from a friendly local marijuana dispensary—high in CBD and lower in THC—and took a toke. Soon the hurt was still there, but it wasn't such a bad thing anymore.

For three days, he'd watched the media turmoil surrounding the assassination of Noah Stone roil and bubble. Unfounded stories of cult rituals and the failure of the Alliance were hurting good people, but he could think of nothing to do. He'd had to change rooms and register under a pseudonym to avoid reporters slavering after him like hounds after a fox.

Hank stood and stretched his good arm, the other at rest in a sling, and then winced. The Chicago wound hadn't opened up, but it was tender. He'd been lucky. Emotion tightened his throat— Noah's last words flashed into his mind. "Help me."

No, he had to stay away from that, it was too fresh, and too powerful.

A flash of light from the dresser caught his eye. Sunlight glittered off his daughter's necklace. He lifted it and stroked the chain with his thumb. So delicate, so fragile, like the child who once . . .

He let the pain rise, and then tried to counter it with the sweetness of her memory. That almost worked. He slipped the necklace into his pocket, went to his window, and gazed out at the green hills and slopes of Ashland under a sky the blue of wildflowers. A beautiful place to be . . . except it wasn't his place. You needed people to belong to a place.

He touched a ring of many colors on his right hand. After Hank made the promise, Benson Spencer had insisted on giving him the Alliance ring Noah Stone had worn. Dreams of Noah's dying face still woke Hank in the night.

Hank turned to his open suitcase. He'd been packed for days. But he had no place to go. And no place to stay. Feeling caged, he rigged his sling and headed out.

Outside, the sun warm on his shoulders, he entered Lithia Park and strolled over a stone bridge. Children tossed bits of bread to the white swan that ruled the pond beneath the bridge.

The sidewalk wound past a lawn where Frisbee players dashed for discs, through the cool shade of tall trees, and skirted Ashland Creek. At a shallow spot, children waded in the rocky streambed and splashed crystalline water while their mothers sat in the sun and chatted.

Hank came upon a playground, and a flash of brown skin snagged his attention. It was Jewel, talking Chloe down a slide. Chloe gave a push and zoomed down to Jewel's waiting arms. She giggled, squirmed free, and raced to climb the slide ladder. Jewel clapped her hands and said, "You go, girl."

Hank slipped behind a tree. He didn't want to upset either of them, and he was sure the sight of him would screw up their fun.

On a sunny summer day at the Lincoln Park Zoo, Amy had ridden on his shoulders and chattered about the pigs and cows and ducks in the Farm-in-the-Zoo. He'd set her down in the petting pen and hovered over her, ready to yank her away from a rambunctious animal. She had petted goats and sheep, and so had he, marveling at the soft feel of wool in its natural state. The memory was warm.

Music started up not far away, and Chloe pointed in its direction. The answer to her question was yes. At a distance, Hank followed them.

At the band shell, a group of seniors pumped out the happy rhythms of Dixieland jazz. They were damn good, and soon attracted a couple dozen people. Jewel sat on the grass, and Chloe danced around her.

When Jewel had taken the auditorium stage to join him in the promise, there'd been a connection between them. He wondered . . . No, that wasn't going to happen.

He turned away and headed back to Main Street. Maybe he'd see a play tonight and then think of where to go tomorrow.

Jewel caught movement out of the corner of her eye and turned in time to see Hank Soldado walking away. She wondered if he'd seen her. Yeah, must have, and no doubt didn't want to have anything to do with her. After sending him to the Keep, she sure couldn't blame him for that.

But that night in the auditorium— She gazed at the sling that cradled his left arm. If only she could tell him, show him how what he'd done set her free to embrace the way of life Noah had offered.

She turned to watch Chloe's antics, but the picture that came to her mind was the wistful way Hank had watched Chloe when he first met her on the Alliance campus. Knowing his history, Jewel understood the longing she'd seen in his eyes and the tears that had spilled. She'd been pretty much wrong about the man six ways from Sunday.

Glancing at his retreating figure, she wished she could help him. She twisted the multicolored Alliance ring she'd added to the collection on her fingers, a gift from Benson Spencer. She laughed at herself. Damn, this promise thing was gettin' to her. But that wasn't all bad, was it?

Chloe danced close and Jewel grabbed her. She crushed her with a hug, fireworks in her heart for the joy in the life she now had.

⚬⚬

At ten o'clock the next morning, Hank's hotel room phone rang. Benson Spencer's energy sizzled out of the receiver. "Hank, Hank, can I grab you for a meeting?"

Hank smiled at an image of Benson pinballing from meeting to meeting. "Depends on who with and what for."

"The Alliance board."

What? Hank said, "What?"

"The Alliance board would like to talk to you."

It couldn't be security, Donovan and Sally were handling that. "Tell me why."

"Nope. How about you trust me on this?"

Benson had him there. "Would buying you those beers I promised do instead?"

Benson laughed. "No, but I'll take you up on the offer after the meeting. Come to Noah's offi—ah, the tower office at ten thirty?"

The man wouldn't be denied. "Ten thirty it is."

When Hank got out of his car at the Alliance campus, the people he passed walked with heads down and shoulders slumped. Well, the Alliance had lost its heart, hadn't it?

He went to the main building—barefoot Becky was on the job, but her smile made it only halfway before it died. He climbed the circular stairs to the office atop the tower.

The place looked naked without Noah's clutter. Benson paced by the windows, and sitting around the coffee table were five people; he recognized three. Judge Edith Crabtree. Faruq Al-Kadri, the Palestinian. And Joe Donovan, who stood and came to him for a handshake.

Joe said, "Shoulder going to be okay?"

Hank nodded and took in the other two people there. A slight Asian woman and a bearded giant of a man were people he'd glimpsed on the campus.

The Asian woman stood and smiled. "Mr. Soldado. Thank you so much for coming. I'm the chairman pro tem, Hoshi Anderson. Coffee?"

"Don't mind if I do."

Al-Kadri fidgeted. "I still don't see what a former security guard can do for us. Our problem is not security, it is how to resurrect a dead body." The bitterness and pain in the man's voice touched Hank.

Benson zipped to the coffeepot and poured a mugful. "'Scuse me, Faruq, but when did the Alliance become a dead body?" He took the coffee to Hank.

"The day Noah Stone died." Al-Kadri loosed a sigh. "He was the heart and soul of us. We were all killed."

Judge Edith glowered at him. "Wrong. The promise is the heart and soul of the Alliance, and it's alive and well." She turned to Hank and smiled. "Good to see you again, Mr. Soldado."

"Me, too, ma'am." What the hell was going on here?

Al-Kadri gave Edith a nod. "All right. I will give you that. It is what Noah would say." His voice tight with anguish, he said, "But we have lost our leader. Our leader! Whom do we follow now?" He pointed at Edith. "You?" He swung his gaze across the other board members. "Any of us?"

Benson pointed at Hank. "Him."

Hank said, "What?" Benson couldn't be serious.

The bearded man spoke, his voice a rumbling bass. "Hold on, here." He glanced at Hank. "No offense, Mr. Soldado"—he eyed the other board members—"but since when is a convicted killer qualified to lead the Alliance?"

Benson raised his hand. "Since right now."

Donovan faced the board members. "Same for me."

"Okay," said the big man, "but your say-so isn't enough. Not for this."

Edith Crabtree said to him, "I think I know what is enough, Gordon, and I think it's the reason Benson and Joe brought Mr. Soldado to us." She eyed the two, and then turned her gaze to Hank. "It's what happened in that auditorium after Noah was shot."

Donovan nodded and Benson said, "Yes."

Hoshi sucked in a breath, and then said, "Of course. The promise."

Edith said, "If I've ever seen a lynch mob, that was it." She shook her head. "I was ready to tie the hangman's knot myself, and I'm a founding member of the Alliance—and a Black one, to boot." Her gaze settled on Hank. "And then your words—Noah's words—reached me."

Gordon said, "So he calmed a crowd down—"

"He turned the promise into a living, healing thing!" Edith's eyes glittered. "I have never witnessed anything like it." She gazed at Al-Kadri. "Noah could have done it."

Hoshi said, "I will always be ashamed of how I wanted to . . . kill that woman." She shuddered, gazed out at the mountains, then straightened and faced them. Her chin lifted. "Then this man opened his soul to us and made the promise."

Hank didn't think of it that way. He'd just done what felt right.

Hoshi's eyes moistened. "I'll be forever grateful, Mr. Soldado. And I hereby nominate you as chairman of the Alliance, to take up the duties and responsibilities once held by Noah Stone."

"Wa-a-a-i-t a minute," Hank said.

Donovan and Benson chorused, "Second the motion."

Edith smiled at them. "You're not board members." She leveled her gaze at Hank. "But I second the motion. Any discussion?"

Al-Kadri shook his head. "I do not believe." He gazed at Hank.

Hank set his coffee mug down. "Damn right there's discussion, and I'll start it by saying I think you people are nuts."

Donovan said, "We're just doing what Noah would have wanted."

Benson ceased pacing and settled next to Donovan. "Noah had such hope for you, Hank."

With effort, Edith pushed up from her chair and came to Hank. She took his hand and tapped his Alliance ring. "You made the promise, didn't you?"

"Yeah."

"Mean it?"

"Yes, but—"

She said, "This is how you help the best you can."

How could he make these people see? Maybe the truth would do it. "Look, I was sent here by a man who wanted Noah Stone gone."

Edith said, "Do you mean dead?"

He thought about it. "No. But that was the result."

Gordon said, "Aha!"

Benson said, "Yet you saved Noah. Twice."

"Yeah, I did, but—"

Edith stepped closer. "Why?"

Why? He didn't know. He shrugged.

The judge said again, "Why?"

She liked to put people on trial, didn't she? "I don't know," he said.

She gazed at him, her dignity and strength undeniable. "That's not good enough. You will tell me why."

Hank searched inside himself. It burst from him. "It wasn't right!"

Edith nodded. "A good start. But why was it wrong?"

She pinned him with her gaze. He dug deeper. He saw Noah Stone's hand extended to him, to help. And he saw how his help made both of them stronger, and how that strength rippled out, person to person.

He said, partly with joy for what he'd found, partly with anguish for what he'd lost, "Because when we help each other, we help ourselves." The promise was two-way. "Living the promise is more honest than altruism, more real than that, more human than that."

He pointed to the judge. "I help you"—he shifted his aim to Gordon—"you help him, it builds." He pointed to himself. "It comes back to me. That's the way it should be. And if it was . . . what our lives could be."

He gazed at each of the board members. "The promise is the answer if we have the guts to make it and to keep it."

Benson and Donovan smiled.

Al-Kadri said, "Now I believe." He turned to Hoshi. "I call for the vote."

Hank wondered if these people had any idea what they were asking. He said, "I don't think you want to do that."

Edith turned her wise eyes on him. "After what you just said? Why not?"

"I'm not qualified. What Noah did was too . . . too valuable to turn over to an amateur."

Benson pointed at Hank. "You're wrong. The night Noah died, I saw you become the promise. You reached out with all the power you brought to the promise and pulled an auditorium of bloodthirsty people to you. You helped them."

Edith nodded. "Benson has it right. It is the promise that must light the way." She smiled. "And, Hank baby, you shine!"

Could they be right? He gazed out the window at the green hills across the valley and imagined he was sitting down across from Noah. "What would you do?"

Noah said, "I can't tell you what to do, but after I thought long and hard about the problems we have with guns and strife, it came to me that maybe I had a duty."

When it was put that way, Hank couldn't argue. Any decent member of society had a duty to try to make things better. He scanned the room. All eyes were on him. They thought he could do this. *Should* do this.

It was his duty, wasn't it? To Noah. To Jewel. To Chloe.

After another hour of wrangling, Hank agreed to give it a try. Then, his shoulder screaming at him to give it a rest, he decided to get someplace where he could sort out his thoughts and feelings. He told the board, "The new chairman is going on a retreat. See you tomorrow."

They protested that there was a lot to do, but he was soon down the spiral staircase and outside. On the way to the parking lot, he saw Jewel on a bench in the shade of an oak tree, eating a sandwich, a brown paper sack beside her. She looked up and, to his surprise, gave a little wave. He walked to her.

She said, "Hey" and pointed to his injured arm.

Before she could ask, he said, "It'll be okay."

"Good." Her gaze flicked to the administration building and back to him. "You working with the Alliance again?"

He laughed. "I guess you could call it that." He discovered that he wanted to talk with her about it. He hadn't had anybody to talk to since . . . since his wife . . . since Marcie. "Listen, can I interest you in a cup of coffee after work?"

She shook her head. "I'm afraid I can't."

Oh, well.

She continued. "Got a going-away party for Franklin." She chuckled. "A TV producer offered him the lead in a new sitcom about a gay taxi driver."

Hank chuckled at the irony. "Well, if you think it's okay, wish him luck for me."

"I think he'd like that."

This was going nowhere. He said, "Well, I gotta go clear my head." He turned away.

Her soft voice stopped him. "About that coffee . . ."

He turned back.

Her smile was warm, her gaze direct and open. "Ah, you'll ask me again, right?"

He grinned. "Oh, yeah."

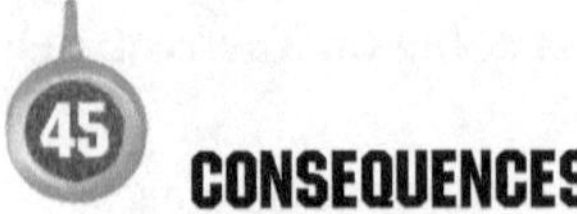

CONSEQUENCES

Mitch sat back in his recliner as he watched the press conference in Ashland get under way, but his gut was snarled up the way it had been since . . . since he'd had a hand in the murders of two people. Nobody had connected him to the colonel, and he hoped to God that they never did. He prayed every day to forget that awful moment, but it was still all there, all the time. Along with guilt like lead weighing ever heavier on his soul.

An announcer from the television caught Mitch's attention with the words, "And now to our coverage of the Alliance press conference in Ashland, Oregon."

Carrie skipped in. "Hey, Daddy. What are you watching?"

"News." He shifted in the chair and patted a spot next to him. "Come watch with me." She snuggled next to him.

The picture cut to Bruce Ball, the network reporter. Behind him was a low stage with a microphone stand. The stage was outdoors, with a backdrop of green hills. It was a sunny, cloudless day. He guessed there must be a hundred people, including a dozen reporters with microphones bunched up front, close to the stage.

Ball said to the camera, "This is the first public appearance by the new head of the Alliance, Hank Soldado, after the shocking murder of the U.S. Attorney General and the assassination of the organization's leader, Noah Stone, on the campus of Southern Oregon University. The aftermath that propelled Mr. Soldado to leadership in the Alliance was caught on amateur video."

Cut—the picture changed to Hank Soldado, standing on the auditorium stage, speaking into a microphone, lines of people stretching out from him on both sides. Bruce Ball's voice-over said, "After the killing of Noah Stone, Soldado, although wounded in trying to prevent the murder, led the audience in something the Alliance calls 'the promise.'"

The clip rolled, and Mitch was sucked back to that auditorium at the words of the promise. The whole audience said it with Soldado.

Ball gazed into the camera. "After her inquiry, the assassin, Colonel Martha Hanson, was sentenced to the Oregon Women's Keep for life."

An image of Marion Smith-Taylor's blood dripping from his hands slammed into Mitch's mind. He grunted with the force of it, then clenched his teeth and willed his focus back to the television. But he knew the horror would be back.

Carrie turned to him, her expression worried. "Daddy?"

"I'm fine, honey, I'm fine."

At the Alliance press conference, a Black man who looked like a football player stepped onto the stage and scanned the crowd. Mitch spotted the tension of a pro searching for danger. Must be Donovan, Soldado's head of security.

The man gestured to the side of the stage, and moments later Hank Soldado strode onstage, dressed in casual slacks and a sport shirt, one arm in a sling. He looked strong and capable, in charge.

He stood before the microphone and gazed at the crowd. The picture zoomed in for a close-up. Recognition of the intensity in Soldado's eyes startled Mitch. He'd seen its like before . . . in Noah Stone on the night of his speech at McCormick Place.

Hank said, "I'm here to reassure all members of the Alliance that we will stay true to the mission begun by Noah Stone." It seemed to Mitch that Soldado's gaze was leveled directly at him. "There are those who thought that what Noah started would end with him. I'm here to tell you that it won't."

Mitch glanced at Carrie. She seemed enraptured by Hank.

Hank scanned the crowd. "The Alliance will keep making the promise, and continue to keep it. That promise gave new life to me, and it can give new life to all of us. The promise is this—I promise to help, the best I can."

Carrie looked to Mitch. "That sounds nice. Doesn't it, Daddy?"

He sighed. "Yes, honey, it does. It does."

Hank said, "Noah was taken before he could do all the things he had planned to help each of us, all of us, onto the road to a better life. One of the things he was most excited about was the announcement he was to make a few days ago.

"The Alliance, by vote of its board and the overwhelming support of its members, endorses Governor Alan Thomas, candidate for president of the United States."

The audience before Hank burst into cheers and applause. Red-white-and-blue signs popped up that said, "Thomas for President."

"We believe that Governor Thomas, as president, will help our nation move forward toward greater justice and greater safety." He gazed into the camera. "Especially as far as guns are concerned."

After what had happened to Noah Stone, Mitch thought Hank had all kinds of guts to stand there, exposed, and say that.

Hank said, "And now I'll take your questions."

Carrie turned to Mitch, her brow wrinkled. "What does he mean about guns, Daddy?"

Mitch clicked the remote and Hank vanished. He took out a mini Tootsie Roll. After raised eyebrows from Carrie, he handed it to her. "It means, sugar, that we're going to have a long talk about guns and their place in our lives." He smiled. "But not today. Why don't you run along and see what your little brother is up to. I've got some thinking to do."

He had some things to make up for, and signing up for the promise was a place to start.

After a half hour of being peppered with questions, Hank held up a hand. He was uncomfortable with the assault by hungry reporters, though he gave honest answers. And the pain in his shoulder had flared up. "That's it, folks. Many thanks, and a good life to you." He did not like this part of the job.

The reporters kept yammering questions, but Hank had no trouble turning away. He headed off the stage and smiled at the sight of Jewel waiting for him, Chloe at her side.

PARTING SHOTS

I did not publish this book to argue about guns

I did it to stimulate thinking about gun violence, self-defense, and our criminal justice system.

Gundown offers thought-starters. not prescriptions for cures. It is about community and the promise.

Our common ground

Whether for or against guns, we all have one thing in common—none of us wants to be shot or to see a loved one hit by a bullet. Let's start there and find ways to stop the fusillade that riddles our society with death and injury.

Gun violence is undeniably epidemic in America

For me, an unending river of tragic headlines sums up the issue of handguns in America.

> **Mistaking her for an intruder, Florida woman shot and killed her 27-year-old daughter**

The woman's husband, a cop, was asleep in their bed. If that handgun hadn't been there, she would have awakened her husband or called the police. No handgun, no young life lost.

> **Ohio man mistakes teen son for intruder, kills him**

He ended his son's life when his son was only fourteen. No handgun, no young life lost.

You could argue that these incidents were just cases of self-defense gone horribly wrong. Yes, we need to defend ourselves, but how about this 2015 study of self-defense that found:

> American gun owners are far more likely to injure themselves or someone else with their firearm than to stop a criminal.

For instance:

2-year-old girl shot in face after gun goes off inside mom's purse

Having a gun doesn't work the way we think it will, or the way the NRA says it does. I have to wonder what would have happened if those parents had had stoppers instead.

Gun violence is *about guns*

You hear people say that guns don't kill people, people kill people.

Yes. But only a handgun could lead to this headline:

Couple left four children in a car with a loaded gun, boy accidentally killed his 7-year-old brother

Picture a person you love dearly and then think of a bullet from your gun accidentally ending their life. It could happen. Wouldn't you give up your gun to prevent that?

9-year-old girl shot in arm by celebratory gunfire

That little girl was leaving church on New Year's Eve. Police said the round "seemed to be from the voluminous amount of gunfire" happening at the time. *Seemed* to be?

Milwaukee 2-year-old fatally shoots mother in back

It was the mom's boyfriend's handgun, and it slid out from under a car seat. Sadly, it wasn't a "smart" gun.

Smart guns can prevent accidental shootings by children, but gun stores won't sell them—a New Jersey dealer was almost driven out of business when he offered them. How about laws requiring every lethal weapon to be a smart gun? Gunmakers would make billions on new or retrofitted guns.

Here's an insight into guns in the home from a 2014 study:

> Bringing a gun into the home *substantially increases the risk for suicide* for all family members and *the risk for women being murdered in the home.*

Half of all suicides are done with guns, and *attempts made with other methods **usually fail**.* How many of those "gunicides" would still be alive if there had been no gun handy?

If you own a handgun or an assault rifle, let me ask you this: Do you *really* need a lethal firearm in your home?

It's about the money

A headline from June 19, 2016:

Orlando shooting makes big profits for gun makers

Yes, the day after forty-nine people were murdered in Orlando, Florida, gun sales and the stock of gun and ammo makers shot up. Whenever mass shootings occur or there is serious discussion of gun control, gun sales soar.

And when we decry the violence and the weaponry used against us, the NRA raises its voice to encourage people to buy more firearms, and to fear losing their guns. It adds to that constant pressure on politicians to stay away from new gun safety legislation. The NRA's lifeblood (money) comes, of course, from gun and ammo makers.

Whatever happens in America regarding guns is in the hands of the people who control firearms in America, gun manufacturers and their subsidiary, the National Rifle Association. Only if they change their ways can anything happen, and the motivation for what they do or don't do is money.

That's why *Gundown* imagines a way for gun makers to make even more gigantic profits if they turn from lethal firearms to nonlethal defensive weapons. The market is there—more and more of us need some form of self-defense. In a sense, they've created it by pushing so many people to buy so many guns.

I ask gun makers, which sounds like a better idea to you: serving the existing and increasingly saturated gun market and living in a country where your kids could be shot at school or you at a movie theater, or becoming hugely wealthy by walking away from that to create and promote nonlethal self-defense weapons?

To the majority of politicians who fail to give this deadly issue the debate and consideration that we the people need because they fear political repercussions, I say how about a little guts? Lives depend on it. The American public and most gun owners support gun safety laws.

Where I come from on guns

I grew up in Texas in the 1950s. I owned guns—BB guns, pellet rifles, a .22 rifle, a shotgun, a .38 revolver—and hunted for many years. I enjoy shooting guns, I'm a good shot, and it's fun. Like most men of that time, I never even questioned my right to have any gun I wanted. When I was sixteen, I bought that .38 revolver by mail order (my parents never knew about it).

I started working on this story about twenty years ago (as I write this, it is 2016). It was sparked by an attack on an elementary school in Stockton, California, when five schoolchildren were killed. It started me thinking about what, if anything, could be done to deal with gun violence. It was clear that gridlocked government was powerless to change things. That led to the insight that the key lies with gunmakers—and the money.

What about self-defense?

Ours is an increasingly dangerous society, and a great deal of the danger exists because, with more than 500 million guns littering our country, criminals, radicalized militants, and the insane can easily obtain weapons to slaughter innocent students or office workers or bystanders or wives and girlfriends. Month after month, year after year, the news reports assault after assault, killing after killing.

In *Gundown*, citizens are encouraged to carry nonlethal defensive guns. A lot of people would feel safer if they had a stopper—I know women who have been raped, and I'm sure they'd like to have delivered a shot of tangle to the attacker's crotch.

If market forces get behind a move to replace lethal firearms with a new kind of defensive weapon that will bring the gun and ammo makers billions in profit, who knows what might happen?

To those who fear ourselves

Some folks fear tyranny from our government. Here's what Sgt. John Love, a Vietnam vet and gun owner says about that:

> "I am a Nam vet, two tours. I own a Dirty Harry style magnum Smith & Wesson, a coach side-by-side 12 gauge, a long rifle, a target pistol, and so forth. I do not need an assault rifle added to my arsenal to protect myself, or thirty rounds jammed in my weapon. I am not living in fear that my government is secretly at war with me and that I am going to have to fight them off at any moment. I am not under any misguided

> misconception that my guns will do me any
> good if my government did come after me. It
> would be like bringing a damn slingshot to a
> guided missile duel. Get over it."

America has the strongest democratic government in the world. There's no need to fear each other, and certainly no need to arm ourselves with military weapons to kill each other. We have peaceful ways to work things out.

If someone does come to "take your guns," it can only happen if a majority of your fellow citizens have voted for them do so. If you accept and exercise the freedoms and benefits of living in a democracy, then you should also live by its rules.

Did you know that conservative Republican president Richard Nixon wanted a federal ban on handguns?

And how about ultraconservative Supreme Court Justice Antonin Scalia, who said,

> "Like most rights, the right secured by the
> Second Amendment is not unlimited . . ."
> It is ". . . not a right to keep and carry any
> weapon whatsoever in any manner whatso-
> ever and for whatever purpose."

Yes, even he concluded that the kinds of guns we own can be regulated and controlled.

We pride ourselves on being a nation that lives by the rule of law. Well, the Constitution does not grant a right to own an assault rifle. The Supreme Court—rule of law—has held that there's no barrier to state laws limiting the nature of guns that can be owned. There's already a 1934 federal law that in effect stopped ownership of machine guns. More recently, in 2016, the Supreme Court ruled that:

> ". . . machine guns are not protected arms
> under the Second Amendment."

There is no legal or constitutional reason we can't ban weapons suitable only for—and created specifically for—killing.

About our criminal justice system

It often doesn't seem to accomplish much in the way of justice. As it says in the story:

> "Defense lawyers distort the truth in order to
> free known criminals. Prosecution lawyers
> do the same in pursuit of conviction. Law-
> yers seek to discredit opposition witnesses,
> not to glean the truth from them. The adver-
> sarial system is about winning, not justice."

About the technology in this story

The stoppers and ammo, brain fingerprinting, and the neurological things that happen in the Repair Shop are based on existing technology.

About the promise in this story

Writing this book changed me. I wrote it as a novel of ideas because I wanted to offer thought-starters that could lead to solutions for the troubles that plague us. Along the way, I found that the core idea of *Gundown*, the promise, had deep meaning for me. So I made the promise, and I live by it as best I can.

For just about everybody I know, the intent of the promise is already a part of their operating systems, and I think the majority of us are good people just like them. But we forget now and then, don't we? Making the promise creates a conscious commitment to live in a certain way, to think about what we do, and how we affect other people. It has helped me remember to be helpful at times when I'm inclined to be the opposite. Making it has made a difference in how I live and relate to others, and it can in yours.

Think of how your day-to-day life could be if most of the people you encountered had made the promise and were living by it. And what could we do if we joined together to work on the kinds of changes we need? The Alliance logo I created is made up of a patchwork of skin colors taken from the photos of 150 people of many races and countries. Chances are you'll find a color very close to yours there.

Make the promise

I promise to help, the best I can.

Review Gundown and pass it along

If *Gundown* resonates with you, please share it with others and post a review on websites such as Amazon, GoodReads, Barnes & Noble, or your own website or blog.

I would like to hear from you, too. Write to ray@rayrhamey. com.

Many thanks, and a good life to you.

ABOUT THE AUTHOR

Ray Rhamey has been a writer all of his professional career, beginning with writing programmed instruction training manuals for an insurance company (mind-numbing). He moved on to advertising and had a terrific career doing that, plus a lot of fun. During those decades of creativity, he started working on screenplays.

Screenwriting took him out of advertising and to "Hollywood." Although he had the talent and skill to craft a professional script and had an agent, he didn't concoct stories anyone was interested in spending millions of dollars to produce. (Although, on the kid side, he was a story editor/scriptwriter at Filmation, and you can still get his video adaptation of *The Little Engine That Could*.)

He moved on to writing novels, and then started doing freelance editing of fiction, a business that has expanded to include book design at crrreative.com. He writes a blog about crafting compelling fiction, *Flogging the Quill*, and has written a book on writing craft titled *Mastering the Craft of Compelling Storytelling*.

Ray grew up in Dallas, Texas, but has since lived, as his grandmother would have said, all over hell and half of Georgia (except he hasn't lived in Georgia). As of this writing, the places he's called home are Dallas and Austin, Texas; Bloomington and Chicago, Illinois; St. Louis, Missouri; Studio City and Van Nuys, California; Ashland, Oregon; Cincinnati, Ohio; Sandy, Utah; Louisville, Kentucky; and Seattle and Pullman, Washington.

I promise to help, the best I can.

NOVELS BY ME I THINK YOU WILL ENJOY

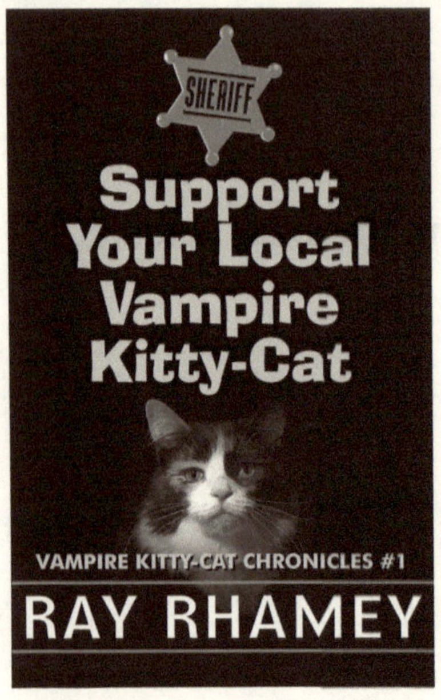

In small-town Bloomsburg Illinois, newbie vampires Patch, a calico tomcat, and Meg, a pinkish human being, are targets for vigilante vampire hunters. Patch and Meg come out of the coffin to campaign for sheriff so they can stop the vampire killers.

On the way to election day, Patch is kidnapped, tried for murder (hey, it was one of those yappy little dogs), there's betrayal at the American Vampire Association, a bloodthirsty preacher has vampicide on his mind, and Patch and Meg are hit with a deadly double-cross.

Support Your Local Vampire Kitty-Cat is serious fun in the way only satire can be. More than that, it's the story of a cat and a young woman who struggle with a curse that is destroying their lives.

Join Patch in a tale rife with action, humor, and what vampire life, so to speak, is really like.

Full disclosure: *Support Your Local Vampire Kitty-Cat* a vastly revised and improved version of its first iteration, *The Vampire Kitty-Cat Chronicles.*

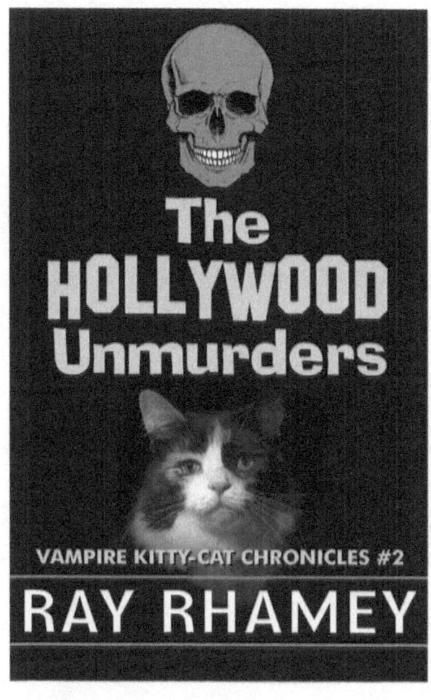

The old vampire saying, "Life doesn't get any easier after you're dead," nails it for vampire kitty-cat Patch when Meg, his vampire partner, is arrested for murder. When the sun comes up, innocent Meg, locked in a jail cell, will be toast.

Worse, her arrest means curtains for Patch. Trapped in their apartment, he can't open the refrigerator to get to their V1 Juice (blood), much less open the bottles.

Opposable thumbs are so handy.

Meg begs Nick, the cop who nabbed her, to help Patch, but he's down on cats. Reciprocally, Meg hates Nick for sending them to their doom.

And Nick is the only one who can save them.

The Hollywood Unmurders is a stand-alone sequel to *Support Your Local Vampire Kitty-Cat.*

The story of a woman, a healer, who loves deeply ... and has lost.

Of a man whose child is in danger ... and who doesn't know how to fight for her.

Of a people who do things that seem like magic—heal, extend life, kill without a touch.

Of a madman who creates a plague to wipe out the human race as vengeance for the death of his son.

Of a Homeland Security agent whose twisted desire for revenge on terrorists lead her to despicable acts.

The Magians are amidst us. A mutation gives them control over natural life energy to extend their lives, to heal or to kill. Their kin have been burned at the stake as witches, so they live apart from the rest of humanity in small scattered clans. But their genes course through the populace, and many of us unknowingly share their heritage.

But now Homeland Security pursues Rhianna, a Magian healer, because they see terrorism in the manifestation of her ability. On the run, she learns that Drago, a Magian clanmaster, will launch a fatal plague that will wipe out "ordinary" people, billions of us, as vengeance for the murder of his son.

And battle is joined ...

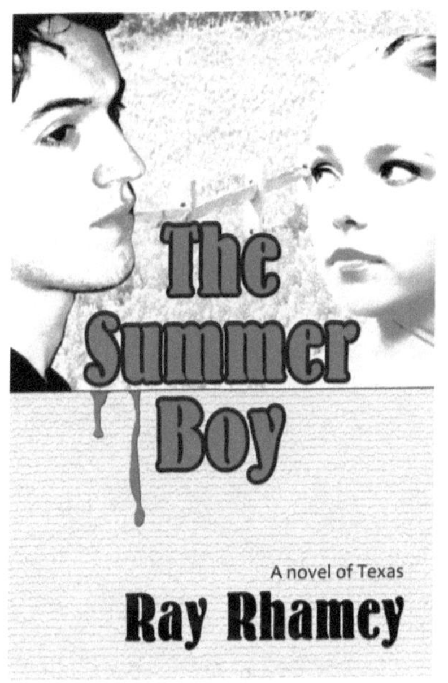

The air was as still as it was hot—only the whir of a grasshopper's flight troubled the quiet. Jesse felt like an overcooked chicken, his meat darn near ready to fall off his bones. Mouth so dry he didn't have enough spit left to swallow, Jesse croaked, "That guy tryin' to kill us?"

Turns out the answer is "not yet." A ranch hand is murdered and bad things start happening to Jesse, just an average kid working on a ranch the summer of 1958.

And then there's Lola; boss's daughter is a firecracker of a girl, and her bold ways send death their way.

It will take all of their heart and courage to survive.

Paperback and Kindle editions of these novels are available on Amazon and through your local bookstore. I hope you'll give them a look. A search works best on Amazon if you look for the title plus my last name.

And I'd appreciate it if you could post a review of *Gundown* on Amazon.

Thanks for reading.